The Best of
James H. Schmitz

Edited by Mark L. Olson

The NESFA Press
Box G, MIT Branch PO
Cambridge, MA 02139-0910
1991

Copyrights

First Edition
3rd printing, December 2000

Library of Congress Catalog Card Number: 91-61064

ISBN: 0-915368-46-3

Copyright Acknowledgments

Contents

Mischief in the Spaceways
by Janet Kagan

For twenty-some years now I've been haunting second-hand bookstores and snapping up every Schmitz novel or collection I luck onto. I thrust copies of *The Demon Breed*, *Agent of Vega*, *A Pride of Monsters*, or *The Universe Against Her* into the hands of friends and I say, "Here, read this — you'll love it!" They do and, as they take up haunting second-hand bookstores in pursuit of everything else Schmitz ever wrote, spare copies get harder and harder to track down.

With this volume, NESFA has come to my rescue. At last, I've a new collection of Schmitz stories to thrust into the hands of friends!

I don't know which stories NESFA has chosen to include here (although I did threaten some poor fellow with Dire Consequences if they left out "The Second Night of Summer"), but I do know you're in for a good time reading them. They're by James H. Schmitz ...

I'd have had it easier if NESFA had asked me to write an afterword. In an afterward, I could have run on for pages, pointing to each story in turn and saying, "Look at that!" and "Catch this!"

But ... an introduction?

I've an ingrained objection to coming between an author and his readers. The objection is all the more heartfelt when that author is James H. Schmitz, a writer I admire above all for his sense of mischief.

Whatever the story, he always found a way to play havoc with his readers' expectations. He could take any cliche and, by turning it upside down, inside out, or back on itself, make you sit up and take notice of things you'd never seen before. And leave you smiling over the discovery as well.

If you've never read his work before, I'll be damned if I'll be the one to spoil the surprises he's got in store for you.

As a reader, I pick up a Schmitz story to reread whenever I need the Good Stuff. As a writer, I'm still trying to figure out how he gets away with some of the things he gets away with — and I reread Schmitz stories in the hope that someday maybe I'll learn enough to get away with it, too.

(This man wrote a story in which the hero sleeps through the conquest of a planet, and wakes no less the hero of the story for having missed the battle. What is "The Truth About Cushgar"? I have got to learn how to get away with things like that!)

Rather than spoil any specific surprises these stories hold in store for you, I'll take this opportunity to flag a handful of purely Schmitzian techniques for you. Chances are you'll be too busy reading the stories to spot them the first time, but you might want to keep your eye out for them when you reread the stories.

Heroes, villains, monsters — they're all here — but Schmitz has worked his fine mischief on each and every one of them. There's never been anyone quite like him, and you're about to have the pleasure of learning why.

HEROES

A word about the "default setting." In computer terminology, the default setting defines how the computer will operate. Default settings are simple enough to change … if you know they're there and if you're willing to take the conscious and deliberate action necessary to change them.

When James H. Schmitz first started writing sf, the default setting for "hero" was white, male, and in his twenties — and a writer didn't change the default setting without good reason.

"Good reason," I regret to say, was biological — or what passed for biological in the cultural stereotyping of the time. If the writer needed a protagonist who would protect a child, the protagonist would be female. If the writer needed a protagonist who was irrationally jealous, the protagonist would be female. If the writer needed a protagonist who was a secretary or a schoolteacher … ditto.

In those rare stories where the default settings were changed, the change was a forced one; and the change in the default setting was itself the point of the story.

Not where Schmitz was concerned. He knew the default settings were there and, to judge from the stories, the knowledge gave him a fierce itch to change the settings to his own specs. The result is the most unconventional collection of heroes you ever saw.

I use the word "heroes" deliberately. A conventional "heroine" was, at the time, little more than the hero's girlfriend. But Schmitz wrote heroes — and many of his best were female.

A complaint I've heard all too often about Schmitz's work is this: "But … but there isn't any reason for Nile Etland to be a woman!" There's no reason for Heinlein's Lorenzo the Magnificent to be a man, either. But that's the reader's default settings speaking.

Flick out of the default settings and there's no reason an interstellar agent can't be female, no reason a career bureaucrat can't have an insatiable sense of curiosity, no reason the ecology of an alien world can't be the hero of the story.

Change the default settings and you might even wind up with a story like "The Second Night of Summer," a particularly mischievous example that's one of my favorites.

Keep your eye on the hero in a Schmitz story — she's not who you expected.

VILLAINS

And neither is the villain ...

If a story has a villain, that means you're reading space opera instead of the "classier" problem-solving sort of sf, right? Not always ... and es–pecially not when it's a Schmitz story, where even a villain can be out of the ordinary.

In 1965, Schmitz wrote "Balanced Ecology," a story in which the villains are clear cutters. You read that right: the villains are people who want to cut down a planet's forests purely for monetary gain. But "Balanced Ecology" is problem-solving sf ... from the point of view of the world at risk.

In "The Custodians," Schmitz gives us an ethical space-pirate in league with a group of arms smugglers as the villain of the piece and then (I suspect he chuckled while he did it) he proceeds to pull off a trick ... No, no, I can't tell you. You've got to see him do it to appreciate it.

Keep your eye on those villains — there's not a preened mustache in the lot.

And while you're at it, keep your eye on what happens to those villains in the end. Contrary to the blood-thirsty conventions of his time (and ours), Schmitz prefers rehabilitation to punishment and treats his villains accordingly.

Even without knowing which stories NESFA's chosen to include here, I guarantee you'll see an example of this treatment. It'd be almost impossible to put together a collection that didn't have one. If the choice had been up to me, I'd have given you "Gone Fishing" as the best example.

Told largely from the villain's point of view, the story at first seems all too predictable. Schmitz seems to telegraph the ending, the fate of the villain ... until he takes the story one step further — to show you what happened after the ending you expected. You're left shaking your head and smiling because you didn't see that coming.

Yes, keep your eye on the villain and on the fate of the villain.

MONSTERS

Agreed; a monster is not the same as a villain. But there was, at the time, a conventional monster. Repulsive to look at, it dripped ichor and smelled accordingly. In all, it was the sort of thing a hero would instinc–tively kill on sight.

"But there was a time," Schmitz wrote, in his introduction to *A Pride of Monsters*, "when the monsters were very real and very close. [...] And the beast remains part of our heritage, unforgotten; it pads through the dark back-ways of our minds, peers out into our dreams. There is a kinship, a bond, between it and us.

"[...] A monster, essentially, is something which appears more formidable than you, with intentions toward you that are at best un-guessable. Perhaps we are trying to regain our monsters. The real ones ..."

Schmitz set out to do exactly that, to help us regain our monsters. He gifted science fiction with a dozen or more of the most memorable monsters ever seen in the field, among them "Greenface," the janandra, the Worm World ...

In *A Tale of Two Clocks*, you'll find my favorite, a monster named Pili. Pili has long golden hair and smells of ripe apples — a scent that raised hairs on the back of my neck for months after I first read the novel. In "Lion Loose," you'll find a Schmitz monster that looks like "a barn door with dirty fur" (and its intentions are so unguessable that I find myself surprised all over again each time I reread the story).

Watch those monsters — they're not what you think.

And watch too the reactions of a Schmitz character confronted by a monster. There's no "instinctive" kill-on-sight. Far from it, as you'll see in the following quote from "The Winds of Time":

"On the other hand, Geftly realized that he wouldn't now be able to bring himself to eject the janandra out of the cargo lock and into the Great Current. Its intentions obviously hadn't been friendly, but its level of intelligence was as good as his own, perhaps somewhat better; and at present it was helpless. To dispose of it as he'd had in mind would therefore be the cold-blooded murder of an equal."

Schmitz just can't keep his hands off those default settings, can he?

FAMILY AND FRIENDS

Here's another odd thing for your consideration. Most action/adventure heroes exist in a vacuum. They may have girlfriends and they most assuredly have sidekicks, but they don't have family and they don't have friends. The difference between a sidekick and a friend is enormous, but the sidekick has become so conventional as to go unnoticed — except by James H. Schmitz.

A Schmitz hero has both friends and family.

Try to imagine a typical Heinlein hero taking a problem to his father. Not easy, is it? But that's Telzey Amberdon's first thought when she believes her friend Gonwil's life may be in danger. What's more, Telzey's father believes her and acts on the belief.

As in real life, not all family members are likeable or even good, but — good or bad — they exist. And family is always something to be taken into consideration. Even a space pirate has a sister. He may not have seen her for some time but she remains, for him, a consideration ... and that makes him a very different sort of space pirate indeed, as you'll see in "The Custodians."

STYLE

Not much of a stylist, Schmitz nevertheless had style. There's something about his choice of words I want you to keep an eye out for. It's yet another example of the mischief inherent in his work (and it's a handy little technique that even the rawest beginning writer can use to good advantage).

He treats each of his characters as an individual. He does so in a deceptively simple fashion that nevertheless adds a depth to his work that many writers of the time lacked.

Even today there are a number of writers who consider gender (at least, the female gender) a perfectly good substitute for character motivation or for exposition. To such a writer, the phrase "being a woman" sums up a female character *in toto*. This is a tic, and the sign of an extremely lazy writer. (It's also a sign of contempt for the reader; the writer assumes you've bought into the same stereotypes and that you won't question them.)

Let me give you an example of common garden-variety laziness: "Being a woman, she couldn't keep the secret." If the divulger of secrets in question had been male, that same lazy writer would have written: "He couldn't keep the secret from Roger Williams — he and Roger had been through too much together."

The first character described reinforces a stereotype and makes the female character "representative" of her entire gender, to its derogation. The second character is an individual with an individual reason for his specific behavior in this instance.

This difference in treatment was once quite common in sf (and a number of writers still do it). Female characters are treated as generic and representative, male characters as specific and individual.

Once again, Schmitz took notice of the stereotyping and took action against it. Gender is not sufficient reason for the behavior of a Schmitz character.

"Jessamine was a sweet and understanding woman," says Schmitz of Telzey's mother, "but she had the streak of conservatism which tended to characterize junior members of the Grand Council of the Federation."

No tics here. Schmitz was not a lazy writer.

In fact, it's a good idea to take any apparent stereotyped behavior or attribute in a Schmitz story as a warning flag. If he makes much of a woman's fashionable wigs, you'll likely find they're concealing some very interesting electronic equipment. If you think you see a black chauffeur, you've been conned. If you think you see Trigger Argee behaving irrationally because she's obsessed by love, you've got one hell of a surprise coming.

To James Schmitz, the stereotyping of other people is always a mistake. A person who stereotypes others lacks the flexibility to deal with the real world. Bigotry is inevitably dangerous to the bigot.

My favorite Schmitz novel this week, *The Demon Breed*, is all about the hazards of bigotry. In it, one of his characters sums up humans this way: "To say that the human is thus and so is almost always to lie automatically. The species, its practices and philosophies remain unpredictable. Individuals vary, and the species varies with circumstances. This instability seems a main source of its strength. We cannot judge it by what it is today or was yesterday. We do not know what it will be tomorrow."

I couldn't put it better myself ... but I'd like to add that he accords the same individuality to his non-human characters as well. And, in so doing, he makes you aware of them as people, even if they look like a stegosaurus without the spine frills.

WHICH BRINGS ME TO THE PLOTS

Here's a plot: Our hero has an old wreck of a cargo ship and one chance to make a go of interstellar trade. If he succeeds, he'll also get the hand of the lady back home in marriage. On his first trip out, he comes across some slave-girls in need of rescue ...

This plot was old when Verne and Wells were children, though in their day the old wreck of a cargo ship would have had tattered sails instead of dented plates. And it's this hoary old chestnut that Schmitz took for the plot of his novella "The Witches of Karres."

"The Witches of Karres" appeared in *Astounding* in December of 1949. In March of 1950, when John W. Campbell, Jr., counted up the votes for best of that issue, he found that the readers had awarded "The Witches of Karres" first place in the Analytical Laboratory — over the formidable competition of Isaac Asimov's "... And Now You Don't" and Robert Heinlein's "Gulf"!

How did Schmitz do that with a story whose every plot turn was cliche? Read *The Witches of Karres* and you'll see for yourself, but I'll give you a hint ... Every time the plot was supposed to take a turn to the right, Schmitz hung a left — or a zig-zag.

The story always opens in a port bar in the midst of an argument. You know what happens next, of course. Our hero has to fight his way out ...

"The Witches of Karres" opens in a spaceport bar. An argument (over which planet, Nikkeldepain or Porlumma, has the sillier name) heats to threats. "But the captain only smiled politely, paid for his two drinks, and left."

And you're left blinking in surprise. No bar fight? That isn't the way this story is supposed to run.

Then the captain rescues those slave-girls ... Schmitz heard the word "girls" (and you didn't). The slave-girls are actually girls, aged fourteen, "five or six," and "nine or ten." (The captain "wasn't very good at estimating them around that age," Schmitz explains.) Worse still, Schmitz gives you the uncomfortable feeling that his captain is rescuing the slavers from the slaves, rather than vice-versa.

Pure action/adventure every step of the way, "The Witches of Karres" can easily be taken at face value and read for the genuine excitement of its galactic sweep. (I've hooked half the kids in my neighborhood on sf with this book.) But watch your own expectations as you read, and you'll read it with double the delight.

Throughout the novella and the additional adventures recounted in the later novel of the same name, Schmitz takes one cliche after another and wrings its tail ... until you howl with laughter. (I warn you, though: reading *The Witches of Karres* will also leave you with a permanent raised eyebrow and a snort of derision for any writer who does the expected in a space opera.)

My vote for the unlikeliest exchange ever written in space opera is still the final exchange between Goth and Captain Pausert in the novella version of "The Witches of Karres." And, no, I'm not going to quote it here. You'll have to find a copy for yourself.

See you in the second-hand bookshop. Psst — you'll want that copy of *The Demon Breed*, too, and *Agent of Vega*, and ...

IN CONCLUSION

I've kept you from the stories quite long enough. Turn the page. Be ready to reset. Keep your eyes open for those twists, your ears open for the sound of a friend's voice, your mind open to all the possibilities of humankind (including those that come in unfamiliar forms) — and sniff the air from time to time for the sweet scent of danger.

Here, read this — you'll love it!

The Best of
James H. Schmitz

Grandpa

A green-winged, downy thing as big as a hen fluttered along the hillside to a point directly above Cord's head and hovered there, twenty feet above him. Cord, a fifteen-year-old human being, leaned back against a skipboat parked on the equator of a world that had known human beings for only the past four Earth years, and eyed the thing speculatively. The thing was, in the free and easy terminology of the Sutang Colonial Team, a swamp bug. Concealed in the downy fur back of the bug's head was a second, smaller, semiparasitical thing, classed as a bug rider.

The bug itself looked like a new species to Cord. Its parasite might or might not turn out to be another unknown. Cord was a natural research man; his first glimpse of the odd flying team had sent endless curiosities thrilling through him. How did that particular phenomenon tick, and why? What fascinating things, once you'd learned about it, could you get it to *do?*

Normally, he was hampered by circumstances in carrying out any such investigation. The Colonial Team was a practical, hardworking outfit — two thousand people who'd been given twenty years to size up and tame down the brand-new world of Sutang to the point where a hundred thousand colonists could be settled on it, in reasonable safety and comfort. Even junior colonial students like Cord were expected to confine their curiosity to the pattern of research set up by the station to which they were attached. Cord's inclination toward independent experiments had got him into disfavor with his immediate superiors before this.

He sent a casual glance in the direction of the Yoger Bay Colonial Station behind him. No signs of human activity about that low, fortresslike bulk in the hill. Its central lock was still closed. In fifteen minutes, it was scheduled to be opened to let out the Planetary Regent, who was in-specting the Yoger Bay Station and its principal activities today.

Fifteen minutes was time enough to find out something about the new bug, Cord decided.

But he'd have to collect it first.

He slid out one of the two handguns holstered at his side. This one was his own property: a Vanadian projectile weapon. Cord thumbed it to position for anesthetic small-game missiles and brought the hovering swamp bug down, drilled neatly and microscopically through the head. As the bug hit the ground, the rider left its back. A tiny scarlet demon, round and bouncy as a rubber ball, it shot toward Cord in three long hops, mouth wide to sink home inch-long, venom-dripping fangs. Rather breathlessly, Cord triggered the gun again and knocked it out in mid-leap. A new species, all right! Most bug riders were harmless plant-eaters, mere suckers of vegetable juice —

"Cord!" A feminine voice.

Cord swore softly. He hadn't heard the central lock click open. She must have come around from the other side of the station.

"Hi, Grayan!" he shouted innocently without looking around. "Come see what I got! New species!"

Grayan Mahoney, a slender, black-haired girl two years older than himself, came trotting down the hillside toward him. She was Sutang's star colonial student, and the station manager, Nirmond, indicated from time to time that she was a fine example for Cord to pattern his own behavior on. In spite of that, she and Cord were good friends, but she bossed him around considerably.

"Cord, you dope!" she scowled as she came up. "Quit acting like a collector! If the Regent came out now, you'd be sunk. Nirmond's been telling her about you!"

"Telling her what?" Cord asked, startled.

"For one," Grayan reported, "that you don't keep up on your assigned work. Two, that you sneak off on one-man expeditions of your own at least once a month and have to be rescued —"

"Nobody," Cord interrupted hotly, "has had to rescue me yet!"

"How's Nirmond to know you're alive and healthy when you just drop out of sight for a week?" Grayan countered. "Three," she resumed checking the items off on slim fingertips, "he complained that you keep private zoological gardens of unidentified and possibly deadly vermin in the woods back of the station. And four ... well, Nirmond simply doesn't want the responsibility for you any more!" She held up the four fingers significantly.

"Golly!" gulped Cord, dismayed. Summed up tersely like that, his record didn't look too good.

"Golly is right! I keep warning you! Now Nirmond wants the Regent to send you back to Vanadia — and there's a starship coming in to New Venus forty-eight hours from now!" New Venus was the Colonial Team's main settlement on the opposite side of Sutang.

"What'll I do?"

"Start acting like you had good sense mainly." Grayan grinned suddenly. "I talked to the Regent, too — Nirmond isn't rid of you yet! But if you louse up on our tour of the Bay Farms today, you'll be off the Team for good!"

She turned to go. "You might as well put the skipboat back; we're not using it. Nirmond's driving us down to the edge of the Bay in a treadcar, and we'll take a raft from there. Don't let them know I warned you!"

Cord looked after her, slightly stunned. He hadn't realized his reputation had become as bad as all that! To Grayan, whose family had served on Colonial Teams for the past four generations, nothing worse was imaginable than to be dismissed and sent back ignominiously to one's own homeworld. Much to his surprise, Cord was discovering now that he felt exactly the same way about it!

Leaving his newly bagged specimens to revive by themselves and flutter off again, he hurriedly flew the skipboat around the station and rolled it back into its stall.

Three rafts lay moored just offshore in the marshy cove, at the edge of which Nirmond had stopped the treadcar. They looked somewhat like exceptionally broad-brimmed, well-worn sugarloaf hats floating out there, green and leathery. Or like lily pads twenty-five feet across, with the upper section of a big, gray-green pineapple growing from the center of each. Plant animals of some sort. Sutang was too new to have had its phyla sorted out into anything remotely like an orderly classification. The rafts were a local oddity which had been investigated and could be regarded as harmless and moderately useful. Their usefulness lay in the fact that they were employed as a rather slow means of transportation about the shallow, swampy waters of the Yoger Bay. That was as far as the Team's interest in them went at present.

The Regent had stood up from the back seat of the car, where she was sitting next to Cord. There were only four in the party; Grayan was up front with Nirmond.

"Are those our vehicles?" The Regent sounded amused.

Nirmond grinned, a little sourly. "Don't underestimate them, Dane! They could become an important economic factor in this region in time. But, as a matter of fact, these three are smaller than I like to use." He was peering about the reedy edges of the cove. "There's a regular monster parked here usually —"

Grayan turned to Cord. "Maybe Cord knows where Grandpa is hiding."

It was well-meant, but Cord had been hoping nobody would ask him about Grandpa. Now they all looked at him.

"Oh, you want Grandpa?" he said, somewhat flustered. "Well, I left him ... I mean I saw him a couple of weeks ago about a mile south from here —"

Grayan sighed. Nirmond grunted and told the Regent, "The rafts tend to stay wherever they're left, providing it's shallow and muddy. They use a hair-root system to draw chemicals and microscopic nourishment directly from the bottom of the bay. Well — Grayan, would you like to drive us there?"

Cord settled back unhappily as the treadcar lurched into motion. Nirmond suspected he'd used Grandpa for one of his unauthorized tours of the area, and Nirmond was quite right.

"I understand you're an expert with these rafts, Cord," Dane said from beside him. "Grayan told me we couldn't find a better steersman, or pilot, or whatever you call it, for our trip today."

"I can handle them," Cord said, perspiring. "They don't give you any trouble!" He didn't feel he'd made a good impression on the Regent so far. Dane was a young, handsome-looking woman with an easy way of talking and laughing, but she wasn't the head of the Sutang Colonial Team for nothing. She looked quite capable of shipping out anybody whose record wasn't up to par.

"There's one big advantage our beasties have over a skipboat, too," Nirmond remarked from the front seat. "You don't have to worry about a snapper trying to climb on board with you!" He went on to describe the stinging ribbon-tentacles the rafts spread around them under water to discourage creatures that might make a meal off their tender underparts. The snapper and two or three other active and aggressive species of the Bay hadn't yet learned it was foolish to attack armed human beings in a boat, but they would skitter hurriedly out of the path of a leisurely perambulating raft.

Cord was happy to be ignored for the moment. The Regent, Nirmond, and Grayan were all Earth people, which was true of most of the members of the Team; and Earth people made him uncomfortable, particularly in groups. Vanadia, his own homeworld, had barely graduated from the status of Earth colony itself, which might explain the difference. All the Earth people he'd met so far seemed dedicated to what Grayan Mahoney called the Big Picture, while Nirmond usually spoke of it as "Our Purpose Here." They acted strictly in accordance with their Team Regulations — sometimes, in Cord's opinion, quite insanely. Because now and then the Regulations didn't quite cover a new situation and then somebody was likely to get killed. In which case, the Regulations would be modified promptly, but Earth people didn't seem otherwise disturbed by such events.

Grayan had tried to explain it to Cord:

"We can't really ever *know* in advance what a new world is going to be like! And once we're there, there's too much to do, in the time we've got, to study it inch by inch. You get your job done, and you take a chance. But if you stick by the Regulations you've got the best chances of surviving anybody's been able to figure out for you —"

Cord felt he preferred to just use good sense and not let Regulations or the job get him into a situation he couldn't figure out for himself.

To which Grayan replied impatiently that he hadn't yet got the Big Picture —

The treadcar swung around and stopped, and Grayan stood up in the front seat, pointing. "That's Grandpa, over there!"

Dane also stood up and whistled softly, apparently impressed by Grandpa's fifty-foot spread. Cord looked around in surprise. He was pretty sure this was several hundred yards from the spot where he'd left the big raft two weeks ago; and as Nirmond said, they didn't usually move about by themselves.

Puzzled, he followed the others down a narrow path to the water, hemmed in by tree-sized reeds. Now and then he got a glimpse of Grandpa's swimming platform, the rim of which just touched the shore. Then the path opened out, and he saw the whole raft lying in sunlit, shallow water; and he stopped short, startled.

Nirmond was about to step up on the platform, ahead of Dane.

"Wait!" Cord shouted. His voice sounded squeaky with alarm. "Stop!"

He came running forward.

They had frozen where they stood, looked around swiftly. Then glanced back at Cord coming up. They were well trained.

"What's the matter, Cord?" Nirmond's voice was quiet and urgent.

"Don't get on that raft — it's changed!" Cord's voice sounded wobbly, even to himself. "Maybe it's not even Grandpa —"

He saw he was wrong on the last point before he'd finished the sentence. Scattered along the rim of the raft were discolored spots left by a variety of heat-guns, one of which had been his own. It was the way you goaded the sluggish and mindless things into motion. Cord pointed at the cone-shaped central projection. "There — his head! He's sprouting!"

"Sprouting?" the station manager repeated uncomprehendingly. Grandpa's head, as befitted his girth, was almost twelve feet high and equally wide. It was armor-plated like the back of a saurian to keep off plant-suckers, but two weeks ago it had been an otherwise featureless knob, like those on all other rafts. Now scores of long, kinky, leafless vines had grown out from all surfaces of the cone, like green wires. Some were drawn up like tightly coiled springs, others trailed limply to the platform and over it. The top of the cone was dotted with angry red buds, rather like pimples, which hadn't been there before either. Grandpa looked unhealthy.

"Well," Nirmond said, "so it is. Sprouting!" Grayan made a choked sound. Nirmond glanced at Cord as if puzzled. "Is that all that was bothering you, Cord?"

"Well, sure!" Cord began excitedly. He hadn't caught the significance of the word "all"; his hackles were still up, and he was shaking. "None of them ever —"

Then he stopped. He could tell by their faces that they hadn't got it. Or rather, that they'd got it all right but simply weren't going to let it change their plans. The rafts were classified as harmless, according to the Regulations. Until proved otherwise, they would continue to be regarded as harmless. You didn't waste time quibbling with the Regulations —

apparently even if you were the Planetary Regent. You didn't feel you had the time to waste.

He tried again. "Look —" he began. What he wanted to tell them was that Grandpa with one unknown factor added wasn't Grandpa any more. He was an unpredictable, oversized lifeform, to be investigated with cautious thoroughness till you knew what the unknown factor meant.

But it was no use. They knew all that. He stared at them helplessly. "I —"

Dane turned to Nirmond. "Perhaps you'd better check," she said. She didn't add, — "to reassure the boy!" but that was what she meant.

Cord felt himself flushing terribly. They thought he was scared — which he was — and they were feeling sorry for him, which they had no right to do. But there was nothing he could say or do now except watch Nirmond walk steadily across the platform. Grandpa shivered slightly a few times, but the rafts always did that when someone first stepped on them. The station manager stopped before one of the kinky sprouts, touched it, and then gave it a tug. He reached up and poked at the lowest of the budlike growths. "Odd-looking things!" he called back. He gave Cord another glance. "Well, everything seems harmless enough, Cord. Coming aboard, everyone?"

It was like dreaming a dream in which you yelled and yelled at people and couldn't make them hear you! Cord stepped up stiff-legged on the platform behind Dane and Grayan. He knew exactly what would have happened if he'd hesitated even a moment. One of them would have said in a friendly voice, careful not to let it sound too contemptuous: "You don't have to come along if you don't want to, Cord!"

Grayan had unholstered her heat-gun and was ready to start Grandpa moving out into the channels of the Yoger Bay.

Cord hauled out his own heat-gun and said roughly, "I was to do that!"

"All right, Cord." She gave him a brief, impersonal smile, as if he were someone she'd met for the first time that day, and stood aside.

They were so infuriatingly polite! He was, Cord decided, as good as on his way back to Vanadia right now.

For a while, Cord almost hoped that something awesome and catastrophic would happen promptly to teach the Team people a lesson. But nothing did. As always, Grandpa shook himself vaguely and experimentally when he felt the heat on one edge of the platform and then decided to withdraw from it, all of which was standard procedure. Under the water, out of sight, were the raft's working sections: short, thick leaf-structures shaped like paddles and designed to work as such, along with the slimy nettle-streamers which kept the vegetarians of the Yoger Bay away, and a jungle of hair roots through which Grandpa sucked nourishments from the mud and the sluggish waters of the Bay, and with which he also anchored himself.

The paddles started churning, the platform quivered, the hair roots were hauled out of the mud; and Grandpa was on his ponderous way.

Cord switched off the heat, reholstered his gun, and stood up. Once in motion, the rafts tended to keep traveling unhurriedly for quite a while. To stop them, you gave them a touch of heat along their leading edge; and they could be turned in any direction by using the gun lightly on the opposite side of the platform.

It was simple enough. Cord didn't look at the others. He was still burning inside. He watched the reed beds move past and open out, giving him glimpses of the misty, yellow and green and blue expanse of the brackish Bay ahead. Behind the mist, to the west, were the Yoger Straits, tricky and ugly water when the tides were running; and beyond the Straits lay the open sea, the great Zlanti Deep, which was another world entirely and one of which he hadn't seen much as yet.

Suddenly he was sick with the full realization that he wasn't likely to see any more of it now! Vanadia was a pleasant enough planet; but the wildness and strangeness were long gone from it. It wasn't Sutang.

Grayan called from beside Dane, "What's the best route from here into the farms, Cord?"

"The big channel to the right," he answered. He added somewhat sullenly, "We're headed for it!"

Grayan came over to him. "The Regent doesn't want to see all of it," she said, lowering her voice. "The algae and plankton beds first. Then as much of the mutated grains as we can show her in about three hours. Steer for the ones that have been doing best, and you'll keep Nirmond happy!"

She gave him a conspiratorial wink. Cord looked after her un-certainly. You couldn't tell from her behavior that anything was wrong. Maybe —

He had a flare of hope. It was hard not to like the Team people, even when they were being rock-headed about their Regulations. Perhaps it was that purpose that gave them their vitality and drive, even though it made them remorseless about themselves and everyone else. Anyway, the day wasn't over yet. He might still redeem himself in the Regent's opinion. Something might happen —

Cord had a sudden cheerful, if improbable, vision of some Bay monster plunging up on the raft with snapping jaws, and of himself alertly blowing out what passed for the monster's brains before anyone else — Nirmond, in particular — was even aware of the threat. The Bay monsters shunned Grandpa, of course, but there might be ways of tempting one of them.

So far, Cord realized, he'd been letting his feelings control him. It was time to start thinking!

Grandpa first. So he'd sprouted — green vines and red buds, purpose unknown, but with no change observable in his behavior-patterns otherwise. He was the biggest raft in this end of the Bay, though all of them had been growing steadily in the two years since Cord had first seen one.

Sutang's seasons changed slowly; its year was somewhat more than five
Earth years long. The first Team members to land here hadn't yet seen a
full year pass.

Grandpa then was showing a seasonal change. The other rafts, not
quite so far developed, would be reacting similarly a little later. Plant
animals — they might be blossoming, preparing to propagate.

"Grayan," he called, "how do the rafts get started? When they're
small, I mean."

Grayan looked pleased; and Cord's hopes went up a little more.
Grayan was on his side again anyway!

"Nobody knows yet," she said. "We were just talking about it. About
half of the coastal marsh-fauna of the continent seems to go through a
preliminary larval stage in the sea." She nodded at the red buds on the
raft's cone. "It looks as if Grandpa is going to produce flowers and let the
wind or tide take the seeds out through the Straits."

It made sense. It also knocked out Cord's still half-held hope that the
change in Grandpa might turn out to be drastic enough, in some way, to
justify his reluctance to get on board. Cord studied Grandpa's armored
head carefully once more — unwilling to give up that hope entirely. There
were a series of vertical gummy black slits between the armor plates,
which hadn't been in evidence two weeks ago either. It looked as if
Grandpa were beginning to come apart at the seams. Which might
indicate that the rafts, big as they grew to be, didn't outlive a full seasonal
cycle, but came to flower at about this time of Sutang's year and died.
However, it was a safe bet that Grandpa wasn't going to collapse into
senile decay before they completed their trip today.

Cord gave up on Grandpa. The other notion returned to him —
Perhaps he *could* coax an obliging Bay monster into action that would
show the Regent he was no sissy!

Because the monsters were there, all right.

Kneeling at the edge of the platform and peering down into the wine-
colored, clear water of the deep channel they were moving through, Cord
could see a fair selection of them at almost any moment.

Some five or six snappers, for one thing. Like big, flattened crayfish,
chocolate-brown mostly, with green and red spots on their carapaced
backs. In some areas they were so thick you'd wonder what they found to
live on, except that they ate almost anything, down to chewing up the mud
in which they squatted. However, they preferred their food in large
chunks and alive, which was one reason you didn't go swimming in the
Bay. They would attack a boat on occasion; but the excited manner in
which the ones he saw were scuttling off toward the edges of the channel
showed they wanted to have nothing to do with a big moving raft.

Dotted across the bottom were two-foot round holes which looked
vacant at the moment. Normally, Cord knew, there would be a head filling
each of those holes. The heads consisted mainly of triple sets of jaws, held
open patiently like so many traps to grab at anything that came within

range of the long, wormlike bodies behind the heads. But Grandpa's passage, waving his stingers like transparent pennants through the water, had scared the worms out of sight, too.

Otherwise, mostly schools of small stuff — and then a flash of wicked scarlet, off to the left behind the raft, darting out from the reeds! Turning its needle-nose into their wake.

Cord watched it without moving. He knew that creature, though it was rare in the Bay and hadn't been classified. Swift, vicious — alert enough to snap swamp bugs out of the air as they fluttered across the surface. And he'd tantalized one with fishing tackle once into leaping up on a moored raft, where it had flung itself about furiously until he was able to shoot it.

No fishing tackle. A handkerchief might just do it, if he cared to risk an arm —

"What fantastic creatures!" Dane's voice just behind him.

"Yellowheads," said Nirmond. "They've got a high utility rating. Keep down the bugs."

Cord stood up casually. It was no time for tricks! The reed bed to their right was thick with yellowheads, a colony of them. Vaguely froggy things, man-sized and better. Of all the creatures he'd discovered in the Bay, Cord liked them least. The flabby, sacklike bodies clung with four thin limbs to the upper sections of the twenty-foot reeds that lined the channel. They hardly ever moved, but their huge, bulging eyes seemed to take in everything that went on about them. Every so often, a downy swamp bug came close enough; and a yellowhead would open its vertical, enormous, tooth-lined slash of a mouth, extend the whole front of its face like a bellows in a flashing strike; and the bug would be gone. They might be useful, but Cord hated them. "Ten years from now we should know what the cycle of coastal life is like," Nirmond said. "When we set up the Yoger Bay Station there were no yellowheads here. They came the following year. Still with traces of the oceanic larval form; but the metamorphosis was almost complete. About twelve inches long —"

Dane remarked that the same pattern was duplicated endlessly elsewhere. The Regent was inspecting the yellowhead colony with field glasses; she put them down now, looked at Cord, and smiled. "How far to the farms?"

"About twenty minutes."

"The key," Nirmond said, "seems to be the Zlanti Basin. It must be almost a soup of life in spring."

"It is," nodded Dane, who had been here in Sutang's spring, four Earth years ago. "It's beginning to look as if the Basin alone might justify colonization. The question is still —" she gestured towards the yellow-heads — "how do creatures like that get there?"

They walked off toward the other side of the raft, arguing about ocean currents. Cord might have followed. But something splashed back of them, off to the left and not too far back. He stayed, watching.

After a moment, he saw the big yellowhead. It had slipped down from its reedy perch, which was what had caused the splash. Almost submerged at the water line, it stared after the raft with huge pale-green eyes. To Cord, it seemed to look directly at him. In that moment, he knew for the first time why he didn't like yellowheads. There was something very like intelligence in that look, an alien calculation. In creatures like that, intelligence seemed out of place. What use could they have for it?

A little shiver went over him when it sank completely under the water and he realized it intended to swim after the raft. But it was mostly excitement. He had never seen a yellowhead come down out of the reeds before. The obliging monster he'd been looking for might be presenting itself in an unexpected way.

Half a minute later, he watched it again, swimming awkwardly far down. It had no immediate intention of boarding, at any rate. Cord saw it come into the area of the raft's trailing stingers. It maneuvered its way between them with curiously human swimming motions, and went out of sight under the platform.

He stood up, wondering what it meant. The yellowhead had appeared to know about the stingers; there had been an air of purpose in every move of its approach. He was tempted to tell the others about it, but there was the moment of triumph he could have if it suddenly came slobbering up over the edge of the platform and he nailed it before their eyes.

It was almost time anyway to turn the raft in toward the farms. If nothing happened before then —

He watched. Almost five minutes, but no sign of the yellowhead. Still wondering, a little uneasy, he gave Grandpa a calculated needling of heat.

After a moment, he repeated it. Then he drew a deep breath and forgot all about the yellowhead.

"Nirmond!" he called sharply.

The three of them were standing near the center of the platform, next to the big armored cone, looking ahead at the farms. They glanced around.

"What's the matter now, Cord?"

Cord couldn't say it for a moment. He was suddenly, terribly scared again. Something *had* gone wrong!

"The raft won't turn!" he told them.

"Give it a real burn this time!" Nirmond said.

Cord glanced up at him. Nirmond, standing a few steps in front of Dane and Grayan as if he wanted to protect them, had begun to look a little strained, and no wonder. Cord already had pressed the gun to three different points on the platform; but Grandpa appeared to have developed a sudden anesthesia for heat. They kept moving out steadily toward the center of the Bay.

Now Cord held his breath, switched the heat on full, and let Grandpa have it. A six-inch patch on the platform blistered up instantly, turned brown, then black —

Grandpa stopped dead. Just like that.

"That's right! Keep burn —" Nirmond didn't finish his order.

A giant shudder. Cord staggered back toward the water. Then the whole edge of the raft came curling up behind him and went down again, smacking the Bay with a sound like a cannon shot. He flew forward off his feet, hit the platform face down, and flattened himself against it. It swelled up beneath him. Two more enormous slaps and joltings. Then quiet. He looked round for the others.

He lay within twelve feet of the central cone. Some twenty or thirty of the mysterious new vines the cone had sprouted were stretched out stiffly toward him now, like so many thin green fingers. They couldn't quite reach him. The nearest tip was still ten inches from his shoes.

But Grandpa had caught the others, all three of them. They were tumbled together at the foot of the cone, wrapped in a stiff network of green vegetable ropes, and they didn't move.

Cord drew his feet up cautiously, prepared for another earthquake reaction. But nothing happened. Then he discovered that Grandpa was back in motion on his previous course. The heat-gun had vanished. Gently, he took out the Vanadian gun.

"Cord? It didn't get you?" It was the Regent.

"No," he said, keeping his voice low. He realized suddenly he'd simply assumed they were all dead. Now he felt sick and shaky.

"What are you doing?"

Cord looked at Grandpa's big armor-plated head with a certain hunger. The cones were hollowed out inside; the station's lab had decided their chief function was to keep enough air trapped under the rafts to float them. But in that central section was also the organ that controlled Grandpa's overall reactions.

He said softly, "I've got a gun and twelve heavy-duty explosive bullets. Two of them will blow that cone apart."

"No good, Cord!" the pain-racked voice told him. "If the thing sinks, we'll die anyway. You have anesthetic charges for that gun of yours?"

He stared at her back. "Yes."

"Give Nirmond and the girl a shot each, before you do anything else. Directly into the spine, if you can. But don't come any closer —"

Somehow, Cord couldn't argue with that voice. He stood up carefully. The gun made two soft spitting sounds.

"All right," he said hoarsely. "What do I do now?"

Dane was silent a moment. "I'm sorry, Cord. I can't tell you that. I'll tell you what I can —"

She paused for some seconds again. "This thing didn't try to kill us, Cord. It could have easily. It's incredibly strong. I saw it break Nirmond's legs. But as soon as we stopped moving, it just held us. They were both unconscious then —

"You've got that to go on. It was trying to pitch you within reach of its vines or tendrils, or whatever they are, too, wasn't it?"

"I think so," Cord said shakily. That was what had happened, of course; and at any moment Grandpa might try again.

"Now it's feeding us some sort of anesthetic of its own through those vines. Tiny thorns. A sort of numbness —" Dane's voice trailed off a moment. Then she said clearly, "Look, Cord — it seems we're food it's storing up! You get that?"

"Yes," he said.

"Seeding time for the rafts. There are analogues. Live food for its seed probably; not for the raft. One couldn't have counted on that. Cord?"

"Yes. I'm here."

"I want," said Dane, "to stay awake as long as I can. But there's really just one other thing — this raft's going somewhere. To some particularly favorable location. And that might be very near shore. You might make it in then; otherwise it's up to you. But keep your head and wait for a chance. No heroics, understand?"

"Sure, I understand," Cord told her. He realized then that he was talking reassuringly, as if it weren't the Planetary Regent but someone like Grayan.

"Nirmond's the worst," Dane said. "The girl was knocked un-conscious at once. If it weren't for my arm — But, if we can get help in five hours or so, everything should be all right. Let me know if anything happens, Cord."

"I will," Cord said gently again. Then he sighted his gun carefully at a point between Dane's shoulder blades, and the anesthetic chamber made its soft, spitting sound once more. Dane's taut body relaxed slowly, and that was all.

There was no point Cord could see in letting her stay awake; because they weren't going anywhere near shore.

The reed beds and the channels were already behind them, and Grandpa hadn't changed direction by the fraction of a degree. He was moving out into the open Bay — and he was picking up company!

So far, Cord could count seven big rafts within two miles of them; and on the three that were closest he could make out a sprouting of new green vines. All of them were traveling in a straight direction; and the common point they were all headed for appeared to be the roaring center of the Yoger Straits, now some three miles away!

Behind the Straits, the cold Zlanti Deep — the rolling fogs, and the open sea! It might be seeding time for the rafts, but it looked as if they weren't going to distribute their seeds in the Bay —

For a human being, Cord was a fine swimmer. He had a gun and he had a knife; in spite of what Dane had said, he might have stood a chance among the killers of the Bay. But it would be a very small chance, at best. And it wasn't, he thought, as if there weren't still other possibilities. He was going to keep his head.

Except by accident, of course, nobody was going to come looking for them in time to do any good. If anyone did look, it would be around the

Bay Farms. There were a number of rafts moored there; and it would be assumed they'd used one of them. Now and then something unexpected happened and somebody simply vanished — by the time it was figured out just what had happened on this occasion, it would be much too late.

Neither was anybody likely to notice within the next few hours that the rafts had started migrating out of the swamps through the Yoger Straits. There was a small weather station a little inland, on the north side of the Straits, which used a helicopter occasionally. It was about as improbable, Cord decided dismally, that they'd use it in the right spot just now as it would be for a jet transport to happen to come in low enough to spot them.

The fact that it was up to him, as the Regent had said, sank in a little more after that! Cord had never felt so lonely.

Simply because he was going to try it sooner or later, he carried out an experiment next that he knew couldn't work. He opened the gun's anesthetic chamber and counted out fifty pellets — rather hurriedly because he didn't particularly want to think of what he might be using them for eventually. There were around three hundred charges left in the chamber then; and in the next few minutes Cord carefully planted a third of them in Grandpa's head.

He stopped after that. A whale might have showed signs of somnolence under a lesser load. Grandpa paddled on undisturbed. Perhaps he had become a little numb in spots, but his cells weren't equipped to distribute the soporific effect of that type of drug.

There wasn't anything else Cord could think of doing before they reached the Straits. At the rate they were moving, he calculated that would happen in something less than an hour; and if they did pass through the Straits, he was going to risk a swim. He didn't think Dane would have disapproved, under the circumstances. If the raft simply carried them all out into the foggy vastness of the Zlanti Deep, there would be no practical chance of survival left at all.

Meanwhile, Grandpa was definitely picking up speed. And there were other changes going on — minor ones, but still a little awe-inspiring to Cord. The pimply-looking red buds that dotted the upper part of the cone were opening out gradually. From the center of most of them protruded now something like a thin, wet, scarlet worm: a worm that twisted weakly, extended itself by an inch or so, rested and twisted again, and stretched up a little farther, groping into the air. The vertical black slits between the armor plates looked somehow deeper and wider than they had been even some minutes ago; a dark, thick liquid dripped slowly from several of them.

Under other circumstances Cord knew he would have been fas—cinated by these developments in Grandpa. As it was, they drew his suspicious attention only because he didn't know what they meant.

Then something quite horrible happened suddenly. Grayan started moaning loudly and terribly and twisted almost completely around.

Afterwards, Cord knew it hadn't been a second before he stopped her struggles and the sounds together with another anesthetic pellet; but the vines had tightened their grip on her first, not flexibly but like the digging, bony green talons of some monstrous bird of prey. If Dane hadn't warned him —

White and sweating, Cord put his gun down slowly while the vines relaxed again. Grayan didn't seem to have suffered any additional harm; and she would certainly have been the first to point out that his murderous rage might have been as intelligently directed against a machine. But for some moments Cord continued to luxuriate furiously in the thought that, at any instant he chose, he could still turn the raft very quickly into a ripped and exploded mess of sinking vegetation.

Instead, and more sensibly, he gave both Dane and Nirmond another shot, to prevent a similar occurrence with them. The contents of two such pellets, he knew, would keep any human being torpid for at least four hours. Five shots —

Cord withdrew his mind hastily from the direction it was turning into; but it wouldn't stay withdrawn. The thought kept coming up again, until at last he had to recognize it:

Five shots would leave the three of them completely unconscious, whatever else might happen to them, until they either died from other causes or were given a counteracting agent.

Shocked, he told himself he couldn't do it. It was exactly like killing them.

But then, quite steadily, he found himself raising the gun once more, to bring the total charge for each of the three Team people up to five. And if it was the first time in the last four years Cord had felt like crying, it also seemed to him that he had begun to understand what was meant by using your head — along with other things.

Barely thirty minutes later, he watched a raft as big as the one he rode go sliding into the foaming white waters of the Straits a few hundred yards ahead, and dart off abruptly at an angle, caught by one of the swirling currents. It pitched and spun, made some headway, and was swept aside again. And then it righted itself once more. Not like some blindly animated vegetable, Cord thought, but like a creature that struggled with intelligent purpose to maintain its chosen direction.

At least, they seemed practically unsinkable —

Knife in hand, he flattened himself against the platform as the Straits roared just ahead. When the platform jolted and tilted up beneath him, he rammed the knife all the way into it and hung on. Cold water rushed suddenly over him, and Grandpa shuddered like a laboring engine. In the middle of it all, Cord had the horrified notion that the raft might release its unconscious human prisoners in its struggle with the Straits. But he underestimated Grandpa in that. Grandpa also hung on.

Abruptly, it was over. They were riding a long swell, and there were three other rafts not far away. The Straits had swept them together, but they seemed to have no interest in one another's company. As Cord stood up shakily and began to strip off his clothes, they were visibly drawing apart again. The platform of one of them was half-submerged; it must have lost too much of the air that held it afloat and, like a small ship, it was foundering.

From this point, it was only a two-mile swim to the shore north of the Straits, and another mile inland from there to the Straits Head Station. He didn't know about the current; but the distance didn't seem too much, and he couldn't bring himself to leave knife and gun behind. The Bay creatures loved warmth and mud, they didn't venture beyond the Straits. But Zlanti Deep bred its own killers, though they weren't often observed so close to shore.

Things were beginning to look rather hopeful.

Thin, crying voices drifted overhead, like the voices of curious cats, as Cord knotted his clothes into a tight bundle, shoes inside. He looked up. There were four of them circling there; magnified seagoing swamp bugs, each carrying an unseen rider. Probably harmless scavengers — but the ten-foot wingspread was impressive. Uneasily, Cord remembered the venomously carnivorous rider he'd left lying beside the station.

One of them dipped lazily and came sliding down toward him. It soared overhead and came back, to hover about the raft's cone.

The bug rider that directed the mindless flier hadn't been interested in him at all! Grandpa was baiting it!

Cord stared in fascination. The top of the cone was alive now with a softly wriggling mass of the scarlet, wormlike extrusions that had started sprouting before the raft left the Bay. Presumably, they looked enticingly edible to the bug rider.

The flier settled with an airy fluttering and touched the cone. Like a trap springing shut, the green vines flashed up and around it, crumpling the brittle wings, almost vanishing into the long soft body —

Barely a second later, Grandpa made another catch, this one from the sea itself. Cord had a fleeting glimpse of something like a small, rubbery seal that flung itself out of the water upon the edge of the raft, with a suggestion of desperate haste — and was flipped on instantly against the cone, where the vines clamped it down beside the flier's body.

It wasn't the enormous ease with which the unexpected kill was accomplished that left Cord standing there, completely shocked. It was the shattering of his hopes to swim to shore from here. Fifty yards away, the creature from which the rubbery thing had been fleeing showed briefly on the surface, as it turned away from the raft; and the glance was all he needed. The ivory-white body and gaping jaws were similar enough to those of the shark of Earth to indicate the pursuer's nature. The important difference was that, wherever the white hunters of the Zlanti Deep went, they went by the thousands.

Stunned by that incredible piece of bad luck, still clutching his bundled clothes, Cord stared toward shore. Knowing what to look for, he could spot the telltale roilings of the surface now — the long, ivory gleams that flashed through the swells and vanished again. Shoals of smaller things burst into the air in sprays of glittering desperation and fell back. He would have been snapped up like a drowning fly before he'd covered a twentieth of that distance!

But almost another full minute passed before the realization of the finality of his defeat really sank in.

Grandpa was beginning to eat!

Each of the dark slits down the sides of the cone was a mouth. So far only one of them was in operating condition, and the raft wasn't able to open that one very wide as yet. The first morsel had been fed into it, however: the bug rider the vines had plucked out of the flier's downy neck fur. It took Grandpa several minutes to work it out of sight, small as it was. But it was a start.

Cord didn't feel quite sane any more. He sat there, clutching his bundle of clothes and only vaguely aware of the fact that he was shivering steadily under the cold spray that touched him now and then, while he followed Grandpa's activities attentively. He decided it would be at least some hours before one of that black set of mouths grew flexible and vigorous enough to dispose of a human being. Under the circumstances, it couldn't make much difference to the other human beings here; but the moment Grandpa reached for the first of them would also be the moment he finally blew the raft to pieces. The white hunters were cleaner eaters, at any rate; and that was about the extent to which he could still control what was going to happen.

Meanwhile, there was the very faint chance that the weather station's helicopter might spot them —

Meanwhile also, in a weary and horrified fascination, he kept debating the mystery of what could have produced such a nightmarish change in the rafts. He could guess where they were going by now; there were scattered strings of them stretching back to the Straits or roughly parallel to their own course, and the direction was that of the plankton-swarming pool of the Zlanti Basin, a thousand miles to the north. Given time, even mobile lily pads like the rafts had been could make that trip for the benefit of their seedlings. But nothing in their structure explained the sudden change into alert and capable carnivores.

He watched the rubbery little seal-thing being hauled up to a mouth next. The vines broke its neck; and the mouth took it in up to the shoulders and then went on working patiently at what was still a trifle too large a bite. Meanwhile, there were more thin cat cries overhead; and a few minutes later, two more sea bugs were trapped almost simultaneously and added to the larder. Grandpa dropped the dead seal-thing and fed himself another bug rider. The second rider left its mount with a sudden hop, sank its teeth viciously into one of the vines that caught it again, and was promptly battered to death against the platform.

Cord felt a resurge of unreasoning hatred against Grandpa. Killing a bug was about equal to cutting a branch from a tree; they had almost no life-awareness. But the rider had aroused his partisanship because of its appearance of intelligent action — and it was in fact closer to the human scale in that feature than to the monstrous life-form that had, mechanically, but quite successfully, trapped both it and the human beings. Then his thoughts had drifted again; and he found himself speculating vaguely on the curious symbiosis in which the nerve systems of two creatures as dissimilar as the bugs and their riders could be linked so closely that they functioned as one organism.

Suddenly an expression of vast and stunned surprise appeared on his face.

Why — now he knew!

Cord stood up hurriedly, shaking with excitement, the whole plan complete in his mind. And a dozen long vines snaked instantly in the direction of his sudden motion, and groped for him, taut and stretching. They couldn't reach him, but their savagely alert reaction froze Cord briefly where he was. The platform was shuddering under his feet, as if in irritation at his inaccessibility; but it couldn't be tilted up suddenly here to throw him within the grasp of the vines, as it could around the edges.

Still, it was a warning! Cord sidled gingerly around the cone till he had gained the position he wanted, which was on the forward half of the raft. And then he waited. Waited long minutes, quite motionless, until his heart stopped pounding and the irregular angry shivering of the surface of the raft-thing died away, and the last vine tendril had stopped its blind groping. It might help a lot if, for a second or two after he next started moving, Grandpa wasn't too aware of his exact whereabouts!

He looked back once to check how far they had gone by now beyond the Straits Head Station. It couldn't, he decided, be even an hour behind them. Which was close enough, by the most pessimistic count — if everything else worked out all right! He didn't try to think out in detail what that "everything else" could include, because there were factors that simply couldn't be calculated in advance. And he had an uneasy feeling that speculating too vividly about them might make him almost incapable of carrying out his plan.

At last, moving carefully, Cord took the knife in his left hand but left the gun holstered. He raised the tightly knotted bundle of clothes slowly over his head, balanced in his right hand. With a long, smooth motion he tossed the bundle back across the cone, almost to the opposite edge of the platform.

It hit with a soggy thump. Almost immediately, the whole far edge of the raft buckled and flapped up to toss the strange object to the reaching vines.

Simultaneously, Cord was racing forward. For a moment, his attempt to divert Grandpa's attention seemed completely successful — then he was pitched to his knees as the platform came up.

He was within eight feet of the edge. As it slapped down again, he threw himself desperately forward.

An instant later, he was knifing down through cold, clear water, just ahead of the raft, then twisting and coming up again.

The raft was passing over him. Clouds of tiny sea creatures scattered through its dark jungle of feeding roots. Cord jerked back from a broad, wavering streak of glassy greenness, which was a stinger, and felt a burning jolt on his side, which meant he'd been touched lightly by another. He bumped on blindly through the slimy black tangles of hair roots that covered the bottom of the raft; then green half-light passed over him, and he burst up into the central bubble under the cone.

Half-light and foul, hot air. Water slapped around him, dragging him away again — nothing to hang on to here! Then above him, to his right, molded against the interior curve of the cone as if it had grown there from the start, the froglike, man-sized shape of the yellowhead.

The raft rider —

Cord reached up and caught Grandpa's symbiotic partner and guide by a flabby hind leg, pulled himself half out of the water, and struck twice with the knife, fast while the pale-green eyes were still opening.

He'd thought the yellowhead might need a second or so to detach itself from its host, as the bug riders usually did, before it tried to defend itself. This one merely turned its head; the mouth slashed down and clamped on Cord's left arm above the elbow. His right hand sank the knife through one staring eye, and the yellowhead jerked away, pulling the knife from his grasp.

Sliding down, he wrapped both hands around the slimy leg and hauled with all his weight. For a moment more, the yellow-head hung on. Then the countless neural extensions that connected it now with the raft came free in a succession of sucking, tearing sounds; and Cord and the yellowhead splashed into the water together.

Black tangle of roots again — and two more electric burns suddenly across his back and legs! Strangling, Cord let go. Below him, for a moment, a body was turning over and over with oddly human motions; then a solid wall of water thrust him up and aside, as something big and white struck the turning body and went on.

Cord broke the surface twelve feet behind the raft. And that would have been that, if Grandpa hadn't already been slowing down.

Alter two tries, he floundered back up on the platform and lay there gasping and coughing awhile. There were no indications that his presence was resented now. A few vine tips twitched uneasily, as if trying to remember previous functions, when he came limping up presently to make sure his three companions were still breathing; but Cord never noticed that.

They were still breathing; and he knew better than to waste time trying to help them himself. He took Grayan's heat-gun from its holster. Grandpa had come to a full stop.

Cord hadn't had time to become completely sane again, or he might have worried now whether Grandpa, violently sundered from his controlling partner, was still capable of motion on his own. Instead, he determined the approximate direction of the Straits Head Station, selected a corresponding spot on the platform, and gave Grandpa a light tap of heat.

Nothing happened immediately. Cord sighed patiently and stepped up the heat a little.

Grandpa shuddered gently. Cord stood up.

Slowly and hesitatingly at first, then with steadfast — though now again brainless — purpose, Grandpa began paddling back toward the Straits Head Station.

Lion Loose...

For twelve years, at a point where three major shipping routes of the Federation of the Hub crossed within a few hours' flight of one another, the Seventh Star Hotel had floated in space, a great golden sphere, gleaming softly in the void through its translucent shells of battle plastic. The Star had been designed to be much more than a convenient transfer station for travelers and freight; for some years after it was opened to the public, it retained a high rating among the more exotic pleasure resorts of the Hub. The Seventh Star Hotel was the place to have been that season, and the celebrities and fat cats converged on it with their pals and hangers-on. The Star blazed with life, excitement, interstellar scandals, tinkled with streams of credits dancing in from a thousand worlds. In short, it had started out as a paying proposition.

But gradually things changed. The Star's entertainment remained as delightfully outrageous as ever, the cuisine as excellent; the accommodations and service were still above reproach. The fleecing, in general, became no less expertly painless. But one had *been* there. By its eighth year, the Star was dated. Now, in its twelfth, it lived soberly off the liner and freighter trade, four fifths of the guest suites shut down, the remainder irregularly occupied between ship departures.

And in another seven hours, if the plans of certain men went through, the Seventh Star Hotel would abruptly wink out of existence.

Some fifty or sixty early diners were scattered about the tables on the garden terraces of Phalagon House, the Seventh Star Hotel's most exclusive eatery. One of them had just finished his meal, sat smoking and regarding a spiraling flow of exquisitely indicated female figures across the garden's skyscape with an air of friendly approval. He was a large and muscular young man, deeply tanned, with shoulders of impressive thickness, an aquiline nose, and dark, reflective eyes.

After a minute or two, he yawned comfortably, put out the cigarette, and pushed his chair back from the table. As he came to his feet, there was a soft bell-note from the table ComWeb. He hesitated, said, "Go ahead."

"Is intrusion permitted?" the ComWeb inquired.

"Depends," the guest said. "Who's calling?"

"The name is Reetal Destone."

He grinned, appeared pleasantly surprised. "Put the lady through."

There was a brief silence. Then a woman's voice inquired softly, "Quillan?"

"Right here, doll! Where —"

"Seal the ComWeb, Quillan."

He reached down to the instrument, tapped the seal button, said, "All right. We're private."

"Probably," the woman's voice said. "But better scramble this, too. I want to be very sure no one's listening."

Quillan grunted, slid his left hand into an inner coat pocket, briefly fingered a device of the approximate size and shape of a cigarette, drew his hand out again. "Scrambling!" he announced. "Now, what —"

"Mayday, Quillan," the soft voice said. "Can you come immediately?"

Quillan's face went expressionless. "Of course. Is it urgent?"

"I'm in no present danger. But we'd better waste no time."

"Is it going to take real hardware? I'm carrying a finger gun at the moment."

"Then go to your rooms and pick up something useful," Reetal said. "This should take real hardware, all right."

"All right. Then where do I go?"

"I'll meet you at your door. I know where it is."

When Quillan arrived, she was standing before the door to his suite, a tall blonde in a sleeveless black and gold sheath; a beautiful body, a warm, lovely, humorous face. The warmth and humor were real, but masked a mind as impersonally efficient as a computer, and a taste for high and dangerous living. When Quillan had last met Reetal Destone, a year and a half before, the taste was being satisfied in industrial espionage. He hadn't heard of her activities since then.

She smiled thoughtfully at him as he came up. "I'll wait outside," she said. "We're not talking here."

Quillan nodded, went on into his living room, selected a gun belt and holstered gun from a suitcase, fastened the belt around his waist under the coat, and came out. "Now what?"

"First a little portal-hopping —"

He followed her across the corridor and into a tube portal, watched as she tapped out a setting. The exit light flashed a moment later; they stepped out into a vacant lounge elsewhere in the same building, crossed it, entered another portal. After three more shifts, they emerged into a long hall, dimly lit, heavily carpeted. There was no one in sight.

"Last stop," Reetal said. She glanced up at his face. "We're on the other side of the Star now, in one of the sections they've closed up. I've established a kind of emergency headquarters here. The Star's nearly broke, did you know?"

"I'd heard of it."

"That appears to be part of the reason for what's going on."

Quillan said, "What's going on?"

Reetal slid her arm through his, said, "Come on. That's my, hm-m-m, unregistered suite over there. Big boy, it's very, very selfish of me, but I was extremely glad to detect your name on the list of newly arrived guests

just now! As to what's going on ... the *Camelot* berths here at midnight,
you know."

Quillan nodded. "I've some business with one of her passengers."

Reetal bent to unlock the entrance door to the indicated suite. "The way
it looks now," she remarked, "the odds are pretty high that you're not
going to keep that appointment."

"Why not?"

"Because shortly after the *Camelot* docks and something's been unloaded from her, the *Camelot* and the Seventh Star Hotel are scheduled to
go *poof!* together. Along with you, me, and some twelve thousand other
people. And, so far, I haven't been able to think of a good way to keep it
from happening."

Quillan was silent a moment. "Who's scheduling the poof?" he asked.

"Some old acquaintances of ours are among them. Come on in. What
they're doing comes under the heading of destroying the evidence."

She locked the door behind them, said, "Just a moment," went over to
the paneled wall, turned down a tiny silver switch. "Room portal," she
said, nodding at the wall. "It might come in handy. I keep it turned off
most of the time."

"Why are you turning it on now?" Quillan asked.

"One of the Star's stewards is working on this with me. He'll be along
as soon as he can get away. Now I'll give you the whole thing as briefly as
I can. The old acquaintances I mentioned are some boys of the
Brotherhood of Beldon. Movaine's here; he's got Marras Cooms and Fluel
with him, and around thirty of the Brotherhood's top guns. Nome
Lancion's coming in on the *Camelot* in person tonight to take charge.
Obviously, with all that brass on the job, they're after something very big.
Just what it is, I don't yet know. I've got one clue, but a rather puzzling
one. Tell you about that later. Do you know Velladon?"

"The commodore here?" Quillan nodded. "I've never met him but I
know who he is."

Reetal said, "He's been manager of the Seventh Star Hotel for the past
nine years. He's involved in the Beldon outfit's operation. So is the chief of
the Star's private security force — his name's Ryter — and half a dozen
other Star executives. They've got plenty of firepower, too; close to half the
entire security force, I understand, including all the officers. That would
come to nearly seventy men. There's reason to believe the rest of the force
was disarmed and murdered by them in the subspace section of the Star
about twelve hours ago. They haven't been seen since then.

"Now, Velladon, aside from his share in whatever they're after, has
another reason for wanting to wipe out the Star in an unexplained blowup.
There I have definite information. Did you know the Mooley brothers
owned the Star?"

"Yes."

"I've been working for the Mooleys the past eight months," Reetal said,
"checking up on employees at Velladon's level for indications of graft.

And it appears the commodore has been robbing them blind here for at least several years."

"Sort of risky thing to try with the Mooleys, from what I hear," Quillan remarked.

"Yes. Very. Velladon had reason to be getting a little desperate about that. Two men were planted here a month ago. One of them is Sher Heraga, the steward I told you about. The other man came in as a bookkeeper. Two weeks ago, Heraga got word out that the bookkeeper had disappeared. Velladon and Ryter apparently got wise to what he was trying to do. So the Mooleys sent me here to find out exactly what was going on before they took action. I arrived four days ago."

She gave a regretful little headshake. "I waited almost a day before contacting Heraga. It seemed advisable to move very cautiously in the matter. But that made it a little too late to do anything. Quillan, for the past three days, the Seventh Star hotel has been locked up like a bank vault. And except for ourselves, only the people who are in on the plot are aware of it."

"The message transmitters are inoperative?" he asked.

Reetal nodded. "The story is that a gravitic storm center in the area has disrupted transmissions completely for the time being."

"What about incoming ships?"

"Yours was the only one scheduled before the *Camelot* arrives. It left again eight hours ago. Nobody here had been let on board. The guests who wanted to apply for outgoing berths were told there were none open, that they'd have to wait for the *Camelot*."

She went over to a desk, unlocked a drawer, took out a sheaf of papers, and handed one of them to Quillan. "That's the layout of the Star," she said. "This five-level building over by the shell is the Executive Block. The Brotherhood and the commodore's men moved in there this morning. The Block is the Star's defense center. It's raid-proofed, contains the control offices and the transmitter and armament rooms. About the standard arrangement. While they hold the Executive Block, they have absolute control of the Star."

"If it's the defense center, it should be practically impossible to do anything about them there," Quillan agreed. "They could close it up, and dump the air out of the rest of the Star in a minute, if they had to. But there must be ... well, what about the lifeboats in the subspace section — and our pals must have a getaway ship stashed away somewhere?"

"They have two ships," Reetal said. "A souped-up armed freighter the Brotherhood came in on, and a large armed yacht which seems to be the commodore's personal property. Unfortunately, they're both in subspace locks."

"Why unfortunately?"

"Because they've sealed off subspace. Try portaling down there, and you'll find yourself looking at a battle-plastic bulkhead. There is no way of getting either to those ships or to the lifeboats."

Quillan lifted his eyebrows. "And that hasn't caused any comment? What about the maintenance crews, the warehouse men, the —"

"All the work crews were hauled out of subspace this morning," Reetal said. "On the quiet, the Star's employees have been told that a gang of raiders was spotted in the warehouse area, and is at present cornered there. Naturally, the matter isn't to be mentioned to the guests, to avoid arousing unnecessary concern. And that explains everything very neatly. The absence of the security men, and why subspace is sealed off. Why the Executive Block is under guard, and can't be entered — and why the technical and office personnel in there don't come out, and don't communicate out. They've been put on emergency status, officially."

"Yunk," Quillan said disgustedly after a moment. "This begins to look like a hopeless situation, doll!"

"True."

"Let's see now —"

Reetal interrupted, "There is one portal still open to subspace. That's in the Executive Block, of course, and Heraga reports it's heavily guarded."

"How does he know?"

"The Block's getting its meals from Phalagon House. He floated a diner in there a few hours ago."

"Well," Quillan said, brightening, "perhaps a deft flavoring of poison —"

Reetal shook her head. "I checked over the hospital stocks. Not a thing there that wouldn't be spotted at once. Unless we can clobber them thoroughly, we can't afford to make them suspicious with a trick like that."

"Poison would be a bit rough on the office help, too," Quillan conceded. "They wouldn't be in on the deal."

"No, they're not. They're working under guard."

"Gas ... no, I suppose not. It would take too long to whip up something that could turn the trick." Quillan glanced at his watch. "If the *Camelot* docks at midnight, we've around six and a half hours left, doll! And I don't find myself coming up with any brilliant ideas. What have you thought of?"

Reetal hesitated a moment. "Nothing very brilliant either," she said then. "But there are two things we might try as a last resort."

"Let's hear them."

"I know a number of people registered in the Star at present who'd be carrying personal weapons. If they were told the facts, I could probably line up around twenty who'd be willing to make a try to get into the Executive Block, and take over either the control offices or the transmitter room. If we got a warning out to the *Camelot*, that would break up the plot. Of course, it wouldn't necessarily save the Star."

"No," Quillan said, "but it's worth trying if we can't think of something better. How would you get them inside?"

"We could crowd twenty men into one of those diner trucks, and Heraga could take us in."

"What kind of people are your pals?"

"A few smugglers and confidence men I've had connections with. Fairly good boys for this sort of thing. Then there's an old millionaire sportsman, with a party of six, waiting to transfer to the *Camelot* for a safari on Jontarou. Old Philmarron isn't all there, in my opinion, but he's dead game and loves any kind of a ruckus. We can count on him and his friends, if they're not too drunk at the moment. Still ... that's not too many to set against something less than a hundred professional guns, even though some of them must be down on the two ships."

"No, not enough." Quillan looked thoughtful. "What's the other idea?"

"Let the cat out of the bag generally. Tell the guests and the employees out here what's going on, and see if somebody can think of something that might be done."

He shook his head. "What you'd set off with that would be anywhere between a riot and a panic. The boys in the Executive Block would simply give us the breathless treatment. Apparently, they prefer to have everything looking quiet and normal when the *Camelot* gets here —"

"But they don't have to play it that way," Reetal agreed. "We might be dead for hours before the liner docks. If they keep the landing lock closed until what they want has been unloaded, nobody on the *Camelot* would realize what had happened before it was too late."

There was a moment's silence. Then Quillan said, "You mentioned you'd picked up a clue to what they're after. What was that?"

"Well, that is a curious thing," Reetal said. "On the trip out here, a young girl name of Solvey Kinmarten attached herself to me. She didn't want to talk much, but I gathered she was newly married, and that her husband was on board and was neglecting her. She's an appealing little thing, and she seemed so forlorn and upset that I adopted her for the rest of the run. After we arrived, of course, I pretty well forgot about the Kin-martens and their troubles.

"A few hours ago, Solvey suddenly came bursting into the suite where I'm registered. She was shaking all over. After I calmed her down a bit, she spilled out her story. She and her husband, Brock Kinmarten, are rest wardens. With another man named Eltak, whom Solvey describes as 'some sort of crazy old coot,' they're assigned to escort two deluxe private rest cubicles to a very exclusive sanatorium on Mezmiali. But Brock told Solvey at the beginning of the trip that this was a very unusual assignment, that he didn't want her even to come near the cubicles. That wouldn't have bothered her so much, she says, but on the way here Brock became increasingly irritable and absent-minded. She knew he was worrying about the cubicles, and she began to wonder whether they weren't involved in something illegal. The pay was very high; they're both getting almost twice the regular warden fee for the job. One day, she found an opportunity to do a little investigating.

"The cubicles are registered respectively to a Lady Pendrake and a Major Pendrake. Lady Pendrake appears to be genuine; the cubicle is unusually large and constructed somewhat differently from the ones with which Solvey was familiar, but it was clear that it had an occupant. However, the life indicator on 'Major Pendrake's' cubicle registered zero when she switched it on. If there was something inside it, it wasn't a living human being.

"That was all she learned at the time, because she was afraid Brock might catch her in the cubicle room. Here in the Star, the cubicles were taken to a suite reserved for Lady Pendrake. The other man, Eltak, stayed in the suite with the cubicles, while the Kinmartens were given other quarters. However, Brock was still acting oddly and spending most of his time in the Pendrake suite. So this morning, Solvey swiped his key to the suite and slipped in when she knew the two men had left it.

"She'd barely got there when she heard Brock and Eltak at the door again. She ran into the next room, and hid in a closet. Suddenly there was a commotion in the front room, and Solvey realized that men from the Star's security force had arrived and were arresting Brock and Eltak. They hauled both of them away, then floated the cubicles out and on a carrier and took them off too, locking the suite behind them.

"Solvey was in a complete panic, sure that she and Brock had become involved in some serious breach of the Warden Code. She waited a few minutes, then slipped out of the Pendrake suite, and looked me up to see if I couldn't help them. I had Heraga check, and he reported that the Kinmarten suite was under observation. Evidently, they wanted to pick up the girl, too. So I tucked her away in one of the suites in this section, and gave her something to put her to sleep. She's there now."

Quillan said, "And where are the prisoners and the cubicles?"

"In the Executive Block."

"How do you know?"

Reetal smiled briefly. "The Duke of Fluel told me."

"Huh? The Brotherhood knows you're here?"

"Relax," Reetal said. "Nobody but Heraga knows I'm working for the Mooleys. I told the Duke I had a big con deal set up when the *Camelot* came in — I even suggested he might like to get in on it. He laughed, and said he had other plans. But he won't mention to anyone that I'm here."

"Why not?"

"Because," Reetal said dryly, "what the Duke is planning to get in on is an hour of tender dalliance. Before the *Camelot* arrives, necessarily. The cold-blooded little skunk!" She hesitated a moment; when she spoke again, her voice had turned harsh and nasal, wicked amusement sounding through it. "Sort of busy at the moment, sweetheart, but we might find time for a drink or two later on in the evening, eh?"

Quillan grunted. "You're as good at the voice imitations as ever. How did you find out about the cubicles?"

"I took a chance and fed him a Moment of Truth."

"With Fluel," Quillan said thoughtfully, "that *was* taking a chance!"

"Believe me, I was aware of it! I've run into card-carrying sadists be–fore, but the Duke's the only one who scares me silly. But it did work. He dropped in for about a minute and a half, and came out without noticing a thing. Meanwhile, I'd got the answers to a few questions. The bomb with which they're planning to mop up behind them already has been planted up here in the normspace section. Fluel didn't know where; armaments experts took care of it. It's armed now. There's a firing switch on each of their ships, and both switches have to be tripped before the thing goes off. Part of what they're after is in those Pendrake rest cubicles —"

"Part of it?" Quillan asked.

"Uh-huh. An even hundred similar cubicles will be unloaded from the *Camelot* — the bulk of the haul; which is why Nome Lancion is supervising things on the liner. I started to ask what was in the cubicles, but I saw Fluel was beginning to lose that blank look they have under Truth, and switched back to light chitchat just before he woke up. Yaco's paying for the job — or rather, it *will* pay for the stuff, on delivery, and no questions asked."

"That's not very much help, is it?" Quillan said after a moment. "Something a big crooked industrial combine like Yaco thinks it can use —"

"It must expect to be able to use it to extremely good advantage," Reetal said. "The Brotherhood will collect thirty million credits for their part of the operation. The commodore's group presumably won't do any worse." She glanced past Quillan toward the room portal. "It's O.K., Heraga! Come in."

Sher Heraga was a lean, dark-skinned little man with a badly bent nose, black curly hair, and a nervous look. He regretted, he said, that he hadn't been able to uncover anything which might be a lead to the location of the bomb. Apparently, it wasn't even being guarded. And, of course, a bomb of the size required here would be quite easy to conceal.

"If they haven't placed guards over it," Reetal agreed, "it'll take blind luck to spot it! Unless we can get hold of one of the men who knows where it's planted —"

There was silence for some seconds. Then Quillan said, "Well, if we can't work out a good plan, we'd better see what we can do with one of the bad ones. Are the commodore's security men wearing uniforms?"

Heraga shook his head. "Not the ones I saw."

"Then here's an idea," Quillan said. "As things stand, barging into the Executive Block with a small armed group can't accomplish much. It might be more interesting than sitting around and waiting to be blown up, but it still would be suicide. However, if we could get things softened up and disorganized in there first — "

"Softened up and disorganized how?" Reetal asked.

"We can use that notion you had of having Heraga float in another diner. This time, I'm on board — in a steward's uniform, in case the guards check."

"They didn't the first time," Heraga said.

"Sloppy of them. Well, they're just gun hands. Anyway, once we're inside I shuck off the uniform and get out. Heraga delivers his goodies, and leaves again —"

Reetal gave him a look. "You'll get shot down the instant you're seen, dope!"

"I think not. There're two groups in there — around a hundred men in all — and they haven't had time to get well acquainted yet. I'll have my gun in sight, and anyone who sees me should figure I belong to the other group, until I run into one of the Brotherhood boys who knows me personally."

"Then that's when you get shot down. I understand the last time you and the Duke of Fluel met, he woke up with lumps."

"The Duke doesn't love me," Quillan admitted. "But there's nothing personal between me and Movaine or Marras Cooms — and I'll have a message for Movaine."

"What kind of a message?"

"I'll have to play that by ear a little. It depends on how things look in there. But I have a few ideas, based on what you've learned of the oper-ation. Now, just what I can do when I get that far, I don't know yet. I'll simply try to louse the deal up as much as I can. That may take time, and, of course, it might turn out to be impossible to get word out to you."

"So what do we do meanwhile?" Reetal asked. "If we start lining up our attack group immediately, and then there's no action for another five or six hours, there's always the chance of a leak, with around twenty people in the know."

"And if there's a leak," Quillan agreed, "we've probably had it. No, you'd better wait with that! If I'm not out, and you haven't heard from me before the Camelot's actually due to dock, Heraga can still take the group — everyone but yourself — in as scheduled."

"Why everyone but me?" Reetal asked.

"If nothing else works, you might find some way of getting a warning to the liner's security force after they've docked. It isn't much of a possibility, but we can't afford to throw it away."

"Yes, I see." Reetal looked reflective. "What do you think, Heraga?"

The little man shrugged. "You told me that Mr. Quillan is not inexperienced in dealing with, ah, his enemies. If he feels he might accomplish something in the Executive Block, I'm in favor of the plan. The situation certainly could hardly become worse."

"That's the spirit!" Quillan approved. "The positive outlook — that's what a thing like this mainly takes. Can you arrange for the diner and the uniform?"

"Oh, yes," Heraga said. "I've had myself put in charge of that detail, naturally."

"Then what can you tell me about the Executive Block's layout?"

Reetal stood up. "Come over to the desk," she said. "We've got diagrams."

"The five levels, as you see," Heraga was explaining a few moments later, "are built directly into the curve of the Star's shells. Level Five, on the top, is therefore quite small. The other levels are fairly extensive. Two, Three, and Four could each accommodate a hundred men comfortably. These levels contain mainly living quarters, private offices, and the like. The Brotherhood men appear to be occupying the fourth level, Velladon's group the second. The third may be reserved for meetings between representatives of the two groups. All three of these levels are connected by single-exit portals to the large entrance area on the ground level.

"The portals stood open when I went in earlier today, and there were about twenty armed men lounging about the entrance ball. I recognized approximately half of them as being members of the Star's security force. The others were unfamiliar." Heraga cleared his throat. "There is a possibility that the two groups do not entirely trust each other."

Quillan nodded. "If they're playing around with something like sixty million CR, anybody would have to be crazy to trust the Brotherhood of Beldon. The transmitter room and the control offices are guarded, too?"

"Yes, but not heavily," Heraga said. "There seem to be only a few men stationed at each of those points. Ostensibly, they're there as a safe-guard — in case the imaginary raiders attempt to break out of the subspace section."

"What's the arrangement of the ordinary walk-in tube portals in the Executive Block?"

"There is one which interconnects the five levels. On each of the lower levels, there are, in addition, several portals which lead out to various points in the Seventh Star Hotel. On the fifth level, there is only one portal of this kind. Except for the portal which operates between the different levels in the Executive Block, all of them have been rendered unusable at present."

"Unusable in what way?"

"They have been sealed off on the Executive Block side."

"Can you get me a diagram of the entry and exit systems those outgoing portals connect with?" Quillan asked. "I might turn one of them usable again."

"Yes, I can do that."

"How about the communication possibilities?"

"The ComWeb system is functioning normally on the second, third, and fourth levels. It has been shut off on the first level — to avoid the spread of 'alarming rumors' by office personnel. There is no ComWeb on the fifth level."

Reetal said, "We'll shift our operating headquarters back to my re-gistered suite then. The ComWebs are turned off in these vacant sections. I'll stay in the other suite in case you find a chance to signal in."

Heraga left a few minutes later to make his arrangements. Reetal smiled at Quillan, a little dubiously.

"Good luck, guy," she said. "Anything else to settle before you start off?"

Quillan nodded. "Couple of details. If you're going to be in your regular suite, and Fluel finds himself with some idle time on hand, he might show up for the dalliance you mentioned."

Reetal's smile changed slightly. Her left hand fluffed the hair at the back of her head, flicked down again. There was a tiny click, and Quillan looked at a small jeweled hair-clasp in her palm, its needle beak pointing at him.

"It hasn't got much range," Reetal said, "but within ten feet it will scramble the Duke's brains just as thoroughly as they need to be scrambled."

"Good enough," Quillan said. "Just don't give that boy the ghost of a chance, doll. He has a rep for playing very unnice games with the ladies."

"I know his reputation." Reetal replaced the tiny gun in her hair. "Anything else?"

"Yes. Let's look in on the Kinmarten chick for a moment. If she's awake, she may have remembered something or other by now that she didn't think to tell you."

They found Solvey Kinmarten awake, and tearfully glad to see Reetal. Quillan was introduced as a member of the legal profession who would do what he could for Solvey and her husband. Solvey frowned prettily, trying very hard to remember anything that might be of use. But it appeared that she had told Reetal all she knew.

The blue and white Phalagon House diner, driven by Heraga, was admitted without comment into the Executive Block. It floated on unchallenged through the big entry hall and into a corridor. Immediately behind the first turn of the corridor, the diner paused a few seconds. Its side door opened and closed. The diner moved on.

Quillan, coatless and with the well-worn butt of a big Miam Devil Special protruding from the holster on his right hip, came briskly back along the corridor. Between fifteen and twenty men, their guns also conspicuously in evidence, were scattered about the entrance hall, expressions and attitudes indicating a curious mixture of boredom and uneasy tension. The eyes of about half of them swiveled around to Quillan when he came into the hall; then, with one exception, they looked indifferently away again.

The exception, leaning against the wall near the three open portals to the upper levels, continued to stare as Quillan came toward him, forehead creased in a deep scowl as if he were painfully ransacking his mind for something. Quillan stopped in front of him.

"Chum," he asked, "any idea where Movaine is at the moment? They just give me this message for him —"

Still scowling, the other scratched his chin and blinked. "Uh ... dunno for sure," he said after a moment. "He oughta be in the third-level conference room with the rest of 'em. Uh ... dunno you oughta barge in there right now, pal! The commodore's *reee-lly* hot about somethin'!"

Quillan looked worried. "Gotta chance it, I guess! Message is pretty important, they say —" He turned, went through the center portal of the three, abruptly found himself walking along a wide, well-lit hall.

Nobody in sight here, or in the first intersecting passage he came to. When he reached the next passage. he heard voices on the right, turned toward them, went by a string of closed doors on both sides until, forty feet on, the passage angled again and opened into a long, high-ceilinged room. The voices came through an open door on the right side of the room. Standing against the wall beside the door were two men whose heads turned sharply toward Quillan as he appeared in the passage. The short, chunky one scowled. The big man next to him, the top of whose head had been permanently seared clear of hair years before by a near miss from a blaster, dropped his jaw slowly. His eyes popped.

"My God!" he said.

"Movaine in there, Baldy?" Quillan inquired, coming up.

"Movaine! He ... you ... how —"

The chunky man took out his gun, waved it negligently at Quillan. "Tell the ape to blow, Perk. He isn't wanted here."

"Ape?" Quillan asked softly. His right hand moved, had the gun by the barrel, twisted, reversed the gun, jammed it back with some violence into the chunky man's stomach. "Ape?" he repeated. The chunky man went white.

"Bad News —" Baldy Perk breathed. "Take it easy! That's Orca. He's the commodore's torpedo. How —"

"Where's Movaine?"

"Movaine ... he ... uh —"

"All right, he's not here. And Lancion can't have arrived yet. Is Cooms in there?"

"Yeah," Baldy Perk said weakly, "Cooms is in there, Quillan."

"Let's go in." Quillan withdrew the gun, slid it into a pocket, smiled down at Orca. "Get it back from your boss, slob. Be seeing you!"

Orca's voice was a husky whisper. "You will, friend! You will!"

The conference room was big and sparsely furnished. Four men sat at the long table in its center. Quillan knew two of them — Marras Cooms, second in command of the Beldon Brotherhood's detachment here, and the Duke of Fluel, Movaine's personal gun. Going by Heraga's de–scriptions, the big, florid-faced man with white hair and flowing white mustaches who was doing the talking was Velladon, the commodore; while the fourth man, younger, wiry, with thinning black hair plastered back across his skull, would be Ryter, chief of the Star's security force.

"What I object to primarily is that the attempt was made without obtaining my consent, and secretly," Velladon was saying, with a toothy grin but in a voice that shook with open fury. "And now it's been made and bungled, you have a nerve asking for our help. The problem is yours — and you better take care of it fast! I can't spare Ryter. If —"

"Cooms," Baldy Perk broke in desperately from the door, "Bad News Quillan's here an' —"

The heads of the four men at the table came around simultaneously. The eyes of two of them widened for an instant. Then Marras Cooms began laughing softly.

"Now everything's happened!" he said.

"Cooms," the commodore said testily, "I prefer not to be interrupted. Now —"

"Can't be helped, commodore," Quillan said, moving forward, Perk shuffling along unhappily beside him. "I've got news for Movaine, and the news can't wait."

"Movaine?" the commodore repeated, blue eyes bulging at Quillan. "Movaine! Cooms, who is this man?"

"You're looking at Bad News Quillan," Cooms said. "A highjacking specialist, with somewhat numerous sidelines. But the point right now is that he isn't a member of the Brotherhood."

"What!" Velladon's big fist smashed down on the table. "Now what kind of a game ... how did he get in here?"

"Well," Quillan said mildly, "I oozed in through the north wall about a minute ago. I —"

He checked, conscious of having created some kind of sensation. The four men at the table were staring up at him without moving. Baldy Perk appeared to be holding his breath. Then the commodore coughed, cleared his throat, drummed his fingers on the table.

He said reflectively: "He could have news — good or bad — at that! For all of us." He chewed on one of his mustache tips, grinned suddenly up at Quillan. "Well, sit down, friend! Let's talk. You can't talk to Movaine, you see. Movaine's, um, had an accident. Passed away suddenly half an hour ago."

"Sorry to hear it," Quillan said. "That's the sort of thing that happens so often in the Brotherhood." He swung a chair around, sat down facing the table. "You're looking well tonight, Fluel," he observed.

The Duke of Fluel, lean and dapper in silver jacket and tight-fitting silver trousers, gave him a wintry smile, said nothing.

"Now, then, friend," Velladon inquired confidentially, "just what was your business with Movaine?"

"Well, it will come to around twenty per cent of the take," Quillan informed him. "We won't argue about a half-million CR more or less. But around twenty per."

The faces turned thoughtful. After some seconds, the commodore asked, "And who's we?"

"A number of citizens," Quillan said, "who have been rather unhappy since discovering that you, too, are interested in Lady Pendrake and her pals. We'd gone to considerable expense and trouble to ... well, her ladyship was scheduled to show up in Mezmiali, you know. And now she isn't going to show up there. All right, that's business. Twenty per — no hard feelings. Otherwise, it won't do you a bit of good to blow up the Star and the liner. There'd still be loose talk — maybe other complications, too. You know how it goes. You wouldn't be happy, and neither would Yaco. Right?"

The commodore's massive head turned back to Cooms. "How well do you know this man, Marras?"

Cooms grinned dryly. "Well enough."

"Is he leveling?"

"He'd be nuts to be here if he wasn't. And he isn't nuts — at least, not that way."

"There might be a question about that," Fluel observed. He looked at the commodore. "Why not ask him for a couple of the names that are in it with him?"

"Hagready and Boltan," Quillan said.

Velladon chewed the other mustache tip. "I know Hagready. If he —"

"I know both of them," Cooms said. "Boltan works highjacking crews out of Orado. Quillan operates there occasionally."

"Pappy Boltan's an old business associate," Quillan agreed. "Reliable sort of a guy. Doesn't mind taking a few chances either."

Velladon's protruding blue eyes measured him a moment. "We can check on those two, you know —"

"Check away," Quillan said.

Velladon nodded. "We will." He was silent for a second or two, then glanced over at Cooms. "There've been no leaks on our side," he remarked. "And they must have known about this for weeks! Of all the inept, bungling —"

"Ah, don't be too hard on the Brotherhood, commodore," Quillan said. "Leaks happen. You ought to know,"

"What do you mean?" Velladon snapped.

"From what we heard, the Brotherhood's pulling you out of a hole here. You should feel rather kindly toward them."

The commodore stared at him reflectively. Then he grinned. "Could be I should," he said. "Did you come here alone?"

"Yes."

The commodore nodded. "If you're bluffing, God help you. If you're not, your group's in. Twenty per. No time for haggling — we can raise Yaco's price to cover it." He stood up, and Ryter stood up with him. "Marras," the commodore went on, "tell him what's happened. If he's half as hot as he sounds, he's the boy to put on that job. Let him get in on a little of the work for the twenty per cent. Ryter, come on. We —"

"One moment, sir," Quillan interrupted. He took Orca's gun by the muzzle from his pocket, held it out to Velladon. "One of your men lost this thing. The one outside the door. If you don't mind — he might pout if he doesn't get it back."

The fifth level of the Executive Block appeared to be, as Heraga had said, quite small. The tiny entry hall, on which two walk-in portals opened, led directly into the large room where the two Pendrake rest cubicles had been placed. One of the cubicles now stood open. To right and left, a narrow passage stretched away from the room, ending apparently in smaller rooms.

Baldy Perk was perspiring profusely.

"Now right here," he said in a low voice, "was where I was standing. Movaine was over there, on the right of the cubicle, and Cooms was beside him. Rubero was a little behind me, hanging on to the punk — that Kinmarten. An' the Duke" — he nodded back at the wide doorspace to the hall — "was standing back there.

"All right. The punk's opened the cubicle a crack, looking like he's about to pass out while he's doin' it. This bearded guy, Eltak, stands in front of the cubicle, holding the gadget he controls the thing with —"

"Where's the gadget now?" Quillan asked.

"Marras Cooms' got it."

"How does it work?"

Baldy shook his head. "We can't figure it out. It's got all kinds of little knobs and dials on it. Push this one an' it squeaks, turn that one an' it buzzes. Like that."

Quillan nodded. "All right. What happened?"

"Well, Movaine tells the old guy to go ahead an' do the demonstrating. The old guy sort of grins and fiddles with the gadget. The cubicle door pops open an' this thing comes pouring out. I never seen nothin' like it! It's like a barn door with dirty fur on it! It swirls up an' around an' — it wraps its upper end clean around poor Movaine. He never even screeches."

"Then everything pops at once. The old guy is laughing like crazy, an' that half-smart Rubero drills him right through the head. I take one shot at the thing, low so's not to hit Movaine, an' then we're all running. I'm halfway to the hall when Cooms tears past me like a rocket. The Duke an' the others are already piling out through the portal. I get to the hall, and there's this terrific smack of sound in the room. I look back ... an' ... an' —" Baldy paused and gulped.

"And what?" Quillan asked.

"There, behind the cubicles, I see poor Movaine stickin' halfway out o' the wall!" Baldy reported in a hushed whisper.

"*Half*way out of the wall?"

"From the waist up he's in it! From the waist down he's dangling into the room! I tell you, I never seen nothin' like it."

"And this Hlat creature —"

"That's gone. I figure the smack I heard was when it hit the wall flat, carrying Movaine. It went on into it. Movaine didn't — at least, the last half of him didn't."

"Well," Quillan said after a pause, "in a way, Movaine got his demonstration. The Hlats can move through solid matter and carry other objects along with them, as advertised. If Yaco can work out how it's done and build a gadget that does the same thing, they're getting the Hlats cheap. What happened then?"

"I told Marras Cooms about Movaine, and he sent me and a half dozen other boys back up here with riot guns to see what we could do for him. Which was nothin', of course." Baldy gulped again. "We finally cut this end of him off with a beam and took it back down."

"The thing didn't show up while you were here?"

Baldy shuddered and said, "Naw."

"And the technician ... Eltak ... was dead?"

"Sure. Hole in his head you could shove your fist through."

"Somebody," Quillan observed, "ought to drill Rubero for that stupid trick!"

"The Duke did — first thing after we got back to the fourth level."

"So the Hlat's on the loose, and all we really have at the moment are the cubicles ... and Rest Warden Kinmarten. Where's he, by the way?"

"He tried to take off when we got down to Level Four, an' somebody cold-conked him. The doc says he ought to be coming around again pretty soon."

Quillan grunted, shoved the Miam Devil Special into its holster, said, "O.K., you stay here where you can watch the room and those passages and the hall. If you feel the floor start moving under you, scream. I'll take a look at the cubicle."

Lady Pendrake's cubicle was about half as big again as a standard one; but, aside from one detail, its outer settings, instruments, and operating devices appeared normal. The modification was a recess almost six feet long and a foot wide and deep, in one side, which could be opened either to the room or to the interior of the rest cubicle, but not simultaneously to both. Quillan already knew its purpose; the supposed other cubicle was a camouflaged food locker, containing fifty-pound slabs of sea beef, each of which represented a meal for the Hlat. The recess made it possible to feed it without allowing it to be seen, or, possibly, attempting to emerge. Kinmarten's nervousness, as reported by his wife, seemed understandable. Any rest warden might get disturbed over such a charge.

Quillan asked over his shoulder, "Anyone find out yet why the things can't get out of a closed rest cubicle?"

"Yeah," Baldy Perk said. "Kinmarten says it's the cubicle's defense fields. They could get through the material. They can't get through the field."

"Someone think to energize the Executive Block's battle fields?" Quil–
lan inquired.

"Yeah. Velladon took care of that before he came screaming up to the
third level to argue with Cooms and Fluel."

"So it can't slip out of the Block unless it shows itself down on the
ground level when the entry lock's open."

"Yeah," Baldy muttered. "But I dunno. Is that good?"

Quillan looked at him. "Well, we *would* like it back."

"Why? There's fifty more coming in on the liner tonight."

"We don't have the fifty yet. If someone louses up that detail —"

"Yawk!" Baldy said faintly. There was a crash of sound as his riot gun
went off. Quillan spun about, hair bristling, gun out. "What happened?"

"I'll swear," Baldy said, white-faced, "I saw something moving along
that passage!"

Quillan looked, saw nothing, slowly replaced the gun "Baldy," he said,
"if you think you see it again, just say so. That's an order! If it comes at us,
we get out of this level fast. But we don't shoot before we have to. If we kill
it, it's no good to us. Got that?"

"Yeah," Baldy said. "But I got an idea now, Bad News." He nodded at
the other cubicle. "Let's leave that meat box open."

"Why?"

"If it's hungry," Baldy explained simply, "I'd sooner it wrapped itself
around a few chunks of sea beef, an' not around me."

Quillan punched him encouragingly in the shoulder. "Baldy," he said,
"in your own way, you *have* had an idea! But we won't leave the meat box
open. When Kinmarten wakes up, I want him to show me how to bait this
cubicle with a piece of sea beef, so it'll snap shut if the Hlat goes inside.
Meanwhile it won't hurt it if it gets a little hungry."

"That," said Baldy, "isn't the way *I* feel about it."

"There must be around a hundred and fifty people in the Executive
Block at present," Quillan said. "Look at it that way! Even if the thing
keeps stuffing away, your odds are pretty good, Baldy."

Baldy shuddered.

Aside from a dark bruise high on his forehead, Brock Kinmarten
showed no direct effects of having been knocked out. However, his face
was strained and his voice not entirely steady. It was obvious that the
young rest warden had never been in a similarly unnerving situation
before. But he was making a valiant effort not to appear frightened and, at
the same time, to indicate that he would co-operate to the best of his ability
with his captors.

He'd regained consciousness by the time Quillan and Perk returned to
the fourth level, and Quillan suggested bringing him to Marras Cooms'
private quarters for questioning. The Brotherhood chief agreed; he was
primarily interested in finding out how the Hlat-control device func–
tioned.

Kinmarten shook his head. He knew nothing about the instrument, he said, except that it was called a Hlat-talker. It was very unfortunate that Eltak had been shot, because Eltak undoubtedly could have told them all they wanted to know about it. If what he had told Kinmarten was true, Eltak had been directly involved in the development of the device.

"Was he some Federation scientist?" Cooms asked, fiddling absently with the mysterious cylindrical object.

"No, sir," the young man said. "But — again if what he told me was the truth — he was the man who actually discovered these Hlats. At least, he was the first man to discover them who wasn't immediately killed by them."

Cooms glanced thoughtfully at Quillan, then asked, "And where was that?"

Kinmarten shook his head again. "He didn't tell me. And I didn't really want to know. I was anxious to get our convoy to its destination, and then to be relieved of the assignment. I ... well, I've been trained to act as Rest Warden to human beings, after all, not to monstrosities!" He produced an uncertain smile, glancing from one to the other of his interrogators. The smile promptly faded out again.

"You've no idea at all then about the place they came from?" Cooms asked expressionlessly.

"Oh, yes," Kinmarten said hastily. "Eltak talked a great deal about the Hlats, and actually — except for its location — gave me a fairly good picture of what the planet must be like. For one thing, it's an uncolonized world, of course. It must be terratype or very nearly so, because Eltak lived there for fifteen years with apparently only a minimum of equipment. The Hlats are confined to a single large island. He discovered them by accident and —"

"What was he doing there?"

"Well, sir, he came from Hyles-Frisian. He was a crim ... he'd been engaged in some form of piracy, and when the authorities began looking for him, he decided it would be best to get clean out of the Hub. He cracked up his ship on this world and couldn't leave again. When he discovered the Hlats and realized their peculiar ability, he kept out of their way and observed them. He found out they had a means of communicating with each other, and that he could duplicate it. That stopped them from harming him, and eventually, he said, he was using them like hunting dogs. They were accustomed to co-operating with one another, because when there was some animal around that was too large for one of them to handle, they would attack it in a group ..."

He went on for another minute or two on the subject. The Hlats — the word meant "rock lion" in one of the Hyles-Frisian dialects, describing a carnivorous animal which had some superficial resemblance to the creatures Eltak had happened on — frequented the seacoast and sub–merged themselves in sand, rocks, and debris, whipping up out of it to seize some food animal, and taking it down with them again to devour it at leisure.

Quillan interrupted, "You heard what happened to the man it attacked on the fifth level?"

"Yes, sir."

"Why would the thing have left him half outside the wall as it did?"

Kinmarten said that it must simply have been moving too fast. It could slip into and out of solid substances without a pause itself, but it needed a little time to restructure an object it was carrying in the same manner. No more time, however, than two or three seconds — depending more on the nature of the object than on its size, according to Eltak.

"It can restructure *anything* in that manner?" Quillan asked.

Kinmarten hesitated. "Well, sir, I don't know. I suppose there might be limitations on its ability. Eltak told me the one we were escorting had been the subject of extensive experimentation during the past year, and that the results are very satisfactory."

"Suppose it carries a living man through a wall. Will the man still be alive when he comes out on the other side, assuming the Hlat doesn't kill him deliberately?"

"Yes, sir. The process itself wouldn't hurt him."

Quillan glanced at Cooms. "You know," he said, "we might be letting Yaco off too cheaply!"

Cooms raised an eyebrow warningly, and Quillan grinned. "Our friend will be learning about Yaco soon enough. Why did Eltak tell the creature to attack, Kinmarten?"

"Sir, I don't know," Kinmarten said. "He was a man of rather violent habits. My impression, however, was that he was simply attempting to obtain a hostage."

"How did he get off that island with the Hlat?"

"A University League explorer was investigating the planet. Eltak contacted them and obtained the guarantee of a full pardon and a large cash settlement in return for what he could tell them about the Hlats. They took him and this one specimen along for experimentation."

"What about the Hlats on the *Camelot*?"

"Eltak said those had been quite recently trapped on the island."

Cooms ran his fingers over the cylinder, producing a rapid series of squeaks and whistles. "That's one thing Yaco may not like," he observed. "They won't have a monopoly on the thing."

Quillan shook his head. "Their scientists don't have to work through red tape like the U-League. By the time the news breaks — if the Federation ever intends to break it — Yaco will have at least a five-year start on everyone else. That's all an outfit like that needs." He looked at Kinmarten. "Any little thing you haven't thought to tell us, friend?" he inquired pleasantly.

A thin film of sweat showed suddenly on Kinmarten's forehead.

"No, sir," he said. "I've really told you everything I know. I —"

"Might try him under dope," Cooms said absently.

"Uh-uh!" Quillan said. "I want him wide awake to help me bait the cubicle for the thing. Has Velladon shown any indication of becoming willing to co-operate in hunting it?"

Cooms gestured with his head. "Ask Fluel! I sent him down to try to patch things up with the commodore. He just showed up again."

Quillan glanced around. The Duke was lounging in the doorway. He grinned slightly, said, "Velladon's still sore at us. But he'll talk to Quillan. Kinmarten here ... did he tell you his wife's on the Star?"

Brock Kinmarten went utterly white. Cooms looked at him, said softly, "No, that must have slipped his mind."

Fluel said, "Yeah. Well, she is. And Ryter says they'll have her picked up inside half an hour. When they bring her in, we really should check on how candid Kinmarten's been about everything."

The rest warden said in a voice that shook uncontrollably, "Gentlemen, my wife knows absolutely nothing about these matters! I swear it! She —"

Quillan stood up. "Well, I'll go see if I can't get Velladon in a better mood. Are you keeping that Hlat-talker, Cooms?"

Cooms smiled. "I am."

"Marras figures," the Duke's flat voice explained, "that if the thing comes into the room and he squeaks at it a few times, he won't get hurt."

"That's possible," Cooms said, unruffled. "At any rate, I intend to hang on to it."

"Well, I wouldn't play around with those buttons too much," Quillan observed.

"Why not?"

"You might get lucky and tap out some pattern that spells 'Come to chow' in the Hlat's vocabulary."

There were considerably more men in evidence on Level Two than on the fourth, and fewer signs of nervousness. The Star men had been told of the Hlat's escape from its cubicle, but weren't taking it too seriously. Quillan was conducted to the commodore and favored with an alarmingly toothy grin. Ryter, the security chief, joined them a few seconds later. Apparently, Velladon had summoned him.

Velladon said, "Ryter here's made a few transmitter calls. We hear Pappy Boltan pulled his outfit out of the Orado area about a month ago. Present whereabouts unknown. Hagready went off on some hush-hush job at around the same time."

Quillan smiled. "Uh-huh! So he did."

"We also," said Ryter, "learned a number of things about you personally." He produced a thin smile. "You lead a busy and — ap-parently — profitable life."

"Business is fair," Quillan agreed. "But it can always be improved."

The commodore turned on the toothy grin. "So all right," he growled, "you're clear. We rather liked what we learned. Eh, Ryter?"

Ryter nodded.

"This Brotherhood of Beldon, now —" The commodore shook his head heavily.

Quillan was silent a moment. "They might be getting sloppy," he said. "I don't know. It's one possibility. They used to be a rather sharp outfit, you know."

"That's what I'd heard!" Velladon chewed savagely on his mustache, asked finally, "What's another possibility?"

Quillan leaned back in his chair. "Just a feeling, so far. But the business with the cubicle upstairs might have angles that weren't mentioned."

They looked at him thoughtfully. Ryter said, "Mind amplifying that?"

"Cooms told me," Quillan said, "that Nome Lancion had given Movaine instructions to make a test with Lady Pendrake on the quiet and find out if those creatures actually can do what they're supposed to do. I think he was telling the truth. Nome tends to be overcautious when it's a really big deal. Unless he's sure of the Hlats, he wouldn't want to be involved in a thing like blowing up the Star and the liner."

The commodore scowled absently. "Uh-huh," he said. "He knows *we* can't back out of it —"

"All right. The Brotherhood's full of ambitious men. Behind Lancion, Movaine was top man. Cooms behind him; Fluel behind Cooms. Suppose that Hlat-control device Cooms is hanging on to so tightly isn't as entirely incomprehensible as they make it out to be. Suppose Cooms makes a deal with Eltak. Eltak tickles the gadget, and the Hlat kills Movaine. Rubero immediately guns down Eltak — and is killed by Fluel a couple of minutes later, supposedly for blowing his top and killing the man who knew how to control the Hlat."

Ryter cleared his throat. "Fluel was Movaine's gun," he observed.

"So he was," Quillan said. "Would you like the Duke to be yours?"

Ryter grinned, shook his head. "No, thanks!"

Quillan looked back at Velladon. "How well are you actually covered against the Brotherhood?"

"Well, *that's* air-tight," the commodore said. "We've got 'em outgunned here. When the liner lands, "we'll be about even. But Lancion won't start anything. We're *too* even. Once we're clear of the Star, we don't meet again. We deal with Yaco individually. The Brotherhood has the Hlats, and we have the trained Federation technicians accompanying them, who ... who —"

"Who alone are supposed to be able to inform Yaco how to control the Hlats," Ryter finished for him. The security chief's face was expres-sionless.

"By God!" the commodore said softly.

"Well, it's only a possibility that somebody's playing dirty," Quillan remarked. "We'd want to be sure of it. But if anyone can handle a Hlat with that control instrument, the Brotherhood has an advantage now that it isn't talking about — it can offer Yaco everything Yaco needs in one package. Of course, Yaco might still be willing to pay for the Hlat technicians. If it didn't, you and Ryter could make the same kind of trouble for it that my friends can."

The color was draining slowly from Velladon's face. "There's a dif—ference," he said. "If *we* threaten to make trouble for Yaco, they'd see to it that our present employers learn that Ryter and I are still alive."

"That's the Mooleys, eh?"

"Yes."

"Tough." Quillan knuckled his chin thoughtfully. "Well, let's put it this way then," he said. "My group doesn't have *that* kind of problem, but if things worked out so that we'd have something more substantial than nuisance value to offer Yaco, we'd prefer it, of course."

Velladon nodded. "Very understandable! Under the circumstances, co-operation appears to be indicated, eh?"

"That's what I had in mind."

"You've made a deal," Velladon said. "Any immediate suggestions?"

Quillan looked at his watch. "A couple. We don't want to make any mistake about this. It's still almost five hours before the *Camelot* pulls in, and until she does you're way ahead on firepower. I wouldn't make any accusations just now. But you might mention to Cooms you'd like to borrow the Hlat gadget to have it examined by some of your technical experts. The way he reacts might tell us something. If he balks, the matter shouldn't be pushed too hard at the moment — it's a tossup whether you or the Brotherhood has a better claim to the thing.

"But then there's Kinmarten, the rest warden in charge of the cubicle. I talked with him while Cooms and Fluel were around, but he may have been briefed on what to say. Cooms mentioned doping him, which could be a convenient way of keeping him shut up, assuming he knows more than he's told. He's one of the personnel you're to offer Yaco. I think you can insist on having Kinmarten handed over to you immediately. It should be interesting again to see how Cooms reacts."

Velladon's big head nodded vigorously. "Good idea!"

"By the way," Quillan said, "Fluel mentioned you've been looking for Kinmarten's wife, the second rest warden on the Pendrake convoy. Found her yet?"

"Not a trace, so far," Ryter said.

"That's a little surprising, too, isn't it?"

"Under the circumstances," the commodore said, "it might not be surprising at all!" He had regained his color, was beginning to look angry. "If they —"

"Well," Quillan said soothingly, we don't *know*. It's just that things do seem to be adding up a little. Now, there's one other point. We should do something immediately about catching that Hlat."

Velladon grunted and picked at his teeth with his thumbnail. "It would be best to get it back in its cubicle, of course. But I'm not worrying about it — just an animal, after all. Even the light hardware those Beldon fancy

Dans carry should handle it. You use a man-sized gun, I see. So do I. If it shows up around here, it gets smeared, that's all. There're fifty more of the beasts on the *Camelot*."

Quillan nodded. "You're right on that. But there's the possibility that it is being controlled by the Brotherhood at present. If it is, it isn't just an animal any more. It could be turned into a thoroughly dangerous nui–sance."

The commodore thought a moment, nodded. "You're right, I suppose. What do you want to do about it?"

"Baiting the cubicle on the fifth level might work. Then there should be life-detectors in the Star's security supplies —"

Ryter nodded. "We have a couple of dozen of them, but not in the Executive Block. They were left in the security building."

The commodore stood up. "You stay here with Ryter," he told Quillan. "There're a couple of other things I want to go over with you two. I'll order the life-detectors from the office here — second passage down, isn't it, Ryter? ... And, Ryter, I have another idea. I'm pulling man in space-armor off the subspace portal and detailing him to Level Five." He grinned at Quillan. "That boy's got a brace of grenades and built-in spray guns! If Cooms is thinking of pulling any funny stunts up there, he'll think again."

The commodore headed briskly down the narrow passageway, his big holstered gun slapping his thigh with every step. The two security guards stationed at the door to the second-level office came to attention as he approached, saluted smartly. He grunted, went in without returning the salutes, and started over toward the ComWeb on a desk at the far end of the big room, skirting the long, dusty-looking black rug beside one wall.

Velladon unbuckled his gun belt, placed the gun on the desk, sat down and switched on the ComWeb.

Behind him, the black rug stirred silently, and rose up.

"You called that one," Ryter was saying seven or eight minutes later, "almost too well!"

Quillan shook his head, poked at the commodore's gun on the desk with his finger, looked about the silent office and back at the door where a small group of security men stood staring in at them.

"Three men gone without a sound!" he said. He indicated the glowing disk of the ComWeb. "He had time enough to turn it on, not time enough to make his call. Any chance of camouflaged portals in this section?"

"No," Ryter said. "I know the location of every portal in the Executive Block. No number of men could have taken Velladon and the two guards without a fight anyway. We'd have heard it. It didn't happen that way."

"Which leaves," Quillan said, "one way it could have happened." He jerked his head toward the door. "Will those men keep quiet?"

"If I tell them to."

"Then play it like this. Two guards have vanished. The Hlat obviously did it. The thing's deadly. That'll keep every man in the group on the alert every instant from now on. But we don't say Velladon has vanished. He's outside in the Star at the moment, taking care of something."

Ryter licked his lips. "What does that buy us?"

"If the Brotherhood's responsible for this —"

"I don't take much stock in coincidences," Ryter said.

"Neither do I. But the Hlat's an animal; it can't tell them it's carried out the job. If they don't realize we suspect them, it gives us some advantage. For the moment, we just carry on as planned, and get rid of the Hlat in one way or another as the first step. The thing's three times as dangerous as anyone suspected — except, apparently, the Brotherhood. Get the life-detectors over here as soon as you can, and slap a space-armor guard on the fifth level."

Ryter hesitated, nodded. "All right."

"Another thing," Quillan said. "Cooms may have the old trick in mind of working from the top down. If he can take you out along with a few other key men, he might have this outfit demoralized to the point of making up for the difference in the number of guns — especially if the Hlat's still on his team. You'd better keep a handful of the best boys you have around here glued to your back from now on."

Ryter smiled bleakly. "Don't worry. I intend to. What about you?"

"I don't think they're planning on giving me any personal attention at the moment. My organization is outside, not here. And it would look odd to the Brotherhood if I started dragging a few Star guards around with me at this point."

Ryter shrugged. "Suit yourself. It's your funeral if you've guessed wrong."

"There was nothing," Quillan told Marras Cooms, "that you could actually put a finger on. It was just that I got a very definite impression that the commodore and Ryter may have something up their sleeves. Velladon's looking too self-satisfied to suit me."

The Brotherhood chief gnawed his lower lip reflectively. He seemed thoughtful, not too disturbed. Cooms might be thoroughly afraid of the escaped Hlat, but he wouldn't have reached his present position in Nome Lancion's organization if he had been easily frightened by what other men were planning.

He said, "I warned Movaine that if Velladon learned we'd checked out the Hlat, he wasn't going to like it."

"He doesn't," Quillan said. "He regards it as something pretty close to an attempted double cross."

Cooms grinned briefly. "It was."

"Of course. The question is, what can he do about it? He's got you outgunned two to one, but if he's thinking of jumping you before Lancion gets here, he stands to lose more men than he can afford to without endangering the entire operation for himself."

Cooms was silent a few seconds. "There's an unpleasant possibility which didn't occur to me until a short while ago," he said then. "The fact is that Velladon actually may have us outgunned here by something like four to one. If that's the case, he can afford to lose quite a few men. In fact, he'd prefer to."

Quillan frowned. "*Four* to one? How's that?"

Cooms said, "The commodore told us he intended to let only around half of the Seventh Star's security force in on the Hlat deal. The other half was supposed to have been dumped out of one of the subspace section's locks early today, without benefit of suits. We had no reason to disbelieve him. Velladon naturally would want to cut down the number of men who got in on the split with him to as many as he actually needed. But if he's been thinking about eliminating us from the game, those other men may still be alive and armed."

Quillan grunted. "I see. You know, that could explain something that looked a little odd to me."

"What was that?" Cooms asked.

Quillan said, "After they discovered down there that two of their guards were missing and decided the Hlat must have been on their level, I tried to get hold of the commodore again. Ryter told me Velladon won't be available for a while, that he's outside in the Star, taking care of something there. I wondered what could be important enough to get Vel–ladon to leave the Executive Block at present, but —"

"Brother, I'm way ahead of you!" Cooms said. His expression hardened. "That doesn't look good. But at least he can't bring in reinforce–ments without tipping us off. We've got our own guards down with theirs at the entrance."

Quillan gave him a glance, then nodded at the wall beyond them. "That's a portal over there, Marras. How many of them on this level?"

"Three or four. Why? The outportals have been plugged, man! Sealed off. Fluel checked them over when we moved in."

"Sure they're sealed." Quillan stood up, went to the portal, stood looking at the panel beside it a moment, then pressed on it here and there, and removed it. "Come over here, friend. I suppose portal work's been out of your line. I'll show you how fast a thing like that can get *un*plugged!"

He slid a pocketbook-sized tool kit out of his belt, snapped it open. About a minute later, the lifeless VACANT sign above the portal flickered twice, then acquired a steady white glow.

"Portal in operation," Quillan announced. "I'll seal it off again now. But that should give you the idea."

Cooms' tongue flicked over his lips. "Could somebody portal through to this level from the Star while the exits are sealed here?"

"If the mechanisms have been set for that purpose, the portals can be opened again at any time from the Star side. The Duke's an engineer of sorts, isn't he? Let him check on it. He should have been thinking of the point himself, as far as that goes. Anyway, Velladon can bring in as many men as he likes to his own level without using the main entrance." He considered. "I didn't see anything to indicate that he's started doing it —"

Marras Cooms shrugged irritably. "That means nothing! It would be easy enough to keep half a hundred men hidden away on any of the lower levels."

"I suppose that's right. Well, if the commodore intends to play rough, you should have some warning anyway."

"What kind of warning?"

"There's Kinmarten and that Hlat-talking gadget, for example," Quillan pointed out. "Velladon would want both of those in his possession and out of the way where they can't get hurt before he starts any shoot-ing."

Cooms looked at him for a few seconds. "Ryter," he said then, "sent half a dozen men up here for Kinmarten just after you got back! Velladon's supposed to deliver the Hlats' attendants to Yaco, so I let them have Kinmarten." He paused. "They asked for the Hlat-talker, too."

Quillan grunted. "Did you give them that?"

"No."

"Well," Quillan said after a moment, "that doesn't necessarily mean that we're in for trouble with the Star group. But it does mean, I think, that we'd better stay ready for it!" He stood up. "I'll get back down there and go on with the motions of getting the hunt for the Hlat organized. Velladon would sooner see the thing get caught, too, of course, so he shouldn't try to interfere with that. If I spot anything that looks suspicious, I'll get the word to you."

"I never," said Orca, unconsciously echoing Baldy Perk, "saw anything like it!" The commodore's chunky little gunman was ashen-faced. The circle of Star men standing around him hardly looked happier. Most of them were staring down at the empty lower section of a suit of space armor which appeared to have been separated with a neat diagonal slice from its upper part.

"Let's get it straight," Ryter said, a little unsteadily. "You say this half of the suit was lying against the wall like *that*?"

"Not exactly," Quillan told him. "When we got up to the fifth level, the suit was stuck against the wall — like that — about eight feet above the floor. That was in the big room where the cubicles are. When Kinmarten and Orca and I finally got the suit worked away from the wall, I expected frankly that we'd find half the body of the guard still inside. But he'd vanished."

Ryter cleared his throat. "Apparently," he said, "the creature drew the upper section of the suit into the wall by whatever means it uses, then stopped applying the transforming process to the metal, and simply moved on with the upper part of the suit and the man."

Quillan nodded. "That's what it looks like."

"But he had *two grenades!*" Orca burst out. "He had sprayguns! How could it get him that way?"

"Brother," Quillan said, "grenades won't help you much if you don't spot what's moving up behind you!"

Orca glared speechlessly at him. Ryter said, "All right! We've lost another man. We're not going to lose any more. We'll station no more guards on the fifth level. Now get everyone who isn't on essential guard duty to the main room, and split 'em up into life-detector units. Five men to each detail, one to handle the detector, four to stay with him, guns out. If the thing comes back to this level, we want to have it spotted the instant it arrives. Orca, you stay here — and keep *your* gun out!"

The men filed out hurriedly. Ryter turned to Quillan. "Were you able to get the cubicle baited?"

Quillan nodded. "Kinmarten figured out how the thing should be set for the purpose. If the Hlat goes in after the sea beef, it's trapped. Of course, if the hunting it's been doing was for food, it mightn't be interested in the beef."

"We don't know," Ryter said, "that the hunting it's been doing was for food."

"No. Did you manage to get the control device from Cooms?"

Ryter shook his head. "He's refused to hand it over."

"If you tried to take it from him," Quillan said, "you might have a showdown on your hands."

"And if this keeps on," Ryter said, "I may prefer a showdown! Another few rounds of trouble with the Hlat, and the entire operation could blow up in our faces! The men aren't used to that kind of thing. It's shaken them up. If we've got to take care of the Brotherhood, I'd rather do it while I still have an organized group. Where did you leave Kinmarten, by the way?"

"He's back in that little room with his two guards," Quillan said.

"Well, he should be all right there. We can't spare —" Ryter's body jerked violently. "*What's that?*"

There had been a single thudding crash somewhere in the level. Then shouts and cursing.

"Main hall!" Quillan said. "Come on!"

The main hall was a jumble of excitedly jabbering Star men when they arrived there. Guns waved about, and the various groups were showing a marked tendency to stand with their backs toward one another and their faces toward the walls.

Ryter's voice rose in a shout that momentarily shut off the hubbub. "*What's going on here?*"

Men turned, hands pointed, voices babbled again. Someone nearby said sharply and distinctly, "... Saw it drop right out of the ceiling!" Far—ther down the hall, another group shifted aside enough to disclose it had been clustered about something which looked a little like the empty shell of a gigantic black beetle.

The missing section of the suit of space armor had been returned. But not its occupant.

Quillan moved back a step, turned, went back down the passage from which they had emerged, pulling the Miam Devil from its holster. Behind him the commotion continued; Ryter was shouting something about getting the life-detector units over there. Quillan went left down the first intersecting corridor, right again on the following one, keeping the gun slightly raised before him. Around the next corner, he saw the man on guard over the portal connecting the building levels facing him, gun pointed.

"What happened?" the guard asked shakily.

Quillan shook his head, coming up. "That thing got another one!"

The guard breathed, "By God!" and lowered his gun a little. Quillan raised his a little, the Miam Devil grunted, and the guard sighed and went down. Quillan went past him along the hall, stopped two doors beyond the portal, and rapped on the locked door.

"Quillan here! Open up!"

The door opened a crack, and one of Kinmarten's guards looked out questioningly. Quillan shot him through the head, slammed on into the room across the collapsing body, saw the second guard wheeling toward him, shot again, and slid the gun back into the holster. Kinmarten, standing beside a table six feet away, right hand gripping a heavy marble ashtray, was staring at him in white-faced shock.

"Take it easy, chum!" Quillan said, turning toward him. "I —"

He ducked hurriedly as the ashtray came whirling through the air toward his head. An instant later, a large fist smacked the side of Kinmarten's jaw. The rest warden settled limply to the floor.

"Sorry to do that, pal," Quillan muttered, stooping over him. "Things are rough all over right now." He hauled Kinmarten upright, bent, and had the unconscious young man across his shoulder. The hall was still empty except for the body of the portal guard. Quillan laid Kinmarten on the carpet before the portal, hauled the guard off into the room, and pulled the door to the room shut behind him as he came out. Picking up Kinmarten, he stepped into the portal with him and jabbed the fifth-level button. A moment later, he moved out into the small dim entry hall on the fifth level, the gun in his right hand again.

He stood there silently for some seconds, looking about him listening. The baited cubicle yawned widely at him from the center of the big room. Nothing seemed to be stirring. Kinmarten went back to the floor. Quillan moved over to the panel which concealed the other portal's mechanisms.

He had the outportal unsealed in considerably less than a minute this time, and slapped the panel gently back in place. He turned back to Kinmarten and started to bend down for him, then straightened quietly again, turning his head.

Had there been a flicker of shadowy motion just then at the edge of his vision, behind the big black cube of the Hlat's food locker? Quillan remained perfectly still, the Miam Devil ready and every sense straining for an indication that the thing was there — or approaching stealthily now, gliding behind the surfaces of floor or ceiling or walls like an underwater swimmer.

But half a minute passed and nothing else happened. He went down on one knee beside Kinmarten, the gun still in his right hand. With his left, he carefully wrestled the rest warden back up across his shoulder, came upright, moved three steps to the side, and disappeared in the outportal.

Reetal Destone unlocked the entry door to her suite and stepped hurriedly inside, letting the door slide shut behind her. She crossed the room to the ComWeb stand and switched on the playback. There was the succession of tinkling tones which indicated nothing had been recorded.

She shut the instrument off again, passing her tongue lightly over her lips. No further messages from Heraga ...

And none from Quillan.

She shook her head, feeling a surge of sharp anxiety, glanced at her watch and told herself that, after all, less than two hours had passed since Quillan had gone into the Executive Block. Heraga reported there had been no indications of disturbance or excitement when he passed through the big entrance hall on his way out. So Quillan, at any rate, had succeeded in bluffing his way into the upper levels.

It remained a desperate play, at best.

Reetal went down the short passage to her bedroom. As she came into the room, her arms were caught from the side at the elbows, pulled suddenly and painfully together behind her. She stood still, frozen with shock.

"In a hurry, sweetheart?" Fluel's flat voice said.

Reetal managed a breathless giggle. "Duke! You startled me! How did you get in?"

She felt one hand move up her arm to her shoulder. Then she was swung about deftly and irresistibly, held pinned back against the wall, still unable to move her arms.

He looked at her a moment, asked, "Where are you hiding it this time?"

"Hiding what, Duke?"

"I've been told sweet little Reetal always carries a sweet little gun around with her in some shape or form or other."

Reetal shook her head, her eyes widening. "Duke, what's the matter? I ..."

He let go of her suddenly, and his slap exploded against the side of her face. Reetal cried out, dropping her head between her hands. Immediately he had her wrists again, and her fingers were jerked away from the jeweled ornament in her hair.

"So that's where it is! " Fluel said. "Thought it might be. Don't get funny again now, sweetheart. Just stay quiet."

She stayed quiet, wincing a little as he plucked the glittering little device out of her hair. He turned it around in his fingers, examining it, smiled and slid it into an inside pocket, and took her arm again. "Let's go to the front room, Reetal," he said almost pleasantly. "We've got a few things to do."

A minute later, she was seated sideways on a lounger, her wrists fastened right and left to its armrests. The Duke placed a pocket recorder on the floor beside her. "This is a crowded evening, sweetheart," he remarked, "which is lucky for you in a way. We'll have to rush things along a little. I'll snap the recorder on in a minute so you can answer questions — No, keep quiet. Just listen very closely now, so you'll know what the right answers are. If you get rattled and gum things up, the Duke's going to get annoyed with you."

He sat down a few feet away from her, hitched his shoulders to straighten out the silver jacket, and lit a cigarette. "A little while after Bad News Quillan turned up just now," he went on, "a few things occurred to me. One of them was that a couple of years ago you and he were operating around Beldon at about the same time. I thought, well, maybe you knew each other; maybe not. And then —"

"Duke," Reetal said uncertainly, "just what are you talking about? I don't know —"

"Shut up." He reached over, tapped her knee lightly with his fingertips. "Of course, if you want to get slapped around, all right. Otherwise, don't interrupt again. Like I said, you're in luck; I don't have much time to spend here. You're getting off very easy. Now just listen.

"Bad News knew a lot about our operation and had a story to explain that. If the story was straight, we couldn't touch him. But I was wondering about the two of you happening to be here on the Star again at the same time. A team maybe, eh? But he didn't mention you as being in on the deal. So what was the idea?

"And then, sweetheart, I remembered something else — and that tied it in. Know that little jolt people sometimes get when they're dropping off to sleep? Of course. Know another time they sometimes get it? When they're snapping back out of a Moment of Truth, eh? I remembered suddenly I'd felt a little jump like that while we were talking today. Might have been a reflex of some kind. Of course, it didn't occur to me at the time you could be pulling a lousy stunt like that on old Duke. Why take a chance on getting your neck broken?

"But, sweetheart, that's the tie-in! Quillan hasn't told it straight. He's got no backing. He's on his own. There's no gang outside somewhere that knows all about our little deal. He got his information right here, from you. And you got it from dumb Duke, eh?"

"Duke," Reetal said quite calmly, "can I ask just one question?"

He stared bleakly at her a moment, then grinned. "It's my night to be big-hearted, I guess. Go ahead."

"I'm not trying to argue. But it simply doesn't make sense. If I learned about this operation you're speaking of from you, what reason could I have to feed you Truth in the first place? There'd be almost a fifty-fifty chance that you'd spot it immediately. Why should I take such a risk? Don't you see?"

Fluel shrugged, dropped his cigarette, and ground it carefully into the carpet with the tip of his shoe.

"You'll start answering those questions yourself almost immediately, sweetheart! Let's not worry about that now. Let me finish. Something happened to Movaine couple of hours ago. Nobody's fault. And something else happened to Marras Cooms just now. That puts me in charge of the operation here. Nice, isn't it? When we found Cooms lying in the hall with a hole through his stupid head, I told Baldy Perk it looked like Bad News had thrown in with the Star boys and done it. Know Baldy? He's Cooms' personal gun. Not what you'd call bright, and he's mighty hot now about Cooms. I left him in charge on our level, with orders to get Quillan the next time he shows up there. Well and good. The boys know Bad News' rep too well to try asking him questions. They won't take chances with him. They'll just gun him down together the instant they see him."

He paused to scuff his shoe over the mark the cigarette had left on the carpet, went on, "But there's Nome Lancion now. He kind of liked Cooms, and he might get suspicious. When there's a sudden vacancy in the organization like that, Nome takes a good look first at the man next in line. He likes to be sure the facts are as stated.

"So now you know the kind of answers from you I want to hear go down on the recorder, sweetheart. And be sure they sound right. I don't want to waste time on replays. You and Quillan were here on the Star. You got some idea of what was happening, realized you were due to be vaporized along with the rest of them after we left. There was no way out of the jam for you unless you could keep the operation from being carried out. You don't, by the way, mention getting any of that information from me. I don't want Lancion to think I'm beginning to get dopey. You and Quillan just cooked up this story, and he managed to get into the Executive Block. The idea being to knock off as many of the leaders as he could, and mess things up."

Fluel picked up the recorder, stood up, and placed it on the chair. "That's all you have to remember. You're a smart girl; you can fill in the details any way you like. Now let's get started —"

She stared at him silently for an instant, a muscle beginning to twitch in her cheek. "If I do that," she said, "if I give you a story Nome will like, what happens next?"

Fluel shrugged. "Just what you're thinking happens next. You're a dead little girl right now, Reetal. Might as well get used to the idea. You'd be dead anyhow four, five hours from now, so that shouldn't make too much difference. What makes a lot of difference is just how unpleasant the thing can get."

She drew a long breath. "Duke, I —"

"You're stalling, sweetheart."

"Duke, give me a break. I really didn't know a thing about this. I —"

He looked down at her for a moment. "I gave you a break," he said. "You've wasted it. Now we'll try it the other way. If we work a few squeals into the recording, that'll make it more convincing to Lancion. He'll figure little Reetal's the type who wouldn't spill a thing like that without a little pressure." He checked himself, grinned. "And that reminds me. When you're talking for the record, use your own voice."

"My own voice?" she half whispered.

"Nome will remember what you sound like — and I've heard that voice imitations are part of your stock in trade. You might think it was cute if Nome got to wondering after you were dead whether that really had been you talking. Don't try it, sweetheart."

He brought a glove out of his jacket pocket, slipped it over his left hand, flexing his fingers to work it into position. Reetal's eyes fastened on the rounded metal tips capping thumb, forefinger, and middle finger of the glove. Her face went gray.

"Duke," she said. "No —"

"Shut up." He brought out a strip of transparent plastic, moved over to her. The gloved hand went into her hair, gripped it, turned her face up. He laid the plastic gag lengthwise over her mouth, pressed it down and released it. Reetal closed her eyes.

"That'll keep it shut," he said. "Now —" His right hand clamped about the back of her neck, forcing her head down and forward almost to her knees. The gloved left hand brushed her hair forwards, then its middle finger touched the skin at a point just above her shoulder blades.

"Right there," Fluel said. The finger stiffened, drove down.

Reetal jerked violently, twisted, squirmed sideways, wrists straining against the grip of the armrests. Her breath burst out of her nostrils, followed by squeezed, whining noises. The metal-capped finger continued to grind savagely against the nerve center it had found.

"Thirty," Fluel said finally. He drew his hand back, pulled her upright again, peeled the gag away from her lips. "Only thirty seconds, sweetheart. Think you'd sooner play along now?"

Reetal's head nodded.

"Fine. Give you a minute to steady up. This doesn't really waste much time, you see —" He took up the recorder, sat down on the chair again, watching her. She was breathing raggedly and shallowly, eyes wide and incredulous. She didn't look at him.

The Duke lit another cigarette.

"Incidentally," he observed, "if you were stalling because you hoped old Bad News might show up, forget it. If the boys haven't gunned him

down by now, he's tied up on a job the commodore gave him to do. He'll
be busy another hour or two on that. He —"

He checked himself. A central section of the wall paneling across the
room from him had just dilated open. Old Bad News stood in the
concealed suite portal, Rest Warden Kinmarten slung across his shoulder.

Both men moved instantly. Fluel's long legs bounced him sideways out
of the chair, right hand darting under his coat, coming out with a gun.
Quillan turned to the left to get Kinmarten out of the way. The big Miam
Devil seemed to jump into his hand. Both guns spoke together.

Fluel's gun thudded to the carpet. The Duke said, "Ah-aa-ah!" in a
surprised voice, rolled up his eyes, and followed the gun down.

Quillan said, stunned, "He was fast! I felt that one parting my hair."

He became very solicitous then — after first ascertaining that Fluel had
left the Executive Block unaccompanied, on personal business. He located
a pain-killer spray in Reetal's bedroom and applied it to the bruised point
below the back of her neck. She was just beginning to relax gratefully, as
the warm glow of the spray washed out the pain and the feeling of
paralysis, when Kinmarten, lying on the carpet nearby, began to stir and
mutter.

Quillan hastily put down the spray.

"Watch him," he cautioned. "I'll be right back. If he sits up, yell. He's a
bit wild at the moment. If he wakes up and sees the Duke lying there, he'll
start climbing the walls."

"What —" Reetal began. But he was gone down the hall.

He returned immediately with a glass of water, went down on one
knee beside Kinmarten, slid an arm under the rest warden's shoulder, and
lifted him to a sitting position.

"Wake up, old pal!" he said loudly. "Come on, wake up! Got some–
thing good for you here —"

"What are you giving him?" Reetal asked, cautiously massaging the
back of her neck.

"Knockout drops. I already had to lay him out once. We want to lock
him up with his wife now, and if he comes to and tells her what's
happened, they'll both be out of their minds by the time we come to let
them out —"

He interrupted himself. Kinmarten's eyelids were fluttering. Quillan
raised the glass to his lips. "Here you are, pal," he said in a deep, soothing
voice. "Drink it! It'll make you feel a lot better."

Kinmarten swallowed obediently, swallowed again. His eyelids
stopped fluttering. Quillan lowered him back to the floor.

"That ought to do it," he said.

"What," Reetal asked, "did happen? The Duke —"

"Tell you as much as I can after we get Kinmarten out of the way. I have
to get back to the Executive Block. Things are sort of teetering on the edge
there." He jerked his head at Fluel's body. "I want to know about him, too,
of course. Think you can walk now?"

Reetal groaned. "I can try," she said.

They found Solvey Kinmarten dissolved in tears once more. She flung herself on her husband's body when Quillan placed him on the bed. "What have those *beasts* done to Brock?" she demanded fiercely.

"Nothing very bad," Quillan said soothingly. "He's, um, under sedation at the moment, that's all. We've got him away from them now, and he's safe ... look at it that way. You stay here and take care of him. We'll have the whole deal cleared up before morning, doll. Then you can both come out of hiding again." He gave her an encouraging wink.

"I'm so very grateful to both of you —"

"No trouble, really. But we'd better get back to work on the thing."

"Heck," Quillan said a few seconds later, as he and Reetal came out on the other side of the portal, "I feel like hell about those two. Nice little characters! Well, if the works blow up, they'll never know it."

"*We'll* know it," Reetal said meaningfully. "Start talking."

He rattled through a brief account of events in the Executive Block, listened to her report on the Duke's visit, scratched his jaw reflectively.

"That might help!" he observed. "They're about ready to jump down each other's throats over there right now. A couple more pushes —" He stood staring down at the Duke's body for a moment. Blood soiled the back of the silver jacket, seeping out from a tear above the heart area. Quillan bent down, got his hands under Fluel's armpits, hauled the body upright.

Reetal asked, startled, "What are you going to do with it?"

"Something useful, I think. And wouldn't that shock the Duke ... the first time he's been of any use to anybody. Zip through the Star's ComWeb directory, doll, and get me the call symbol for Level Four of the Executive Block!"

Solvey Kinmarten dimmed the lights a trifle in the bedroom, went back to Brock, rearranged the pillows under his head, and bent down to place her lips tenderly to the large bruises on his forehead and the side of his jaw. Then she brought a chair up beside the bed, and sat down to watch him.

Perhaps a minute later, there was a slight noise behind her. Startled, she glanced around, saw something huge, black, and shapeless moving swiftly across the carpet of the room toward her.

Solvey quietly fainted.

"Sure you know what to say?" Quillan asked.

Reetal moistened her lips. "Just let me go over it in my mind once more." She was sitting on the floor, on the right side of the ComWeb stand, her face pale and intent. "You know," she said, "this makes me feel a little queasy somehow, Quillan! And suppose they don't fall for it?"

"They'll fall for it!" Quillan was on his knees in front of the stand, supporting Fluel's body, which was sprawled half across it, directly before the lit vision screen. An outflung arm hid the Duke's face from the screen.

"You almost had *me* thinking I was listening to Fluel when you did the take-off on him this evening. A dying man can be expected to sound a little odd, anyway." He smiled at her encouragingly. "Ready now?"

Reetal nodded nervously, cleared her throat.

Quillan reached across Fluel, tapped out Level Four's call symbol on the instrument, ducked back down below the stand. After a moment, there was a click.

Reetal produced a quavering, agonized groan. Somebody else gasped.

"Duke!" Baldy Perk's voice shouted. "What's happened?"

"Baldy Perk!" Quillan whispered quickly.

Reetal stammered hoarsely, "The c-c-commodore, Baldy! Shot me ... shot Marras! They're after ... Quillan ... now!"

"I thought Bad News ... Baldy sounded stunned.

"Was w-wrong, Baldy," Reetal croaked. "Bad News ... with us! Bad News ... pal! The c-c-comm —"

Beneath the ComWeb stand the palm of Quillan's right hand thrust sharply up and forward. The stand tilted, went crashing back to the floor. Fluel's body lurched over with it. The vision screen shattered. Baldy's roaring question was cut off abruptly.

"Great stuff, doll!" Quillan beamed, helping Reetal to her feet. "You sent shudders down my back!"

"Down mine, too!"

"I'll get him out of here now. Ditch him in one of the shut-off sections. Then I'll get back to the Executive Block. If Ryter's thought to look into Kinmarten's room, they'll really be raving on both sides there now!"

"Is that necessary?" Reetal asked. "For you to go back, I mean. Somebody besides Fluel might have become suspicious of you by now."

"Ryter might," Quillan agreed. "He's looked like the sharpest of the lot right from the start. But we'll have to risk that. We've got all the makings of a shooting war there now, but we've got to make sure it gets set off before somebody thinks of comparing notes. If I'm around, I'll keep jolting at their nerves."

"I suppose you're right. Now, our group —"

Quillan nodded. "No need to hold off on that any longer, the way things are moving. Get on another ComWeb and start putting out those Mayday messages right now! As soon as you've rounded the boys up —"

"That might," Reetal said, "take a little less than an hour."

"Fine. Then move them right into the Executive Block. With just a bit of luck, one hour from now should land them in the final stages of a beautiful battle on the upper levels. Give them my description and Ryter's, so we don't have accidents."

"Why Ryter's?"

"Found out he was the boy who took care of the bomb-planting detail. We want him alive. The others mightn't know where it's been tucked away. Heraga says the clerical staff and technicians in there are all wearing the white Star uniforms. Anyone else who isn't in one of those uniforms is fair game —" He paused. "Oh, and tip them off about the Hlat! God only knows what that thing will be doing when the ruckus starts."

"What about sending a few men in through the fifth-level portal, the one you've unplugged?"

Quillan considered, shook his head. "No. Down on the ground level is where we want them. They'd have to portal there again from the fifth, and a portal is too easy to seal off and defend. Now let's get a blanket or something to tuck Fluel into. I don't want to feel conspicuous if I run into somebody on the way."

Quillan emerged cautiously from the fifth-level portal in the Executive Block a short while later, came to a sudden stop just outside it. In the big room beyond the entry hall, the door of the baited cubicle was closed, and the life-indicator on the door showed a bright steady green glow.

Quillan stared at it a moment, looking somewhat surprised, then went quietly into the room and bent to study the cubicle's instruments. A grin spread slowly over his face. The trap had been sprung. He glanced at the deep-rest setting and turned it several notches farther down.

"Happy dreams, Lady Pendrake!" he murmured. "That takes care of you. What an appetite! And now —"

As the Level Four portal dilated open before him, a gun blazed from across the hall. Quillan flung himself out and down, rolled to the side, briefly aware of a litter of bodies and tumbled furniture farther up the hall. Then he was flat on the carpet, gun out before him, pointing back at the overturned, ripped couch against the far wall from which the fire had come.

A hoarse voice bawled, "Bad News — hold it!"

Quillan hesitated, darting a glance right and left. Men lying about everywhere, the furnishings a shambles. "That you, Baldy?" he asked.

"Yeah," Baldy Perk half sobbed. "I'm hurt —"

"What happened?"

"*Star* gang jumped us. Portaled in here — spitballs and riot guns! Bad News, we're clean wiped out! Everyone that was on this level —"

Quillan stood up, holstering the gun, went over to the couch, and moved it carefully away from the wall. Baldy was crouched behind it, kneeling on the blood-soaked carpet, gun in his right hand. He lifted a white face, staring eyes, to Quillan.

"Waitin' for 'em to come back," he muttered. "Man, I'm not for long! Got hit twice. Near passed out a couple of times already."

"What about your boys on guard downstairs?"

"Same thing there, I guess ... or they'd have showed up. They got Cooms and the Duke, too! Man, it all happened fast!"

"And the crew on the freighter?"

"Dunno about them."

"You know the freighter's call number?"

"Huh? Oh, yeah. Sure. Never thought of that," Baldy said wearily. He seemed dazed now.

"Let's see if you can stand."

Quillan helped the big man to his feet. Baldy hadn't bled too much outwardly, but he seemed to have estimated his own condition correctly. He wasn't for long. Quillan slid an arm under his shoulders.

"Where's a ComWeb?" he asked.

Baldy blinked about. "Passage there —" His voice was beginning to thicken.

The ComWeb was in the second room up the passage. Quillan eased Perk into the seat before it. Baldy's head lolled heavily forward, like a drunken man's. "What's the number?" Quillan asked.

Baldy reflected a few seconds, blinking owlishly at the instrument, then told him. Quillan tapped out the number, flicked on the vision screen, then stood aside and back, beyond the screen's range.

"Yeah, Perk?" a voice said some seconds later. "Hey, *Perk* ... Perk, what's with ya?"

Baldy spat blood, grinned. "Shot —" he said.

"*What?*"

"Yeah." Baldy scowled, blinking. "Now, lessee — Oh, yeah. Star gang's gonna jump ya! Watch it!"

"What?"

"Yeah, watch —" Baldy coughed, laid his big head slowly down face forward on the ComWeb stand, and stopping moving.

"Perk! Man, wake up! Perk!"

Quillan quietly took out the gun, reached behind the stand and blew the ComWeb apart. He wasn't certain what the freighter's crew would make of the sudden break in the connection, but they could hardly regard it as reassuring. He made a brief prowl then through the main sections of the level. Evidence everywhere of a short and furious struggle, a struggle between men panicked and enraged almost beyond any regard for self-preservation. It must have been over in minutes. He found that the big hall portal to the ground level had been sealed, whether before or after the shooting he couldn't know. There would have been around twenty members of the Brotherhood on the level. None of them had lived as long as Baldy Park, but they seemed to have accounted for approximately an equal number of the Star's security force first.

Five Star men came piling out of the fifth-level portal behind him a minute or two later, Ryter in the lead. Orca behind Ryter. All five held leveled guns.

"You won't need the hardware," Quillan assured them. "It's harmless enough now. Come on in."

They followed him silently up to the cubicle, stared uncompre-hendingly at dials and indicators. "The thing's back inside there, all right!" Ryter said. He looked at Quillan. "Is this where you've been all the time?"

"Sure. Where else?" The others were forming a half-circle about him, a few paces back.

"Taking quite a chance with that Hlat, weren't you?" Ryter remarked.

"Not too much. I thought of something." Quillan indicated the out–portal in the hall. "I had my back against that. A portal's space-break, not solid matter. It couldn't come at me from behind. And if it attacked from any other angle" — he tapped the holstered Miam Devil lightly, and the gun in Orca's hand jerked upward a fraction of an inch — "there aren't many animals that can swallow more than a bolt or two from that baby and keep coming."

There was a moment's silence. Then Orca said thoughtfully, "That would work!"

"Did it see you?" Ryter asked.

"It couldn't have. First *I* saw of it, it was sailing out from that corner over there. It slammed in after that chunk of sea beef so fast, it shook the cubicle. And that was that." He grinned. "Well, most of our troubles should be over now!"

One of the men gave a brief, nervous laugh. Quillan looked at him curiously. "Something, chum?"

Ryter shook his head. "Something is right! Come on downstairs again, Bad News. This time we have news for you —"

The Brotherhood guards on the ground level had been taken by surprise and shot down almost without losses for the Star men. But the battle on the fourth level had cost more than the dead left up there. An additional number had returned with injuries that were serious enough to make them useless for further work.

"It's been expensive," Ryter admitted. "But one more attack by the Hlat would have left me with a panicked mob on my hands. If we'd realized it was going to trap itself —"

"I wasn't so sure that would work either," Quillan said. "Did you get Kinmarten back?"

"Not yet. The chances are he's locked up somewhere on the fourth level. Now the Hlat's out of the way, some of the men have gone back up there to look for him. If Cooms thought he was important enough to start a fight over, I want him back."

"How about the crew on the Beldon ship?" Quillan asked. "Have they been cleaned up?"

"No," Ryter said. "We'll have to do that now, of course."

"How many of them?"

"Supposedly twelve. And that's probably what it is."

"If they know or suspect what's happened," Quillan said, "twelve men can give a boarding party in a lock a remarkable amount of trouble."

Ryter shrugged irritably. "I know, but there isn't much choice. Lancion's bringing in the other group on the *Camelot*. We don't want to have to handle both of them at the same time."

"How are you planning to take the freighter?"

"When the search party comes back down, we'll put every man we can spare from guard duty here on the job. They'll be instructed to be careful about it ... if they can wind up the matter within the next several hours, that will be early enough. We can't afford too many additional losses now. But we should come out with enough men to take care of Lancion and handle the shipment of Hlats. And that's what counts."

"Like me to take charge of the boarding party?" Quillan inquired. "That sort of thing's been a kind of specialty of mine."

Ryter looked at him without much expression on his face. "I under–stand that," he said. "But perhaps it would be better if you stayed up here with us."

The search party came back down ten minutes later. They'd looked through every corner of the fourth level. Kinmarten wasn't there, either dead or alive. But one observant member of the group had discovered, first, that the Duke of Fluel was also not among those present, and, next, that one of the four outportals on the level had been unsealed. The exit on which the portal was found to be set was in a currently unused hall in the General Offices building on the other side of the Star. From that hall, almost every other section of the Star was within convenient portal range.

None of the forty-odd people working in the main control office on the ground level had actually witnessed any shooting; but it was apparent that a number of them were uncomfortably aware that something quite extraordinary must be going on. They were a well-disciplined group, however. An occasional uneasy glance toward one of the armed men lounging along the walls, some anxious faces, were the only noticeable indications of tension. Now and then, there was a brief, low-pitched conversation at one of the desks.

Quillan stood near the center of the office, Ryter and Orca a dozen feet from him on either side. Four Star guards were stationed along the walls. From the office one could see through a large doorspace cut through both sides of a hall directly into the adjoining transmitter room. Four more guards were in there. Aside from the men in the entrance hall and at the subspace portal, what was available at the moment of Ryter's security force was concentrated at this point.

The arrangement made considerable sense; and Quillan gave no sign of being aware that the eyes of the guards shifted to him a little more frequently than to any other point in the office, or that none of them had moved his hand very far away from his gun since they had come in here. But that also made sense. In the general tension area of the Executive Block's ground level, a specific point of tension — highly charged though undetected by the noninvolved personnel — was the one provided by the presence of Bad News Quillan here. Ryter was more than suspicious by now; the opened portal on the fourth level, the disappearance of Kinmarten and the Duke, left room for a wide variety of speculations. Few of those speculations could be very favorable to Bad News. Ryter obviously preferred to let things stand as they were until the Beldon freighter was taken and the major part of his group had returned from the subspace sections of the Star. At that time, Bad News could expect to come in for some very direct questioning by the security chief.

The minutes dragged on. Under the circumstances, a glance at his watch could be enough to bring Ryter's uncertainties up to the explosion point, and Quillan also preferred to let things stand as they were for the moment. But he felt reasonably certain that over an hour had passed since he'd left Reetal; and so far there had been no hint of anything unusual occurring in the front part of the building. The murmur of voices in the main control office continued to eddy about him. There were indications that in the transmitter room across the hall messages had begun to be exchanged between the Star and the approaching liner.

A man sitting at a desk near Quillan stood up presently, went out into the hall, and disappeared. A short while later, the white-suited figure returned and picked up the interrupted work. Quillan's glance went over the clerk, shifted on. He felt something tighten up swiftly inside him. There was a considerable over-all resemblance, but *that* wasn't the man who had left the office.

Another minute or two went by. Then two other uniformed figures appeared at the opening to the hall, a sparse elderly man, a blond girl. They stood there talking earnestly together for some seconds, then came slowly down the aisle toward Quillan. It appeared to be an argument about some detail of her work. The girl frowned, stubbornly shaking her head. Near Quillan they separated, started off into different sections of the office. The girl, glancing back, still frowning, brushed against Ryter. She looked up at him, startled.

"I'm sorry," she said.

Ryter scowled irritably, started to say something, suddenly appeared surprised. Then his eyes went blank and his knees buckled under him.

The clerk sitting at the nearby desk whistled shrilly.

Quillan wheeled, gun out and up, toward the wall behind him. The two guards there were still lifting their guns. The Miam Devil grunted disapprovingly twice, and the guards went down. Noise crashed from the hall ... heavy sporting rifles. He turned again, saw the two other guards stumbling backward along the far wall. Feminine screaming erupted around the office as the staff dove out of sight behind desks, instrument stands, and filing cabinets. The elderly man stood above Orca, a sap in his hand and a pleased smile on his face.

In the hallway, four white-uniformed men had swung about and were pointing blazing rifles into the transmitter room. The racketing of the gunfire ended abruptly and the rifles were lowered again. The human din in the office began to diminish, turned suddenly into a shocked, strained silence. Quillan realized the blond girl was standing at his elbow.

"Did you get the rest of them?" he asked quickly, in a low voice.

"Everyone who was on this level," Reetal told him. "There weren't many of them."

"I know. But there's a sizable batch still in the subspace section. If we can get the bomb disarmed, we'll just leave them sealed up there. How long before you can bring Ryter around?"

"He'll be able to talk in five minutes."

Quillan had been sitting for some little while in a very comfortable chair in what had been the commodore's personal suite on the Seventh Star, broodingly regarding the image of the *Camelot* in a huge wall screen. The liner was still over two hours' flight away but would arrive on schedule. On the Star, at least in the normspace section, everything was quiet; and in the main control offices and in the transmitter room normal working conditions had been restored.

A room portal twenty feet away opened suddenly, and Reetal Destone stepped out.

"So there you are!" she observed.

Quillan looked mildly surprised, then grinned. "I'd hate to have to try to hide from you!" he said.

"Hm-m-m!" said Reetal. She smiled. "What are you drinking?"

He nodded at an open liquor cabinet near the screen. "Velladon was leaving some excellent stuff behind. Join me?"

"Hm-m-m." She went to the cabinet, looked over the bottles, made her selection, and filled a glass. "One has the impression," she remarked, "that you *were* hiding from me."

"One does? I'd have to be losing my cotton-picking mind —"

"Not necessarily." Reetal brought her drink over to his chair, sat down on the armrest with it. "You might just have a rather embarrassing problem to get worked out before you give little Reetal a chance to start asking questions about it."

Quillan looked surprised. "What gave you that notion?"

"Oh," Reetal said, "adding things up gave me that notion ... Care to hear what the things were?"

"Go ahead, doll."

"First," said Reetal, "I understand that a while ago, after you'd first sent me off to do some little job for you, you were in the transmitter room having a highly private — shielded and scrambled — conversation with somebody on board the *Camelot*."

"Why, yes," Quillan said. "I was talking to the ship's security office. They're arranging to have a Federation police boat pick up what's left of the commodore's boys and the Brotherhood in the subspace section."

"And that," said Reetal, "is where that embarrassing little problem begins. Next, I noticed, as I say, that you were showing this tendency to avoid a chance for a private talk between us. And after thinking about that for a little, and also about a few other things which came to mind at around that time, I went to see Ryter."

"Now why — ?"

Reetal ran her fingers soothingly through his hair. "Let me finish, big boy. I found Ryter and Orca in a highly nervous condition. And do you know why they're nervous? They're convinced that some time before the *Camelot* gets here, you're going to do them both in."

"Hm-m-m," said Quillan.

"Ryter," she went on, "besides being nervous, is also very bitter. In retrospect, he says, it's all very plain what you've done here. You and your associates — a couple of tough boys named Hagready and Boltan, and others not identified — are also after these Hlats. The Duke made some mention of that, too, you remember. The commodore and Ryter bought the story you told them because a transmitter check produced the information that Hagready and Boltan had, in fact, left their usual work areas and gone off on some highly secret business about a month ago.

"Ryter feels that your proposition — to let your gang in on the deal for twenty per cent, or else — was made in something less than good faith. He's concluded that when you learned of the operation being planned by Velladon and the Brotherhood, you and your pals decided to obstruct them and take the Hlats for delivery to Yaco yourselves, without cutting anybody in. He figures that someone like Hagready or Boltan is coming in on the *Camelot* with a flock of sturdy henchmen to do just that. You, personally, rushed to the Seventh Star to interfere as much as you could here. Ryter admits reluctantly that you did an extremely good job of interfering. He says it's now obvious that every move you made since you showed up had the one purpose of setting the Star group and the Brotherhood at each other's throats. And now that they've practically wiped each other out, you and your associates can go on happily with your original plans.

"But, of course, you can't do that if Ryter and Orca are picked up alive by the Federation cops. The boys down in the subspace section don't matter; they're ordinary gunhands and all they know is that you were somebody who showed up on the scene. But Ryter could, and certainly would, talk —"

"Ah, he's too imaginative," Quillan said, taking a swallow of his drink. "I never heard of the Hlats before I got here. As I told you, I'm on an entirely different kind of job at the moment. I had to make up some kind of story to get an in with the boys, that's all."

"So you're not going to knock those two weasels off?"

"No such intentions. I don't mind them sweating about it till the Feds arrive, but that's it."

"What about Boltan and Hagready?"

"What about them? I did happen to know that if anyone started asking questions about those two, he'd learn that neither had been near his regular beat for close to a month."

"I'll bet!" Reetal said cryptically.

"What do you mean by that?"

"Hm-m-m," she said. "Bad News Quillan! A really tough boy, for sure. You know, I didn't believe for an instant that you were after the Hlats —"

"Why not?"

Reetal said, "I've been on a couple of operations with you, and you'd be surprised how much I've picked up about you from time to time on the side. Swiping a shipment of odd animals and selling them to Yaco, that could be Bad News, in character. Selling a couple of hundred human beings — like Brock and Solvey Kinmarten — to go along with the animals to an outfit like Yaco would not be in character."

"So I have a heart of gold," Quillan said.

"So you fell all over your own big feet about half a minute ago!" Reetal told him. "Bad News Quillan — with no interest whatsoever in the Hlats — still couldn't afford to let Ryter live to talk about him to the Feds, big boy!"

Quillan looked reflective for a moment. "Dirty trick!" he observed. "For that, you might freshen up my glass."

Reetal took both glasses over to the liquor cabinet, freshened them up, and settled down on the armrest of the chair again. "So there we're back to the embarrassing little problem," she said.

"Ryter?"

"No, idiot. We both know that Ryter is headed for Rehabilitation. Fifteen years or so of it, at a guess. The problem is little Reetal who has now learned a good deal more than she was ever intended to learn. Does she head for Rehabilitation, too?"

Quillan took a swallow of his drink and set the glass down again. "Are you suggesting," he inquired, "that I might be, excuse the expression, a cop?"

Reetal patted his head. "Bad News Quillan! Let's look back at his record. What do we find? A shambles, mainly. Smashed-up organizations, outfits, gangs. Top-level crooks with suddenly vacant expressions and unexplained holes in their heads. Why go on? The name is awfully well earned! And nobody realizing anything because the ones who do realize it suddenly ... well, where *are* Boltan and Hagready at the moment?"

Quillan sighed. "Since you keep bringing it up — Hagready played it smart, so he's in Rehabilitation. Be cute if Ryter ran into him there some day. Pappy Boltan didn't want to play it smart. I'm not enough of a philosopher to make a guess at where he might be at present. But I knew he wouldn't be talking."

"All right," Reetal said, "we've got that straight. Bad News is Intel–ligence of some kind. Federation maybe, or maybe one of the services. It doesn't matter, really, I suppose. Now, what about me?"

He reached out and tapped his glass with a fingertip. "That about you, doll. You filled it. I'm drinking it. I may not think quite as fast as you do, but I still think. Would I take a drink from a somewhat lawless and very clever lady who really believed I had her lined up for Rehabilitation? Or who'd be at all likely to blab out something that would ruin an old pal's reputation?"

Reetal ran her fingers through his hair again. "I noticed the deal with the drink," she said. "I guess I just wanted to hear you say it. You don't tell on me, I don't tell on you. Is that it?"

"That's it," Quillan said. "What Ryter and Orca want to tell the Feds doesn't matter. It stops there; the Feds will have the word on me before they arrive. By the way, did you go wake up the Kinmartens yet?"

"Not yet," Reetal said. "Too busy getting the office help soothed down and back to work."

"Well, let's finish these drinks and go do that, then. The little doll's almost bound to be asleep by now, but she might still be sitting there biting nervously at her pretty knuckles."

Major Heslet Quillan, of Space Scout Intelligence, was looking unhappy. "We're still searching for them everywhere," he explained to Klayung, "but it's a virtual certainty that the Hlat got them shortly before it was trapped."

Klayung, a stringy, white-haired old gentleman, was an operator of the Psychology Service, in charge of the shipment of Hlats the *Camelot* had brought in. He and Quillan were waiting in the vestibule of the Seventh Star's rest cubicle vaults for Lady Pendrake's cubicle to be brought over from the Executive Block.

Klayung said reflectively, "Couldn't the criminals with whom you were dealing here have hidden the couple away somewhere?"

Quillan shook his head. "There's no way they could have located them so quickly. I made half a dozen portal switches when I was taking Kinmarten to the suite. It would take something with a Hlat's abilities to follow me over that route and stay undetected. And it must be an un-usually cunning animal to decide to stay out of sight until I'd led it where it wanted to go."

"Oh, they're intelligent enough," Klayung agreed absently. "Their average basic I.Q. is probably higher than that of human beings. A somewhat different type of mentality, of course. Well, when the cubicle arrives, I'll question the Hlat and we'll find out."

Quillan looked at him. "Those control devices make it possible to hold two-way conversations with the things?"

"Not exactly," Klayung said. "You see, major, the government authorities who were concerned with the discovery of the Hlats realized it would be almost impossible to keep some information about them from getting out. The specimen which was here on the Star has been stationed at various scientific institutions for the past year; a rather large number of people were involved in investigating it and experimenting with it. In consequence, several little legends about them have been deliberately built up. The legends aren't entirely truthful, so they help to keep the actual facts about the Hlats satisfactorily vague.

"The Hlat-talker is such a legend. Actually, the device does nothing. The Hlats respond to telepathic stimuli, both among themselves and from other beings, eventually begin to correlate such stimuli with the meanings of human speech."

"Then you —" Quillan began.

"Yes. Eltak, their discoverer, was a fairly good natural telepath. If he hadn't been abysmally lazy, he might have been very good at it. I carry a variety of the Service's psionic knickknacks about with me, which gets me somewhat comparable results."

He broke off as the vestibule portal dilated widely. Lady Pendrake's cubicle floated through, directed by two gravity crane operators behind it. Klayung stood up.

"Set it there for the present, please," he directed the operators. "We may call for you later if it needs to be moved again."

He waited until the portal had closed behind the men before walking over to the cubicle. He examined the settings and readings at some length.

"Hm-m-m, yes," he said, straightening finally. His expression became absent for a few seconds; then he went on. "I'm beginning to grasp the situation, I believe. Let me tell you a few things about the Hlats, major. For one, they form quite pronounced likes and dislikes. Eltak, for example, would have been described by most of his fellow men as a rather offensive person. But the Hlats actually became rather fond of him during the fifteen or so years he lived on their island.

"That's one point. The other has to do with their level of intelligence. We discovered on the way out here that our charges had gained quite as comprehensive an understanding of the functioning of the cubicles that had been constructed for them as any human who was not a technical specialist might do. And —"

He interrupted himself, stood rubbing his chin for a moment.

"Well, actually," he said, "that should be enough to prepare you for a look inside the Hlat's cubicle."

Quillan gave him a somewhat surprised glance. "I've been told it's ugly as sin," he remarked. "But I've seen some fairly revolting-looking mon-sters before this."

Klayung coughed. "That's not exactly what I meant," he said. "I ... well, let's just open the thing up. Would you mind, major?"

"Not at all." Quillan stepped over to the side of the cubicle, unlocked the door switch, and pulled it over. They both moved back a few feet, before the front of the cubicle. A soft humming came for some seconds from the door's mechanisms; then it suddenly swung open. Quillan stooped to glance inside, straightened instantly again, hair bristling.

"*Where is it?*" he demanded, the Miam Devil out in his hand.

Klayung looked at him thoughtfully. "Not very far away, I believe. But I can assure you, major, that it hasn't the slightest intention of attacking us — or anybody else — at present."

Quillan grunted, looked back into the cubicle. At the far end, the Kinmartens lay side by side, their faces composed. They appeared to be breathing regularly.

"Yes," Klayung said, "they're alive and unharmed." He rubbed his chin again. "And I think it would be best if we simply closed the cubicle now. Later we can call a doctor over from the hospital to put them under sedation before they're taken out. They've both had thoroughly unnerving experiences, and it would be advisable to awaken them gradually to avoid emotional shock."

He moved over to the side of the cubicle, turned the door switch back again. "And now for the rest of it," he said. "We may as well sit down again, major. This may take a little time.

"Let's look at the thing for a moment from the viewpoint of the Hlat," he resumed when he was once more comfortably seated. "Eltak's death took it by surprise. It hadn't at that point grasped what the situation in the Executive Block was like. It took itself out of sight for the moment, killing one of the gang leaders in the process, then began prowling about the various levels of the building, picking up information from the minds and conversation of the men it encountered. In a fairly short time, it learned enough to understand what was planned by the criminals; and it arrived at precisely your own conclusion … that it might be possible to reduce and demoralize the gangs to the extent that they would no longer be able to carry out their plan. It began a systematic series of attacks on them with that end in mind.

"But meanwhile you had come into the picture. The Hlat was rather puzzled by your motive at first because there appeared to be an extraordinary degree of discrepancy between what you were saying and what you were thinking. But after observing your activities for a while, it began to comprehend what you were trying to do. It realized that your approach was more likely to succeed than its own, and that further action on its side might interfere with your plans. But there remained one thing for it to do.

"I may tell you in confidence, major, that another legend which has been spread about these Hlats is their supposed inability to escape from the cubicles. Even their attendants are supplied with this particular bit of misinformation. Actually, the various force fields in the cubicles don't hamper them in the least. The cubicles are designed simply to protect the Hlats and keep them from being seen; and rest cubicles, of course, can be taken anywhere without arousing undue curiosity.

"You mentioned that the Kinmartens are very likable young people. The Hlat had the same feeling about them; they were the only human beings aside from Eltak with whose minds it had become quite familiar. There was no assurance at this point that the plans to prevent a bomb from being exploded in the Star would be successful, and the one place where human beings could hope to survive such an explosion was precisely the interior of the Hlat's cubicle, which had been constructed to safeguard its occupant against any kind of foreseeable accident.

"So the Hlat sprang your cubicle trap, removed the bait, carried the Kinmartens inside, and whipped out of the cubicle again before the rest current could take effect on it. It concluded correctly that everyone would decide it had been recaptured. After that, it moved about the Executive Block, observing events there and prepared to take action again if that appeared to be advisable. When you had concluded your operation successfully, it remained near the cubicle, waiting for me to arrive."

Quillan shook his head. "That's quite an animal!" he observed after some seconds. "You say it's in our general vicinity now?"

"Yes," Klayung said. "It followed the cubicle down here, and has been drifting about the walls of the vestibule while we ... well, while I talked."

"Why doesn't it show itself?"

Klayung cleared his throat. "For two reasons," he said. "One is that rather large gun you're holding on your knees. It saw you use it several times, and after all the shooting in the Executive Block, you see —"

Quillan slid the Miam Devil into its holster. "Sorry," he said. "Force of habit, I guess. Actually, of course, I've understood for some minutes now that I wasn't ... well, what's the other reason?"

"I'm afraid," Klayung said, "that you offended it with your remark about its appearance. Hlats may have their share of vanity. At any rate, it seems to be sulking."

"Oh," said Quillan. "Well, I'm sure," he went on rather loudly, "that it understands I received the description from a prejudiced source. I'm quite willing to believe it was highly inaccurate."

"Hm-m-m," said Klayung. "That seems to have done it, major. The wall directly across from us —"

Something like a ripple passed along the side wall of the vestibule. Then the wall darkened suddenly, turned black. Quillan blinked, and the Hlat came into view. It hung, spread out like a spider, along half the length of the vestibule wall. Something like a huge, hairy amoeba in overall appearance, though the physical structures under the coarse, black pelt must be of very unamoebalike complexity. No eyes were in sight, but Quillan had the impression of being regarded steadily. Here and there, along the edges and over the surface of the body, were a variety of flexible extensions.

Quillan stood up, hitched his gun belt into position, and started over toward the wall.

"Lady Pendrake," he said, "honored to meet you. Could we shake hands?"

Just Curious

Roy Litton's apartment was on the eighteenth floor of the Torrell Arms. It was a pleasant place which cost him thirty-two thousand dollars a year. The living room had a wide veranda which served in season as a sun deck. Far below was a great park. Beyond the park, drawn back to a respectful distance from the Torrell Arms, was the rest of the city.

"May I inquire," Roy Litton said to his visitor, "from whom you learned about me?"

The visitor's name was Jean Merriam. She was a slender, expensive brunette, about twenty-seven. She took a card from her handbag and slid it across the table to Litton. "Will that serve as an introduction?" she asked.

Litton studied the words scribbled on the card and smiled. "Yes," he said, "that's quite satisfactory. I know the lady's handwriting well. In what way can I help you?"

"I represent an organization," Jean said, "which does discreet inves— tigative work."

"You're detectives?"

She shrugged, smiled. "We don't refer to ourselves as detectives, but that's the general idea. Conceivably your talents could be very useful to us. I'm here to find out whether you're willing to put them at our disposal from time to time. If you are, I have a test assignment for you. You don't mind, do you?"

Litton rubbed his chin. "You've been told what my standard fee is?"

Jean Merriam opened the handbag again, took out a check, and gave it to him. Litton read it carefully, nodded. "Yes," he said, and laid the check on the table beside him. "Ten thousand dollars. You're in the habit of paying such sums out of your personal account?"

"The sum was put in my account yesterday for this purpose."

"Then what do you, or your organization, want me to do?"

"I've been given a description of how you operate, Mr. Litton, but we don't know how accurate the description is. Before we retain you, I'd like you to tell me exactly what you do."

Litton smiled. "I'm willing to tell you as much as I know."

She nodded. "Very well. I'll decide on the basis of what you say whether or not your services might be worth ten thousand dollars to the organization. Once I offer you the assignment and you accept it, we're committed. The check will be yours when the assignment is completed."

"Who will judge when it has been completed?"

"You will," said Jean. "Naturally there will be no further assignments if we're not satisfied with the results of this one. As I said, this is a test. We're gambling. If you're as good as I've been assured you are, the gamble should pay off. Fair enough?"

Litton nodded. "Fair enough, Miss Merriam." He leaned back in his chair. "Well, then — I sometimes call myself a 'sensor' because the word describes my experiences better than any other word I can think of. I'm not specifically a mind reader. I can't predict the future. I don't have second sight. But under certain conditions, I turn into a long-range sensing device with a limited application. I have no theoretical explanation for it. I can only say what happens.

"I work through contact objects; that is, material items which have had a direct and extensive physical connection with the persons I investigate. A frequently worn garment is the obvious example. Eyeglasses would be excellent. I once was able to use an automobile which the subject had driven daily for about ten months. Through some such object I seem to become, for a time which varies between approximately three and five minutes, the person in question." Litton smiled. "Naturally I remain here physically, but my awareness is elsewhere.

"Let me emphasize that during this contact period I *am* — or seem to be — the other person. I am not conscious of Roy Litton or of what Roy Litton is doing. I have never heard of him and know nothing of his sensing ability. I am the other person, aware only of what he is aware of, doing what he is doing, thinking what he is thinking. If, meanwhile, you were to speak to the body sitting here, touch it, even cause it severe pain — which has been done experimentally — I wouldn't know it. When the time is up, the contact fades and I am back. Then I know who I am and can recall my experience and report on it. Essentially, that's the process."

Jean Merriam asked, "To what extent do you control the process?"

"I can initiate it or not initiate it. I'm never drawn out of myself unless I intend to be drawn out of myself. That's the extent of my control. Once it begins, the process continues by itself and concludes itself. I have no way of affecting its course."

Jean said reflectively, "I don't wish to alarm you, Mr. Litton. But mightn't you be running the risk of remaining permanently lost in somebody else's personality ... unable to return to your own?"

Litton laughed. "No. I know definitely that can't happen, though I don't know why. The process simply can't maintain itself for much more than five minutes. On the other hand, it's rarely terminated in less than three."

"You say that during the time of contact you think what the other person thinks and are aware of what he's aware of?"

"That's correct."

"Only that? If we employed you to investigate someone in this manner, we usually would need quite specific information. Wouldn't we have to be extremely fortunate if the person happened to think of that particular matter in the short time you shared his mind?"

"No," said Litton. "Conscious thoughts quite normally have thousands of ramifications and shadings the thinker doesn't know about. When the contact dissolves, I retain his impressions and it is primarily these ramifications and shadings I then investigate. It is something like developing a vast number of photographic prints. Usually the information my clients want can be found in those impressions in sufficient detail."

"What if it can't be found?"

"Then I make a second contact. On only one occasion, so far, have I been obliged to make three separate contacts with a subject to satisfy the client's requirements. There is no fee for additional contacts."

Jean Merriam considered a moment. "Very well," she said. She brought a small box from the handbag, opened it, and took out a ring, which she handed to Litton. "The person in whom the organization is interested," she said, "was wearing this ring until four weeks ago. Since then it's been in a safe. The safe was opened yesterday and the ring taken from it and placed in this box. Would you consider it a suitable contact object?"

Litton held the ring in his palm an instant before replying. "Eminently suitable!" he said then.

"You can tell by touching such objects?"

"As a rule. If I get no impression, it's a waste of time to proceed. If I get a negative impression, I refuse to proceed."

"A negative impression?"

Litton shrugged. "A feeling of something that repels me. I can't de-scribe it more definitely."

"Does it mean that the personality connected with the object is a repellent one?"

"Not necessarily. I've merged with some quite definitely repellent personalities in the course of this work. That doesn't disturb me. The feeling I speak of is a different one."

"It frightens you?"

"Perhaps." He smiled. "However, in this case there is no such feeling. Have you decided to offer me the assignment?"

"Yes, I have," Jean Merriam said. "Now then, I've been told nothing about the person connected with the ring. Since very few men could get it on, and very few children would wear a ring of such value, I assume the owner is a woman — but I don't know even that. The reason I've been told nothing is to make sure I'll give you no clues, inadvertently or otherwise." She smiled. "Even if you were a mind reader, you see, you could get no significant information from me. We want to be certain of the authenticity of your talent."

"I understand," Litton said. "But you must know what kind of information your organization wants to gain from the contact?"

Jean nodded. "Yes, of course. We want you to identify the subject by name and tell us where she can be found. The description of the locality should be specific. We also want to learn as much as we can about the subject's background, her present activities and interests, and any people with whom she is closely involved. The more details you can give us about such people, the better. In general, that's all. Does it seem like too difficult an assignment?"

"Not at all," Litton said. "In fact, I'm surprised you want no more. Is that kind of information really worth ten thousand dollars to you?"

"I've been told," Jean said, "that if we get it within the next twenty-four hours, it will be worth a great deal more than ten thousand dollars."

"I see." Litton settled comfortably in the chair, placed his clasped hands around the ring on the table, enclosing it. "Then, if you like, Miss Merriam, I'll now make the contact."

"No special preparations?" she inquired, watching him.

"Not in this case." Litton nodded toward a heavily curtained alcove in the wall on his left. "That's what I call my withdrawal room. When I feel there's reason to expect difficulties in making a contact, I go in there. Observers can be disturbing under such circumstances. Otherwise, no preparations are necessary."

"What kind of difficulties could you encounter?" Jean asked.

"Mainly, the pull of personalities other than the one I want. A contact object may be valid, but contaminated by associations with other people. Then it's a matter of defining and following the strongest attraction, which is almost always that of the proper owner and our subject. Incidentally, it would be advantageous if you were prepared to record my report."

Jean tapped the handbag. "I'm recording our entire conversation, Mr. Litton."

He didn't seem surprised. "Very many of my clients do," he remarked. "Very well, then, let's begin ..."

"How long did it take him to dream up this stuff?" Nick Garland asked.

"Four minutes and thirty-two seconds," Jean Merriam said.

Garland shook his head incredulously. He took the transcript she'd made of her recorded visit to Roy Litton's apartment from the desk and leafed through it again. Jean watched him, her face expressionless. Garland was a big gray-haired bear of a man, coldly irritable at present — potentially dangerous.

He laid the papers down, drummed his fingers on the desk. "I still don't want to believe it," he said, "but I guess I'll have to. He hangs on to Caryl Chase's ring for a few minutes, then he can tell you enough about her to fill five typed, single-spaced pages ... That's what happened?"

Jean nodded. "Yes, that's what happened. He kept pouring out details about the woman as if he'd known her intimately half her life. He didn't hesitate about anything. My impression was that he wasn't guessing about anything. He seemed to know."

Garland grunted. "Max thinks he knew." He looked up at the man standing to the left of the desk. "Fill Jean in, Max. How accurate is Litton?"

Max Jewett said, "On every point we can check out, he's completely accurate."

"What are the points you can check out?" Jean asked.

"The ring belongs to Caryl Chase. She's thirty-two. She's Phil Chase's wife, currently estranged. She's registered at the Hotel Arve, Geneva, Switzerland, having an uneasy off-and-on affair with one William Haskell, British ski nut. He's jealous, and they fight a lot. Caryl suspects Phil has detectives looking for her, which he does. Her daughter Ellie is hidden away with friends of Caryl's parents in London. Litton's right about the ring. Caryl got it from her grandmother on her twenty-first birthday and had worn it regularly since. When she ran out on Phil last month, she took it off and left it in her room safe. Litton's statement, that leaving it was a symbolic break with her past life, makes sense." Jewett shrugged. "That's about it. Her psychoanalyst might be able to check out some of the rest of what you got on tape. We don't have that kind of information."

Garland growled, "We don't need it. We got enough for now."

Jean exchanged a glance with Jewett. "You feel Litton's genuine, Mr. Garland?"

"He's genuine. Only Max and I knew we were going to test him on Caryl. If he couldn't do what he says he does, you wouldn't have got the tape. There's no other way he could know those things about her." Garland's face twisted into a sour grimace. "I thought Max had lost his marbles when he told me it looked like Phleger had got his information from some kind of swami. But that's how it happened. Frank Phleger got Litton to tap my mind something like two or three months ago. He'd need that much time to get set to make his first move."

"How much have you lost?" Jean asked.

He grunted. "Four, five million. I can't say definitely yet. That's not what bothers me." His mouth clamped shut, a pinched angry line. His eyes shifted bleakly down to the desk, grew remote, lost focus.

Jean Merriam watched him silently. Inside that big skull was stored information which seemed sometimes equal to the intelligence files of a central bank. Nick Garland's brain was a strategic computer, a legal library. He was a multimillionaire, a brutal genius, a solitary and cunning king beast in the financial jungle — a jungle he allowed to become barely aware he existed. Behind his secretiveness he remained an unassailable shadow. In the six years Jean had been working for him she'd never before seen him suffer a setback; but if they were right about Litton, this was more than a setback. Garland's mind had been opened, his plans analyzed, his strengths and weaknesses assessed by another solitary king beast — a lesser one, but one who knew exactly how to make the greatest possible use of the information thus gained — and who had begun to do it. So Jean waited and wondered.

"Jean," Garland said at last. His gaze hadn't shifted from the desk. "Yes?"

"Did Litton buy your story about representing something like a detective agency?"

"He didn't seem to question it," Jean said. "My impression was that he
doesn't particularly care who employs him, or for what purpose."

"He'll look into anyone's mind for a price?" It was said like a bitter
curse.

"Yes ... his price. What are you going to do?"

Garland's shoulders shifted irritably. "Max is trying to get a line on
Phleger."

Jean glanced questioningly at Jewett. Jewett told her, "Nobody seems
to have any idea where Frank Phleger's been for the past three weeks. We
assume he dropped out of sight to avoid possible repercussions. The
indications are that we're getting rather close to him."

"I see," Jean said uncomfortably. The king beasts avoided rough play
as a matter of policy, usually avoided conflict among themselves, but
when they met in a duel there were no rules.

"Give that part of it three days," Garland's voice said. She looked
around, found him watching her with a trace of what might be irony, back
at any rate from whatever brooding trance he'd been sunk in. "Jean, call
Litton sometime tomorrow."

"All right."

"Tell him the boss of your detective organization wants an appointment with him. Ten o'clock, three days from now."

She nodded, said carefully, "Litton could become extremely valuable
to you, Mr. Garland."

"He could," Garland agreed. "Anyway, I want to watch the swami
perform. We'll give him another assignment."

"Am I to accompany you?"

"You'll be there, Jean. So will Max."

"I keep having the most curiously definite impression," Roy Litton
observed, "that I've met you before."

"You have," Garland said amiably.

Litton frowned, shook his head. "It's odd I should have forgotten the
occasion!"

"The name's Nick Garland," Garland told him.

Still frowning, Litton stared at him across the table. Then abruptly his
face paled. Jean Merriam, watching from behind her employer, saw
Litton's eyes shift to her, from her to Max Jewett, and return at last,
hesitantly, to Garland's face. Garland nodded wryly.

"I was what you call one of your subjects, Mr. Litton," he said. "I can't
give you the exact date, but it should have been between two and three
months ago. You remember now?"

Litton shook his head. "No. After such an interval it would be
impossible to be definite about it, in any case. I keep no notes and the
details of a contact very quickly grow blurred to me." His voice was

guarded; he kept his eyes on Garland's. "Still, you seemed familiar to me at once as a person. And your name seems familiar. It's quite possible that you have been, in fact, a contact subject."

"I was," Garland said. "We know that. That's why we're here."

Litton cleared his throat. "Then the story Miss Merriam told me at her first visit wasn't true."

"Not entirely," Garland admitted. "She wasn't representing a detective outfit. She represented me. Otherwise, she told the truth. She was sent here to find out if you could do what we'd heard you could do. We learned that you could. Mr. Litton, you've cost me a great deal of money. But I'm not too concerned about that now, because, with your assistance, I'll make it back. And I'll make a great deal more besides. You begin to get the picture?"

Relief and wariness mingled for an instant in Litton's expression. "Yes, I believe I do."

"You'll get paid your regular fees, of course," Garland told him. "The fact is, Mr. Litton, you don't charge enough. What you offer is worth more than ten thousand a shot. What you gave Frank Phleger was worth enormously more."

"Frank Phleger?" Litton said.

"The client who paid you to poke around in my mind. No doubt he wouldn't have used his real name. It doesn't matter. Let's get on to your first real assignment for me. Regular terms. This one isn't a test. It's to bring up information I don't have and couldn't get otherwise. All right?"

Litton nodded, smiled. "You have a suitable contact object?"

"We brought something that should do," Garland said. "Max, give Mr. Litton the belt."

Jean Merriam looked back toward Jewett. Garland hadn't told her what Litton's assignment was to be, had given her no specific instructions, but she'd already turned on the recorder in her handbag. Jewett was taking a large plastic envelope from the briefcase he'd laid beside his chair. He came over to the table, put the envelope before Litton, and returned to his place.

"Can you tell me specifically what you want to know concerning this subject?" Litton asked.

"To start with," Garland said, "just give us whatever you can get. I'm interested in general information."

Litton nodded, opened the plastic envelope, and took out a man's leather belt with a broad silver buckle. Almost immediately an expression of distaste showed in his face. He put the belt on the table, looked over at Garland.

"Mr. Garland," he said, "Miss Merriam may have told you that on occasion I'm offered a contact object I can't use. Unfortunately, this belt is such an object."

"What do you mean?" Garland asked. "Why can't you use it?"

"I don't know. It may be something about the belt itself, and it may be the person connected with it." Litton brushed the belt with his fingers. "I simply have a very unpleasant feeling about this object. It repels me." He smiled apologetically. "I'm afraid I must refuse to work with it."

"Well, now," Garland said, "I don't like to hear that. You've cost me a lot, you know. I'm willing to overlook it, but I do expect you to be cooperative in return."

Litton glanced at him, swallowed uneasily. "I understand — and I assure you you'll find me cooperative. If you'll give me some other assignment, I assure you —"

"No," Garland said. "No, right now I want information about this particular person, not somebody else. It's too bad if you don't much like to work with the belt, but that's your problem. We went to a lot of trouble to get the belt for you. Let me state this quite clearly, Mr. Litton. You owe me the information, and I think you'd better get it now."

His voice remained even, but the menace in the words was undis—guised. The king beast was stepping out from cover, and Jean's palms were suddenly wet. She saw Litton's face whiten.

"I suppose I do owe it to you," Litton said after a moment. He hesitated again. "But this isn't going to be easy."

Garland snorted. "You're getting ten thousand dollars for a few minutes' work!"

"That isn't it. I …" Litton shook his head helplessly, got to his feet. He indicated the curtained alcove at the side of the room. "I'll go in there. At best, this will be a difficult contact to attempt. I can't be additionally distracted by knowing that three people are staring at me."

"You'll get the information?" Garland asked.

Litton looked at him, said sullenly, "I always get the information." He picked up the belt, went to the alcove, and disappeared through the curtains.

Garland turned toward Jean Merriam. "Start timing him," he said.

She nodded, checked her watch. The room went silent, and im—mediately Jean felt a heavy oppression settle on her. It was almost as if the air had begun to darken around them. Frightened, she thought, *Nick hates that freak … Has he decided to kill him?*

She pushed the question away and narrowed her attention to the almost inaudible ticking of the tiny expensive watch. After a while she realized that Garland was looking at her again. She met his eyes, whispered, "Three minutes and ten seconds." He nodded.

There was a sound from within the alcove. It was not particularly loud, but in the stillness it was startling enough to send a new gush of fright through Jean. She told herself some minor piece of furniture, a chair, a small side table, had fallen over, been knocked over on the carpeting. She was trying to think of some reason why Litton should have knocked over a chair in there when the curtains before the alcove were pushed apart. Litton moved slowly out into the room.

He stopped a few feet from the alcove. He appeared dazed, half-stunned, like a man who'd been slugged hard in the head and wasn't sure what had happened. His mouth worked silently, his lips writhing in slow, stiff contortions as if trying to shape words that couldn't be pronounced. Abruptly he started forward. Jean thought for a moment he was returning to the table, but he went past it, pace quickening, on past Garland and herself without glancing at either of them. By then he was almost running, swaying from side to side in long staggering steps, and she realized he was hurrying toward the French doors which stood open on the wide veranda overlooking the park. Neither Garland nor Jewett moved from their chairs, and Jean, unable to speak, twisted around to look after Litton as they were doing. She saw him run across the veranda, strike the hip-high railing without checking, and go on over.

The limousine moved away from the Torrell Arms through the sunlit park, Jewett at the wheel, Garland and Jean Merriam in the back seat. There was no siren wail behind them, no indication of disturbance, nothing to suggest that anyone else was aware that a few minutes ago a man had dropped into the neatly trimmed park shrubbery from the eighteenth floor of the great apartment hotel.

"You could have made use of him," Jean said. "He could have been of more value to you than anyone else in the world. But you intended to kill him from the start, didn't you?"

Garland didn't reply for a moment. Then he said, "I could have made use of him, sure. So could anyone else with ten thousand dollars to spare, or some way to put pressure on him. I don't need somebody like Litton to stay on top. And I don't like the rules changed. When Phleger found Litton, he started changing them. It could happen again. Litton had to be taken out."

"Max could have handled that," Jean said. Her hands had begun to tremble again; she twisted them tightly together around the strap of the handbag. "What did you do to get Litton to kill himself?"

Garland shook his head. "I didn't intend him to kill himself. Max was to take care of him afterward."

"You did something to him."

Garland drew a long sighing breath. "I was just curious," he said. "There's something I wonder about now and then. I thought Litton might be able to tell me, so I gave him the assignment."

"What assignment? He became someone else for three minutes. What happened to him?"

Garland's head turned slowly toward her. She noticed for the first time that his face was almost colorless. "That was Frank Phleger's belt," he said. "Max's boys caught up with him last night. Phleger's been dead for the last eight hours."

The Second Night of Summer

On the night after the day that brought summer officially to the land of Wend, on the planet of Noorhut, the shining lights were seen again in the big hollow at the east end of Grimp's father's farm.

Grimp watched them for more than an hour from his upstairs room. The house was dark, but an occasional murmur of voices floated up to him through the windows below. Everyone in the farmhouse was looking at the lights.

On the other farms around and in the village, which was over a hill and another two miles up the valley, every living soul who could get within view of the hollow was probably doing the same. For a time, the agitated yelling of the Village Guardian's big pank-hound had sounded clearly over the hill, but he had quieted down then very suddenly — or had *been* quieted down, more likely, Grimp suspected. The Guardian was dead-set against anyone making a fuss about the lights — and that included the pank-hound, too.

There was some excuse for the pank-hound's excitement, though. From the window, Grimp could see there were a lot more lights tonight than had turned up in previous years — big, brilliant-blue bubbles, drifting and rising and falling silently all about the hollow. Sometimes one would lift straight up for several hundred feet, or move off over the edge of the hollow for about the same distance, and hang there suspended for a few minutes, before floating back to the others. That was as far as they ever went away from the hollow.

There was, in fact, no need for the Halpa detector-globes to go any farther than that to get the information wanted by those who had sent them out, and who were listening now to the steady flow of brief reports, in some Halpa equivalent of human speech-thought, coming back to them through the globes:

"No signs of hostile activity in the vicinity of the breakthrough point. No weapons or engines of power within range of detection. The area shows no significant alterations since the last investigation. Sharp curiosity among those who observe us consciously — traces of alarm and suspicion. But no overt hostility."

The reports streamed on without interruption, repeating the same bits of information automatically and incessantly, while the globes floated and dipped soundlessly above and about the hollow.

Grimp continued to watch them, blinking sleepily now and then, until a spreading glow over the edge of the valley announced that Noorhut's Big Moon was coming up slowly, like a Planetary Guardian, to make its own inspection of the lights. The globes began to dim out then, just as they always had done at moonrise in the preceding summers; and even before the top rim of the Big Moon's yellow disk edged over the hills, the hollow was completely dark.

Grimp heard his mother starting up the stairs. He got hurriedly into bed. The show was over for the night and he had a lot of pleasant things to think about before he went to sleep.

Now that the lights had showed up, his good friend Grandma Erisa Wannattel and her patent-medicine trailer were sure to arrive, too. Sometime late tomorrow afternoon, the big draft-trailer would come rolling up the valley road from the city. For that was what Grandma Wannattel had done the past four summers — ever since the lights first started appearing above the hollow for the few nights they were to be seen there each year. And since four years were exactly half of Grimp's whole life, that made Grandma's return a mathematical certainty for him.

Other people, of course, like the Village Guardian, might have a poor opinion of Grandma, but just hanging around her and the trailer and the gigantic, exotic-looking rhinocerine pony that pulled it was, in Grimp's opinion, a lot better even than going to the circus.

And vacations started the day after tomorrow! The whole future just now, in fact, looked like one good thing after another, extending through a vista of summery infinities.

Grimp went to sleep happily.

At about the same hour, though at a distance greater than Grimp's imagination had stretched as yet, eight large ships came individually out of the darkness between the stars that was their sea, and began to move about Noorhut in a carefully timed pattern of orbits. They stayed much too far out to permit any instrument of space-detection to suspect that Noorhut might be their common center of interest.

But that was what it was. Though the men who crewed the eight ships bore the people of Noorhut no ill will, hardly anything could have looked less promising for Noorhut than the cargo they had on board.

Seven of them were armed with a gas which was not often used any more. A highly volatile lethal catalyst, it sank to the solid surface of a world over which it was freed and spread out swiftly there to the point where its presence could no longer be detected by any chemical means. However, its effect of drawing the final breath almost imperceptibly out of all things that were oxygen-breathing was not noticeably reduced by diffusion.

The eighth ship was equipped with a brace of torpedoes, which were normally released some hours after the gas-carriers dispersed their invisible death. They were quite small torpedoes, since the only task remaining for them would be to ignite the surface of the planet that had been treated with the catalyst.

All those things might presently happen to Noorhut. But they would happen only if a specific message was flashed from it to the circling squadron — the message that Noorhut already was lost to a deadly foe who must, at any cost now, be prevented from spreading out from it to other inhabited worlds.

Next afternoon, right after school, as Grimp came expectantly around the bend of the road at the edge of the farm, he found the village policeman sitting there on a rock, gazing tearfully down the road.

"Hello, Runny," said Grimp, disturbed. Considered in the light of gossip he'd overheard in the village that morning, this didn't look so good for Grandma. It just didn't look good.

The policeman blew his nose on a handkerchief he carried tucked into the front of his uniform, wiped his eyes, and gave Grimp an annoyed glance.

"Don't *you* call me Runny, Grimp!" he said, replacing the hand-kerchief. Like Grimp himself and most of the people on Noorhut, the policeman was brown-skinned and dark-eyed, normally a rather good-looking young fellow. But his eyes were swollen and red-rimmed now; and his nose, which was a bit larger than average, anyway, was also red and swollen and undeniably runny. He had hay-fever bad.

Grimp apologized and sat down thoughtfully on the rock beside the policeman, who was one of his numerous cousins. He was about to mention that he had overheard Vellit using the expression when she and the policeman came through the big Leeth-flower orchard above the farm the other evening — at a much less leisurely rate than was their custom there. But he thought better of it. Vellit was the policeman's girl for most of the year, but she broke their engagement regularly during hay-fever season and called him cousin instead of dearest.

"What are you doing here?" Grimp asked bluntly instead.

"Waiting," said the policeman.

"For what?" said Grimp, with a sinking heart.

"Same individual you are, I guess," the policeman told him, hauling out the handkerchief again. He blew. "This year she's going to go right back where she came from or get pinched."

"Who says so?" scowled Grimp.

"The Guardian, that's who," said the policeman. "That good enough for you?"

"He can't do it!" Grimp said hotly. "It's our farm, and she's got all her licenses."

"He's had a whole year to think up a new list she's got to have," the policeman informed him. He fished in the breast-pocket of his uniform, pulled out a folded paper, and opened it. "He put thirty-four items down here I got to check — she's bound to miss on one of them."

"It's a dirty trick!" said Grimp, rapidly scanning as much as he could see of the list.

"Let's us have more respect for the Village Guardian, Grimp!" the policeman said warningly.

"Uh-huh," muttered Grimp. "Sure ..." If Runny would just move his big thumb out of the way. But what a list! Trailer; rhinocerine pony (beast, heavy draft, imported); patent medicines; household utensils; fortune-telling; pets; herbs; miracle-healing —

The policeman looked down, saw what Grimp was doing, and raised the paper out of his line of vision. "That's an official document," he said, warding Grimp off with one hand and tucking the paper away with the other. "Let's us not get our dirty hands on it."

Grimp was thinking fast. Grandma Wannattel did have framed licenses for some of the items he'd read hanging around inside the trailer, but certainly not thirty-four of them.

"Remember that big skinless werret I caught last season?" he asked.

The policeman gave him a quick glance, looked away again, and wiped his eyes thoughtfully. The season on werrets would open the following week and he was as ardent a fisherman as anyone in the village — and last summer Grimp's monster werret had broken a twelve-year record in the valley.

"Some people," Grimp said idly, staring down the valley road to the point where it turned into the woods, "would sneak after a person for days who's caught a big werret, hoping he'd be dumb enough to go back to that pool."

The policeman flushed and dabbed the handkerchief gingerly at his nose.

"Some people would even sit in a haystack and use spyglasses, even when the hay made them sneeze like crazy," continued Grimp quietly.

The policeman's flush deepened. He sneezed.

"But a person isn't that dumb," said Grimp. "Not when he knows there's anyway two werrets there six inches bigger than the one he caught."

"Six inches?" the policeman repeated a bit incredulously — eagerly.

"Easy," nodded Grimp. "I had a look at them again last week."

It was the policeman's turn to think. Grimp idly hauled out his sling-shot, fished a pebble out of his small-pebble pocket, and knocked the head off a flower twenty feet away. He yawned negligently.

"You're pretty good with that slingshot," the policeman remarked. "You must be just about as good as the culprit that used a slingshot to ring the fire-alarm signal on the defense unit bell from the top of the school-house last week."

"That'd take a pretty good shot," Grimp admitted.

"And who then," continued the policeman, "dropped pepper in his trail, so the pank-hound near coughed off his head when we started to track him. The Guardian," he added significantly, "would like to have a clue about that culprit, all right."

"Sure, sure," said Grimp, bored. The policeman, the Guardian, and probably even the pank-hound, knew exactly who the culprit was; but they wouldn't be able to prove it in twenty thousand years. Runny just had to realize first that threats weren't going to get him anywhere near a record werret.

Apparently, he had; he was settling back for another bout of thinking. Grimp, interested in what he would produce next, decided just to leave him to it ...

Then Grimp jumped up suddenly from the rock.

"There they are!" he yelled, waving the slingshot.

A half-mile down the road, Grandma Wannattel's big, silvery trailer had come swaying out of the woods behind the rhinocerine pony and turned up toward the farm. The pony saw Grimp, lifted its head, which was as long as a tall man, and bawled a thunderous greeting. Grandma Wannattel stood up on the driver's seat and waved a green silk handkerchief.

Grimp started sprinting down the road.

The werrets should turn the trick — but he'd better get Grandma informed, just the same, about recent developments here, before she ran into Runny.

Grandma Wannattel flicked the pony's horny rear with the reins just before they reached the policeman, who was waiting at the side of the road with the Guardian's check-list unfolded in his hand.

The pony broke into a lumbering trot, and the trailer swept past Runny and up around the bend of the road, where it stopped well within the boundaries of the farm. They climbed down and Grandma quickly unhitched the pony. It waddled, grunting, off the road and down into the long, marshy meadow above the hollow. It stood still there, cooling its feet.

Grimp felt a little better. Getting the trailer off community property gave Grandma a technical advantage. Grimp's people had a favorable opinion of her, and they were a sturdy lot who enjoyed telling off the Guardian any time he didn't actually have a law to back up his orders. But on the way to the farm, she had confessed to Grimp that, just as he'd feared, she didn't have anything like thirty-four licenses. And now the policeman was coming up around the bend of the road after them, blowing his nose and frowning.

"Just let me handle him alone," Grandma told Grimp out of the corner of her mouth.

He nodded and strolled off into the meadow to pass the time with the pony. She'd had a lot of experience in handling policemen.

"Well, well, young man," he heard her greeting his cousin behind him. "That looks like a bad cold you've got."

The policeman sneezed.

"Wish it were a cold," he said resignedly. "It's hay-fever. Can't do a thing with it. Now I've got a list here —"

"Hay-fever?" said Grandma. "Step up into the trailer a moment. We'll fix that."

"About this list —" began Runny, and stopped. "You think you got something that would fix it?" he asked skeptically. "I've been to I don't know how many doctors and they didn't help any."

"Doctors!" said Grandma. Grimp heard her heels click up the metal steps that led into the back of the trailer. "Come right in, won't take a moment."

"Well —" said Runny doubtfully, but he followed her inside.

Grimp winked at the pony. The first round went to Grandma.

"Hello, pony," he said.

His worries couldn't reduce his appreciation of Grandma's fabulous draft-animal. Partly, of course, it was just that it was such an enormous beast. The long, round barrel of its body rested on short legs with wide, flat feet which were settled deep in the meadow's mud by now. At one end was a spiky tail and at the other a very big, wedge-shaped head, with a blunt, badly chipped horn set between nose and eyes. From nose to tail and all around, it was covered with thick, rectangular, horny plates, a mottled green-brown in color.

Grimp patted its rocky side affectionately. He loved the pony most for being the ugliest thing that had ever showed up on Noorhut. According to Grandma, she had bought it from a bankrupt circus which had imported it from a planet called Treebel; and Treebel was supposed to be a world full of hot swamps, inexhaustibly explosive volcanoes, and sulphurous stenches.

One might have thought that after wandering around melting lava and under rainfalls of glowing ashes for most of its life, the pony would have considered Noorhut pretty tame. But though there wasn't much room for expression around the solid slab of bone supporting the horn, which was the front of its face, Grimp thought it looked thoroughly contented with its feet sunk out of sight in Noorhut's cool mud.

"You're a big fat pig!" he told it fondly.

The pony slobbered out a long, purple tongue and carefully parted his hair.

"Cut it out!" said Grimp. "Ugh!"

The pony snorted, pleased, curled its tongue about a huge clump of weeds, pulled them up, and flipped them into its mouth, roots, mud, and all. It began to chew.

Grimp glanced at the sun and turned anxiously to study the trailer. If she didn't get rid of Runny soon, they'd be calling him back to the house for supper before he and Grandma got around to having a good talk. And they weren't letting him out of doors these evenings, while the shining lights were here.

He gave the pony a parting whack, returned quietly to the road, and sat down out of sight near the back door of the trailer, where he could hear what was going on.

"... so about the only thing the Guardian could tack on you now," the policeman was saying, "would be a Public Menace charge. If there's any trouble about the lights this year, he's likely to try that. He's not a bad Guardian, you know, but he's got himself talked into thinking you're sort of to blame for the lights showing up here every year."

Grandma chuckled. "Well, I try to get here in time to see them every summer," she admitted. "I can see how that might give him the idea."

"And of course," said the policeman, "we're all trying to keep it quiet about them. If the news got out, we'd be having a lot of people coming here from the city, just to look. No one but the Guardian minds you being here, only you don't want a lot of city people tramping around your farms."

"Of course not" agreed Grandma. "And I certainly haven't told anyone about them myself."

"Last night," the policeman added, "everyone was saying there were twice as many lights this year as last summer. That's what got the Guardian so excited."

Chafing more every minute, Grimp had to listen then to an extended polite argument about how much Runny wanted to pay Grandma for her hay-fever medicines, while she insisted he didn't owe her anything at all. In the end, Grandma lost and the policeman paid up — much too much to take from any friend of Grimp's folks, Grandma protested to the last. And then, finally, that righteous minion of the law came climbing down the trailer steps again, with Grandma following him to the door.

"How do I look, Grimp?" he beamed cheerfully as Grimp stood up.

"Like you ought to wash your face sometime," Grimp said tactlessly, for he was fast losing patience with Runny. But then his eyes widened in surprise.

Under a coating of yellowish grease, Runny's nose seemed to have returned almost to the shape it had out of hay-fever season, and his eyelids were hardly puffed at all! Instead of flaming red, those features, furthermore, now were only a delicate pink in shade. Runny, in short, was almost handsome again.

"Pretty good, eh?" he said. "Just one shot did it. And I've only got to keep the salve on another hour. Isn't that right, Grandma?"

"That's right," smiled Grandma from the door, clinking Runny's money gently out of one hand into the other. "You'll be as good as new then."

"Permanent cure, too," said Runny. He patted Grimp benevolently on the head. "And next week we go werret-fishing, eh, Grimp?" he added greedily.

"I guess so," Grimp said, with a trace of coldness. It was his opinion that Runny could have been satisfied with the hay-fever cure and forgotten about the werrets.

"It's a date!" nodded Runny happily and took his greasy face whistling down the road. Grimp scowled after him, half-minded to reach for the slingshot then and there and let go with a medium stone at the lower rear of the uniform. But probably he'd better not.

"Well, that's that," Grandma said softly.

At that moment, up at the farmhouse, a cow horn went "Whoop-whoop!" across the valley.

"Darn," said Grimp. "I knew it was getting late, with him doing all that talking! Now they're calling me to supper." There were tears of disappointment in his eyes.

"Don't let it fuss you, Grimp," Grandma said consolingly. "Just jump up in here a moment and close your eyes."

Grimp jumped up into the trailer and closed his eyes expectantly.

"Put out your hands," Grandma's voice told him.

He put out his hands, and she pushed them together to form a cup. Then something small and light and furry dropped into them, caught hold of one of Grimp's thumbs, with tiny, cool fingers, and chittered.

Grimp's eyes popped open.

"It's a lortel!" he whispered, overwhelmed.

"It's for you!" Grandma beamed.

Grimp couldn't speak. The lortel looked at him from a tiny, black, human face with large blue eyes set in it, wrapped a long, furry tail twice around his wrist, clung to his thumb with its fingers, and grinned and squeaked.

"It's wonderful!" gasped Grimp. "Can you really teach them to talk?"

"Hello," said the lortel.

"That's all it can say so far," Grandma said. "But if you're patient with it, it'll learn more."

"I'll be patient," Grimp promised, dazed. "I saw one at the circus this winter, down the valley at Laggand. They said it could talk, but it never said anything while I was there."

"Hello!" said the lortel.

"Hello!" gulped Grimp.

The cow horn whoop-whooped again.

"I guess you'd better run along to supper, or they might get mad," said Grandma.

"I know," said Grimp. "What does it eat?"

"Bugs and flowers and honey and fruit and eggs, when it's wild. But you just feed it whatever you eat yourself."

"Well, good-by," said Grimp. "And golly — thanks, Grandma."

He jumped out of the trailer. The lortel climbed out of his hand, ran up his arm, and sat on his shoulder, wrapping its tail around its neck.

"It knows you already," Grandma said. "It won't run away."

Grimp reached up carefully with his other hand and patted the lortel.

"I'll be back early tomorrow," he said. "No school … They won't let me out after supper as long as those lights keep coming around."

The cow horn whooped for the third time, very loudly. This time it meant business.

"Well, good-by," Grimp repeated hastily. He ran off, the lortel hanging on to his shirt collar and squeaking.

Grandma looked after him and then at the sun, which had just touched the tops of the hills with its lower rim.

"Might as well have some supper myself," she remarked, apparently to no one in particular. "But after that I'll have to run out the go-buggy and create a diversion."

Lying on its armor-plated belly down in the meadow, the pony swung its big head around toward her. Its small yellow eyes blinked questioningly. "What makes you think a diversion will be required?" its voice asked into her ear. The ability to produce such ventriloquial effects was one of the talents that made the pony well worth its considerable keep to Grandma.

"Weren't you listening?" she scolded. "That policeman told me the Guardian's planning to march the village's defense unit up to the hollow after supper, and start them shooting at the Halpa detector-globes as soon as they show up."

The pony swore an oath meaningless to anyone who hadn't been raised on the planet Treebel. It stood up, braced itself, and began pulling its feet out of the mud in a succession of loud, sucking noises.

"I haven't had an hour's straight rest since you talked me into tramping around with you eight years ago!" it complained.

"But you've certainly been seeing life, like I promised," Grandma smiled.

The pony slopped in a last, enormous tongueful of wet weeds. "That I have!" it said, with emphasis.

It came chewing up to the road.

"I'll keep a watch on things while you're having your supper," it told her.

As the uniformed twelve-man defense unit marched in good order out of the village, on its way to assume a strategic position around the hollow on Grimp's father's farm, there was a sudden, small explosion not very far off.

The Guardian, who was marching in the lead with a gun over his shoulder and the slavering pank-hound on a leash, stopped short. The unit broke ranks and crowded up behind him.

"What was that?" the Guardian inquired.

Everybody glanced questioningly around the rolling green slopes of the valley, already darkened with evening shadows. The pank-hound sat down before the Guardian, pointed its nose at the even darker shadows in the woods ahead of them, and growled.

"Look!" a man said, pointing in the same direction.

A spark of bright green light had appeared on their path, just where it entered the woods. The spark grew rapidly in size, became as big as a human head — then bigger! Smoky green streamers seemed to be pouring out of it ...

"I'm going home right now," someone announced at that point, sensibly enough.

"Stand your ground!" the Guardian ordered, conscious of the beginnings of a general withdrawal movement behind him. He was an old soldier. He unslung his gun, cocked it, and pointed it. The pank-hound got up on his six feet and bristled.

"Stop!" the Guardian shouted at the green light.

It expanded promptly to the size of a barrel, new streamers shooting out from it and fanning about like hungry tentacles.

He fired.

"*Run!*" everybody yelled then. The pank-hound slammed backward against the Guardian's legs, upsetting him, and streaked off after the retreating unit. The green light had spread outward jerkily into the shape of something like a many-armed, writhing starfish, almost the size of the trees about it. Deep, hooting sounds came out of it as it started drifting down the path toward the Guardian.

He got up on one knee and, in a single drumroll of sound, emptied all thirteen charges remaining in his gun into the middle of the starfish. It hooted more loudly, waved its arms more wildly, and continued to advance.

He stood up quickly then, slung the gun over his shoulder, and joined the retreat. By the time the unit reached the first houses of the village, he was well up in the front ranks again. And a few minutes later, he was breathlessly organizing the local defenses, employing the tactics that had shown their worth in the raids of the Laggand Bandits nine years before.

The starfish, however, was making no attempt to follow up the valley people's rout. It was still on the path at the point where the Guardian had seen it last, waving its arms about and hooting menacingly at the silent trees.

"That should do it, I guess," Grandma Wannattel said. "Before the first projection fizzles out, the next one in the chain will start up where they can see it from the village. It ought to be past midnight before anyone starts bothering about the globes again. Particularly since there aren't going to be any globes around tonight — that is, if the Halpa attack-schedule has been correctly estimated."

"I wish we were safely past midnight right now," the rhinocerine pony worriedly informed her. Its dark shape stood a little up the road from the trailer, outlined motionlessly like a ponderous statue against the red evening sky. Its head was up; it looked as if it were listening. Which it was, in its own way — listening for any signs of activity from the hollow.

"No sense getting anxious about it," Grandma remarked. She was perched on a rock at the side of the road, a short distance from the pony, with a small black bag slung over her shoulder. "We'll wait here another hour till it's good and dark and then go down to the hollow. The breakthrough might begin a couple of hours after that."

"It *would* have to be us again!" grumbled the pony. In spite of its size, its temperament was on the nervous side. And while any companion of Zone Agent Wannattel was bound to run regularly into situations that were far from soothing, the pony couldn't recall any previous experience that had looked as extremely unsoothing as the prospects of the night-hours ahead. On far-off Vega's world of Jeltad, in the planning offices of the Department of Galactic Zones, the decision to put Noorhut at stake to win one round in mankind's grim war with the alien and mysterious Halpa might have seemed as distressing as it was unavoidable. But the pony couldn't help feeling that the distress would have become a little more acute if Grandma's distant employers had happened to be standing right here with the two of them while the critical hours approached.

"I'd feel a lot better myself if Headquarters hadn't picked us for this particular operation," Grandma admitted. "Us and Noorhut ..."

Because, by what was a rather singular coincidence, considering how things stood there tonight, the valley was also Grandma's home. She had been born, quite some while before, a hundred and eighty miles farther inland, at the foot of the dam of the great river Wend, which had given its name to the land, and nowadays supplied it with almost all its required power.

Erisa Wannattel had done a great deal of traveling since she first became aware of the fact that her varied abilities and adventuresome nature needed a different sort of task to absorb them than could be found on Noorhut, which was progressing placidly up into the final stages of a rounded and balanced planetary civilization. But she still liked to consider the Valley of the Wend as her home and headquarters, to which she returned as often as her work would permit. Her exact understanding of the way people there thought about things and did things also made them easy for her to manipulate; and on occasion that could be very useful.

In most other places, the means she had employed to turn the Guardian and his troop back from the hollow probably would have started a panic or brought armed ships and radiation guns zooming up for the kill within minutes. But the valley people had considered it just another local emergency. The bronze alarm bell in the village had pronounced a state of siege, and cow horns passed the word up to the outlying farms. Within minutes, the farmers were pelting down the roads to the village with their families and guns; and, very soon afterward, everything quieted down again. Guard lines had been set up by then, with the women and children quartered in the central buildings, while the armed men had settled down to watching Grandma's illusion projections — directional video narrow beams — from the discreet distance marked by the village boundaries.

If nothing else happened, the people would just stay there till morning and then start a cautious investigation. After seeing mysterious blue lights dancing harmlessly over Grimp's farm for four summers, this section of Wend was pretty well conditioned to fiery apparitions. But even if they got too adventurous, they couldn't hurt themselves on the projections, which were designed to be nothing but very effective visual displays.

What it all came to was that Grandma had everybody in the neighborhood rounded up and immobilized where she wanted them.

In every other respect, the valley presented an exceptionally peaceful twilight scene to the eye. There was nothing to show that it was the only present point of contact between forces engaged in what was probably a war of intergalactic proportions — a war made wraith-like but doubly deadly by the circumstance that, in over a thousand years, neither side had found out much more about the other than the merciless and devastating finality of its forms of attack. There never had been any actual battles between Mankind and the Halpa, only alternate and very thorough massacres — all of them, from Mankind's point of view, on the wrong side of the fence.

The Halpa alone had the knowledge that enabled them to reach their human adversary. That was the trouble. But, apparently, they could launch their attacks only by a supreme effort, under conditions that existed for periods of less than a score of years, and about three hundred years apart as Mankind measured time.

It was hard to find any good in them, other than the virtue of persistence. Every three hundred years, they punctually utilized that brief period to execute one more thrust, carefully prepared and placed, and carried out with a dreadfully complete abruptness, against some new point of human civilization — and this time the attack was going to come through on Noorhut.

"Something's starting to move around in that hollow!" the pony announced suddenly. "It's not one of their globe-detectors."

"I know," murmured Grandma. "That's the first of the Halpa themselves. They're going to be right on schedule, it seems. But don't get nervous. They can't hurt anything until their transmitter comes through and revives them. We've got to be particularly careful now not to frighten them off. They seem to be even more sensitive to emotional tensions in their immediate surroundings than the globes."

The pony made no reply. It knew what was at stake and why eight big ships were circling Noorhut somewhere beyond space-detection tonight. It knew, too, that the ships would act only if it was discovered that Grandma had failed. But —

The pony shook its head uneasily. The people on Treebel had never become civilized to the point of considering the possibility of taking calculated risks on a planetary scale — not to mention the fact that the lives of the pony and of Grandma were included in the present calculation. In the eight years it had been accompanying her on her travels, it had developed a tremendous respect for Erisa Wannattel's judgment and prowess. But, just the same, frightening the Halpa off, if it still could be done, seemed like a very sound idea right now to the pony.

As a matter of fact, as Grandma well knew, it probably could have been done at this stage by tossing a small firecracker into the hollow. Until they had established their planetary foothold, the Halpa took extreme precautions. They could spot things in the class of radiation weapons a hundred miles away, and either that or any suggestion of local aggressiveness or of long-range observation would check the invasion attempt on Noorhut then and there.

But one of the principal reasons she was here tonight was to see that nothing *did* happen to stop it. For this assault would only be diverted against some other world then, and quite probably against one where the significance of the spying detector-globes wouldn't be understood before it was too late. The best information system in the Galaxy couldn't keep more than an insignificant fraction of its populations on the alert for dangers like that —

She bounced suddenly to her feet and, at the same instant, the pony swung away from the hollow toward which it been staring. They both stood for a moment then, turning their heads about, like baffled hounds trying to fix a scent on the wind.

"It's Grimp!" Grandma exclaimed.

The rhinocerine pony snorted faintly. "Those are his thought images, all right," it agreed. "He seems to feel you need protection. Can you locate him?"

"Not yet," said Grandma anxiously. "Yes, I can. He's coming up through the woods on the other side of the hollow, off to the left. The little devil!" She was hustling back to the trailer. "Come on, I'll have to ride you there. I can't even dare use the go-buggy this late in the day."

The pony crouched beside the trailer while she quickly snapped on its saddle from the top of the back steps. Six metal rings had been welded into the horny plates of its back for this purpose, so it was a simple job. Grandma clambered aloft, hanging onto the saddle's hand-rails.

"Swing wide of the hollow!" she warned. "This could spoil everything. But make all the noise you want. The Halpa don't care about noise as such — it has to have emotional content before they get interested — and the quicker Grimp spots us, the easier it will be to find him."

The pony already was rushing down into the meadow at an amazing rate of speed — it took a lot of very efficient muscle to drive as heavy a body as that through the gluey swamps of Treebel. It swung wide of the hollow and of what it contained, crossed a shallow bog farther down the meadow with a sound like a charging torpedo-boat, and reached the woods.

It had to slow down then, to avoid brushing off Grandma.

"Grimp's down that slope somewhere," Grandma said. "He's heard us."

"They're making a lot of noise!" Grimp's thought reached them suddenly and clearly. He seemed to be talking to someone. "But we're not scared of them, are we?"

"Bang-bang!" another thought-voice came excitedly.

"It's the lortel," Grandma and the pony said together.

'That's the stuff!' Grimp resumed approvingly. "We'll slingshot them all if they don't watch out. But we'd better find Grandma soon."

"Grimp!" shouted Grandma. The pony backed her up with a roaring call.

"Hello?" came the lortel's thought.

"Wasn't that the pony?" asked Grimp. "All right — let's go that way."

"Here we come, Grimp!" Grandma shouted as the pony descended the steep side of a ravine with the straightforward technique of a rockslide.

'That's Grandma!" thought Grimp. "Grandma!" he yelled. "Look out! There's monsters all around!"

"What you missed!" yelled Grimp, dancing around the pony as Grandma Wannattel scrambled down from the saddle. "There's monsters all around the village and the Guardian killed one and I slingshot another till he fizzled out and I was coming to find you —"

"Your mother will be worried!" began Grandma as they rushed into each other's arms.

"No," grinned Grimp. "All the kids are supposed to be sleeping in the school house, and she won't look there till morning, and the schoolteacher said the monsters were all" — he slowed down cautiously — "ho-lucy-nations. But he wouldn't go look when the Guardian said they'd show him one. He stayed right in bed! But the Guardian's all right — he killed one and I slingshot another and the lortel learned a new word. Say 'bang-bang,' lortel!" he invited.

"Hello!" squeaked the lortel.

"Aw," said Grimp disappointedly. "He can say it, though. And I've come to take you to the village so the monsters don't get you. Hello, pony!"

"Bang-bang," said the lortel distinctly.

"See?" cried Grimp. "He isn't scared at all — he's a real brave lortel! If we see some monsters don't you get scared either, because I've got my slingshot," he said, waving it bloodthirstily, "and two back pockets still full of medium stones. The way to do it is to kill them all!"

"It sounds like a pretty good idea, Grimp," Grandma agreed. "But you're awfully tired now."

"No, I'm not!" Grimp said, surprised. His right eye sagged shut and then his left and he opened them both with an effort and looked at Grandma."

"That's right," he admitted. "I am ..."

"In fact," said Grandma, "you're asleep!"

"No, I'm n —" objected Grimp. Then he sagged toward the ground, and Grandma caught him.

"In a way I hate to do it," she panted, wrestling him aboard the pony, which had lain down and flattened itself as much as it could to make it easier. "He'd probably enjoy it. But we can't take a chance. He's a husky little devil, too," she groaned, giving a final boost, "and those ammunition pockets don't make him any lighter!" She clambered up again herself and noticed that the lortel had transferred itself to her coat collar.

The pony stood up cautiously.

"Now what?" it said.

"Might as well go straight to the hollow," said Grandma, breathing hard. "We'll probably have to wait around there a few hours, but if we're careful it won't do any harm."

"Did you find a good deep pond?" Grandma asked the pony a little later, as it came squishing up softly through the meadow behind her to join her at the edge of the hollow.

"Yes," said the pony. "About a hundred yards back. That should be close enough. How much more waiting do you think we'll have to do?"

Grandma shrugged carefully. She was sitting in the grass with what, by daylight, would have been a good view of the hollow below. Grimp was asleep with his head on her knees; and the lortel, after catching a few bugs in the grass and eating them, had settled down on her shoulder and dozed off too.

"I don't know," she said. "It's still three hours till Big Moonrise, and it's bound to be some time before then. Now you've found a waterhole, we'll just stay here together and wait. The one thing to remember is not to let yourself start getting excited about them."

The pony stood huge and chunky beside her, its forefeet on the edge of the hollow, staring down. Muddy water trickled from its knobby flanks. It had brought the warm mud-smells of a summer pond back with it to hang in a cloud about them.

There was vague, dark, continuous motion at the bottom of the hollow. A barely noticeable stirring in the single big pool of darkness that filled it.

"If I were alone," the pony said, "I'd get out of here! I know when I ought to be scared. But you've taken psychological control of my reactions, haven't you?"

"Yes," said Grandma. "It'll be easier for me, though, if you help along as much as you can. There's really no danger until their transmitter has come through."

"Unless," said the pony, "they've worked out some brand-new tricks in the past few hundred years."

"There's that," Grandma admitted. "But they've never tried changing their tricks on us yet. If it were *us* doing the attacking, we'd vary our methods each time, as much as we could. But the Halpa don't seem to think just like we do about anything. They wouldn't still be so careful if they didn't realize they were very vulnerable at this point."

"I hope they're right about that!" the pony said briefly.

Its head moved then, following the motion of something that sailed flutteringly out of the depths of the hollow, circled along its far rim, and descended again. The inhabitants of Treebel had a much deeper range of dark-vision than Grandma Wannattel, but she was also aware of that shape.

"They're not much to look at," the pony remarked. "Like a big, dark rag of leather, mostly."

"Their physical structure is believed to be quite simple," Grandma agreed slowly. The pony was tensing up again, and it was best to go on talking to it, about almost anything at all. That always helped, even though the pony knew her much too well by now to be really fooled by such tricks.

"Many very efficient life-forms aren't physically complicated, you know," she went on, letting the sound of her voice ripple steadily into its mind. "Parasitical types, particularly. It's pretty certain, too, that the Halpa have the hive-mind class of intelligence, so what goes for the nerve-systems of most of the ones they send through to us might be nothing much more than secondary reflex-transmitters ..."

Grimp stirred in his sleep at that point and grumbled. Grandma looked down at him. "You're sound asleep!" she told him severely, and he was again.

"You've got plans for that boy, haven't you?" the pony said, without shifting its gaze from the hollow.

"I've had my eye on him," Grandma admitted, "and I've already recommended him to Headquarters for observation. But I'm not going to make up my mind about Grimp till next summer, when we've had more time to study him. Meanwhile, we'll see what he picks up naturally from the lortel in the way of telepathic communication and sensory extensions. I think Grimp's the kind we can use."

"He's all right," the pony agreed absently. "A bit murderous, though, like most of you ..."

"He'll grow out of it!" Grandma said, a little annoyedly, for the subject of human aggressiveness was one she and the pony argued about frequently. "You can't hurry developments like that along too much. All of Noorhut should grow out of that stage, as a people, in another few hundred years. They're about at the turning-point right now —"

Their heads came up together, then, as something very much like a big, dark rag of leather came fluttering up from the hollow and hung in the dark air above them. The representatives of the opposing powers that were meeting on Noorhut that night took quiet stock of one another for a moment.

The Halpa was about six feet long and two wide, and considerably less than an inch thick. It held its position in the air with a steady, rippling motion, like a bat the size of a man. Then, suddenly, it extended itself with a snap, growing taut as a curved sail.

The pony snorted involuntarily. The apparently featureless shape in the air turned towards it and drifted a few inches closer. When nothing more happened, it turned again and fluttered quietly back down into the hollow.

"Could it tell I was scared?" the pony asked uneasily.

"You reacted just right," Grandma said soothingly. "Startled suspicion at first, and then just curiosity, and then another start when it made that jump. It's about what they'd expect from creatures that would be hanging around the hollow now. We're like cows to them. They can't tell what things are by their looks, like we do —"

But her tone was thoughtful, and she was more shaken than she would have cared to let the pony notice. There had been something indescribably menacing and self-assured in the Halpa's gesture. Almost certainly, it had only been trying to draw a reaction of hostile intelligence from them, probing, perhaps, for the presence of weapons that might be dangerous to its kind.

But there was a chance — a tiny but appalling chance — that the things *had* developed some drastically new form of attack since their last break-through, and that they already were in control of the situation ...

In which case, neither Grimp nor anyone else on Noorhut would be doing any more growing-up after tomorrow.

Each of the eleven hundred and seventeen planets that had been lost to the Halpa so far still traced a fiery, forbidding orbit through space — torn back from the invaders only at the cost of depriving it, by humanity's own weapons, of the conditions any known form of life could tolerate.

The possibility that this might also be Noorhut's future had loomed as an ugly enormity before her for the past four years. But of the nearly half a hundred worlds which the Halpa were found to be investigating through their detector-globes as possible invasion points for this period, Noorhut finally had been selected by Headquarters as the one where local conditions were most suited to meet them successfully. And that meant in a manner which must include the destruction of their only real invasion weapon, the fabulous and mysterious Halpa transmitter. Capable as they undoubtedly were, they had shown in the past that they were able or willing to employ only one of those instruments for each period of attack. Destroying the transmitter meant therefore that humanity would gain a few more centuries to figure out a way to get back at the Halpa before a new attempt was made.

So on all planets but Noorhut the detector-globes had been encouraged carefully to send back reports of a dangerously alert and well-armed population. On Noorhut, however, they had been soothed along ... and just as her home-planet had been chosen as the most favorable point of encounter, so was Erisa Wannattel herself selected as the agent most suited to represent humanity's forces under the conditions that existed there.

Grandma sighed gently and reminded herself again that Headquarters was as unlikely to miscalculate the overall probability of success as it was to select the wrong person to achieve it. There was only the tiniest, the most theoretical, of chances that something might go wrong and that she would end her long career with the blundering murder of her own home-world.

But there was that chance.

"There seem to be more down there every minute!" the pony was saying.

Grandma drew a deep breath.

"Must be several thousand by now," she acknowledged. "It's getting near breakthrough time, all right, but those are only the advance forces." She added, "Do you notice anything like a glow of light down there, towards the center?"

The pony stared a moment. "Yes," it said. "But I would have thought that was way under the red for you. Can you see it?"

"No," said Grandma. "I get a kind of a feeling, like heat. That's the transmitter beginning to come through. I think we've got them!"

The pony shifted its bulk slowly from side to side.

"Yes," it said resignedly, "or they've got us."

"Don't think about that," Grandma ordered sharply and clamped one more mental lock shut on the foggy, dark terrors that were curling and writhing under her conscious thoughts, threatening to emerge at the last moment and paralyze her actions.

She had opened her black bag and was unhurriedly fitting together something composed of a few pieces of wood and wire, and a rather heavy, stiff spring ...

"Just be ready," she added.

"I've been ready for an hour," said the pony, shuffling its feet unhappily.

They did no more talking after that. All the valley had become quiet about them. But slowly the hollow below was filling up with a black, stirring, slithering tide. Bits of it fluttered up now and then like strips of black smoke, hovered a few yards above the mass, and settled again.

Suddenly, down in the center of the hollow, there was something else.

The pony had seen it first, Grandma Wannattel realized. It was staring in that direction for almost a minute before she grew able to distinguish something that might have been a group of graceful miniature spires. Semi-transparent in the darkness, four small domes showed at the corners, with a larger one in the center. The central one was about twenty feet high and very slender.

The whole structure began to solidify swiftly ...

The Halpa Transmitter's appearance of crystalline slightness was perhaps the most mind-chilling thing about it. For it brought instantly a jarring sense of what must be black distance beyond all distances, reaching back unimaginably to its place of origin. In that unknown somewhere, a prodigiously talented and determined race of beings had labored for human centuries to prepare and point some stupendous gun ... and were able then to bridge the vast interval with nothing more substantial than this dark sliver of glass that had come to rest suddenly in the valley of the Wend.

But, of course, the Transmitter was all that was needed; its deadly poison lay in a sluggish, almost inert mass about it. Within minutes from now, it would waken to life, as similar transmitters had wakened on other nights on those lost and burning worlds. And in much less than minutes after that, the Halpa invaders would be hurled by their slender machine to every surface section of Noorhut — no longer inert, but quickened into a ravening, almost indestructible form of vampiric life, dividing and subdividing in its incredibly swift cycle of reproduction, fastening to feed anew, growing and dividing again —

Spreading, at that stage, much more swiftly than it could be exterminated by anything but the ultimate weapons!

The pony stirred suddenly, and she felt the wave of panic roll up in it. "It's the Transmitter, all right," Grandma's thought reached it quickly. "We've had two descriptions of it before. But we can't be sure it's *here* until it begins to charge itself. Then it lights up — first at the edges, and then at the center. Five seconds after the central spire lights up, it will be energized too much to let them pull it back again. At least they couldn't pull it back after that, the last time they were observed. And then we'd better be ready —"

The pony had been told all that before. But as it listened it was quieting down again.

"And you're going to go on sleeping!" Grandma Wannattel's thought told Grimp next. "No matter what you hear or what happens, you'll sleep on and know nothing at all any more until I wake you up ..."

Light surged up suddenly in the Transmitter — first into the four outer spires, and an instant later into the big central one, in a sullen red glow. It lit the hollow with a smoky glare. The pony took two startled steps backwards.

"Five seconds to go!" whispered Grandma's thought. She reached into her black bag again and took out a small plastic ball. It reflected the light from the hollow in dull crimson gleamings. She let it slip down carefully inside the shaftlike frame of the gadget she had put together of wood and wire. It clicked into place there against one end of the compressed spring.

Down below, they lay now in a blanket fifteen feet thick over the wet ground, like big, black, water-sogged leaves swept up in circular piles about the edges of the hollow. The tops and sides of the piles were stirring and shivering and beginning to slide down toward the Transmitter.

"... five, and go!" Grandma said aloud. She raised the wooden catapult to her shoulder.

The pony shook its blunt-horned head violently from side to side, made a strangled, bawling sound, surged forward, and plunged down the steep side of the hollow in a thundering rush.

Grandma aimed carefully and let go.

The blanket of dead-leaf things was lifting into the air ahead of the pony's ground-shaking approach in a weightless, silent swirl of darkness, which instantly blotted both the glowing Transmitter and the pony's shape from sight. The pony roared once as the blackness closed over it. A second later, there was a crash like the shattering of a hundred-foot mirror — and at approximately the same moment, Grandma's plastic ball exploded somewhere in the center of the swirling swarm.

Cascading fountains of white fire filled the whole of the hollow. Within the fire, a dense mass of shapes fluttered and writhed frenziedly like burning rags. From down where the fire boiled fiercest rose continued sounds of brittle substances suffering enormous violence. The pony was trampling the ruined Transmitter, making sure of its destruction.

"Better get out of it!" Grandma shouted anxiously. "What's left of that will all melt now anyway!"

She didn't know whether it heard her or not. But a few seconds later, it came pounding up the side of the hollow again. Blazing from nose to rump, it tramped past Grandma, plunged through the meadow behind her, shedding white sheets of fire that exploded the marsh grass in its tracks, and hurled itself headlong into the pond it had selected previously. There was a great splash accompanied by sharp hissing noises. Pond and pony vanished together under billowing clouds of steam.

"That was pretty hot!" its thought came to Grandma.

She drew a deep breath.

"Hot as anything that ever came out of a volcano!" she affirmed. "If you'd played around in it much longer, you'd have fixed up the village with roasts for a year."

"I'll just stay here for a while, till I've cooled off a bit," said the pony.

Grandma found something strangling her then, and discovered it was the lortel's tail. She unwound it carefully. But the lortel promptly reanchored itself with all four hands in her hair. She decided to leave it there. It seemed badly upset.

Grimp, however, slept on. It was going to take a little maneuvering get him back into the village undetected before morning, but she would figure that out by and by. A steady flow of cool night air was being drawn past them into the hollow now and rising out it again in boiling, vertical columns of invisible heat. At the bottom of the deluxe blaze she'd lit down there, things still seemed to be moving about — but very slowly. The Halpa were tough organisms, all right, though not nearly so tough, when you heated them up with a really good incendiary, as were the natives of Treebel.

She would have to make a final check of the hollow around dawn, of course, when the ground should have cooled off enough to permit it — but her century's phase of the Halpa War did seem to be over. The defensive part of it, at any rate —

Wet, munching sounds from the pond indicated the pony felt comfortable enough by now to take an interest in the parboiled vegetation it found floating around it. Everything had turned out all right.

So she settled down carefully on her back in the long marsh grass without disturbing Grimp's position too much, and just let herself faint for a while.

By sunrise, Grandma Wannattel's patent-medicine trailer was nine miles from the village and rolling steadily southwards up the valley road through the woods. As usual, she was departing under a cloud.

Grimp and the policeman had showed up early to warn her. The

Guardian was making use of the night's various unprecedented disturbances to press through a vote on a Public Menace charge against Grandma in the village; and since everybody still felt rather excited and upset, he had a good chance just now of getting a majority.

Grimp had accompanied her far enough to explain that this state of affairs wasn't going to be permanent. He had it all worked out.

Runny's new immunity to hay-fever had brought him and the pretty Vellit to a fresh understanding overnight; they were going to get married five weeks from now. As a married man, Runny would then be eligible for the post of Village Guardian at the harvest elections — and between Grimp's cousins and Vellit's cousins, Runny's backers would just about control the vote. So when Grandma got around to visiting the valley again next summer, she needn't worry any more about police interference or official disapproval ...

Grandma had nodded approvingly. That was about the kind of neighborhood politics she'd begun to play herself at Grimp's age. She was pretty sure by now that Grimp was the one who eventually would become her successor, and the guardian not only of Noorhut and the star-system to which Noorhut belonged, but of a good many other star-systems besides. With careful schooling, he ought to be just about ready for the job by the time she was willing, finally, to retire.

An hour after he had started back to the farm, looking suddenly a little forlorn, the trailer swung off the valley road into a narrow forest path. Here the pony lengthened its stride, and less than five minutes later they entered a curving ravine, at the far end of which lay something that Grimp would have recognized instantly, from his one visit to the nearest port city, as a small spaceship.

A large round lock opened soundlessly in its side as they approached. The pony came to a stop. Grandma got down from the driver's seat and unhitched it. The pony walked into the lock, and the trailer picked its wheels off the ground and floated in after it. Grandma Wannattel walked in last, and the lock closed quietly on her heels.

The ship lay still a moment longer. Then it was suddenly gone. Dead leaves went dancing for a while about the ravine, disturbed by the breeze of its departure.

In a place very far away — so far that neither Grimp nor his parents nor anyone in the village except the schoolteacher had ever heard of it — a set of instruments began signalling for attention. Somebody answered them.

Grandma's voice announced distinctly:

"This is Zone Agent Wannattel's report on the successful conclusion of the Halpa operation on Noorhut —"

High above Noorhut's skies, eight great ships swung instantly out of their watchful orbits about the planet and flashed off again into the blackness of the boundless space that was their sea and their home.

Novice

There was, Telzey Amberdon thought, someone besides TT and herself in the garden. Not, of course, Aunt Halet, who was in the house waiting for an early visitor to arrive, and not one of the servants. Someone or something else must be concealed among the thickets of magnificently flowering native Jontarou shrubs about Telzey.

She could think of no other way to account for Tick-Tock's spooked behavior — nor, to be honest about it, for the manner her own nerves were acting up without visible cause this morning.

Telzey plucked a blade of grass, slipped the end between her lips, and chewed it gently, her face puzzled and concerned. She wasn't ordinarily afflicted with nervousness. Fifteen years old, genius level, brown as a berry and not at all bad looking in her sunbriefs, she was the youngest member of one of Orado's most prominent families and a second-year law student at one of the most exclusive schools in the Federation of the Hub. Her physical, mental, and emotional health, she'd always been informed, was excellent. Aunt Halet's frequent cracks about the inherent instability of the genius level could be ignored; Halet's own stability seemed questionable at best.

But none of that made the present odd situation any less disagreeable ...

The trouble might have begun, Telzey decided, during the night, within an hour after they arrived from the spaceport at the guest house Halet had rented in Port Nichay for their vacation on Jontarou. Telzey had retired at once to her second-story bedroom with Tick-Tock; but she barely got to sleep before something awakened her again. Turning over, she discovered TT reared up before the window, her forepaws on the sill, big cat-head outlined against the star-hazed night sky, staring fixedly down into the garden.

Telzey, only curious at that point, climbed out of bed and joined TT at the window. There was nothing in particular to be seen, and if the scents and minor night-sounds which came from the garden weren't exactly what they were used to, Jontarou was after all an unfamiliar planet. What else would one expect here?

But Tick-Tock's muscular back felt tense and rigid when Telzey laid her arm across it, and except for an absent-minded dig with her forehead against Telzey's shoulder, TT refused to let her attention be distracted from whatever had absorbed it. Now and then a low, ominous rumble came from her furry throat, a half-angry, half-questioning sound. Telzey began to feel a little uncomfortable. She managed finally to coax Tick-Tock away from the window, but neither of them slept well the rest of the night. At breakfast, Aunt Halet made one of her typical nasty-sweet remarks.

"You look so fatigued, dear — as if you were under some severe mental strain ... which, of course, you might be," Halet added musingly. With her gold-blond hair piled high on her head and her peaches and cream complexion, Halet looked fresh as a daisy herself ... a malicious daisy. "Now wasn't I right in insisting to Jessamine that you needed a vacation away from that terribly intellectual school?" She smiled gently.

"Absolutely," Telzey agreed, restraining the impulse to fling a spoonful of egg yolk at her father's younger sister. Aunt Halet often inspired such impulses, but Telzey had promised her mother to avoid actual battles on the Jontarou trip, if possible. After breakfast, she went out into the back garden with Tick-Tock, who immediately walked into a thicket, camouflaged herself, and vanished from sight. It seemed to add up to something. But what?

Telzey strolled about the garden a while, maintaining a pretense of nonchalant interest in Jontarou's flowers and colorful bug life. She experienced the most curious little chills of alarm from time to time, but discovered no signs of a lurking intruder, or of TT either. Then, for half an hour or more, she'd just sat cross-legged in the grass, waiting quietly for Tick-Tock to show up of her own accord. And the big lunkhead hadn't obliged.

Telzey scratched a tanned kneecap, scowling at Port Nichay's park trees beyond the garden wall. It seemed idiotic to feel scared when she couldn't even tell whether there was anything to be scared about! And, aside from that, another unreasonable feeling kept growing stronger by the minute now. This was to the effect she should be doing some unstated but specific thing ...

In fact, that Tick-Tock *wanted* her do some specific thing!

Completely idiotic!

Abruptly, Telzey closed her eyes, thought sharply, "Tick-Tock?" and waited — suddenly very angry at herself for having given in to her fancies to this extent — for whatever might happen.

She had never really established that she was able to tell, by a kind of symbolic mind-picture method, like a short waking dream, approximately what TT was thinking and feeling. Five years before, when she'd discovered Tick-Tock — an odd-looking and odder-behaved stray kitten then — in the woods near the Amberdons' summer home on Orado, Telzey had thought so. But it might never have been more than a colorful play of her imagination; and after she got into law school and grew increasingly absorbed in her studies, she almost forgot the matter again.

Today, perhaps because she was disturbed about Tick-Tock's behavior, the customary response was extraordinarily prompt. The warm glow of sunlight shining through her closed eyelids faded out quickly and was replaced by some inner darkness. In the darkness there appeared then an image of Tick-Tock sitting a little way off beside an open door in an old stone wall, green eyes fixed on Telzey. Telzey got the impression that TT was inviting her to go through the door, and, for some reason, the thought frightened her.

Again, there was an immediate reaction. The scene with Tick-Tock and the door vanished; and Telzey felt she was standing in a pitch-black room, knowing that if she moved even one step forwards, something that was waiting there silently would reach out and grab her.

Naturally, she recoiled ... and at once found herself sitting, eyes still closed and the sunlight bathing her lids, in the grass of the guest house garden.

She opened her eyes, looked around. Her heart was thumping rapidly. The experience couldn't have lasted more than four or five seconds, but it had been extremely vivid, a whole, compact little nightmare. None of her earlier experiments at getting into mental communication with TT had been like that.

It served her right, Telzey thought, for trying such a childish stunt at the moment! What she should have done at once was to make a methodical search for the foolish beast — TT was bound to be *somewhere* nearby — locate her behind her camouflage, and hang on to her then until this nonsense in the garden was explained! Talented as Tick-Tock was at blotting herself out, it usually was possible to spot her if one directed one's attention to shadow patterns. Telzey began a surreptitious study of the flowering bushes about her.

Three minutes later, off to her right, where the ground was banked beneath a six-foot step in the garden's terraces, Tick-Tock's outline suddenly caught her eye. Flat on her belly, head lifted above her paws, quite motionless, TT seemed like a transparent wraith stretched out along the terrace, barely discernible even when stared at directly. It was a convincing illusion; but what seemed to be rocks, plant leaves, and sun-splotched earth seen through the wraith-outline was simply the camouflage pattern TT had printed for the moment on her hide. She could have changed it completely in an instant to conform to a different background.

Telzey pointed an accusing finger.

"See you!" she announced, feeling a surge of relief which seemed as unaccountable as the rest of it.

The wraith twitched one ear in acknowledgment, the head outlines shifting as the camouflaged face turned towards Telzey. Then the inwardly uncamouflaged, very substantial-looking mouth opened slowly, showing Tick-Tock's red tongue and curved white tusks. The mouth stretched in a wide yawn, snapped shut with a click of meshing teeth, became indistinguishable again. Next, a pair of camouflaged lids drew back from TT's round, brilliant-green eyes. The eyes stared across the lawn at Telzey.

Telzey said irritably, "Quit clowning around, TT!"

The eyes blinked, and Tick-Tock's natural bronze-brown color sud–denly flowed over her head, down her neck, and across her body into legs and tail. Against the side of the terrace, as if materializing into solidity at that moment, appeared two hundred pounds of supple, rangy, long-tailed cat ... or catlike creature. TT's actual origin had never been established. The best guesses were that what Telzey had found playing around in the woods five years ago was either a biological experiment which had got away from a private laboratory on Orado, or some spaceman's lost pet, brought to the capital planet from one of the remote colonies beyond the Hub. On top of TT's head was a large, fluffy pompom of white fur, which might have looked ridiculous on another animal, but didn't on her. Even as a fat kitten, hanging head down from the side of a wall by the broad sucker pads in her paws, TT had possessed enormous dignity.

Telzey studied her, the feeling of relief fading again. Tick-Tock, ordinarily the most restful and composed of companions, definitely was still tensed up about something. That big, lazy yawn a moment ago, the attitude of stretched-out relaxation ... all pure sham!

"What *is* eating you?" she asked in exasperation.

The green eyes stared at her, solemn, watchful, seeming for that fleeting instant quite alien. And why, Telzey thought, should the old question of what Tick-Tock really was pass through her mind just now? After her rather alarming rate of growth began to taper off last year, nobody had cared any more.

For a moment, Telzey had the uncanny certainty of having had the answer to this situation almost in her grasp. An answer which appeared to involve the world of Jontarou, Tick-Tock, and of all unlikely factors — Aunt Halet.

She shook her head. TT's impassive green eyes blinked.

Jontarou? The planet lay outside Telzey's sphere of personal interests, but she'd read up on it on the way here from Orado. Among all the worlds of the Hub, Jontarou was *the* paradise for zoologists and sportsmen, a gigantic animal preserve, its continents and seas swarming with mag-nificent game. Under Federation law, it was being retained deliberately in the primitive state in which it had been discovered. Port Nichay, the only city, actually the only inhabited point on Jontarou, was beautiful and quiet, a pattern of vast but elegantly slender towers, each separated from the others by four or five miles of rolling parkland and interconnected by the threads of transparent skyways. Near the horizon, just visible from the garden, rose the tallest towers of all, the green and gold spires of the Shikaris' Club, a center of Federation affairs and of social activity. From the aircar which brought them across Port Nichay the evening before, Telzey had seen occasional strings of guest houses, similar to the one Halet had rented, nestling along the park slopes.

Nothing very sinister about Port Nichay or green Jontarou, surely!

Halet? That blond, slinky, would-be Machiavelli? What could —?

Telzey's eyes narrowed reflectively. There'd been a minor occurrence — at least, it had seemed minor — before the spaceliner docked last night. A young woman from one of the newscasting services had asked for an interview with the daughter of Federation Councilwoman Jessamine Amberdon. This happened occasionally; and Telzey had no objections until the newshen's gossipy persistence in inquiring about the "unusual pet" she was bringing to Port Nichay with her began to be annoying. TT might be somewhat unusual, but that was not a matter of general interest; and Telzey said so. Then Halet moved smoothly into the act and held forth on Tick-Tock's appearance, habits, and mysterious antecedents, in considerable derail.

Telzey had assumed that Halet was simply going out of her way to be irritating, as usual. Looking back on the incident, however, it occurred to her that the chatter between her aunt and the newscast woman had sounded oddly stilted — almost like something the two might have rehearsed.

Rehearsed for what purpose? Tick-Tock ... Jontarou.

Telzey chewed gently on her lower lip. A vacation on Jontarou for the two of them and TT had been Halet's idea, and Halet had enthused about it so much that Telzey's mother at last talked her into accepting. Halet, Jessamine explained privately to Telzey, had felt they were intruders in the Amberdon family, had bitterly resented Jessamine's political honors and, more recently, Telzey's own emerging promise of brilliance. This invitation was Halet's way of indicating a change of heart. Wouldn't Telzey oblige?

So Telzey had obliged, though she took very little stock in Halet's change of heart. She wasn't, in fact, putting it past her aunt to have some involved dirty trick up her sleeve with this trip to Jontarou. Halet's mind worked like that.

So far there had been no actual indications of purposeful mischief. But logic did seem to require a connection between the various puzzling events here ... A newscaster's rather forced-looking interest in Tick-Tock — Halet could easily have paid for that interview. Then TT's disturbed behavior during their first night in Port Nichay, and Telzey's own formless anxieties and fancies in connection with the guest house garden.

The last remained hard to explain. But Tick-Tock ... and Halet ... might know something about Jontarou that she didn't know.

Her mind returned to the results of the half-serious attempt she'd made to find out whether there was something Tick-Tock "wanted her to do." An open door? A darkness where somebody waited to grab her if she took even one step forwards? It couldn't have had any significance. Or could it?

So you'd like to try magic, Telzey scoffed at herself. Baby games ... How far would you have got at law school if you'd asked TT to help with your problems?

Then why had she been thinking about it again?

She shivered, because an eerie stillness seemed to settle on the garden. From the side of the terrace, TT's green eyes watched her.

Telzey had a feeling of sinking down slowly into a sunlit dream, into something very remote from law school problems.

"Should I go through the door?" she whispered.

The bronze cat-shape raised its head slowly. TT began to purr.

Tick-Tock's name had been derived in kittenhood from the manner in which she purred — a measured, oscillating sound, shifting from high to low, as comfortable and often as continuous as the unobtrusive pulse of an old clock. It was the first time, Telzey realized now, that she had heard the sound since their arrival on Jontarou. It went on for a dozen seconds or so, then stopped. Tick-Tock continued to look at her.

It appeared to have been an expression of definite assent ...

The dreamlike sensation increased, hazing over Telzey's thoughts. If there was nothing to this mind-communication thing, what harm could symbols do? This time, she wouldn't let them alarm her. And if they did mean something ...

She closed her eyes.

The sunglow outside faded instantly. Telzey caught a fleeting picture of the door in the wall, and knew in the same moment that she'd already passed through it.

She was not in the dark room then, but poised at the edge of a brightness which seemed featureless and without limit, spread out around her with a feeling-tone like "sea" or "sky." But it was an unquiet place. There was a sense of unseen things on all sides watching her and waiting.

Was this another form of the dark room — a trap set up in her mind? Telzey's attention did a quick shift. She was seated in the grass again; the sunlight beyond her closed eyelids seemed to shine in quietly through rose-tinted curtains. Cautiously, she let her awareness return to the bright area; and *it* was still there. She had a moment of excited elation. She was controlling this! And why not, she asked herself. These things were happening in *her* mind, after all!

She would find out what they seemed to mean; but she would be in no rush to ...

An impression as if, behind her, Tick-Tock had thought, "Now I can help again!"

Then a feeling of being swept swiftly, irresistibly forwards, thrust out and down. The brightness exploded in thundering colors around her. In fright, she made the effort to snap her eyes open, to be back in the garden; but now she couldn't make it work. The colors continued to roar about her, like a confusion of excited, laughing, triumphant voices. Telzey felt caught in the middle of it all, suspended in invisible spider webs. Tick-Tock seemed to be somewhere nearby, looking on. Faithless, treacherous TT!

Telzey's mind made another wrenching effort, and there was a change. She hadn't got back into the garden, but the noisy, swirling colors were gone and she had the feeling of reading a rapidly moving microtape now, though she didn't actually see the tape.

The tape, she realized, was another symbol for what was happening, a symbol easier for her to understand. There were voices, or what might be voices, around her; on the invisible tape she seemed to be reading what they said.

A number of speakers, apparently involved in a fast, hot argument about what to do with her. Impressions flashed past ...

Why waste time with her? It was clear that kitten-talk was all she was capable of! ... Not necessarily; that was a normal first step. Give her a little time! ... But what — exasperatedly — could *such* a small-bite *possibly* know that would be of significant value?

There was a slow, blurred, awkward-seeming interruption. Its content was not comprehensible to Telzey at all, but in some unmistakable manner it was defined as Tick-Tock's thought.

A pause as the circle of speakers stopped to consider whatever TT had thrown into the debate.

Then another impression ... one that sent a shock of fear through Telzey as it rose heavily into her awareness. Its sheer intensity momentarily displaced the tape-reading symbolism. A savage voice seemed to rumble:

"Toss the tender small-bite to *me*" — malevolent crimson eyes fixed on Telzey from somewhere not far away — "and let's be done here!"

Startled, stammering protest from Tick-Tock, accompanied by gusts of laughter from the circle. Great sense of humor these characters had, Telzey thought bitterly. That crimson-eyed thing wasn't joking at all!

More laughter as the circle caught her thought. Then a kind of majority opinion found sudden expression:

"Small-bite *is* learning! No harm to wait — We'll find out quickly — Let's ..."

The tape ended; the voices faded; the colors went blank. In whatever jumbled-up form she'd been getting the impressions at that point — Telzey couldn't have begun to describe it — the whole thing suddenly stopped.

She found herself sitting in the grass, shaky, scared, eyes open. Tick-Tock stood beside the terrace, looking at her. An air of hazy unreality still hung about the garden.

She might have flipped! She didn't think so; but it certainly seemed possible! Otherwise ... Telzey made an attempt to sort over what had happened.

Something *had* been in the garden! Something had been inside her mind. Something that was at home on Jontarou.

There'd been a feeling of perhaps fifty or sixty of these ... well, beings. Alarming beings! Reckless, wild, hard ... and that red-eyed nightmare! Telzey shuddered.

They'd contacted Tick-Tock first, during the night. TT understood them better than she could. Why? Telzey found no immediate answer.

Then Tick-Tock had tricked her into letting her mind be invaded by these beings. There must have been a very definite reason for that.

She looked over at Tick-Tock. TT looked back. Nothing stirred in Telzey's thoughts. Between *them* there was still no direct communication.

Then how had the beings been able to get through to her?

Telzey wrinkled her nose. Assuming this was real, it seemed clear that the game of symbols she'd made up between herself and TT had provided the opening. Her whole experience just now had been in the form of symbols, translating whatever occurred into something she could consciously grasp.

"Kitten-talk" was how the beings referred to the use of symbols; they seemed contemptuous of it. Never mind, Telzey told herself; they'd agreed she was learning.

The air over the grass appeared to flicker. Again she had the impression of reading words off a quickly moving, not quite visible tape.

"You're being taught and you're learning," was what she seemed to read. "The question was whether you were capable of partial understanding, as your friend insisted. Since you were, everything else that can be done will be accomplished very quickly."

A pause, then with a touch of approval, "You're a well-formed mind, small-bite! Odd and with incomprehensibilities, but well-formed —"

One of the beings, and a fairly friendly one — at least not unfriendly. Telzey framed a tentative mental question. "Who are you?"

"You'll know very soon." The flickering ended; she realized she and the question had been dismissed for the moment. She looked over at Tick-Tock again.

"Can't *you* talk to me now, TT?" she asked silently.

A feeling of hesitation.

"Kitten-talk!" was the impression that formed itself with difficulty. It was awkward, searching; but it came unquestionably from TT. "Still learning, too, Telzey!" TT seemed half anxious, half angry. "We —"

A sharp buzz-note reached Telzey's ears, wiping out the groping thought-impression. She jumped a little, glanced down. Her wrist-talker was signaling. For a moment, she seemed poised uncertainly between a world where unseen, dangerous-sounding beings referred to one as small-bite and where TT was learning to talk, and the familiar other world where wrist-communicators buzzed periodically in a matter-of-fact manner. Settling back into the more familiar world, she switched on the talker.

"Yes?" she said. Her voice sounded husky.

"Telzey, dear," Halet murmured honey-sweet from the talker, "would you come back into the house, please? The living room — We have a visitor who very much wants to meet you."

Telzey hesitated, eyes narrowing. Halet's visitor wanted to meet *her*?

"Why?" she asked.

"He has something *very* interesting to tell you, dear." The edge of triumphant malice showed for an instant, vanished in murmuring sweetness again. "So please hurry!"

"All right." Telzey stood up. "I'm coming."

"Fine, dear!" The talker went dead.

Telzey switched off the instrument, noticed that Tick-Tock had chosen to disappear meanwhile.

Flipped? She wondered, starting up towards the house. It was clear Aunt Halet had prepared some unpleasant surprise to spring on her, which was hardly more than normal behavior for Halet. The other business? She couldn't be certain of anything there. Leaving out TT's strange actions — which might have a number of causes, after all — that entire string of events could have been created inside her head. There was no contradictory evidence so far.

But it could do no harm to take what *seemed* to have happened at face value. Some pretty grim event might be shaping up, in a very real way, around here ...

"You reason logically!" The impression now was of a voice speaking to her, a voice that made no audible sound. It was the same being who'd addressed her a minute or two ago.

The two worlds between which Telzey had felt suspended seemed to glide slowly together and become one.

"I go to law school," she explained to the being, almost absently.

Amused agreement. "So we heard."

"What do you want of me?" Telzey inquired.

"You'll know soon enough."

"Why not tell me now?" Telzey urged. It seemed about to dismiss her again.

Quick impatience flared at her. "Kitten-pictures! Kitten-thoughts! Kitten-talk! Too slow, too slow! YOUR pictures — too much YOU! Wait till the ..."

Circuits close ... channels open ... obstructions clear? What *had* it said? There'd been only the blurred image of a finicky, delicate, but perfectly normal technical operation of some kind.

" ... Minutes now!" the voice concluded. A pause, then another thought tossed carelessly at her. "This is more important to you, small-bite, than to *us!*" The voice impression ended as sharply as if a communicator had snapped off.

Not *too* friendly! Telzey walked on towards the house, a new fear growing inside her ... a fear like the awareness of a storm gathered nearby, still quiet — deadly quiet, but ready to break.

"Kitten-pictures!" A voice seemed to jeer distantly, a whispering in the park trees beyond the garden wall.

Halet's cheeks were lightly pinked; her blue eyes sparkled. She looked downright stunning, which meant to anyone who knew her that the worst side of Halet's nature was champing at the bit again. On uninformed males it had a dazzling effect, however; and Telzey wasn't surprised to find their visitor wearing a tranced expression when she came into the living room. He was a tall, outdoorsy man with a tanned, bony face, a neatly trained black mustache, and a scar down one cheek which would have seemed dashing if it hadn't been for the stupefied look. Beside his chair stood a large, clumsy instrument which might have been some kind of telecamera.

Halet performed introductions. Their visitor was Dr. Droon, a zoologist. He had been tuned in on Telzey's newscast interview on the liner the night before, and wondered whether Telzey would care to discuss Tick-Tock with him.

"Frankly, no," Telzey said.

Dr. Droon came awake and gave Telzey a surprised look. Halet smiled easily.

"My niece doesn't intend to be discourteous, doctor," she explained.

"Of course not," the zoologist agreed doubtfully.

"It's just," Halet went on, "that Telzey is a little, oh, sensitive where Tick-Tock is concerned. In her own way, she's attached to the animal. Aren't you, dear?"

"Yes," Telzey said blandly.

"Well, we hope this isn't going to disturb you too much, dear." Halet glanced significantly at Dr. Droon. "Dr. Droon, you must understand, is simply doing ... well, there is something very important he must tell you now."

Telzey transferred her gaze back to the zoologist. Dr. Droon cleared his throat. "I, ah, understand, Miss Amberdon, that you're unaware of what kind of creature your, ah, Tick-Tock is?"

Telzey started to speak, then checked herself, frowning. She had about to state that she knew exactly what kind of creature TT was ... but she didn't, of course!

Or did she? She ...

She scowled absent-mindedly at Dr. Droon, biting her lip.

"Telzey!" Halet prompted gently.

"Huh?" Telzey said. "Oh ... please go on, doctor!"

Dr. Droon steepled his fingers. "Well," he said, "she ... your pet ... is, ah, a young crest cat. Nearly full grown now, apparently, and —"

"Why, yes!" Telzey cried.

The zoologist looked at her. "You knew that —"

"Well, not really," Telzey admitted. "Or sort of." She laughed, her cheeks flushed. "This is the most ... go ahead, please! Sorry I interrupted." She stared at the wall beyond Dr. Droon with a rapt expression.

The zoologist and Halet exchanged glances. Then Dr. Droon resumed cautiously. The crest cats, he said, were a species native to Jontarou. Their existence had been known for only eight years. The species appeared to have had a somewhat limited range — the Baluit mountains on the other side of the huge continent on which Port Nichay had been built ...

Telzey barely heard him. A very curious thing was happening. For every sentence Dr. Droon uttered, a dozen other sentences appeared in her awareness. More accurately, it was as if an instantaneous smooth flow of information relevant to whatever he said arose continuously from what might have been almost her own memory, but wasn't. Within a minute or two, she knew more about the crest cats of Jontarou than Dr. Droon could have told her in hours ... much more than he'd ever known.

She realized suddenly that he'd stopped talking, that he had asked her a question. "Miss Amberdon?" he repeated now, with a note of uncertainty.

"Yar-rrr-REE!" Telzey told him softly. "I'll drink your blood!"

"Eh?"

Telzey blinked, focused on Dr. Droon, wrenching her mind away from a splendid view of the misty-blue peaks of the Baluit range.

"Sorry," she said briskly. "Just a joke!" She smiled. "Now what were you saying?"

The zoologist looked at her in a rather odd manner for a moment. "I was inquiring," he said then, "whether you were familiar with the sporting rules established by the various hunting associations of the Hub in connection with the taking of game trophies?"

Telzey shook her head. "No, I never heard of them."

The rules, Dr. Droon explained, laid down the type of equipment ... weapons, spotting and tracking instruments, number of assistants, and so forth ... a sportsman could legitimately use in the pursuit of any specific type of game. "Before the end of the first year after their discovery," he went on, "the Baluit crest cat had been placed in the ultra-equipment class."

"What's ultra-equipment?" Telzey asked.

"Well," Dr. Droon said thoughtfully, "it doesn't quite involve the use of full battle armor ... not quite! And, of course, even with that classification the sporting principle of mutual accessibility must be observed."

"Mutual ... oh, I see!" Telzey paused as another wave of silent information rose into her awareness; went on, "So the game has to be able to get at the sportsman too, eh?"

"That's correct. Except in the pursuit of various classes of flying animals, a shikari would not, for example, be permitted the use of an aircar other than as a means of simple transportation. Under these conditions, it was soon established that crest cats were being obtained by sportsmen who went after them at a rather consistent one-to-one ratio."

Telzey's eyes widened. She'd gathered something similar from her other information source but hadn't quite believed it. "One hunter killed for each cat bagged?" she said. "That's pretty rough sport, isn't it?"

"Extremely rough sport!" Dr. Droon agreed dryly. "In fact, when the statistics were published, the sporting interest in winning a Baluit cat trophy appears to have suffered a sudden and sharp decline. On the other hand, a more scientific interest in these remarkable animals was coincidingly created, and many permits for their acquisition by the agents of museums, universities, public and private collections were issued. Sporting rules, of course, do not apply to that activity."

Telzey nodded absently. "I see! *They* used aircars, didn't they? A sort of heavy knockout gun —"

"Aircars, long-range detectors, and stunguns are standard equipment in such work," Dr. Droon acknowledged. "Gas and poison are employed, of course, as circumstances dictate. The collectors were relatively successful for a while.

"And then a curious thing happened. Less than two years after their existence became known, the crest cats of the Baluit range were extinct! The inroads made on their numbers by man cannot begin to account for this, so it must be assumed that a sudden plague wiped them out. At any rate, not another living member of the species has been seen on Jontarou until you landed here with your pet last night."

Telzey sat silent for some seconds. Not because of what he had said, but because the other knowledge was still flowing into her mind. On one very important point *that* was at variance with what the zoologist had stated; and from there a coldly logical pattern was building up. Telzey didn't grasp the pattern in complete detail yet, but what she saw of it stirred her with a half incredulous dread.

She asked, shaping the words carefully but with only a small part of her attention on what she was really saying, "Just what does all that have to do with Tick-Tock, Dr. Droon?"

Dr. Droon glanced at Halet, and returned his gaze to Telzey. Looking very uncomfortable but quite determined, he told her, "Miss Amberdon, there is a Federation law which states that when a species is threatened with extinction. any available survivors must be transferred to the Life Banks of the University League, to insure their indefinite preservation. Under the circumstances, this law applies to, ah, Tick-Tock!"

So that had been Halet's trick. She'd found out about the crest cats, might have put in as much as a few months arranging to make the discovery of TT's origin on Jontarou seem a regrettable mischance — something no one could have foreseen or prevented. In the Life Banks, from what Telzey had heard of them, TT would cease to exist as an individual awareness while scientists tinkered around with the possibilities of reconstructing her species.

Telzey studied her aunt's carefully sympathizing face for an instant, asked Dr. Droon, "What about the other crest cats you said were collected before they became extinct here? Wouldn't they be enough for what the Life Banks need?"

He shook his head. "Two immature male specimens are known to exist, and they are at present in the Life Banks. The others that were taken alive at the time have been destroyed ... often under nearly disastrous circumstances. They are enormously cunning, enormously savage creatures, Miss Amberdon! The additional fact that they can conceal themselves to the point of being virtually indetectable except by the use of instruments makes them one of the most dangerous animals known. Since the young female which you raised as a pet has remained docile ... so far ... you may not really be able to appreciate that."

"Perhaps I can," Telzey said. She nodded at the heavy-looking instrument standing beside his chair. "And that's — ?"

"It's a life detector combined with a stungun, Miss Amberdon. I have no intention of harming your pet, but we can't take chances with an animal of that type. The gun's charge will knock it unconscious for several minutes — just long enough to let me secure it with paralysis belts."

"You're a collector for the Life Banks, Dr. Droon?"

"That's correct."

"Dr. Droon," Halet remarked, "has obtained a permit from the Planetary Moderator, authorizing him to claim Tick-Tock for the University League and remove her from the planet, dear. So you see there is simply nothing we can do about the matter! Your mother wouldn't like us to attempt to obstruct the law, would she?" Halet paused. "The permit should have your signature, Telzey, but I can sign in your stead if necessary."

That was Halet's way of saying it would do no good to appeal to Jontarou's Planetary Moderator. She'd taken the precaution of getting his assent to the matter first.

"So now if you'll just call Tick-Tock, dear ..." Halet went on.

Telzey barely heard the last words. She felt herself stiffening slowly, while the living room almost faded from her sight. Perhaps, in that instant, some additional new circuit had closed in her mind, or some additional new channel had opened, for TT's purpose in tricking her into contact with the reckless, mocking beings outside was suddenly and numbingly clear.

And what it meant immediately was that she'd have to get out of the house without being spotted at it, and go some place where she could be undisturbed for half an hour.

She realized that Halet and the zoologist were both staring at her.

"Are you ill, dear?"

"No." Telzey stood up. It would be worse than useless to try to tell these two anything! Her face must be pretty white at the moment — she could feel it — but they assumed, of course, that the shock of losing TT had just now sunk in on her,

"I'll have to check on that law you mentioned before I sign anything," she told Dr. Droon.

"Why, yes ..." He started to get out of his chair. "I'm sure that can be arranged, Miss Amberdon!"

"Don't bother to call the Moderator's office," Telzey said. "I brought my law library along. I'll look it up myself." She turned to leave the room.

"My niece," Halet explained to Dr. Droon, who was beginning to look puzzled, "attends law school. She's always so absorbed in her studies ... Telzey?"

"Yes, Halet?" Telzey paused at the door.

"I'm very glad you've decided to be sensible about this, dear. But don't take too long, will you? We don't want to waste Dr. Droon's time."

"It shouldn't take more than five or ten minutes," Telzey told her agreeably. She closed the door behind her, and went directly to her bedroom on the second floor. One of her two valises was still unpacked. She locked the door behind her, opened the unpacked valise, took out a pocket edition law library and sat down at the table with it.

She clicked on the library's viewscreen, tapped the clearing and index buttons. Behind the screen, one of the multiple rows of pinhead tapes shifted slightly as the index was flicked into reading position. Half a minute later, she was glancing over the legal section on which Dr. Droon had based his claim. The library confirmed what he had said.

Very neat of Halet, Telzey thought, very nasty ... and pretty idiotic! Even a second-year law student could think immediately of two or three ways in which a case like that could have been dragged out in the Federation's courts for a couple of decades before the question of handing Tick-Tock over to the Life Banks became too acute.

Well, Halet simply wasn't really intelligent. And the plot to shanghai TT was hardly even a side issue now.

Telzey snapped the tiny library shut, fastened it to the belt of her sunsuit, and went over to the open window. A two-foot ledge passed beneath the window, leading to the roof of a patio on the right. Fifty yards beyond the patio, the garden ended in a natural-stone wall. Behind it lay one of the big wooded park areas which formed most of the ground level of Port Nichay.

Tick-Tock wasn't in sight. A sound of voices came from ground-floor windows on the left. Halet had brought her maid and chauffeur along; and a chef had showed up in time to make breakfast this morning, as part of the city's guest house service. Telzey took the empty valise to the window, set it on end against the left side of the frame, and let the window slide down until its lower edge rested on the valise. She went back to the house guard-screen panel beside the door, put her finger against the lock button, and pushed.

The sound of voices from the lower floor was cut off as outer doors and windows slid silently shut all about the house. Telzey glanced back at the window. The valise had creaked a little as the guard field drove the frame down on it, but it was supporting the thrust. She returned to the window, wriggled feet foremost through the opening, twisted around, and got a footing on the ledge.

A minute later, she was scrambling quietly down a vine-covered patio trellis to the ground. Even after they discovered she was gone, the guard screen would keep everybody in the house for some little while. They'd either have to disengage the screen's main mechanisms and start poking around in them, or force open the door to her bedroom and get the lock unset. Either approach would involve confusion, upset tempers, and generally delay any organized pursuit.

Telzey edged around the patio and started towards the wall, keeping close to the side of the house so she couldn't be seen from the windows. The shrubbery made minor rustling noises as she threaded her way through it ... and then there was a different stirring which might have been no more than a slow, steady current of air moving among the bushes behind her. She shivered involuntarily but didn't look back.

She came to the wall, stood still, measuring its height, jumped and got an arm across it, swung up a knee, and squirmed up and over. She came down on her feet with a small thump in the grass on the other side, glanced back once at the guest house, crossed a path, and went on among the park trees.

Within a few hundred yards, it became apparent that she had an escort. She didn't look around for them, but spread out to right and left like a skirmish line, keeping abreast with her, occasional shadows slid silently through patches of open, sunlit ground, disappeared again under the trees. Otherwise, there was hardly anyone in sight. Port Nichay's human residents appeared to make almost no personal use of the vast parkland spread out beneath their tower apartments; and its traffic moved over the airways, visible from the ground only as rainbow-hued ribbons which bisected the sky between the upper tower levels. An occasional private aircar went by overhead.

Wisps of thought which were not her own thoughts flicked through Telzey's mind from moment to moment as the silent line of shadows moved deeper into the park with her. She realized she was being sized up, judged, evaluated again. No more information was coming through; they had given her as much information as she needed. In the main perhaps, they were simply curious now. This was the first human mind they'd been able to make heads or tails of, and that hadn't seemed deaf and silent to their form of communication. They were taking time out to study it. They'd been assured she would have something of genuine importance to tell them; and there was some derision about that. But they were willing to wait a little, and find out. They were curious and they liked games. At the moment, Telzey and what she might try to do to change their plans was the game on which their attention was fixed.

Twelve minutes passed before the talker on Telzey's wrist began to buzz. It continued to signal off and on for another few minutes, then stopped. Back in the guest house they couldn't be sure yet whether she wasn't simply locked inside her room and refusing to answer them. But Telzey quickened her pace.

The park's trees gradually become more massive, reached higher above her, stood spaced more widely apart. She passed through the morning shadow of the residential tower nearest the guest house, and emerged from it presently on the shore of a small lake. On the other side of the lake, a number of dappled grazing animals like long-necked, tall horses lifted their heads to watch her. For some seconds they seemed only mildly interested, but then a breeze moved across the lake, crinkling the surface of the water; and as it touched the opposite shore, abrupt panic exploded among the grazers. They wheeled, went flashing away in effortless twenty-foot strides, and were gone among the trees.

Telzey felt a crawling along her spine. It was the first objective indication she'd had of the nature of the company she had brought to the lake, and while it hardly came as a surprise, for a moment her urge was to follow the example of the grazers.

"Tick-Tock?" she whispered, suddenly a little short of breath.

A single up-and-down purring note replied from the bushes on her right. TT was still around, for whatever good that might do. Not too much, Telzey thought, if it came to serious trouble. But the knowledge was somewhat reassuring ... and this, meanwhile, appeared to be as far as she needed to get from the guest house. They'd be looking for her by aircar presently, but there was nothing to tell them in which direction to turn first.

She climbed the bank of the lake to a point where she was screened by both thick, green shrubbery and the top of a single immense tree from the sky, sat down on some dry, mossy growth, took the law library from her belt, opened it, and placed it in her lap. Vague stirrings indicated that her escort was also settling down in an irregular circle about her; and apprehension shivered on Telzey's skin again. It wasn't that their attitude was hostile; they were simply overawing. And no one could predict what they might do next. Without looking up, she asked a question in her mind.

"Ready?"

Sense of multiple acknowledgment, variously tinged — sardonic; interestedly amused; attentive; doubtful. Impatience quivered through it too, only tentatively held in restraint, and Telzey's forehead was suddenly wet. Some of them seemed on the verge of expressing disapproval with what was being done here —

Her fingers quickly flicked in the index tape, and the stir of feeling about her subsided, their attention captured again for the moment. Her thoughts became to some degree detached, ready to dissect another problem in the familiar ways and present the answers to it. Not a very involved problem essentially, but this time it wasn't a school exercise. Her company waited, withdrawn, silent, aloof once more, while the index blurred, checked, blurred and checked. Within a minute and a half, she had noted a dozen reference symbols. She tapped in another of the pinhead tapes, glanced over a few paragraphs, licked salty sweat from her lip, and said in her thoughts, emphasizing the meaning of each detail of the sentence so that there would be no misunderstanding, "This is the Federation law that applies to the situation which existed originally on this planet ..."

There were no interruptions, no commenting thoughts, no intrusions of any kind, as she went step by step through the section, turned to another one, and another. In perhaps twelve minutes she came to the end of the last one, and stopped. Instantly, argument exploded about her.

Telzey was not involved in the argument; in fact, she could grasp only scraps of it. Either they were excluding her deliberately, or the exchange was too swift, practiced, and varied to allow her to keep up. But their vehemence was not encouraging. And was it reasonable to imagine that the Federation's laws would have any meaning for minds like these? Telzey snapped the library shut with fingers that had begun to tremble, and placed it on the ground. Then she stiffened. In the sensations washing about her, a special excitement rose suddenly, a surge of almost gleeful wildness that choked away her breath. Awareness followed of a pair of malignant crimson eyes fastened on her, moving steadily closer. A kind of nightmare paralysis seized Telzey — they'd turned her over to that red-eyed horror! She sat still, feeling mouse-sized.

Something came out with a crash from a thicket behind her. Her muscles went tight. But it was TT who rubbed a hard head against her shoulder, took another three stiff-legged steps forward, and stopped between Telzey and the bushes on their right, back rigid, neck fur erect, tail twisting.

Expectant silence closed in about them. The circle was waiting. In the greenery on the right something made a slow, heavy stir.

TT's lips peeled back from her teeth. Her head swung towards the motion, ears flattening, transformed to a split, snarling demon-mask. A long shriek ripped from her lungs, raw with fury, blood lust, and challenge.

The sound died away. For some seconds the tension about them held; then came a sense of gradual relaxation mingled with a partly amused approval. Telzey was shaking violently. It had been, she was telling herself, a deliberate test ... not of herself, of course, but of TT. And Tick-Tock had passed with honors. That *her* nerves had been half ruined in the process would seem a matter of no consequence to this rugged crew ...

She realized next that someone here was addressing her personally.

It took a few moments to steady her jittering thoughts enough to gain a more definite impression than that. This speaker, she discovered then, was a member of the circle of whom she hadn't been aware before. The thought-impressions came hard and cold as iron — a personage who was very evidently in the habit of making major decisions and seeing them carried out. The circle, its moment of sport over, was listening with more than a suggestion of deference. Tick-Tock, far from conciliated, green eyes still blazing, nevertheless was settling down to listen, too.

Telzey began to understand.

Her suggestions, Iron Thoughts informed her, might appear without value to a number of foolish minds here, but *he* intended to see they were given a fair trial. Did he perhaps hear, he inquired next of the circle, throwing in a casual but horridly vivid impression of snapping spines and slashed shaggy throats spouting blood, any objection to that?

Dead stillness all around. There was, definitely, no objection! Tick-Tock began to grin like a pleased kitten.

That point having been settled in an orderly manner now, Iron Thoughts went on coldly to Telzey, what specifically did she propose they should do?

Halet's long, pearl-gray sportscar showed up above the park trees twenty minutes later. Telzey, face turned down towards the open law library in her lap, watched the car from the corner of her eyes. She was in plain view, sitting beside the lake, apparently absorbed in legal research. Tick-Tock, camouflaged among the bushes thirty feet higher up the bank, had spotted the car an instant before she did and announced the fact with a three-second break in her purring. Neither of them made any other move.

The car was approaching the lake but still a good distance off. Its canopy was down, and Telzey could just make out the heads of three people inside. Delquos, Halet's chauffeur, would be flying the vehicle, while Halet and Dr. Droon looked around for her from the sides. Three hundred yards away, the aircar began a turn to the right. Delquos didn't like his employer much; at a guess, he had just spotted Telzey and was trying to warn her off.

Telzey closed the library and put it down, picked up a handful of pebbles, and began flicking them idly, one at a time, into the water. The aircar vanished to her left.

Three minutes later, she watched its shadow glide across the surface of the lake towards her. Her heart began to thump almost audibly, but she didn't look up. Tick-Tock's purring continued, on its regular, unhurried note. The car came to a stop almost directly overhead. After a couple of seconds, there was a clicking noise. The purring ended abruptly.

Telzey climbed to her feet as Delquos brought the car down to the bank of the lake. The chauffeur grinned ruefully at her. A side door had been opened, and Halet and Dr. Droon stood behind it. Halet watched Telzey with a small smile while the naturalist put the heavy life-detector-and-stungun device carefully down on the floorboards.

"If you're looking for Tick-Tock," Telzey said, "she isn't here."

Halet just shook her head sorrowfully.

"There's no use lying to us, dear! Dr. Droon just stunned her."

They found TT collapsed on her side among the shrubs, wearing her natural color. Her eyes were shut; her chest rose and fell in a slow breathing motion. Dr. Droon, looking rather apologetic, pointed out to Telzey that her pet was in no pain, that the stungun had simply put her comfortably to sleep. He also explained the use of the two sets of webbed paralysis belts which he fastened about TT's legs. The effect of the stun charge would wear off in a few minutes, and contact with the inner surfaces of the energized belts would then keep TT anesthetized and unable to move until the belts were removed. She would, he repeated, be suffering no pain throughout the process.

Telzey didn't comment. She watched Delquos raise TT's limp body above the level of the bushes with a gravity hoist belonging to Dr. Droon, and maneuver her back to the car, the others following. Delquos climbed into the car first, opened the big trunk compartment in the rear. TT was slid inside and the trunk compartment locked.

"Where are you taking her?" Telzey asked sullenly as Delquos lifted the car into the air.

"To the spaceport, dear," Halet said. "Dr. Droon and I both felt it would be better to spare your feelings by not prolonging the matter unnecessarily."

Telzey wrinkled her nose disdainfully, and walked up the aircar to stand behind Delquos' seat. She leaned against the back of the seat for an instant. Her legs felt shaky.

The chauffeur gave her a sober wink from the side.

"That's a dirty trick she's played on you, Miss Telzey!" he murmured. "I tried to warn you."

"I know." Telzey took a deep breath. "Look, Delquos, in just a minute something's going to happen! It'll look dangerous, but it won't be. Don't let it get you nervous ... right?"

"Huh?" Delquos appeared startled, but kept his voice low. "Just *what's* going to happen?"

"No time to tell you. Remember what I said."

Telzey moved back a few steps from the driver's seat, turned around, said unsteadily, "Halet ... Dr. Droon —"

Halet had been speaking quietly to Dr. Droon; they both looked up.

"If you don't move, and don't do anything stupid," Telzey said rapidly, "you won't get hurt. If you do ... well, I don't know! You see, there's another crest cat in the car ..." In her mind she added, "Now!"

It was impossible to tell in just what section of the car Iron Thoughts had been lurking. The carpeting near the rear passenger seats seemed to blur for an instant. Then he was there, camouflage dropped, sitting on the floorboards five feet from the naturalist and Halet.

Halet's mouth opened wide; she tried to scream but fainted instead. Dr. Droon's right hand started out quickly towards the big stungun device beside his seat. Then he checked himself and sat still, ashen-faced.

Telzey didn't blame him for changing his mind. She felt he must be a remarkably brave man to have moved at all. Iron Thoughts, twice as broad across the back as Tick-Tock, twice as massively muscled, looked like a devil-beast even to her. His dark-green marbled hide was criss-crossed with old scar patterns; half his tossing crimson crest appeared to have been ripped away. He reached out now in a fluid, silent motion, hooked a paw under the stungun, and flicked upwards. The big instrument rose in an incredibly swift, steep arc eighty feet into the air, various parts flying away from it, before it started curving down towards the treetops below the car. Iron Thoughts lazily swung his head around and looked at Telzey with yellow fire-eyes.

"Miss Telzey! Miss Telzey!" Delquos was muttering behind her. "You're *sure* it won't ..."

Telzey swallowed. At the moment, she felt barely mouse-sized again. "Just relax!" she told Delquos in a shaky voice. "He's really quite t-t-t-tame."

Iron Thoughts produced a harsh but not unamiable chuckle in her mind.

The pearl-gray sportscar, covered now by its streamlining canopy, drifted down presently to a parking platform outside the suite of offices of Jontarou's Planetary Moderator, on the fourteenth floor of the Shikaris' Club Tower. An attendant waved it on into a vacant slot.

Inside the car, Delquos set the brakes, switched off the engine, asked, "Now what?"

"I think," Telzey said reflectively, "we'd better lock you in the trunk compartment with my aunt and Dr. Droon while I talk to the Moderator."

The chauffeur shrugged. He'd regained most of his aplomb during the unhurried trip across the parklands. Iron Thoughts had done nothing but sit in the center of the car, eyes half shut, looking like instant death enjoying a dignified nap and occasionally emitting a ripsawing noise which might have been either his style of purring or a snore. And Tick-Tock, when Delquos peeled the paralysis belts off her legs at Telzey's direction, had greeted him with her usual reserved affability. What the chauffeur was suffering from at the moment was intense curiosity, which Telzey had done nothing to relieve.

"Just as you say, Miss Telzey," he agreed. "I hate to miss whatever you're going to be doing here, but if you *don't* lock me up now, Miss Halet will figure I was helping you and fire me as soon as you let her out."

Telzey nodded, then cocked her head in the direction of the rear compartment. Faint sounds coming through the door indicated that Halet had regained consciousness and was having hysterics.

"You might tell her," Telzey suggested, "that there'll be a grown-up crest cat sitting outside the compartment door." This wasn't true, but neither Delquos nor Halet could know it. "If there's too much racket before I get back, it's likely to irritate him ..."

A minute later, she set both car doors on lock and went outside, wishing she were less informally clothed. Sunbriefs and sandals tended to make her look juvenile.

The parking attendant appeared startled when she approached him with Tick-Tock striding alongside.

"They'll never let you into the offices with that thing, miss," he informed her. "Why, it doesn't even have a collar!"

"Don't worry about it," Telzey told him aloofly.

She dropped a two-credit piece she'd taken from Halet's purse into his hand, and continued on towards the building entrance. The attendant squinted after her, trying unsuccessfully to dispel an odd impression that the big catlike animal with the girl was throwing a double shadow.

The Moderator's chief receptionist also had some doubts about TT, and possibly about the sunbriefs, though she seemed impressed when Telzey's identification tag informed her she was speaking to the daughter of Federation Councilwoman Jessamine Amberdon.

"You feel you can discuss this ... emergency ... only with the Moderator himself, Miss Amberdon?" she repeated.

"Exactly," Telzey said firmly. A buzzer sounded as she spoke. The receptionist excused herself and picked up an earphone. She listened a moment, said blandly, "Yes ... Of course ... Yes, I understand," replaced the earphone, and stood up, smiling at Telzey.

"Would you come with me, Miss Amberdon?" she said. "I think the Moderator will see you immediately ..."

Telzey followed her, chewing thoughtfully at her lip. This was easier than she'd expected — in fact, too easy! Halet's work? Probably. A few comments to the effect of "A highly imaginative child ... overexcitable," while Halet was arranging to have the Moderator's office authorize Tick-Tock's transfer to the Life Banks, along with the implication that Jessamine Amberdon would appreciate a discreet handling of any disturbance Telzey might create as a result.

It was the sort of notion that would appeal to Halet —

They passed through a series of elegantly equipped offices and hallways, Telzey grasping TT's neck-fur in lieu of a leash, their appearance creating a tactfully restrained wave of surprise among secretaries and clerks. And if somebody here and there was troubled by a fleeting, uncanny impression that not one large beast but two seemed to be trailing the Moderator's visitor down the aisles, no mention was made of what could have been only a momentary visual distortion. Finally, a pair of sliding doors opened ahead, and the receptionist ushered Telzey into a large, cool balcony garden on the shaded side of the great building. A tall, gray-haired man stood up from the desk at which he was working, and bowed to Telzey. The receptionist withdrew again.

"My pleasure, Miss Amberdon," Jontarou's Planetary Moderator said. "Be seated, please." He studied Tick-Tock with more than casual interest while Telzey was settling herself into a chair, added, "And what may I and my office do for you?"

Telzey hesitated. She'd observed his type on Orado in her mother's circle of acquaintances — a senior diplomat, a man not easy to impress. It was a safe bet that he'd had her brought out to his balcony office only to keep her occupied while Halet was quietly informed where the Amberdon problem child was and requested to come over and take charge.

What she had to tell him now would have sounded rather wild even if presented by a presumably responsible adult. She could provide proof, but until the Moderator was already nearly sold on her story, that would be a very unsafe thing to do. Old Iron Thoughts was backing her up, but if it didn't look as if her plans were likely to succeed, he would be willing to ride herd on his devil's pack just so long ...

Better start the ball rolling without any preliminaries, Telzey decided. The Moderator's picture of her must be that of a spoiled, neurotic brat in a stew about the threatened loss of a pet animal. He expected her to start arguing with him immediately about Tick-Tock.

She said, "Do you have a personal interest in keeping the Baluit crest cats from becoming extinct?"

Surprise flickered in his eyes for an instant. Then he smiled.

"I admit I do, Miss Amberdon," he said pleasantly. "I should like to see the species re-established. I count myself almost uniquely fortunate in having had the opportunity to bag two of the magnificent brutes before disease wiped them out on the planet."

The last seemed a less than fortunate statement just now. Telzey felt a sharp tingle of alarm, then sensed that in the minds which were drawing the meaning of the Moderator's speech from her mind there had been only a brief stir of interest.

She cleared her throat, said, "The point is that they weren't wiped out by disease."

He considered her quizzically, seemed to wonder what she was trying to lead up to. Telzey gathered her courage, plunged on, "Would you like to hear what did happen?"

"I should be much interested, Miss Amberdon," the Moderator said without change of expression. "But first, if you'll excuse me a moment ..."

There had been some signal from his desk which Telzey hadn't noticed, because he picked up a small communicator now, said, "Yes?" After a few seconds, he resumed, "That's rather curious, isn't it? ... Yes, I'd try that ... No, that shouldn't be necessary ... Yes, please do. Thank you." He replaced the communicator, his face very sober; then, his gaze flicking for an instant to TT, he drew one of the upper desk drawers open a few inches, and turned back to Telzey.

"Now, Miss Amberdon," he said affably, "you were about to say? About these crest cats ..."

Telzey swallowed. She hadn't heard the other side of the conversation, but she could guess what it had been about. His office had called the guest house, had been told by Halet's maid that Halet, the chauffeur, and Dr. Droon were out looking for Miss Telzey and her pet. The Moderator's office had then checked on the sportscar's communication number and attempted to call it. And, of course, there had been no response.

To the Moderator, considering what Halet would have told him, it must add up to the grim possibility that the young lunatic he was talking to had let her three-quarters-grown crest cat slaughter her aunt and the two men when they caught up with her! The office would be notifying the police now to conduct an immediate search for the missing aircar.

When it would occur to them to look for it on the Moderator's parking terrace was something Telzey couldn't know. But if Halet and Dr. Droon were released before the Moderator accepted her own version of what had occurred, and the two reported the presence of wild crest cats in Port Nichay, there would be almost no possibility of keeping the situation under control. Somebody was bound to make some idiotic move, and the fat would be in the fire ...

Two things might be in her favor. The Moderator seemed to have the sort of steady nerve one would expect in a man who had bagged two Baluit crest cats. The partly opened desk drawer beside him must have a gun in it; apparently he considered that a sufficient precaution against an attack by TT. He wasn't likely to react in a panicky manner. And the mere fact that he suspected Telzey of homicidal tendencies would make him give the closest attention to what she said. Whether he believed her then was another matter, of course.

Slightly encouraged, Telzey began to talk. It did sound like a thoroughly wild story, but the Moderator listened with an appearance of intent interest. When she had told him as much as she felt he could be expected to swallow for a start, he said musingly, "So they weren't wiped out — they went into hiding! Do I understand you to say they did it to avoid being hunted?"

Telzey chewed her lip frowningly before replying. "There's something about that part I don't quite get," she admitted. "Of course I don't quite get either why you'd want to go hunting ... twice ... for something that's just as likely to bag you instead!"

"Well, those are, ah, merely the statistical odds," the Moderator explained. "If one has enough confidence you see —"

"I don't really. But the crest cats seem to have felt the same way — at first. They were getting around one hunter for every cat that got shot. Humans were the most exciting game they'd ever run into.

"But then that ended, and the humans started knocking them out with stunguns from aircars where they couldn't be got at, and hauling them off while they were helpless. After it had gone on for a while, they decided to keep out of sight.

"But they're still around ... thousands and thousands of them! Another thing nobody's known about them is that they weren't only in the Baluit mountains. There were crest cats scattered all through the big forests along the other side of the continent."

"Very interesting," the Moderator commented. "Very interesting, indeed!" He glanced towards the communicator, then returned his gaze to Telzey, drumming his fingers lightly on the desk top.

She could tell nothing at all from his expression now, but she guessed he was thinking hard. There was supposed to be no native intelligent life in the legal sense on Jontarou, and she had been careful to say nothing so far to make the Baluit cats look like more than rather exceptionally intelligent animals. The next — rather large — question should be how she'd come by such information.

If the Moderator asked her that, Telzey thought, she could feel she'd made a beginning at getting him to buy the whole story.

"Well," he said abruptly, "if the crest cats are not extinct or threatened with extinction, the Life Banks obviously have no claim on your pet." He smiled confidingly at her. "And that's the reason you're here, isn't it?"

"Well, no," Telzey began, dismayed. "I —"

"Oh, it's quite all right, Miss Amberdon! I'll simply rescind the permit which was issued for the purpose. You need feel no further concern about that." He paused. "Now, just one question ... do you happen to know where your aunt is at present?"

Telzey had a dead, sinking feeling. So he hadn't believed a word she said. He'd been stalling her along until the aircar could be found.

She took a deep breath. "You'd better listen to the rest of it."

"Why, is there more?" the Moderator asked politely.

"Yes. The important part! The kind of creatures they are, they wouldn't go into hiding indefinitely just because someone was after them."

Was there a flicker of something beyond watchfulness in his expression? "What would they do, Miss Amberdon?" he asked quietly.

"If they couldn't get at the men in the aircars and couldn't com—municate with them" — the flicker again! — "they'd start looking for the place the men came from, wouldn't they? It might take them some years to work their way across the continent and locate us here in Port Nichay. But supposing they did it finally and a few thousand of them are sitting around in the parks down there right now? They could come up the side of these towers as easily as they go up the side of a mountain. And supposing they'd decided that the only way to handle the problem was to clean out the human beings in Port Nichay?"

The Moderator stared at her in silence a few seconds. "You're saying," he observed then, "that they're rational beings — above the Critical I.Q. level."

"Well," Telzey said, "legally they're rational. I checked on that. About as rational as we are, I suppose."

"Would you mind telling me now how you happen to know this?"

"They told me," Telzey said.

He was silent again, studying her face. "You mentioned, Miss Amberdon, that they have been unable to communicate with other human beings. This suggests then that you are a xenotelepath ..."

"I am?" Telzey hadn't heard the term before. "If it means that I can tell what the cats are thinking, and they can tell what I'm thinking, I guess that's the word for it." She considered him, decided she had him almost on the ropes, went on quickly.

"I looked up the laws, and told them they could conclude a treaty with the Federation which would establish them as an Affiliated Species ... and that would settle everything the way they would want it settled, without trouble. Some of them believed me. They decided to wait until I could talk to you. If it works out, fine! If it doesn't" — she felt her voice falter for an instant — "they're going to cut loose fast!"

The Moderator seemed undisturbed. "What am I supposed to do?"

"I told them you'd contact the Council of the Federation on Orado."

"Contact the Council?" he repeated coolly. "With no more proof of this story than your word, Miss Amberdon?"

Telzey felt a quick, angry stirring begin about her, felt her face whiten.

"All right," she said. "I'll give you proof! I'll have to now. But that'll be it. Once they've tipped their hand all the way, you'll have about thirty seconds left to make the right move. I hope you remember that!"

He cleared his throat. "I —"

"NOW!" Telzey said.

Along the walls of the balcony garden, beside the ornamental flower stands, against the edges of the rock pool, the crest cats appeared. Perhaps thirty of them. None quite as physically impressive as Iron Thoughts, who stood closest to the Moderator; but none very far from it. Motionless as rocks, frightening as gargoyles, they waited, eyes glowing with hellish excitement.

"This is *their* council, you see," Telzey heard herself saying.

The Moderator's face had also paled. But he was, after all, an old shikari and a senior diplomat. He took an unhurried look around the circle, said quietly, "Accept my profound apologies for doubting you, Miss Am—berdon!" and reached for the desk communicator.

Iron Thoughts swung his demon head in Telzey's direction. For an instant, she picked up the mental impression of a fierce yellow eye closing in an approving wink.

"... An open transmitter line to Orado," the Moderator was saying into the communicator. "The Council. And snap it up! Some very important visitors are waiting ..."

The offices of Jontarou's Planetary Moderator became an extremely busy and interesting area then. Quite two hours passed before it occurred to anyone to ask Telzey again whether she knew where her aunt was at present.

Telzey smote her forehead.

"Forgot all about that!" she admitted, fishing the sportscar's keys out of the pocket of her sunbriefs. "They're out on the parking platform ..."

The preliminary treaty arrangements between the Federation of the Hub and the new Affiliated Species of the Planet of Jontarou were formally ratified two weeks later, the ceremony taking place on Jontarou, in the Champagne Hall of the Shikaris' Club.

Telzey was able to follow the event only by news viewer in her ship-cabin, she and Halet being on the return trip to Orado by then. She wasn't too interested in the treaty's details — they conformed almost exactly to what she had read out to Iron Thoughts and his co-chiefs and companions in the park. It was the smooth bridging of the wide language gap between the contracting parties by a row of interpreting machines and a handful of human xenotelepaths which held her attention.

As she switched off the viewer, Halet came wandering in from the adjoining cabin.

"I was watching it, too!" Halet observed. She smiled. "I was hoping to see dear Tick-Tock."

Telzey looked over at her. "Well, TT would hardly be likely to show up in Port Nichay," she said. "She's having too good a time now finding out what life in the Baluit range is like."

"I suppose so," Halet agreed doubtfully, sitting down on a hassock. "But I'm glad she promised to get in touch with us again in a few years. I'll miss her."

Telzey regarded her aunt with a reflective frown. Halet meant it quite sincerely, of course; she had undergone a profound change of heart during the past two weeks. But Telzey wasn't without some doubts about the actual value of a change of heart brought on by telepathic means. The learning process the crest cats had started in her mind appeared to have continued automatically several days longer than her rugged teachers had really intended; and Telzey had reason to believe that by the end of that time she'd developed associated latent abilities of which the crest cats had never heard. She'd barely begun to get it all sorted out yet, but ... as an example ... she'd found it remarkably easy to turn Halet's more obnoxious attitudes virtually upside down. It had taken her a couple of days to get the hang of her aunt's personal symbolism, but after that there had been no problem.

She was reasonably certain she'd broken no laws so far, though the sections in the law library covering the use and abuse of psionic abilities were veiled in such intricate and downright obscuring phrasing — deliberately, Telzey suspected — that it was really difficult to say what they did mean. But even aside from that, there were a number of arguments in favor of exercising great caution.

Jessamine, for one thing, was bound to start worrying about her sister-in-law's health if Halet turned up on Orado in her present state of mind, even though it would make for a far more agreeable atmosphere in the Amberdon household.

"Halet," Telzey inquired mentally, "do you remember what an all-out stinker you used to be?"

"Of course, dear," Halet said aloud. "I can hardly wait to tell dear Jessamine how much I regret the many times I ..."

"Well," Telzey went on, still verbalizing it silently, "I think you'd really enjoy life more if you were, let's say, about halfway between your old nasty self and the sort of sickening-good kind you are now."

"Why, Telzey!" Halet cried out with dopey amiability. "What a delightful idea!"

"Let's try it," Telzey said.

There was silence in the cabin for some twenty minutes then while she went painstakingly about remolding a number of Halet's character traits for the second time. She still felt some misgiving about it; but if it became necessary, she probably could always restore the old Halet *in toto*.

These, she told herself, definitely were powers one should treat with respect! Better rattle through law school first; then, with that out of the way, she could start hunting around to see who in the Federation was qualified to instruct a genius-level novice in the proper handling of psionics ...

MERLE INSINGA '90

Balanced Ecology

The diamondwood tree farm was restless this morning. Ilf Cholm had been aware of it for about an hour but had said nothing to Auris, thinking he might be getting a summer fever or a stomach upset and imagining things and that Auris would decide they should go back to the house so Ilf's grandmother could dose him. But the feeling continued to grow, and by now Ilf knew it was the farm.

Outwardly, everyone in the forest appeared to be going about their usual business. There had been a rainfall earlier in the day; and the tumbleweeds had uprooted themselves and were moving about in the bushes, lapping water off the leaves. Ilf had noticed a small one rolling straight towards a waiting slurp and stopped for a moment to watch the slurp catch it. The slurp was of average size, which gave it a tongue-reach of between twelve and fourteen feet, and the tumbleweed was already within range.

The tongue shot out suddenly, a thin, yellow flash. Its tip flicked twice around the tumbleweed, jerked it off the ground and back to the feed opening in the imitation tree stump within which the rest of the slurp was concealed. The tumbleweed said "Oof!" in the surprised way they always did when something caught them, and went in through the opening. After a moment, the slurp's tongue tip appeared in the opening again and waved gently around, ready for somebody else of the right size to come within reach.

Ilf, just turned eleven and rather small for his age, was the right size for this slurp, though barely. But, being a human boy, he was in no danger. The slurps of the diamondwood farms on Wrake didn't attack humans. For a moment, he was tempted to tease the creature into a brief fencing match. If he picked up a stick and banged on the stump with it a few times, the slurp would become annoyed and dart its tongue out and try to knock the stick from his hand.

But it wasn't the day for entertainment of that kind. Ilf couldn't shake off his crawly, uncomfortable feeling, and while he had been standing there, Auris and Sam had moved a couple of hundred feet farther uphill, in the direction of the Queen Grove, and home. He turned and sprinted after them, caught up with them as they came out into one of the stretches of grassland which lay between the individual groves of diamondwood trees.

Auris, who was two years, two months, and two days older than Ilf, stood on top of Sam's semiglobular shell, looking off to the right towards the valley where the diamondwood factory was. Most of the world of Wrake was on the hot side, either rather dry or rather steamy; but this was cool mountain country. Far to the south, below the valley and the foothills behind it, lay the continental plain, shimmering like a flat, green-brown sea. To the north and east were higher plateaus, above the level where the diamondwood liked to grow. Ilf ran past Sam's steadily moving bulk to the point where the forward rim of the shell made a flat upward curve, close enough to the ground so he could reach it.

Sam rolled a somber brown eye back for an instant as Ilf caught the shell and swung up on it, but his huge beaked head didn't turn. He was a mossback, Wrake's version of the turtle pattern, and, except for the full-grown trees and perhaps some members of the clean-up squad, the biggest thing on the farm. His corrugated shell was overgrown with a plant which had the appearance of long green fur; and occasionally when Sam fed, he would extend and use a pair of heavy arms with three-fingered hands, normally held folded up against the lower rim of the shell.

Auris had paid no attention to Ilf's arrival. She still seemed to be watching the factory in the valley. She and Ilf were cousins but didn't resemble each other. Ilf was small and wiry, with tight-curled red hair. Auris was slim and blond, and stood a good head taller than he did. He thought she looked as if she owned everything she could see from the top of Sam's shell; and she did, as a matter of fact, own a good deal of it — nine tenths of the diamondwood farm and nine tenths of the factory. Ilf owned the remaining tenth of both.

He scrambled up the shell, grabbing the moss-fur to haul himself along, until he stood beside her. Sam, awkward as he looked when walking, was moving at a good ten miles an hour, clearly headed for the Queen Grove. Ilf didn't know whether it was Sam or Auris who had decided to go back to the house. Whichever it had been, he could feel the purpose of going there.

"They're nervous about something," he told Auris, meaning the whole farm. "Think there's a big storm coming?"

"Doesn't look like a storm," Auris said.

Ilf glanced about the sky, agreed silently. "Earthquake, maybe?"

Auris shook her head. "It doesn't feel like earthquake."

She hadn't turned her gaze from the factory. Ilf asked, "Something going on down there?"

Auris shrugged. "They're cutting a lot today," she said. "They got in a limit order."

Sam swayed on into the next grove while Ilf considered the information. Limit orders were fairly unusual; but it hardly explained the general uneasiness. He sighed, sat down, crossed his legs, and looked about. This was a grove of young trees, fifteen years and less. There was plenty of open space left between them. Ahead, a huge tumbleweed was dying, making happy, chuckling sounds as it pitched its scarlet seed pellets far out from its slowly unfolding leaves. The pellets rolled hurriedly farther away from the old weed as soon as they touched the ground. In a twelve-foot circle about their parent, the earth was being disturbed, churned, shifted steadily about. The clean-up squad had arrived to dispose of the dying tumbleweed; as Ilf looked, it suddenly settled six or seven inches deeper into the softened dirt. The pellets were hurrying to get beyond the reach of the clean-up squad so they wouldn't get hauled down, too. But half-grown tumbleweeds, speckled yellow-green and ready to start their rooted period, were rolling through the grove towards the disturbed area. They would wait around the edge of the circle until the clean-up squad finished, then move in and put down their roots. The ground where the squad had worked recently was always richer than any other spot in the forest.

Ilf wondered, as he had many times before, what the cleanup squad looked like. Nobody ever caught so much as a glimpse of them. Riquol Cholm, his grandfather, had told him of attempts made by scientists to catch a member of the squad with digging machines. Even the smallest ones could dig much faster than the machines could dig after them, so the scientists always gave up finally and went away.

"Ilf, come in for lunch!" called Ilf's grandmother's voice.

Ilf filled his lungs, shouted, "Coming, grand —"

He broke off, looked up at Auris. She was smirking.

"Caught me again," Ilf admitted. "Dumb humbugs!" He yelled, "Come out, Lying Lou! I know who it was."

Meldy Cholm laughed her low, sweet laugh, a silverbell called, and the giant greenweb of the Queen Grove sounded its deep harp note, more or less all together. Then Lying Lou and Gabby darted into sight, leaped up on the mossback's hump. The humbugs were small, brown, bobtailed animals, built with spider leanness and very quick. They had round skulls, monkey faces, and the pointed teeth of animals who lived by catching and killing other animals. Gabby sat down beside Ilf, inflating and deflating his voice pouch, while Lou burst into a series of rattling, clicking, spitting sounds.

"They've been down at the factory?" Ilf asked.

"Yes," Auris said. "Hush now. I'm listening."

Lou was jabbering along at the rate at which the humbugs chattered among themselves, but this sounded like, and was, a recording of human voices played back at high speed. When Auris wanted to know what people somewhere were talking about, she sent the humbugs off to listen. They remembered everything they heard, came back and repeated it to her at their own speed, which saved time. Ilf, if he tried hard, could understand scraps of it. Auris understood it all. She was hearing now what the people at the factory had been saying during the morning.

Gabby inflated his voice pouch part way, remarked in Grandfather Riquol's strong, rich voice, "My, my! We're not being quite on our best behavior today, are we, Ilf?"

"Shut up," said Ilf.

"Hush now," Gabby said in Auris' voice. "I'm listening." He added in Ilf's voice, sounding crestfallen, "Caught me again!" then chuckled nastily.

Ilf made a fist of his left hand and swung fast. Gabby became a momentary brown blur, and was sitting again on Ilf's other side. He looked at Ilf with round, innocent eyes, said in a solemn tone, "We must pay more attention to details, men. Mistakes can be expensive!"

He'd probably picked that up at the factory. Ilf ignored him. Trying to hit a humbug was a waste of effort. So was talking back to them. He shifted his attention to catching what Lou was saying; but Lou had finished up at that moment. She and Gabby took off instantly in a leap from Sam's back and were gone in the bushes. Ilf thought they were a little jittery and erratic in their motions today, as if they, too, were keyed up even more than usual. Auris walked down to the front lip of the shell and sat on it, dangling her legs. Ilf joined her there.

"What were they talking about at the factory?" he asked.

"They did get in a limit order yesterday," Auris said. "And another one this morning. They're not taking any more orders until they've filled those two."

"That's good, isn't it?" Ilf asked.

"I guess so."

After a moment, Ilf asked, "Is that what *they're* worrying about?"

"I don't know," Auris said. But she frowned.

Sam came lumbering up to another stretch of open ground, stopped while he was still well back among the trees. Auris slipped down from the shell, said, "Come on but don't let them see you," and moved ahead through the trees until she could look into the open. Ilf followed her as quietly as he could.

"What's the matter?" he inquired. A hundred and fifty yards away, on the other side of the open area, towered the Queen Grove, its tops dancing gently like armies of slender green spears against the blue sky. The house wasn't visible from here; it was a big one-story bungalow built around the trunks of a number of trees deep within the grove. Ahead of them lay the road which came up from the valley and wound on through the mountains to the west.

Auris said, "An aircar came down here a while ago... There it is!"

They looked at the aircar parked at the side of the road on their left, a little distance away. Opposite the car was an opening in the Queen Grove where a path led to the house. Ilf couldn't see anything very interesting about the car. It was neither new nor old, looked like any ordinary aircar. The man sitting inside it was nobody they knew.

"Somebody's here on a visit," Ilf said.

"Yes," Auris said. "Uncle Kugus has come back."

Ilf had to reflect an instant to remember who Uncle Kugus was. Then it came to his mind in a flash. It had been some while ago, a year or so. Uncle Kugus was a big, handsome man with thick, black eyebrows, who always smiled. He wasn't Ilf's uncle but Auris'; but he'd had presents for both of them when he arrived. He had told Ilf a great many jokes. He and Grandfather Riquol had argued on one occasion for almost two hours about something or other; Ilf couldn't remember now what it had been. Uncle Kugus had come and gone in a tiny, beautiful, bright yellow aircar, had taken Ilf for a couple of rides in it, and told him about winning races with it. Ilf hadn't had too bad an impression of him.

"That isn't him," he said, "and that isn't his car."

"I know. He's in the house," Auris said. "He's got a couple of people with him. They're talking with Riquol and Meldy."

A sound rose slowly from the Queen Grove as she spoke, deep and resonant, like the stroke of a big, old clock or the hum of a harp. The man in the aircar turned his head towards the grove to listen. The sound was repeated twice. It came from the giant greenweb at the far end of the grove and could be heard all over the farm, even, faintly, down in the valley when the wind was favorable. Ilf said, "Lying Lou and Gabby were up here?"

"Yes. They went down to the factory first, then up to the house."

"What are they talking about in the house?" Ilf inquired.

"Oh, a lot of things." Auris frowned again. "We'll go and find out, but we won't let them see us right away."

Something stirred beside Ilf. He looked down and saw Lying Lou and Gabby had joined them again. The humbugs peered for a moment at the man in the aircar, then flicked out into the open, on across the road, and into the Queen Grove, like small, flying shadows, almost impossible to keep in sight. The man in the aircar looked about in a puzzled way, apparently uncertain whether he'd seen something move or not.

"Come on," Auris said.

Ilf followed her back to Sam. Sam lifted his head and extended his neck. Auris swung herself upon the edge of the undershell beside the neck, crept on hands and knees into the hollow between the upper and lower shells. Ilf climbed in after her. The shell-cave was a familiar place. He'd scuttled in there many times when they'd been caught outdoors in one of the violent electric storms which came down through the mountains from the north or when the ground began to shudder in an earthquake's first rumbling. With the massive curved shell above him and the equally massive flat shell below, the angle formed by the cool, leathery wall which was the side of Sam's neck and the front of his shoulder seemed like the safest place in the world to be on such occasions.

The undershell tilted and swayed beneath Ilf now as the mossback started forward. He squirmed around and looked out through the opening between the shells. They moved out of the grove, headed towards the road at Sam's steady walking pace. Ilf couldn't see the aircar and wondered why Auris didn't want the man in the car to see them. He wriggled uncomfortably. It was a strange, uneasy-making morning in every way.

They crossed the road, went swishing through high grass with Sam's ponderous side-to-side sway like a big ship sailing over dry land, and came to the Queen Grove. Sam moved on into the green-tinted shade under the Queen Trees. The air grew cooler. Presently he turned to the right, and Ilf saw a flash of blue ahead. That was the great thicket of flower bushes, in the center of which was Sam's sleeping pit.

Sam pushed through the thicket, stopped when he reached the open space in the center to let Ilf and Auris climb out of the shell-cave. Sam then lowered his fore-legs, one after the other, into the pit, which was lined so solidly with tree roots that almost no earth showed between them, shaped like a mold to fit the lower half of his body, tilted forward, drawing neck and head back under his shell, slid slowly into the pit, straightened out, and settled down. The edge of his upper shell was now level with the edge of the pit, and what still could be seen of him looked simply like a big, moss-grown boulder. If nobody came to disturb him, he might stay there unmoving the rest of the year. There were mossbacks in other groves of the farm which had never come out of their sleeping pits or given any indication of being awake since Ilf could remember. They lived an enormous length of time and a nap of half a dozen years apparently meant nothing to them.

Ilf looked questioningly at Auris. She said, "We'll go up to the house and listen to what Uncle Kugus is talking about."

They turned into a path which led from Sam's place to the house. It had been made by six generations of human children, all of whom had used Sam for transportation about the diamondwood farm. He was half again as big as any other mossback around and the only one whose sleeping pit was in the Queen Grove. Everything about the Queen Grove was special, from the trees themselves, which were never cut and twice as thick and almost twice as tall as the trees of other groves, to Sam and his blue flower thicket, the huge stump of the Grandfather Slurp not far away, and the giant greenweb at the other end of the grove. It was quieter here; there were fewer of the other animals. The Queen Grove, from what Riquol Cholm had told Ilf, was the point from which the whole diamondwood forest had started a long time ago.

Auris said, "We'll go around and come in from the back. They don't have to know right away that we're here ..."

"Mr. Terokaw," said Riquol Cholm, "I'm sorry Kugus Ovin persuaded you and Mr. Bliman to accompany him to Wrake on this business. You've simply wasted your time. Kugus should have known better. I've discussed the situation quite thoroughly with him on other occasions."

"I'm afraid I don't follow you, Mr. Cholm," Mr. Terokaw said stiffly. "I'm making you a businesslike proposition in regard to this farm of diamondwood trees — a proposition which will be very much to your advantage as well as to that of the children whose property the Diamondwood is. Certainly you should at least be willing to listen to my terms!"

Riquol shook his head. It was clear that he was angry with Kugus but attempting to control his anger.

"Your terms, whatever they may be, are not a factor in this," he said. "The maintenance of a diamondwood forest is not entirely a business proposition. Let me explain that to you — as Kugus should have done.

"No doubt you're aware that there are less than forty such forests on the world of Wrake and that attempts to grow the trees elsewhere have been uniformly unsuccessful. That and the unique beauty of diamondwood products, which has never been duplicated by artificial means, is, of course, the reason that such products command a price which compares with that of precious stones and similar items."

Mr. Terokaw regarded Riquol with a bleak blue eye, nodded briefly. "Please continue, Mr. Cholm."

"A diamondwood forest," said Riquol, "is a great deal more than an assemblage of trees. The trees are a basic factor, but still only a factor, of a closely integrated, balanced natural ecology. The manner of independence of the plants and animals that make up a diamondwood forest is not clear in all details, but the interdependence is a very pronounced one. None of the involved species seem able to survive in any other environment. On the other hand, plants and animals not naturally a part of this ecology will not thrive if brought into it. They move out or vanish quickly. Human beings appear to be the only exception to that rule."

"Very interesting," Mr. Terokaw said dryly.

"It is," said Riquol. "It is a very interesting natural situation and many people, including Mrs. Cholm and myself, feel it should be preserved. The studied, limited cutting practiced on the diamondwood farms at present acts towards its preservation. That degree of harvesting actually is beneficial to the forests, keeps them moving through an optimum cycle of growth and maturity. They are flourishing under the hand of man to an extent which was not usually attained in their natural, untouched state. The people who are at present responsible for them — the farm owners and their associates — have been working for some time to have all diamondwood forests turned into Federation preserves, with the right to harvest them retained by the present owners and their heirs under the same carefully supervised conditions. When Auris and Ilf come of age and can sign an agreement to that effect, the farms will in fact become Federation preserves. All other steps to that end have been taken by now.

"That, Mr. Terokaw, is why we're not interested in your business proposition. You'll discover, if you wish to sound them out on it, that the other diamondwood farmers are not interested in it either. We are all of one mind in that matter. If we weren't, we would long since have accepted propositions essentially similar to yours."

There was silence for a moment. Then Kugus Ovin said pleasantly, "I know you're annoyed with me, Riquol, but I'm thinking of Auris and Ilf in this. Perhaps in your concern for the preservation of a natural phenomenon, you aren't sufficiently considering their interests."

Riquol looked at him, said, "When Auris reaches maturity, she'll be an extremely wealthy young woman, even if this farm never sells another cubic foot of diamondwood from this day on. Ilf would be sufficiently well-to-do to make it unnecessary for him ever to work a stroke in his life — though I doubt very much he would make such a choice."

Kugus smiled. "There are degrees even to the state of being extremely wealthy," he remarked. "What my niece can expect to gain in her lifetime from this careful harvesting you talk about can't begin to compare with what she would get at one stroke through Mr. Terokaw's offer. The same, of course, holds true of Ilf."

"Quite right," Mr. Terokaw said heavily. "I'm generous in my business dealings, Mr. Cholm. I have a reputation for it. And I can afford to be generous because I profit well from my investments. Let me bring another point to your attention. Interest in diamondwood products throughout the Federation waxes and wanes, as you must be aware. It rises and falls. There are fashions and fads. At present, we are approaching the crest of a new wave of interest in these products. This interest can be properly stimulated and exploited, but in any event we must expect it will have passed its peak in another few months. The next interest peak might develop six years from now, or twelve years from now. Or it might never develop since there are very few natural products which cannot eventually be duplicated and usually surpassed by artificial methods, and there is no good reason to assume that diamondwood will remain an exception indefinitely.

"We should be prepared, therefore, to make the fullest use of this bonanza while it lasts. I am prepared to do just that, Mr. Cholm. A cargo ship full of cutting equipment is at present stationed a few hours' flight from Wrake. This machinery can be landed and in operation here within a day after the contract I am offering you is signed. Within a week, the forest can be leveled. We shall make no use of your factory here, which would be entirely inadequate for my purpose. The diamondwood will be shipped at express speeds to another world where I have adequate processing facilities set up. And we can hit the Federation's main markets with the finished products the following month."

Riquol Cholm said, icily polite now, "And what would be the reason for all that haste, Mr. Terokaw?"

Mr. Terokaw looked surprised. "To insure that we have no competition, Mr. Cholm. What else? When the other diamondwood farmers here discover what has happened, they may be tempted to follow our example. But we'll be so far ahead of them that the diamondwood boom will be almost entirely to our exclusive advantage. We have taken every precaution to see to that. Mr. Bliman, Mr. Ovin and I arrived here in the utmost secrecy today. No one so much as suspects that we are on Wrake, much less what our purpose is. I make no mistakes in such matters, Mr. Cholm!"

He broke off and looked around as Meldy Cholm said in a troubled voice, "Come in, children. Sit down over there. We're discussing a matter which concerns you."

"Hello, Auris!" Kugus said heartily. "Hello, Ilf! Remember old Uncle Kugus?"

"Yes," Ilf said. He sat down on the bench by the wall beside Auris, feeling scared.

"Auris," Riquol Cholm said, "did you happen to overhear anything of what was being said before you came into the room?"

Auris nodded. "Yes." She glanced at Mr. Terokaw, looked at Riquol again. "He wants to cut down the forest."

"It's your forest and Ilf's, you know. Do you want him to do it?"

"Mr. Cholm, please!" Mr. Terokaw protested. "We must approach this properly. Kugus, show Mr. Cholm what I'm offering."

Riquol took the document Kugus held out to him, looked over it. After a moment, he gave it back to Kugus. "Auris," he said, "Mr. Terokaw, as he's indicated, is offering you more money than you would ever be able to spend in your life for the right to cut down your share of the forest. Now ... do you want him to do it?"

"No," Auris said.

Riquol glanced at Ilf, who shook his head. Riquol turned back to Mr. Terokaw.

"Well, Mr. Terokaw," he said, "there's your answer. My wife and I don't want you to do it, and Auris and Ilf don't want you to do it. Now ..."

"Oh, come now, Riquol!" Kugus said, smiling. "No one can expect either Auris or Ilf to really understand what's involved here. When they come of age —"

"When they come of age," Riquol said, "they'll again have the opportunity to decide what they wish to do." He made a gesture of distaste. "Gentlemen, let's conclude this discussion. Mr. Terokaw, we thank you for your offer, but it's been rejected."

Mr. Terokaw frowned, pursed his lips.

"Well, not so fast, Mr. Cholm," he said. "As I told you, I make no mistakes in business matters. You suggested a few minutes ago that I might contact the other diamondwood farmers on the planet on the subject but predicted that I would have no better luck with them."

"So I did," Riquol agreed. He looked puzzled.

"As a matter of fact," Mr. Terokaw went on, "I already have contacted a number of these people. Not in person, you understand, since I did not want to tip off certain possible competitors that I was interested in diamondwood at present. The offer was rejected, as you indicated it would be. In fact, I learned that the owners of the Wrake diamondwood farms are so involved in legally binding agreements with one another that it would be very difficult for them to accept such an offer even if they wished to do it."

Riquol nodded, smiled briefly. "We realized that the temptation to sell out to commercial interests who would not be willing to act in accordance with our accepted policies could be made very strong," he said. "So we've made it as nearly impossible as we could for any of us to yield to temptation."

"Well," Mr. Terokaw continued, "I am not a man who is easily put off. I ascertained that you and Mrs. Cholm are also bound by such an agreement to the other diamondwood owners of Wrake not to be the first to sell either the farm or its cutting rights to outside interests, or to exceed the established limits of cutting. But you are not the owners of this farm. These two children own it between them."

Riquol frowned. "What difference does that make?" he demanded. "Ilf is our grandson. Auris is related to us and our adopted daughter."

Mr. Terokaw rubbed his chin.

"Mr. Bliman," he said, "please explain to those people what the legal situation is."

Mr. Bliman cleared his throat. He was a tall, thin man with fierce dark eyes, like a bird of prey. "Mr. and Mrs. Cholm," he began, "I work for the Federation Government and am a specialist in adoptive procedures. I will make this short. Some months ago, Mr. Kugus Ovin filed the necessary papers to adopt his niece, Auris Luteel, citizen of Wrake. I conducted the investigation which is standard in such cases and can assure you that no official record exists that you have at any time gone through the steps of adopting Auris."

"What?" Riquol came half to his feet. Then he froze in position for a moment, settled slowly back in his chair. "What is this? Just what kind of trick are you trying to play?" he said. His face had gone white.

Ilf had lost sight of Mr. Terokaw for a few seconds, because Uncle Kugus had suddenly moved over in front of the bench on which he and Auris were sitting. But now he saw him again and he had a jolt of fright. There was a large blue and silver gun in Mr. Terokaw's hand, and the muzzle of it was pointed very steadily at Riquol Cholm.

"Mr. Cholm," Mr. Terokaw said, "before Mr. Bliman concludes his explanation, allow me to caution you! I do not wish to kill you. This gun, in fact, is not designed to kill. But if I pull the trigger, you will be in excruciating pain for some minutes. You are an elderly man and it is possible that you would not survive the experience. This would not inconvenience us very seriously. Therefore, stay seated and give up any thoughts of summoning help ... Kugus, watch the children. Mr. Bliman, let me speak to Mr. Het before you resume."

He put his left hand up to his face, and Ilf saw he was wearing a wrist-talker. "Het," Mr. Terokaw said to the talker without taking his eyes off

Riquol Cholm, "you are aware, I believe, that the children are with us in the house?"

The wrist-talker made murmuring sounds for a few seconds, then stopped.

"Yes," Mr. Terokaw said. "There should be no problem about it. But let me know if you see somebody approaching the area ..." He put his hand back down on the table. "Mr. Bliman, please continue."

Mr. Bliman cleared his throat again.

"Mr. Kugus Ovin," he said, "is now officially recorded as the parent by adoption of his niece, Auris Luteel. Since Auris has not yet reached the age where her formal consent to this action would be required, the matter is settled."

"Meaning," Mr. Terokaw added, "that Kugus can act for Auris in such affairs as selling the cutting rights on this tree farm. Mr. Cholm, if you are thinking of taking legal action against us, forget it. You may have had certain papers purporting to show that the girl was your adopted child filed away in the deposit vault of a bank. If so, those papers have been destroyed. With enough money, many things become possible. Neither you nor Mrs. Cholm nor the two children will do or say anything that might cause trouble to me. Since you have made no rash moves, Mr. Bliman will now use an instrument to put you and Mrs. Cholm painlessly to sleep for the few hours required to get you off this planet. Later, if you should be questioned in connection with this situation, you will say about it only what certain psychological experts will have impressed on you to say, and within a few months, nobody will be taking any further interest whatever in what is happening here today.

"Please do not think that I am a cruel man. I am not. I merely take what steps are required to carry out my purpose. Mr. Bliman, please proceed!"

Ilf felt a quiver of terror. Uncle Kugus was holding his wrist with one hand and Auris' wrist with the other, smiling reassuringly down at them. Ilf darted a glance over to Auris' face. She looked as white as his grandparents but she was making no attempt to squirm away from Kugus, so Ilf stayed quiet, too. Mr. Bliman stood up, looking more like a fierce bird of prey than ever, and stalked over to Riquol Cholm, holding something in his hand that looked unpleasantly like another gun. Ilf shut his eyes. There was a moment of silence, then Mr. Terokaw said, "Catch him before he falls out of the chair. Mrs. Cholm, if you will just settle back comfortably ..."

There was another moment of silence. Then, from beside him, Ilf heard Auris speak.

It wasn't regular speech but a quick burst of thin, rattling gabble, like human speech speeded up twenty times or so. It ended almost immediately.

"What's that? What's that?" Mr. Terokaw said, surprised.

Ilf's eyes flew open as something came in through the window with a whistling shriek. The two humbugs were in the room, brown blurs flicking here and there, screeching like demons. Mr Terokaw exclaimed something in a loud voice and jumped up from the chair, his gun swinging this way and that. Something scuttled up Mr. Bliman's back like a big spider, and he yelled and spun away from Meldy Cholm lying slumped back in her chair. Something ran up Uncle Kugus' back. He yelled, letting go of Ilf and Auris, and pulled out a gun of his own. "Wide aperture !" roared Mr. Terokaw, whose gun was making loud, thumping noises. A brown shadow swirled suddenly about his knees. Uncle Kugus cursed, took aim at the shadow, and fired.

"Stop that, you fool!" Mr. Terokaw shouted. "You nearly hit me."

"Come," whispered Auris, grabbing Ilf's arm. They sprang up from the bench and darted out the door behind Uncle Kugus' broad back.

"Het!" Mr. Terokaw's voice came bellowing down the hall behind them. "Up in the air and look out for those children! They're trying to get away. If you see them start to cross the road, knock 'em out. Kugus — after them! They may try to hide in the house."

Then he yowled angrily, and his gun began making the thumping noises again. The humbugs were too small to harm people, but their sharp little teeth could hurt and they seemed to be using them now.

"In here," Auris whispered, opening a door. Ilf ducked into the room with her, and she closed the door softly behind them. Ilf looked at her, his heart pounding wildly.

Auris nodded at the barred window. "Through there! Run and hide in the grove. I'll be right behind you ..."

"Auris! Ilf!" Uncle Kugus called in the hall. "Wait — don't be afraid. Where are you?" His voice still seemed to be smiling. Ilf heard his footsteps hurrying along the hall as he squirmed quickly sideways between two of the thick wooden bars over the window, dropped to the ground. He turned, darted off towards the nearest bushes. He heard Auris gabble something to the humbugs again, high and shrill, looked back as he reached the bushes and saw her already outside, running towards the shrubbery on his right. There was a shout from the window. Uncle Kugus was peering out from behind the bars, pointing a gun at Auris. He fired. Auris swerved to the side, was gone among the shrubs. Ilf didn't think she had been hit.

"They're outside!" Uncle Kugus yelled. He was too big to get through the bars himself.

Mr. Terokaw and Mr. Bliman were also shouting within the house. Uncle Kugus turned around, disappeared from the window.

"Auris!" Ilf called, his voice shaking with fright.

"Run and hide, Ilf!" Auris seemed to be on the far side of the shrubbery, deeper in the Queen Grove.

Ilf hesitated, started running along the path that led to Sam's sleeping pit, glancing up at the open patches of sky among the treetops. He didn't see the aircar with the man Het in it. Het would be circling around the Queen Grove now, waiting for the other men to chase them into sight so he could knock them out with something. But they could hide inside Sam's shell and Sam would get them across the road. "Auris, where are you?" Ilf cried.

Her voice came low and clear from behind him. "Run and hide, Ilf!"

Ilf looked back. Auris wasn't there but the two humbugs were loping up the path a dozen feet away. They darted past Ilf without stopping, disappeared around the turn ahead. He could hear the three men yelling for him and Auris to come back. They were outside, looking around for them now, and they seemed to be coming closer.

Ilf ran on, reached Sam's sleeping place. Sam lay there unmoving, like a great mossy boulder filling the pit. Ilf picked up a stone and pounded on the front part of the shell.

"Wake up!" he said desperately. "Sam, wake up!"

Sam didn't stir. And the men were getting closer. Ilf looked this way and that, trying to decide what to do.

"Don't let them see you," Auris called suddenly.

"That was the girl over there," Mr. Terokaw's voice shouted. "Go after her, Bliman!"

"Auris, watch out!" Ilf screamed, terrified.

"Aha! And here's the boy, Kugus. This way! Het," Mr. Terokaw yelled triumphantly, "come down and help us catch them! We've got them spotted ..."

Ilf dropped to hands and knees, crawled away quickly under the branches of the blue flower thicket, and waited, crouched low. He heard Mr. Terokaw crashing through the bushes towards him and Mr. Bliman braying, "Hurry up, Het! Hurry up!" Then he heard something else. It was the sound the giant greenweb sometimes made to trick a flock of silver-bells into fluttering straight towards it, a deep drone which suddenly seemed to be pouring down from the trees and rising up from the ground.

Ilf shook his head dizzily. The drone faded, grew up again. For a moment, he thought he heard his own voice call, "Auris, where are you?" from the other side of the blue flower thicket. Mr. Terokaw veered off in that direction, yelling something to Mr. Bliman and Kugus. Ilf backed farther away through the thicket, came out on the other side, climbed to his feet, and turned.

He stopped. For a stretch of twenty feet ahead of him, the forest floor was moving, shifting and churning with a slow, circular motion, turning lumps of deep brown mold over and over.

Mr. Terokaw came panting into Sam's sleeping place, red-faced, glaring about, the blue and silver gun in his hand. He shook his head to clear the resonance of the humming air from his brain. He saw a huge, moss-covered boulder tilted at a slant away from him but no sign of Ilf.

Then something shook the branches of the thicket behind the boulder. "Auris!" Ilf's frightened voice called.

Mr. Terokaw ran around the boulder, leveling the gun. The droning in the air suddenly swelled to a roar. Two big gray, three-fingered hands came out from the boulder on either side of Mr. Terokaw and picked him up.

"Awk!" he gasped, then dropped the gun as the hands folded him, once, twice, and lifted him towards Sam's descending head. Sam opened his large mouth, closed it, swallowed. His neck and head drew back under his shell and he settled slowly into the sleeping pit again.

The greenweb's roar ebbed and rose continuously now, like a thousand harps being struck together in a bewildering, quickening beat. Human voices danced and swirled through the din, crying, wailing, screeching. Ilf stood at the edge of the twenty-foot circle of churning earth outside the blue flower thicket, half stunned by it all. He heard Mr. Terokaw bellow to Mr. Bliman to go after Auris, and Mr. Bliman squalling to Het to hurry. He heard his own voice nearby call Auris frantically and then Mr. Terokaw's triumphant yell: "This way! Here's the boy, Kugus!"

Uncle Kugus bounded out of some bushes thirty feet away, eyes staring, mouth stretched in a wide grin. He saw Ilf, shouted excitedly, and ran towards him. Ilf watched, suddenly unable to move. Uncle Kugus took four long steps out over the shifting loam between them, sank ankle-deep, knee-deep. Then the brown earth leaped in cascades about him, and he went sliding straight down into it as if it were water, still grinning, and disappeared. In the distance, Mr. Terokaw roared, "This way!" and Mr. Bliman yelled to Het to hurry up. A loud, slapping sound came from the direction of the stump of the Grandfather Slurp. It was followed by a great commotion in the bushes around there; but that only lasted a moment. Then, a few seconds later, the greenweb's drone rose and thinned to the wild shriek it made when it had caught something big and faded slowly away ...

Ilf came walking shakily through the opening in the thickets to Sam's sleeping place. His head still seemed to hum inside with the greenweb's drone but the Queen Grove was quiet again; no voices called anywhere. Sam was settled into his pit. Ilf saw something gleam on the ground near the front end of the pit. He went over and looked at it, then at the big, moss-grown dome of Sam's shell.

"Oh, Sam," he whispered, "I'm not sure we should have done it ..."

Sam didn't stir. Ilf picked up Mr. Terokaw's blue and silver gun gingerly by the barrel and went off with it to look for Auris. He found her at the edge of the grove, watching Het's aircar on the other side of the road. The aircar was turned on its side and about a third of it was sunk in the ground. At work around and below it was the biggest member of the clean-up squad Ilf had ever seen in action.

They went up to the side of the road together and looked on while the aircar continued to shudder and turn and sink deeper into the earth. Ilf suddenly remembered the gun he was holding and threw it over on the ground next to the aircar. It was swallowed up instantly there. Tumbleweeds came rolling up to join them and clustered around the edge of the circle, waiting. With a final jerk, the aircar disappeared. The disturbed section of earth began to smooth over. The tumbleweeds moved out into it.

There was a soft whistling in the air, and from a Queen Tree at the edge of the grove a hundred and fifty feet away, a diamondwood seedling came lancing down, struck at a slant into the center of the circle where the aircar had vanished, stood trembling a moment, then straightened up. The tumbleweeds nearest it moved respectfully aside to give it room. The seedling shuddered and unfolded its first five-fingered cluster of silver-green leaves. Then it stood still.

Ilf looked over at Auris. "Auris," he said, "should we have done it?"

Auris was silent a moment.

"Nobody did anything," she said then. "They've just gone away again." She took Ilf's hand. "Let's go back to the house and wait for Riquol and Meldy to wake up."

The organism that was the diamondwood forest grew quiet again. The quiet spread back to its central mind unit in the Queen Grove, and the unit began to relax towards somnolence. A crisis had been passed — perhaps the last of the many it had foreseen when human beings first arrived on the world of Wrake.

The only defense against Man was Man. Understanding that, it had laid its plans. On a world now owned by Man, it adopted Man, brought him into its ecology, and its ecology into a new and again successful balance.

This had been a final flurry. A dangerous attack by dangerous humans. But the period of danger was nearly over, would soon be for good a thing of the past.

It had planned well, the central mind unit told itself drowsily. But now, since there was no further need to think today, it would stop thinking …

Sam the mossback fell gratefully asleep.

The Custodians

McNulty was a Rilf. He could pass for human if one didn't see him undressed; but much of the human appearance of the broad, waxy-pale face and big hands was the result of skillful surgery. Since the Rilf surgeons had only a vague notion of what humans considered good looks, the face wasn't pleasant, but it would do for business purposes. The other Rilf characteristic McNulty was obliged to disguise carefully was his odor — almost as disagreeable to human nostrils as the smell of humans was to him. Twice a day, therefore, he anointed himself with an effective deodorant. The human smells he put up with stoically.

Probably no sort of measures could have made him really attractive to humans. There was nothing too obviously wrong about his motions, but they weren't quite right either. He had an excellent command of English and spoke four other human languages well enough to make himself understood, but always with an underlying watery gurgle which brought something like a giant bullfrog to mind. To some people McNulty was alarming; to others he was repulsive. Not that he cared very much about such reactions. The humans with whom he dealt professionally were not significantly influenced by them.

To Jake Hiskey, for example, captain and owner of the spaceship *Prideful Sue*, McNulty looked, sounded, and smelled like a million dollars. Which was approximately what he would be worth, if Hiskey managed things carefully for the next few days. Hence the skipper was smiling bemusedly as he poked the door buzzer of McNulty's cabin.

"Who is it?" the door speaker inquired in McNulty's sloppy voice.

"Jake. I've got news — good news!"

The lock snicked and the door swung open for Hiskey. As he stepped through, he saw another door at the far end of the cabin close abruptly. Beyond it were the living quarters of the other Rilf currently on the *Prideful Sue*, who went by the name of Barnes and whose olfactory sense was more seriously affronted by humans than McNulty's. Barnes might be second in command of McNulty's tribe of Rilf mercenaries, or possibly a female and McNulty's mate. Assuming that McNulty was male, which was by no means certain. Rilfs gave out very little information about themselves, and almost all that was known of their species was that it had a dilly of a natural weapon and a strong interest in acquiring human currency with which to purchase advanced products of human technology. Hence the weapon was hired out on a temporary basis to human groups who knew about it and could afford it.

"You will excuse Barnes," McNulty said, looking over at Hiskey from a table where he sat before a tapeviewer. "He is indisposed."

"Of course," said Hiskey. He added curiously, "What are you studying up on now?" McNulty and Barnes never missed an opportunity to gather information pertinent to their profession.

"Recent Earthplanet history," replied McNulty. "The past three years. I must say the overall situation looks most favorable!"

Hiskey grinned. "It sure does! For us ..."

McNulty shut off the tapeviewer. "During the past two ship days," he remarked, "I have recorded news reports of forty-two of these so-called miniwars on the planet. Several others evidently are impending. Is that normal?"

"Actually it sounds like a fairly quiet period," Hiskey said. "But we might liven it up!" He pulled out a chair, sat down. "Of course I haven't been near Earthsystem for around eight years, and I haven't paid too much attention to what's been going on here. But on the planet it's obviously the same old stuff. It's been almost a century since the world government fizzled out; and the city states, the rural territories, the sea cities, the domes, the subterranes and what-not have been batting each other around ever since. They'll go on doing it for quite a while. Don't worry about that."

"I am not worrying," McNulty said. "The employment possibilities here appear almost unlimited, as you assured us they would be. What is this good news of which you spoke, Jake? Have your Earth contacts found a method of getting us down on the planet without further delay?"

"No," said Hiskey. "It will be at least five days before they have everything arranged. They're playing this very quietly. We don't want to alert anybody before you and your boys are set up and ready to go into action."

McNulty nodded. "I understand."

"Now here's what's happened," Hiskey went on. "This station we've stopped at is a branch of Space U. The navigator shuttled over to it half an hour ago to find out where he can get in touch with his sister. She's connected with Space U — a student, I suppose — and, of course, he hasn't seen her for the past eight years."

"She is what is known as a graduate student," said McNulty, who disliked vagueness. "Her name is Elisabeth and she is three Earth years younger than Gage. I heard him discuss the matter with you yesterday, and he mentioned those things specifically."

"I guess he did, at that," said Hiskey. "Anyway, he was told on the Space U station that she's a guest on a private asteroid at present, and he contacted her there by transmitter. The asteroid people offered to pick him up so he could spend a few days with his sister as their guest. Gage called me and I told him to say we'd deliver him to the asteroid's lock in the *Prideful Sue,* since we've got time to kill before we can get scheduled through the System check stations anyway. So that's been arranged. And when we get there, I'll see to it that I'm invited down to the asteroid with Gage."

"That is the good news?" McNulty asked blankly.

Hiskey grinned. "There's a little more to it than that. Did your tapes tell you anything about Earthsystem's asteroid estates?"

"Yes. They were mentioned briefly twice," McNulty said. "I gathered their inhabitants retain only tenuous connections with the planetary culture and do not engage in belligerent projects. I concluded that they were of no interest to us."

"Well, start getting interested," Hiskey told him. "Each of those asteroids is a little world to itself. They're completely independent of both Earthplanet and Earthsystem. They got an arrangement with Earthsystem which guarantees their independent status as long as they meet certain conditions. From what Gage's sister told him, the asteroid she's on is a kind of deluxe spacegoing ranch. It belongs to a Professor Alston ... a handful of people, some fancy livestock, plenty of supplies."

"And what business could we have with such people?" inquired McNulty.

"I think they'll be useful. I told you the one thing that might bug our plans right now is to have the System Police get too curious about the *Prideful Sue* while we're hanging around here for the next five or six days."

"So you did," said McNulty. "And I now have a question about that. According to these tapes, Earthsystem has no jurisdiction over Earthplanet. Why then should the System Police attempt to control or investigate what Earth imports?"

Hiskey shrugged. "For my money they're busybodies. The SP got kicked off Earth for good something like forty years ago, but it still acts like it's responsible for what happens there. And it's got muscle enough to control the space of the system. Earth doesn't like that but can't do much about it. If the System Police got an idea of why we're bringing in a shipload of Rilfs to Earth, they'd never let us go down. As long as we do nothing to make them suspicious, they probably won't bother us — but we can't really count on it. However, if we move the *Prideful Sue* down beneath the force fields around Professor Alston's asteroid, she'll be out of sight and out of the SP's jurisdiction. By Earthsystem's own ruling, they *can't* bother us even if they have reason to think we're there."

"You believe Professor Alston will permit you to land the ship?"

"No, I doubt he'd extend his hospitality that far. But it'll be difficult for him to avoid inviting me down for an hour or so, as Harold Gage's captain. When I mention we have a very interesting alien on board — first representative of his kind to reach Earthsystem, who has an intellectual curiosity about the human private asteroids — he'll invite *you* down. Half the crew can crowd into the skiff with you then and stay hidden in it till we want them."

McNulty gurgled interestedly. "You mentioned a handful of people —"

"From all I've heard, there'd be at most fifty even on a really big estate. Probably no more than half that. They don't like to be crowded on the asteroids — one reason most of them got off Earth to start with was that they wanted privacy and one place they could still buy it, if they had money enough, was in space."

"There should be then," said McNulty, "a most efficient and compact system of controls."

"You get the idea, McNulty. Those asteroids are set up like ships. That's what they've been turned into — big ships. Mostly they coast on solar orbit, but they can maneuver to some extent on their own."

"Then, as on a ship," McNulty continued, "the main controls will be concentrated for maximum efficiency within a limited area. It should take us at most an hour or two to gain a practical understanding of their use and operation."

"Might take you less than that," said Hiskey. Perhaps because of a congenital deficiency in inventive imagination, Rilf technology was at a primitive level as compared with the human one. But there was nothing wrong with their ability to learn, and McNulty, like most of them, was intensely interested in human gadgetry and very quick to grasp its function and principles. There wasn't much about the *Prideful Sue's* working innards he didn't know by now. "We needn't make any final decisions before you and I have checked the situation," Hiskey pointed out. "But it should be a cinch. We take over the control section, block the communication system, and we have the asteroid."

"That part of it may well be easy," McNulty agreed. "However, I would expect serious problems to follow."

"What kind of problems?"

"These asteroid people obviously do not isolate themselves completely from Earthsystem. They converse by transmitter. They receive guests. If these activities suddenly stop and no response is obtained from the asteroid, the System Police certainly should grow suspicious. With or without jurisdiction, they will investigate."

Hiskey shook his head. "No, they won't, McNulty. That's what makes this easy for us."

"Please explain," said McNulty.

"A private asteroid — any private asteroid — is expected to go out of communication from time to time. They're one of Solar U's science projects. They seal their force field locks, shut off their transmitters; and when they open up again is entirely up to them. I've heard some have stayed incommunicado for up to ten years, and the minimum shutoff period's supposed to be not less than one month out of every year. What they're out to prove I don't know. But nobody's going to be upset if they discover suddenly that they're not able to get through to Professor Alston and his asteroid. They'll just settle back to wait until he's open to contact again."

McNulty reflected for a considerable time. "That does indeed sound like a favorable situation," he stated abruptly then. "Excuse us, Jake." He went on, without shifting his eyes from Hiskey's face, in the Rilf speech which sounded more like heavy sloshings of water than anything else. When he paused, Barnes's voice responded in kind from a wall speaker. The exchange continued for a minute or two. Then McNulty nodded ponderously at Hiskey.

"Barnes agrees that your plan is an excellent one, Jake. The elimination of the humans now in possession of the asteroid should present no great difficulty."

Hiskey looked startled. "I hadn't planned on killing them unless they try to give us a fight."

"Oh, but killing them is quite necessary," McNulty said.

"Why? We'll need the place only a few days."

"Jake, consider! On the ship which has trailed yours to Earthsystem and is now stationed outside it beyond the patrol range of the System Police are fifty-five Rilfs and their equipment — our army. Four of them have been humanized in appearance as Barnes and I are. The others are obviously not human. The System Police must not be permitted to encounter them."

"Of course not," Hiskey agreed. "But if we're prepared to whisk them down to Earth as soon as they move into the system, the SP isn't going to have time to encounter them."

"I understand," McNulty said. "However, your plan gives us the opportunity to cover ourselves against any deceit or treachery which might be considered by our Earth employers. With perhaps a third of our army left waiting in space, prepared to act, nobody will attempt to renege on contracted payments. And where could a better concealed base be found for our reserve and their ship than such an asteroid, only a few hours from Earth? And we can't afford to have prisoners on that base who would have to be constantly and closely guarded to make sure they cause no trouble. There is too much at stake."

Hiskey said slowly, "Yeah. I guess I see your point."

"Nor," continued McNulty, "can we destroy some and spare others. A single surviving witness might become most inconvenient eventually. Therefore, we must also kill Gage's sister. Since Gage will make a great deal of money as a participant in our operation, he may not object too strongly to that."

Hiskey stared at him for a moment.

"Some things you just don't get, McNulty," he remarked. "Harold Gage is going to object like hell to having his sister killed!"

"He will? Well, I must accept your opinion on the point," said McNulty. "It follows then —"

"I know. We'd have had to get rid of Gage anyway. He wouldn't go along with taking over the asteroid even if his sister weren't there and it wasn't a killing job. We were friends once, but he's been giving me a lot of trouble like that. Now we're in Earthsystem, we don't need a navigator. He goes with the asteroid people."

"That will not cause trouble among your men?"

Hiskey shook his head. "He hasn't had a friend on board for the past two years. We needed him, that's all. If he's eliminated, everybody gets that much better a split. There'll be no trouble."

"I'd gained the impression," McNulty observed, "that he was a rather dangerous person."

"He's a bad boy to go up against with a gun," Hiskey said. "But he won't be wearing guns on a friendly visit to a private asteroid, will he? No, you needn't worry about Gage."

McNulty said he was glad to hear it. He added, "There is, incidentally, an additional advantage to disposing of the asteroid humans. Before I demonstrate the toziens to our prospective employers, they should be exercised. At present, after their long idleness on shipboard, they have become sluggish."

Hiskey grimaced. "I thought those things were always ready to go. "

"No. Permit me." McNulty reached into the front of his coat, paused with his hand just out of sight, made an abrupt shrugging motion. For an instant there was a glassy glittering in the opening of the coat. Then it was gone, and something moved with a hard droning sound along the walls of the cabin behind Hiskey. He sat very still, not breathing, feeling blood drain slowly from his face.

"Do not be disturbed, Jake," said McNulty. "The drug I give you and your crew makes you as immune as a Rilf to the toziens' killing reaction." He lifted his hand. "Ah, now! It becomes conditioned. It adjusts! We no longer hear it."

The drone was thinning to a whisper; and as McNulty stopped speaking, there was a sudden complete silence. But the unseen thing still moved about the cabin. Hiskey felt abrupt brief stirrings of air to right and left of his face, as if the tozien were inspecting him; and in spite of McNulty's assurance he sat frozen and rigid.

"Well, enough of this," McNulty said. Hiskey didn't know what means the Rilf had of summoning the tozien back to him, but for a moment he saw it motionless on the front of McNulty's coat, a clinging glassy patch about the size of a man's hand. Then it disappeared beneath the coat and McNulty closed the coat, and Hiskey breathed again.

"That illustrates my point," McNulty told him. "The tozien remained audible while I might have counted to twenty, slowly. They are all like that now."

Hiskey wiped his forehead. "If they adjust in a few seconds, I can't see it makes much practical difference."

McNulty shook his head reprovingly.

"Those few seconds might give someone time to be warned, find shelter, and escape, Jake! In a tozien attack there should be no escape for foreign life which is not already behind thick walls or enclosed in strong armor. That is the beauty of it! On my last contract I was in a crowd of alert armed men when I released my toziens. In an instant the air was fun of a thousand invisible silent knives, striking simultaneously. Some of the humans gasped as they died, but there were no screams. A clean piece of work! That is how it must be when we demonstrate the toziens to our Earth employers. And since I will be the demonstrator, I shall blood my swarm on the asteroid, on its humans and their livestock, and then they will be ready again."

"Well, that part of it is your business," Hiskey said, rather shakily.

Along the perennial solar orbit it shared with Earthplanet, the Alston asteroid soared serenely through space. Earth was never visible from the asteroid because the sun remained between them. The asteroid's inhabitants had no regrets about that; they were satisfied with what they could see, as they might be. The surface of what had been a ragged chunk of metal and mineral had been tamed into an unobtrusively cultivated great garden. The outer atmosphere was only two hundred yards thick, held in by a shell of multiple force fields; but looking up, one would have found it difficult to say how it differed from the day and night skies of Earth. Breezes blew and clouds drifted; and a rainfall could be had on order. And if clouds, breezes, sky blueness, and rainfall weren't entirely natural phenomena, who cared? Or, at least, cared very much ...

It had cost a great deal of money initially to bring the asteroid over from the Belt and install the machines which transformed its surface into a facsimile section of Earth, planted Earth gravity at its core, set it on Earth's orbit and gave it measured momentum and a twenty-four-hour spin. It cost considerably more money to bring in soil, selected plants, selected animals, along with all the other appurtenances of enclosed but very comfortable and purposeful human habitation and activity. But once everything had been set up, it cost nothing to keep the asteroid going. It was self-powered, very nearly self-maintaining and self-sustaining. A variety of botanical projects initiated by Professor Derek Alston, its present owner, incidentally produced crops of spices disposed of in Earthsystem, which more than covered current expenses.

On this morning Derek Alston sat cross-legged by the side of a miniature lake, listening to and sometimes taking part in the conversation between his wife Sally and Sally's friend, Elisabeth Gage. Sally was a slightly tousled bronze blonde and Elisabeth had straight long jet-black hair sweeping about her shoulders, but Derek kept noticing points of resemblance between the two, in structure, motions, and mannerisms, almost as if they had been rather closely related, say first cousins. Though they were, Derek thought, in fact simply two excellent examples of the type of tall comely young women Earthsystem seemed to produce in increasing numbers each year. They had been fellow students at Solar U before Sally's marriage a little less than a year ago now, and, until Elisabeth arrived yesterday at the asteroid, they hadn't met in person since then. From what Sally had told him, Derek already knew a good deal about Elisabeth before he saw her.

The talk, naturally, mainly was about Elisabeth's brother who should reach the asteroid in another hour or so. There was, Derek knew, in what was being said and in what was not being said between these two, a trace of awkwardness and uncertainty. Essentially, of course, it was an occasion for festivities and rejoicing. Elisabeth was happy. There was no question about that. Her face was filled with her reflections ... dreamy dazed smiles, cheeks glowing, eyes brimming briefly now and then. Her brother was the only surviving member of her family, and they'd been very close throughout her childhood. And now there'd been eight years of separation, and she hadn't known until Harold called that he'd come back to Earthsystem, or was even planning to come back. She'd had no reason to expect him. So she was happy, melting in happiness in fact. And Sally shared sympathetically in her friend's feelings.

But there was the other side to this matter. It wasn't to be mentioned now, but it couldn't be dismissed either ...

"His voice hasn't changed at all —" Elizabeth had just said. There was a tiny silence then, because she had touched, inadvertently, the other side of the matter, and it seemed to Derek the right moment to speak.

"Only twenty-eight years old," he remarked. "Your brother's very young to have put eight years of outsystem travel behind him."

Elisabeth looked at him a moment and smiled. "Yes, I suppose he is," she said. "He was just twenty when he was graduated from navigation school at the SP Academy. Dad was with the SP in Mars Underground, and I know he thought Harold would stay with the force. But after Dad died, Earthsystem looked too tame to Harold. He wanted real adventure and he wanted to make his fortune. Captain Hiskey was putting together his crew just then, and Harold signed as navigator. The pay wasn't much, but the crew was to share in ship's profits." She gave a small shrug. "I'm afraid Harold hasn't made his fortune yet, but he's certainly had adventures. Even from the little he's told me, I know the ship often must have been doing very risky work."

"What were Captain Hiskey's qualifications for that kind of work — for outsystem commerce generally?" Derek asked.

Elisabeth's eyes flickered. "Harold said Hiskey had been first officer on a big transsolar transport. Then he got money enough to buy his own ship." She hesitated. "I guess they've tried about anything they could. But they never had a good enough streak of luck to do much better than break even ... or else they'd get good luck mixed up with bad. Perhaps Harold will stay in Earthsystem now. But I have a feeling he won't. He was always very stubborn when he set himself a goal."

"You heard from him regularly?"

"No, not regularly. Not very often either. I've had seven message-packs from him in eight years. Somebody would get back to Earthsystem and drop the pack off at Mars Underground or Solar U, and I'd receive it that way. The last one was just six months ago. It didn't say a word about the ship coming back. That's why I can still hardly believe Harold's here."

The eyes had begun to brim again. Sally said quickly, "Perhaps he wasn't sure he'd be coming back and didn't want to build up your hopes."

Elisabeth nodded. "I suppose that was it. And ..."

Derek drew back mentally from what she was saying. An independent outsystem trader — not a very large ship, from what Elisabeth had told them. A crew working mainly on a gamble, willing to try anything, each man out to make his fortune, hit the big money by some means. At least some of the men on Captain Hiskey's ship had pursued that objective for eight years without getting there.

Man played it dirty and rough on Earth, held back only by a few general rules which none dared break. In the outsystems the same games were played, as extensions of those on Earth, perhaps somewhat dirtier and rougher, with no enforceable rules of any kind. Drop an adventurous, eager twenty-year-old into that kind of thing after the quiet order of Mars Underground, the disciplines of the SP Academy ... well, it might shape the twenty-year-old in one way or another, but shape him it would, thoroughly and fast, if he was to survive. Eight years should have worked quite a few changes in Harold Gage. The changes needn't have been evident in the message-packs Elisabeth had received. But she was intelligent, and she knew in general what the outsystems were like. And so, unwillingly, she was apprehensive of what she would find in her brother.

It bothered Derek because he liked Elisabeth and thought that whatever her expectations were, she might still be in for a shock. He checked his watch, got to his feet, smiled at his wife and guest, and excused himself. A few minutes later, seated at a transmitter, he dialed a number.

"Lieutenant Pierce," a voice said. "Who is calling?"

"This is Derek Alston, Mike."

"And what can the System Police do for Professor Alston today?" asked Michael Pierce.

"Do you have anything on an outsystem tramp trader called *Prideful Sue*? Captain-owner's name is Hiskey. He might have checked in a day or two ago."

"Hold on," Pierce told him.

Perhaps a minute passed before his voice resumed. "There's a ship by that name and of that description in the territory, Derek. She's Earthplanet registry. Last SP check was ten years ago. No record of present owners. First reported as having arrived from transsolar three days ago. We have a mild interest in the ship because the captain evidently has no intention of checking in or going through Customs. Of course, an SP check isn't compulsory if his business is only and directly with Earthplanet and if we have no reason to suspect Class A contraband. However, he keeps shifting about the system as if he preferred to keep out of our way. Do you feel we should give him more attention?"

"I have no definite reason to think so," Derek said. "But possibly you should."

A number of things were disturbing Harold Gage. One of them was that Jake Hiskey had invited himself down on the asteroid with him. Jake had made no mention of such plans until the *Prideful Sue* eased in to a stop on the coordinates given them in the Alston asteroid's gravity field and went on space anchor. Then Harold came forward to the comm room; and there was Jake, freshly shaved and in dress uniform, talking to the Alstons on viz screen. The matter was already settled. How Jake wangled the invitation Harold didn't know, but he was downright charming when he wanted to be; and undoubtedly he'd made the Alstons feel it would be impossibly rude not to include him in the party. Jake switched off the screen, looked at Harold's face, and grinned.

"Hell, Harold," he said. "You're not begrudging an old friend a few hours' look at sheer luxury, are you?"

"No," Harold said. "But in this case I felt I was already imposing on Elisabeth's friends."

"Ah — don't be so sensitive. They invited you, didn't they? And Professor Alston and that sweet-looking wife of his will get a boot out of me. These millionaire hermits must get mighty bored on their pretty-pretty asteroids where nothing ever happens. We're transsolar spacers, man! We've been places and done things it would curl their hair to think about. We're romantic!" He clapped Harold on the shoulder. "Come on! They told me your sister's waiting at the lock. Hey, this is one place we don't have to wear guns when we stick our noses outside — seems odd, doesn't it?"

And then they were down; and there, first of all, was Elisabeth — not a girl any more but, startlingly, a beautiful woman. Harold wasn't even sure he would have recognized her if she hadn't run towards him, laughing and crying a little, as he stepped out of the skiff, and clung to him for long seconds. And there were the Alstons, pleasant people who immediately took Jake in hand and smoothly dissociated him and themselves from the Gages, so that in only minutes Harold and Elisabeth were wandering about alone in this sunlit, rather dreamlike garden of an asteroid.

He'd been afraid there'd be an awkwardness between them, but none developed. Elisabeth was a completely honest person, of the kind whose expression hides nothing because there is rarely anything in their minds they want to hide. She studied him frankly and gravely, his eyes, his mouth, his motions, listened to his voice and its inflections, her face telling him meanwhile that she realized he'd changed and something of the manner in which he'd changed, and that she was accepting it, perhaps with regret but without judgment and with no loss of affection. He knew, too, that this was a matter it wouldn't be necessary to talk about, now or later ... later meaning after the business on Earthplanet was concluded. What was left then was that he always would have to be a little careful of what he said to her, careful not to reveal too much. Because what Elisabeth didn't know, couldn't possibly know, was just how extensive the change had been.

He told himself it couldn't have been helped. In the outsystems it could hardly have worked out otherwise. For a while they'd remained fairly selective about what they did with the *Prideful Sue*. If a job looked too raw, they didn't touch it. But they weren't making money, or not enough, and the raw jobs began to look less unacceptable. Then some of the crew dropped out, and some got killed, and the replacements were outsystem boys with outsystem ideas. On occasion they'd come close to straight raiding then; and if it had been up to Jake Hiskey alone, what difference was left finally mightn't have mattered enough to count. But a first-class navigator was the most valuable man on the ship in the outsystems; and Harold was a first-class navigator by then. If he hadn't been one, he still would have been the most valuable man on the *Prideful Sue*; Hiskey had come to depend on him more and more. So he could put a stop to an operation if it looked too bad, and from time to time he did. It didn't get him liked on board; but, as it happened, he'd also developed a first-class gun hand. If necessary the hand might get a little more blood on it, and Navigator Gage would get his way.

This last move now, the big one, the one which was to make the whole past eight years pay off extremely well, importing McNulty's mercenaries and their devastating weapon, the Rilf toziens, to Earthplanet — he'd thought about it long and hard and had been at the point of backing out more than once. Hiskey, whose idea it had been, argued that it was a perfectly legitimate enterprise. It was, without question. Earthplanet's criterion of permissible weaponry was the guaranteed limitation of effect. A tozien strike had an active period of less than two days, a target radius of less than twenty miles. It fell well within the allowable range.

And it would have the value of a completely unexpected innovation. Earthplanet hadn't yet heard of the Rilfs. Hiskey had contacts who knew how to handle this kind of thing to best advantage all around. Everyone involved would share in the cut, and the cut was going to be a very large one. Of course, after the first dozen miniwars came to an abrupt end, that part of it would be over. McNulty would be in general demand and could get along without middlemen. There'd be no further payoffs to the crew of the *Prideful Sue*. But down to the last man on board, they'd be more than wealthy enough to retire.

It was, Jake Hiskey pointed out, no more of a dirty business, if one wanted to call it that, than other operations they'd carried out. The Earth gangs periodically slaughtered one another, and there was very little to

choose between them. What great difference did it make to hand some of
them a new weapon?

It wasn't much of an argument, but what decided Harold was that this
was Jake Hiskey's last chance and that Jake knew it and was desperate. He
was fifteen years older than Harold and looked a decade older than that.
The outsystems had leached his nerve from him at last. If Harold pulled
out, Hiskey wouldn't be able to handle the deal with the Rilfs, wouldn't be
able to work a troop of them back to Earthsystem. He was no longer
capable of it. And when one had flown and fought a ship for eight years
with a man, had backed him and been backed by him in tight spots enough
to do for a lifetime, it was difficult to turn away from him when he was
finished. So all right, Harold had thought finally, one more play, dirty as it
might be. Then he and Jake could split. There was nothing really left of
their friendship; that had eroded along the line. If the SP didn't manage to
block them, they'd get the Rilfs to Earth. Afterwards they couldn't be
touched by Earthsystem, even if it became known what role they'd played.
They'd have done nothing illegal.

And he could hope the role they'd played wouldn't become known.
He'd told Elisabeth the *Prideful Sue* had returned to Earthsystem on very
big and very hush-hush business, something he wasn't free to talk about,
and that if the deal was concluded successfully he might be taking a long
vacation from spacefaring. She seemed delighted with that and didn't ask
for details, and Harold inquired what she'd been doing these eight years,
because none of the message-packs she'd sent ever had caught up with
him, and soon Elisabeth was talking and laughing freely and easily. For a
short while, the past years seemed almost to fade, as if they were strolling
about a park in Mars Underground rather than on this fabulous garden
asteroid where handsome horned beasts stepped out now and then from
among the trees to gaze placidly at them as they went by ...

"Mr. Gage! Elisabeth!"

He stopped, blinking. It was like an optical illusion. There was a steep
smooth cliff of rock to the left of the path they were following; and in it,
suddenly, an opening had appeared, a doorway, and Sally Alston had
stepped out of it and was coming towards them, smiling. "I looked for you
in the scanners," she told Elisabeth. Then she turned to Harold. "Mr. Gage,
why didn't you let us know you had this extraordinary alien person on
board? If Captain Hiskey hadn't mentioned —"

"Alien person?" Elisabeth interrupted.

"Why, yes! Somebody called a Rilf. Derek is certain Solar U has no
record of the species, and Captain Hiskey and Mr. Gage are taking him to
Earthplanet on a commercial mission for his people. It's really an historical
event!"

Harold stared at her, completely dumbfounded. Had Jake gone out of
his mind to mention McNulty and the Rilfs to the Alstons? Elisabeth gave

him a quick glance which asked whether this was the big hush-hush business he'd been talking about.

"He's even given himself a human name," Sally told Elisabeth. "McNulty!" She smiled at Harold. "I must admit I find him a little shivery!"

"He's here?" Harold heard himself saying. "McNulty's *here*, on the asteroid?"

"Of course! We invited him down. When Captain Hiskey —"

"How long's he been here?"

She looked at him, startled by his tone. "Why, about twenty minutes. Why?"

"No," Harold said. "Don't ask questions." He took each of them by an arm, began to walk them quickly towards the opening in the cliff. "Do you know exactly where McNulty is at the moment?"

"Well, they — my husband and Captain Hiskey and McNulty — probably are in the control room now. McNulty was saying how interested he'd be in seeing how the asteroid was operated."

That tied it. "You didn't send up for him?" Harold asked. "The ship's skiff brought him down?"

"Yes, it did. But what is the matter, Mr. Gage? Is —"

"And the skiff's still here?" Harold said. "It's inside the field lock?"

"I suppose so. I don't know."

"All right," Harold said. He stopped before the opening. "Now listen carefully because we're not likely to have much time!" He drew a quick deep breath. "First, where is the control room?"

"In the building in the space lock section," Sally said. "The administration building. You saw it when you came down." They were watching him, expressions puzzled and alarmed.

Harold nodded. "Yes, I remember. Now — you and everyone else on the asteroid is in very serious danger. McNulty is a real horror. He has a special weapon. The only way you can stay reasonably safe from it is to hide out behind good solid locked doors. I hope you'll have some way of warning Professor Alston and whoever else is around to do the same thing. Anyone who is in the open, isn't behind walls, when McNulty cuts loose won't have a chance. Not for a moment! Unless he belongs to the *Prideful Sue*'s crew. If you can get to a transmitter in the next few minutes, call the SP and tell them to come here and get in any way they can — in space armor. But transmitters aren't going to stay operable very long. You'll have to hurry." He looked at their whitened faces. "Don't think I'm crazy! The only reason Hiskey would have told you about McNulty, and the only reason McNulty would have showed himself, is that they've decided between them to take over the place."

"But why?" cried Sally.

"Because we're the next thing to lousy pirates. Because they think they can use this asteroid." Harold started to turn away. "Now get inside, seal that door tight, move fast, and with luck you'll stay alive."

So this was one place guns wouldn't be needed! In mentioning that, Jake Hiskey had made sure his navigator wouldn't — quite out of habit and absentmindedly — be going down armed to the peaceful Alston asteroid and to the reunion with his sister. He knew this was a job I couldn't buy, Harold thought. Even if Elisabeth hadn't been involved — He'd set off at a long lope as soon as the camouflaged door in the cliff snapped shut. The asteroid surface in this area was simulated hilly ground, slopes rising and dipping, occasional smooth slabs of meteorite rock showing through. Clusters of trees, shrubbery, cultivated grassy ground ... The space lock section couldn't be more than a few hundred yards away, but he couldn't see it from here. Neither could anyone in the open see him approaching. Sally Alston had said she'd located them by using scanners. Hiskey and McNulty could spot him by the same means, but they wouldn't be looking for him before they'd secured the control room. Standard raiding procedure ... hit the nerve center of an installation as quickly as possible; take it, and the rest is paralyzed, helpless, silenced.

He checked an instant. A curious sensation, like a vibrating pressure on his eardrums, a tingling all through his nerves; it continued a few seconds, faded, returned, faded again ... and the herd came suddenly around the side of the hill ahead of him. Some fifteen large gray-brown animals, a kind of antelope with thick corkscrew horns, running hard and fast. In the moment he saw them, startled, he took it for an indication that McNulty had released the toziens — and knew immediately it wasn't that. Nothing ran from toziens; there was no time. The herd crossed his path with a rapid drumming of hoofs, pounded through thickets, wheeled and appeared about to slam head-on into a vertical cliff wall. At the last moment an opening was there in the rock, similar to the one out of which Sally Alston had stepped, five or six times as wide. The beasts plunged through it, shouldering and jostling one another, and the opening vanished behind the last of them.

It all seemed to have happened in an instant. He ran on, wondering. That odd sensation, switching on and off — an alert signal? An alarm to which even the animals here were conditioned to respond immediately, in a predetermined manner, a "take cover!" that cleared the surface level of anything capable of reacting to it in moments ... it indicated a degree of efficiency and preparedness he wouldn't have attributed to these asteroid dwellers. What sort of emergencies could they expect here?

He saw no more fleeing beasts, or any beasts at all; and in perhaps another minute the tingling irritation in his nerves had ended. The space-lock section couldn't be far away. He'd been cutting across the slopes, avoiding the leisurely winding and intersecting paths along which he'd come with Elisabeth, and keeping to cover when it didn't slow him down. At last then, coming out of a grove of trees on the crest of one of the little hills, he saw the administration building ahead — or rather one corner of it, warm brown, edged with gleaming black, the rest concealed behind trees. There was no one in sight, but he moved cautiously now, staying within the shrubbery. A hundred feet on, he came to a point which overlooked the landing area beneath the space lock. The *Prideful Sue*'s skiff stood in the center of the area, entry port open. Otherwise the section looked deserted.

Above the skiff nothing showed but the simulated Earth sky. If the space lock through the energy carriers englobing the asteroid had been activated, it would have been visible — a ring of frozen fire from below, a glowing cylinder from where Harold stood, the cylinder's thickness depending on the degree to which the lock was expanded. Undoubtedly it could be expanded enough to let in the *Prideful Sue*, and undoubtedly Hiskey had just that in mind. But whatever else he might have accomplished so far, he hadn't yet got around to bringing down the ship.

The skiff wasn't large, but eight or nine men with raiding gear — about half the crew — could have been crammed in with McNulty and left waiting in concealment until they received Hiskey's signal to emerge and go into action. The open entry lock indicated they'd already received the signal, were now inside the administration building. In other words, at some point within the past few minutes the attack on the asteroid had begun. Barnes, the second Rilf, and the rest of the crew were still on the ship. If they joined the group on the asteroid, the situation might become nearly hopeless. As things stood, it seemed quite bad enough, but at least there'd been no sign as yet of the Rilf toziens. It was possible that if Jake Hiskey met no significant resistance from Alston's people, he would prefer not to turn this into a killing operation.

But he'll want to get me in any case, Harold thought. To keep me from interfering ...

They hadn't had time to try to locate him with scanners, but somebody might have been posted outside the administration building to ambush him if he showed up here. The most likely spot for a watcher seemed the cluster of trees and bushes which screened the building —

A blue and golden bird twice the size of a pigeon burst out of the undergrowth six feet ahead and launched itself upwards with a strong beat of wings. Startled — that might easily have advertised his approach — Harold dropped to a deep crouch, glancing after the bird. It rose swiftly to a point about thirty feet above the ground. There something struck and destroyed it.

It seemed as abrupt as an explosion. The flying shape changed to sprays of blood and colorful ribbons and rags which were slashed and scattered again and again in the same instant, then left to fall back to earth. So it was a killing operation after all and McNulty had turned loose his toziens. Not, of course, all of them. There were thousands packed away in his thick nonhuman thorax; and only a small fraction of that number were required to sweep the surface of the asteroid and any sections of the interior open to intrusion clear of animal life large enough to attract their attention. They could have been released only moments ago or he would have been made aware of their presence — as he was aware of it now. An eerie whispering about him, now here, now there, as the toziens darted down in turn in their invisible speed towards this living flesh, sensed the Rilf drug which protected him as it protected all those who manned the *Prideful Sue,* and swerved away. But everyone else on the asteroid who had not found shelter had died or was dying in these seconds.

Starting forwards again, he shut that thought away. Jake Hiskey and McNulty, having begun the slaughter, would finish it. They'd be in the control room at present, securing their hold on the asteroid. That done, they'd bring in the ship and start looking for holed-up survivors.

The man Hiskey had selected to act as lookout at the building was Tom Connick. Not the brightest, but an excellent shot and normally steady as a rock — a good choice as an assassin. He stood, screened by a thicket, thirty feet from what seemed to be the only entrance into the building, a gun ready in his hand. They knew Harold wasn't armed; and if he wanted to get into the administration building, he'd have to come past the thicket, within easy range for Connick. It must have seened as simple as that.

McNulty's toziens, however, had provided a complication. Connick's usual calm was not in evidence. He kept making small abrupt motions, bobbing his head, flinching right or left, jerking up the gun and putting it down again. Harold could appreciate his feelings. He, too, was still drawing the interest of the invisible swarm; every few seconds there would be a momentary indication that a tozien was nearby, and each time his flesh crawled though he knew, as Connick did, that theoretically they were protected from the little horrors. The thought remained that some tozien or other might not realize in time that they were protected. But at present that was all to his advantage. Connick darted glances this way and that, now and then half turning to see what was in back of him; but he was looking for the wrong kind of danger. So in the end Harold rose quietly from the undergrowth ten steps behind Connick with a sizable rock in either hand.

He lobbed the left-hand rock gently upwards. It lifted in a steep arc above Connick's head and came down in front of him. And, for a moment, Connick's nerves snapped. He uttered a frightened sound, a stifled squeal, jabbed the gun forward, shoulders hunching, attention frozen by the deadly dark moving thing which had appeared out of nowhere. It was doubtful whether he even heard the brief rustle of the thicket as Harold came up behind him. Then the edge of the second rock smashed through his skull.

And now there was a gun for Harold, and for Jake Hiskey one man less he might presently send out to look for surviving asteroid people. Harold found a recharger for the gun in one of Connick's pockets. There'd been some question in his mind whether there mightn't be a second man around, though he had studied the vicinity thoroughly before moving in on Connick. But nothing stirred, so Connick's death had not been observed. He could expect to find somebody else stationed inside the building entrance, as a standard precaution.

He started quickly towards the building, then checked. On the far side of the space-lock area there was a faint greenish shimmering in the air, which hadn't been there before. Harold stared at it sharply, looked around. Behind him, too, much closer, barely a hundred feet away — like a nearly invisible curtain hanging from the simulated sky, fitted against the irregularities of the ground below. He pointed Connick's gun into the air, triggered it for an instant. There was a momentary puff of brightness as the charge hit the immaterial curtain. More distantly to the right, and beyond the administration building to the left, was the same shimmering aerial effect.

Energy screens. Activated within the past few minutes. By whom? They enclosed the space-lock section, boxed it in. If they'd been thrown up before the tozien swarm appeared in the section, then McNulty's weapon was still confined here unless it had found an entry to the asteroid's interior from within the building. And the screens might have gone up just in time to do that; he'd been too involved in his wary approach to the building area to have noticed what happened behind him. There was suddenly some real reason for hope ... because this fitted in with the silently pervasive alert signal which had come so quickly after his warning to Sally Alston, with concealed doors opening and closing on the surface and animals streaming off it into the interior. The asteroid had defenses, and somebody was using them — which did not make it any less urgent to do something about the *Prideful Sue*'s crew and its Rilf allies before the defenses were broken down.

There was someone waiting inside the entrance. It was Dionisio.

"What's slowing you men down in there, Dionisio?" Navigator Gage demanded curtly, striding towards him. "Why aren't you moving?"

Dionisio was considerably more intelligent than Connick, but, besides being also badly fretted by the toziens, he was, for a moment, confused. He'd been told the navigator was among those to get it here; but he'd also been told that the navigator was unarmed and had no idea of what was going to happen. And here the navigator came walking up, casually holding a gun at half-ready, looking annoyed and impatient, which was standard for him on an operation, and sounding as if he were very much in on the deal. And, of course, there was the further consideration that the navigator was an extremely fast and accurate man with a gun. So Dionisio blinked, licked his lips, cleared his throat, finally began, "Well ... uh —"

"The skipper's got the control room cleaned up?"

"Well, sir, I guess so."

"You *guess* so?"

"I wasn't there," Dionisio said sullenly, eyes fixed with some nervousness on the gun Navigator Gage was waving around rather freely. "I was in the skiff. There was that funny feeling we all got. Right after that we got the skipper's signal. So we came out. The skipper tells us to start looking around for the people."

"The people in the building?"

"Uh-huh. The skipper and McNulty were in the control room. There were five, six of the people here with them. And then the skipper looks around, and there's *nobody* there."

The navigator's lip curled. "You're implying they disappeared? Just like that?"

"Looks like it," said Dionisio warily.

"Everybody in the building?"

"Uh-huh."

"So what are they doing in there now?"

"Blowing in the walls. Looking for, uh, doors."

"Looking for doors!" repeated Navigator Gage, total disgust in his voice. "And what are *you* doing up *here?*"

Dionisio swallowed. "I'm to, uh, look out to see if somebody comes."

"With the toziens around? You out of your mind? Who's in the skiff? Have the rest of them come down from the ship?"

"No. There's nobody in the —"

And then Dionisio stopped talking and twitched his gunbarrel up very quickly. Because Navigator Gage had glanced back towards the skiff out in the landing area just then; and while this was a kind of odd situation, Dionisio was positive the skipper anyhow wanted Navigator Gage dead, and he himself had no slightest use for the navigator. So up came the gun, and it was Dionisio who was dead in the same moment, because Navigator Gage had, after all, not glanced away to the extent of not being able to catch the motion.

Beyond the entry a lit hallway extended back into the building. Harold thought he'd heard distant human voices in there while he was talking to Dionisio, but at the moment there was silence. He checked quickly through the man's gear, found a folded gas-breather and fitted that over his face. He took off his suit coat, put on Dionisio's faded brown jacket, slapped Dionisio's visor cap on his head, and set it at the jaunty angle Dionisio favored. As he finished, there was a remote heavy thump from within the building, followed in seconds by another. Jake Hiskey was still having holes blown out of the walls, looking for the hidden passages through which Professor Alston and the people working in the administration building had vanished when they got the alert signal. He should find them if he kept at it long enough. And as soon as they had the space-lock controls figured out, they'd haul down the *Prideful Sue* with the heavier raiding equipment she carried.

Dionisio's gun was the only other useful item here. Harold pocketed it, pulled the body over against the entry wall where it wouldn't be visible from within the building, and set off quickly along the long hallway. Glassy motion flickered for an instant before his eyes; the toziens were still around. Now a series of five doors on the right — all locked. Ahead the hall made a turn to the right. As he came towards the corner, he heard men's voices again, at least three or four, mingled in a short burst of jabbering, harsh with excitement. Hiskey's voice among them? The ammonia smell of jolt bombs began to tingle faintly in his nostrils.

He went around the corner without hesitating or slowing his stride. The gas-breather covered half his face; and while Dionisio was about an inch shorter, they were similar enough in general build that he could be accepted as Dionisio for a few moments by men with their attention on other things. Sixty feet ahead, rubble covered the hall floor, chunks of colorful plastic masonry shaken by jolt bombs out of a great jagged hole in the left wall. Only two men in sight, standing waiting in tensed attitudes behind a semiportable gun pointed at the hole. Jake Hiskey's voice now, raw with impatient anger: "Hurry it up! Hurry it up!" A glow spilled from the hole and there was the savage hiss of cutters. Bomb fumes hung thick in the air. Hiskey and at least four of the crew here. Wait till you're right among them.

One of the men at the semiportable glanced around as Harold came up, looked away again. He went past them. The hole drove deep into the wall; evidently they'd uncovered a passage but found it sealed a few yards farther on, and the sealing material was holding. Three men were at work in there with Hiskey. The cutters blazed and a broken conduit spat vicious shorted power ... And what damn fool had left two unused jolt bombs lying on this boulder of plastic? Harold scooped them up in passing, glanced back and saw Hiskey staring open-mouthed over at him, then clawing for his gun.

Harold dropped behind the boulder, thumbed the stud on one of the little bombs and pitched it over into the opening of the hole. The second one went in the general direction of the semiportable. Their successive shock waves rammed at his eardrums, lifted the boulder against him. Clouds of dust filled the hall. After a moment he took out one of his guns and stood up.

They lay where the double shock had caught and battered them. Hiskey had been coming for him, had nearly reached the boulder when he was smashed down. Harold looked at the bloodied head and was surprised by a wash of heavy regret, a brief but intensely vivid awareness of that bright yesterday in which Jake Hiskey and he first swung their ship out past the sun, headed towards high adventure. *Too bad, Jake,* he thought. *Too bad that in eight years the adventure soured so that it's ending here like this.*

McNulty and one or at most two of the original landing group left. Finish it up now before their reinforcements get here —

McNulty at any rate should be in the control room.

Harold went on along the hallway. No sounds anywhere. An open door. He approached it cautiously, looked in. A sizable office, half a dozen desks spaced out, machine stands, wall files — two of these left open. Not many minutes ago, people had been working here. Then the asteroid's

alarm reached them, and like ghosts they'd vanished. At the far side of the
office was another door. As he started towards it, two men stood suddenly
in the doorframe. Guns went off; Harold dropped behind the nearest desk.
Across the room, the two had taken cover as quickly.

A real gun fight now, fast and vicious. The crewmen were Harding and
Ruse, two of the *Prideful Sue's* best hands. The office furniture, in spite of
its elegant appearance, was of tough solid plastic; but within a minute it
was hammered half to pieces. Harold had emptied the charge in one of his
guns before he got Harding. Ruse was still pouring it at him, battering the
shielding desk. There was no way to reach back at him from here. Harold
took a chance finally, shifting to another desk in a crouching leap, felt pain
jar up from the heel of his right leg as he reached cover. Not an
immediately crippling charge, though any hit of that kind was bad
enough. Now, however, lying half across the desk, he had the advantage
and could pour it on Ruse and did. Pinned behind his cover, Ruse kept
firing furiously but ineffectively. At last he stopped firing and tried to
duplicate Harold's trick, and Harold got him in the open. The second gun
hissed out emptily instants later.

Ruse had rolled on behind a low console. Only his legs were in sight.
He seemed to be sprawled loosely on his side, and the legs weren't
moving. It might be a trick, though Harold didn't think so. He knew he'd
caught Ruse with a head shot; and even at minimum charge that should
have been almost instantly fatal. But he stayed where he was and reached
back carefully with one hand to get the gun recharger he'd taken from
Connick out of his pocket. A moment's fumbling told him it was no longer
there. At some point along the line it had been jolted from the pocket and
lost.

But Harding should have a recharger. Harold slid back slowly off the
desk and turned towards Harding's body.

And there, coming towards him in a soft heavy rush across the littered
office, clutching a thick metal spike in one human-looking hand, was
McNulty.

Harold slipped back behind the desk. McNulty lunged across the desk
with the spike, then lumbered around it; and as he came on, his big shape
seemed to be blurring oddly from moment to moment. Then a hard deep
droning noise swelled in the air, and Harold knew the Rilf's thorax was
spewing out its store of toziens.

The purpose was immediately obvious. The toziens couldn't touch
him, but they provided a distraction. In an instant Harold seemed
enclosed in roaring thunders, and the office had turned into something
seen through a shifting syrupy liquid. McNulty, in addition, hardly
needed help. He was clumsy but strong and fast; his broad white face kept
looming up distortedly in the tozien screen near Harold. For a nightmarish
minute or two, it was all Harold could do to keep some sizable piece of
office equipment between the Rilf and himself. McNulty didn't give him a
chance to get near Ruse's or Harding's guns. Then finally McNulty

stumbled on a broken chair and fell; and with the tozien storm whirling about him, Harold managed to wrench the spike away from the Rilf. As McNulty came back up on his feet, he moved in, the spike gripped in both hands, and rammed it deep into what, if McNulty had been human, would have been McNulty's abdomen. He had no idea where McNulty's vital organs were or what they were like, but the spike reached one of them. McNulty's mouth stretched wide. If he made any sound, it was lost in the droning uproar. His big body swayed left and right; then he went down heavily on his back and lay still, the spike's handle sticking up out of him. His eyes remained open.

Harold leaned back for an instant against the edge of a desk, gasping for breath. The toziens still boiled around, sounding like a swarm of gigantic metallic insects, but they seemed to have drawn away a little; he began to see the office more clearly. Then one of them appeared suddenly on McNulty's chest. It stayed there, quivering. Another appeared, and another. In a minute, McNulty's body was covered with them, clustering, shifting about, like flies gathering thick on carrion. Harold's skin crawled as he watched them. They were specialized cells produced by the Rilf body, pliable or steel-hard and razor-edged, depending on what they were doing. McNulty's remote ancestor had been a hunting animal, too awkward perhaps to overtake nimble prey, which had evolved a method of detaching sections of itself to carry out the kill, not unlike the hawks men had trained on old Earth to hunt on sight. McNulty still had been able to use his toziens in that manner, releasing one or more under an inhibition which impelled them to return to him after bringing down a specific victim. Their use by the thousands for uninhibited wholesale slaughter evidently had been a more recent Rilf development, perhaps not attained until they had acquired a civilization and scientific methods. Under those conditions, the toziens ranged over an area of a dozen miles, destroying whatever life they found for almost fifty hours, until their furious energy was exhausted and they died.

Harding had been carrying a recharger, and Harold replenished his guns with it before placing it in his pocket. He looked over once more at McNulty's body, motionless under its glittering blanket, and left the office by the door opposite to the one through which he had entered. Not all the toziens had returned to McNulty. An unidentifiable number still darted about, and some stayed near Harold, attracted by his motion. He knew it because they weren't inaudible now but continued to make droning or whiffing sounds as they had during McNulty's attack. Perhaps McNulty's death was having an effect on their life processes. At any rate, they no longer seemed to have any particular interest in him.

Limping a little because of the charge he'd stopped in his heel, he followed the narrow passage beyond the door to another doorway. There, at the bottom of a short flight of steps, the brightly lit deserted control room whispered and hummed. Harold hurried down the steps, looked around.

He found the space-lock controls almost immediately. And they were a puzzler. The instruments indicated that the lock was open to its fullest extent. But the screen view of the landing area showed only the skiff standing there, and the screen view of the force-field sections containing the space lock showed it wasn't activated, was shut tight. He shifted the controls quickly back and forth. There was no change in the screens. He scowled at the indicators, left them at the shut and secured mark, turned to other instruments nearby, began manipulating them.

In a minute, he had the answer. He sat down at a console, heard himself make a short laughing sound. No wonder Jake Hiskey had worked so furiously to break through into the hidden passages leading into the interior of the asteroid. For every practical purpose, the control room was dead. Power was here, the gadgetry appeared to be operating. But it did and could do nothing. None of it. Nothing at all.

He drew a long slow breath, looked up at the ceiling.

"Is somebody listening?" he asked aloud. "Can you see me here?"

There was a momentary excited babble of voices, male and female. Elisabeth? He discovered the speaker then, ten feet away. "Elisabeth?" he asked, a sudden rawness in his throat.

"Yes, I'm here, Harold. We're *all* here!" Elisabeth's voice told him. "Harold, we couldn't *see* you. We didn't know what was happening out —"

"The scanners, Mr. Gage." That was Alston. "The scanning circuits in that section have been shorted. We were afraid of drawing attention to you by speaking. And —"

"I understand," Harold said. "Better let me talk first because this thing isn't finished. Captain Hiskey and the men he smuggled down here from the ship are dead. So is McNulty — the Rilf. But McNulty's weapon isn't dead and should stay effective for the next two days — make it two and a half, to be safe. You can't come into this section before then, and you can't go anywhere else on the asteroid where it might have spread. It can't hurt me, but any of you would be killed immediately."

"Just what is this biological weapon?" Alston's voice asked.

Harold told him briefly about the toziens, added, "You may have thrown up those screen barriers about this section fast enough to trap them here. But if you didn't, they're all over the surface of the asteroid. And if they're given an opening anywhere, they'll come pouring down into it."

"Fortunately," Alston said, "they have been trapped in the space-lock section. Thanks to your prompt warning, Mr. Gage."

"What makes you sure?"

"They were registering on biological sensing devices covering that section until the scanners went off. The impressions were difficult to define but match your description. Every section of the asteroid is compartmentalized by energy screens at present, and no similar impressions have been obtained elsewhere. Nevertheless, we shall take no chances. We'll remain sealed off from the surface for the next sixty hours."

"You seem to have an override on the instruments here," Harold said.

"An automatic override," Alston acknowledged. "It cuts in when the asteroid shifts to emergency status. The possibility of a successful raid always had to be considered. So there is an interior control room."

Harold sighed. Jake Hiskey and McNulty, he thought, hadn't been alone in underestimating these people. Well, let's get the mess cleaned up ... "You've asked the SP to do something about the *Prideful Sue?*"

"Yes," Alston said. "They'll be here within a few hours."

Tozien whirring dipped past Harold's face, moved off. "She has heavier armament than they might expect," he said. "Eight men and another Rilf on board. Our gunnery isn't the worst. But tell them to give her a chance."

"I'll do that. And I'll advise the police to take precautions."

"Yes, they should. There's one more thing then. We guided a Rilf ship here and left it outside Earthsystem. It's manned by more than half a hundred Rilfs. We've been negotiating to have them take a hand for pay in Earth's miniwars. They may still try to go ahead with the deal. I think they should be turned back."

"Where is that ship now?" Alston sounded startled.

"No fixed position. But it should be moving into Earthsystem to rendezvous on your orbit. If the SP look for it, they'll find it."

Alston began to reply, but his voice blurred out for Harold. Almost as he'd stopped speaking, something had slammed into his back, below his right shoulder blade. The impact threw him out of the chair. He went on down to the floor, rolled over, twisting, on his left side, stopped, and had one of the guns in his right hand, pointed up.

Jake Hiskey's face was a smiling red mask as he leaned against the doorframe at the end of the room. There was a gun in his hand too, and he fired before Harold did. The charge shuddered into the transmitter stand behind Harold and crept quickly down. Harold pulled the trigger then, and Hiskey was flung back and fell beyond the doorframe, out of sight. Harold sucked air back into lungs that seemed tight as a clenched fist in his chest. Spent gun ... or the hit where he'd taken it should have killed him outright. Jake had been too groggy to check that detail. Not that it was going to make very much difference.

Well, Jake, he thought, *perhaps that wasn't really the worst solution.*

The big room swung in circles overhead as he pulled himself against the stand and sat up. Then a voice was crying his name. Elisabeth.

"It's all right," Harold announced thickly, idiotically. "I stopped a hit, that's all."

Questions.

"Captain Hiskey wasn't quite as dead as I believed," he explained. "He's dead enough now. "

The voices grew blurred. Harold decided he was, definitely, finished. It might take a while. But the charge, spent though it had been, would start him hemorrhaging. In an hour or two heart and lungs should be dying mush. Wicked guns, thorough guns —

" ... Immediate medical attention ..."

Oh, sure.

But he was listening now to what they were telling him, and abruptly he became alarmed. "No one can come in here," he said. "I told you why. Not even in armor. Lift the screens anywhere while the toziens are alive, and they'll pour through. They're too fast to stop. You'll have to wait till you know they're dead."

Then there was, they said, another way. Between this section and the next was a small emergency personnel lock — if he could follow their instructions, if he could reach it. A suit of armor couldn't pass through it, but Harold could. And once he was inside the lock, sensing devices would establish with complete reliability whether any Rilf toziens had entered it with him.

Harold considered that. It seemed foolproof.

"All right," he said. "We'll see if it works." He began struggling up to his feet. "Just keep those screens down."

Some while later he reached the main entry to the control room, glanced down at Jake Hiskey, and turned to the right, as they'd said. Toziens went with him, drawn towards the only thing that still moved in the section. There came a passage, and another one, and a door, and, behind the door, a small room. Harold entered the room and looked around. "I think I'm there," he said aloud.

"Yes, you're in the right room," Alston's voice told him. "You won't see the lock until it opens, but it's in the center of the wall directly opposite the door."

"Don't open it yet," Harold said. "They're here, too."

He got across the room. As Alston had told him, there was nothing in the smooth bare wall to suggest an emergency lock behind it, but he was lined up with the center of the door on the other side, as well as he could make it out; and he should be within a few feet, at most, of the lock.

"Professor Alston," he said.

"Yes?"

"I'm in front of the lock now. Wait till I give you the word. Then open it fast."

"We're ready," Alston said. "We'll know when you're inside."

Harold fished the two guns from his pockets, took them by their barrels in one hand, turned around. Supporting himself against the wall with his other hand, he lifted the guns and began waving them about. Tozien droning drew in towards the motion, thickening, zigzagging back and forth above and in front of him. Then he pitched the guns towards the far corner of the room. The droning darted off with them. They hit the wall with a fine crash, went clattering to the floor. The air seethed noisily above them there.

"Now!" Harold said.

He saw the narrow dark opening appear in the wall two feet away, stumbled into it. After that, he seemed to go on stumbling down through soft darkness.

At first there was nothing. Then came an occasional vague awareness of time passing. A great deal of time ... years of it, centuries of it ... seemed to drift by steadily and slowly. Shadows began to appear, and withdrew again. Now and then a thought turned up. Some thoughts attracted other thoughts, clusters of them. Finally he found he had acquired a few facts. Facts had great value, he realized; they could be fitted together to form solid structures.

Carefully, painstakingly, he drew in more facts. His thoughts took to playing about them like schools of fish, shifting from one fact to another. Then there came a point at which it occurred to him that he really had a great many facts on hand now, and should start lining them up and putting them in order.

So he started doing it.

The first group was easy to assemble. In the process, he remembered suddenly having been told all this by one of the shadows:

The men left on the *Prideful Sue* had elected to put up a fight when the System Police boats arrived, and they'd put up a good one. (They should have, a stray thought added as an aside; he'd trained them.) But in the end the *Prideful Sue* was shot apart, and there'd been no survivors.

The Rilf ship, edging into Earthsystem, turned sullenly back when challenged. By the time it faded beyond the instrument range of its SP escort, it was a quarter of a light-year away from the sun, traveling steadily out.

That seemed to clear up one parcel of facts.

Other matters were more complex. He himself, for example — first just lying there, then riding about on one of the small brown cattle which had once been a wild species of Earth, finally walking again — remained something of a puzzle. There were periods when he was present so to speak, and evidently longer, completely vacant periods into which he dropped from time to time. When he came out of them, he didn't know where he'd been. He hadn't noticed it much at first; but then he began to find it disturbing.

"Well," Elisabeth said gently — she happened to be there when he started thinking seriously about this odd practice he'd developed — "the doctor said that, aside from more obvious physical damage, your nervous system got quite a bad jolt from that gun charge. But you *are* recovering, Harold."

So he was recovering. He decided to be satisfied with that. "How long has it been?" he asked.

"Not quite four weeks," said Elizabeth. She smiled. "You're really doing very well, Harold. What would you like me to show you today?"

"Let's look at some more of the things they're doing downstairs," Harold said.

Professor Derek Alston's asteroid also remained something of an enigma. In Mars Underground, and in the SP Academy's navigation school, the private asteroids had been regarded much as they were on Earthplanet, as individually owned pleasure resorts of the very rich which maintained no more contact with the rest of humanity than was necessary. Evidently they preferred to have that reputation. Elisabeth had told him it wasn't until she'd been a Solar U student for a few years that she'd learned gradually that the asteroids performed some of the functions of monasteries and castles in Earth's Middle Ages, built to preserve life, knowledge, and culture through the turbulence of wars and other disasters. They were storehouses of what had become, or was becoming, now lost on Earth, and their defenses made them very secure citadels. The plants and animals of the surface levels were living museums. Below the surface was a great deal more than that. In many respects they acted as individual extensions of Solar U, though they remained independent of it.

All of which seemed true, from what he had seen so far. But the thought came occasionally that it still mightn't be the complete picture. There were the projects, for one thing. This miniature planet, for all that it was an insignificant speck of cosmic debris, had, on the human scale, enormous quantities of cubic space. Very little of the space was in practical use, and that was used in an oddly diffused manner. There were several central areas which in their arrangement might have been part of a residential section of Mars Underground. Having lived mainly on an interstellar ship for the past eight years, Harold found himself reflecting on the fact that if the asteroid's population had been around a hundred times its apparent size, it would not have been unduly crowded. Elsewhere were the storerooms; and here Elisabeth loved to browse, and Harold browsed with her, though treasures of art and literature and the like were of less interest to him. Beautiful things perhaps, but dead.

And then the projects — Step into a capsule, a raindrop-shaped shell, glide through a system of curving tunnels, checking here and there to be fed through automatic locks; and you came to a project. Two or three or at most four people would be conducting it; they already knew who you were, but you were introduced, and they showed you politely around. Elisabeth's interest in what they had to show was moderate. Harold's kept growing.

"You're running some rather dangerous experiments here," he remarked eventually to Derek Alston. This was on another day. There'd been only a scattered few of those blank periods lately.

Derek shook his head. "I don't run them," he said. "They're Solar U and SP projects. The asteroid merely provides facilities."

"Why do you let them set themselves up here?"

Derek Alston shrugged. "They have to be set up somewhere. If there should be some disastrous miscalculation, our defensive system will contain the damage and reduce the probable loss in human lives."

And the asteroid had, to be sure, a remarkable defensive system. For any ordinary purpose it seemed almost excessive. Harold had studied it and wondered again.

"In Eleven," he said, "they're working around with something on the order of a solar cannon. If they slip up on that one, you might find your defensive system strained."

Derek looked over at him.

"I believe you weren't supposed to know the purpose of that device," he said idly.

"They were a little misleading about that, as a matter of fact," said Harold. "But I came across something similar in the outsystems once."

"Yes, I imagine you've learned a great deal more there than they ever taught in navigation school." Derek scratched his head and looked owlish. "If you were to make a guess, what would you say was the real purpose of maintaining such projects on our asteroid? After all, I have to admit that the System Police and Solar U are capable of providing equally suitable protective settings for them."

"The impression I've had," Harold told him, "is that they're being kept a secret from somebody. They're not the sort of thing likely to be associated with a private asteroid."

"No, not at all. Your guess is a good one. There are men, and there is mankind. Not quite the same thing. Mankind lost a major round on Earthplanet in this century and exists there only in fragments. And though men go to the outsystems, mankind hasn't reached them yet."

"You think it's here?"

"Here in Solar U, in the System Police, in major centers like Mars Underground. And on the private asteroids. Various shapes of the same thing. Yes, mankind is here, what's left of it at the moment. It has regrouped in Earthsystem and is building up."

Harold considered that. "Why make it a conspiracy?" he asked then. "Why not be open about it?"

Because it's dangerous to frighten men. Earthplanet regards Earthsystem as an irritation. But it looks at our lack of obvious organization and purpose, our relatively small number, and it doesn't take alarm. It knows it would take disproportionate effort, tremendous unified effort, to wipe us out, and we don't seem worth it. So Earth's men continue with their grinding struggles and maneuverings which eventually are to give somebody control of the planet. By that time Earthsystem's mankind should not be very much concerned about Earthplanet's intentions towards it. The projects you've seen are minor ones. We move farther ahead of them every year, and our population grows steadily. Even now I doubt that the planet's full resources would be sufficient to interfere seriously with that process. But for the present we must conceal the strength we have and the strength we are obtaining. We want no trouble with Earth. Men will have their way there for a time, and then, whatever their designs, mankind will begin to evolve from them again, as it always does. It is a hardy thing. We can wait ..."

And that, Harold decided, had been upper echelon information, given him by one who might be among Earthsystem's present leaders. Elisabeth and Sally Alston had a general understanding of the situation but did not seem to be aware of the underlying purpose. Professor Alston evidently had made him an offer.

He thought about it, and presently a feeling began to grow in him, something like loss, something like loneliness. Elisabeth appeared to sense it and was disturbed.

Then another day. A gun was in his hand again, and in his other hand were the last three of a dozen little crystal globes he'd picked up in one of the machine shops. He swung them up, and they went flying away along a massive wall of asteroid rock. As they began to drop again, the gun snaked out and, in turn, each of the globes sparkled brightly and vanished.

He'd been aware of Derek Alston coming up from behind him before he fired; and now he pocketed the gun and turned.

"Very pretty shooting, friend!" Derek remarked. "I never was able to develop much skill with a handgun myself, but I enjoy watching an expert."

Harold shrugged. "I had the time, and the motivation, to put in a great deal of practice."

"No doubt." Derek held up a sheaf of papers. "Your final medical and psychological reports! It appears you've come all the way back. Care to look them over?"

Harold shook his head. "No. I've known for a couple of days that I'd come all the way back." He patted the pocket which held the gun. "This was a test."

They regarded each other a moment. And now, Harold wondered, how was he going to say it? The Alstons had been more than generous hosts, and Derek took pride in what Earthsystem was accomplishing — with very good reason.

But he'd moved for eight years among the stars. And in spite of all the plans that had gone sour, and the ugliness which tarnished and finally destroyed the *Prideful Sue*, he'd found there what he'd been looking for. Earthsystem seemed dwindled and small. He couldn't possibly come back to it.

Make it brief, he thought.

"I'm not sure what I'll do next," he told Derek Alston. "But I'm shipping transsolar again."

"Well, I should hope so!" said Derek promptly.

"I was wondering whether you'd understand ... Elisabeth in particular."

"Of course she understands! I do — we all do!" Derek smiled. "But before you start talking of leaving, there's one more project I must show you. It's one you should appreciate ..."

They stepped, a minute later, out of a capsule deep in the bowels of the asteroid, and went along a passage with steel bulkheads. A massive lock opened at their approach, and lights came on.

"Come on in and look around," Derek said. "This is our third control room. Not too many people know we have it."

Harold looked around the shining place. First incredulously, then with something like growing awe. He glanced at Derek Alston. "Mind if I check these?" he asked.

"Not at all. Go ahead."

Once, some two years before, he'd been in the control room of Earthplanet's biggest, newest, and proudest outsystem transport. What he'd seen then was dwarfed, made trifling and clumsy, by what was here. His skin shivered with a lover's delight. "You have power to go with it?" he asked presently.

"We have the power."

"Where's the asteroid going on interstellar drives?"

"I told you mankind hadn't got to the outsystems yet," Derek said. "But it's ready to move there. We've been preparing for it. The outsystems won't know for a while that we're around — not till we're ready to let them know it."

"This asteroid is moving to the outsystems?"

"Not this one. Not for some years. We still have functions to perform here. But a few others — the first will be ready to start within the next three months. They can use an experienced transsolar navigator. They think they can also use a fighting captain with an outsystem background. If you're interested, I'll take you over to one of them this afternoon."

Harold drew in a long, deep breath.

"I'm interested," he said.

Sour Note on Palayata

Bayne Duffold, Assistant Secretary of the Hub Systems' Outposts Department, said that the entire proposed operation was not only illegal but probably unethical. Conceivably, it might lead to anything from the scientific murder of a single harmless Palayatan native to open warfare with an opponent of completely unknown potential.

Pilch, acting as spokesman for the Hub's Psychological Service Ship stationed off Palayata, heard him out patiently. "All that is very true, Excellency," she said then. "That is why you were instructed to call in the Service."

Assistant Secretary Duffold bit his thumbtip and frowned. It was true that the home office had instructed him, rather reluctantly, to call in the Service; but he had made no mention of that part of it to Pilch. And the girl already had jolted him with the information that a Psychological Service operator had been investigating the Palayatan problem on the planet itself during the past four months. "We figured Outposts was due to ask for a little assistance here about this time," was the way she had put it.

"I can't give my consent to your plan," Duffold said with finality, "until I've had the opportunity to investigate every phase of it in person."

The statement sounded foolish as soon as it was out. The remarkably outspoken young woman sitting on the other side of his desk was quite capable of reminding him that the Psychological Service, once it had been put on an assignment, did not need the consent of an Outposts assistant secretary for any specific operation. Or anybody else's consent, for that matter. It was one reason that nobody really liked the Service.

But Pilch said pleasantly, "Oh, we've arranged to see that you have the opportunity, of course! We'll be having a conference on the ship, spaceside" — she glanced at her timepiece — "four hours from now, for that very purpose. We particularly want to know what Outposts' viewpoint on the matter is."

And that was another reason they were disliked: they invariably did try to get the consent of everyone concerned for what they were doing! It made it difficult to accuse them of being arbitrary.

"Well —" said Duffold. There was really no way for him to avoid accepting the invitation. Besides, while he shared the general feeling of distaste for Psychological Service and its ways, he found Pilch herself and the prospect of spending a half day or so in her company very attractive. The Outposts Station's feminine complement on Palayata, while a healthy lot, hadn't been picked for good looks; and there was something about

Pilch, something bright and clean, that made him regret momentarily that she wasn't connected with a less morbid line of work. "Kidnaping and enforced interrogation of a friendly alien on his own world!" Duffold shook his head. "That's being pretty heavy-handed, you know!"

"No doubt," said Pilch. "But you know nobody has been able to persuade a Palayatan to leave the planet, so why waste time trying? We need the ship's equipment for the investigation, and it might be safer if the ship is a long way out from Palayata while it's going on." She stood up. "Will you be ready to hop as soon as I've picked up Wintan?"

"Hop? Wintan?" Duffold, getting to his feet, looked startled. "Oh, I see. Wintan's the operator you've had working on the planet. All right. Where will I meet you?"

"Space transport," said Pilch. "Ramp Nineteen. Half an hour from now." She was at the office entrance by then; and he said hurriedly, "Oh, by the way —"

Pilch looked back. "Yes?"

"You've been here two days," Duffold said. "Have they bothered you at all?"

She didn't ask what he meant. "No," she said. Black-fringed gray eyes looked at him out of a face from which every trace of expression was suddenly gone, as she added quietly, "But of course I've had a great deal of psychological conditioning —"

There hadn't been any need to rub that in, Duffold thought, flushing angrily. She knew, of course, how he felt about the Service — how any normal human being felt about it! Wars had been fought to prevent the psychological control of Hub citizens on any pretext; and then, when the last curious, cultish cliques of psychologists had been dissolved, it had turned out to be a matter of absolute necessity to let them resume their activities. So they were still around, with their snickering questioning of the dignity of Man and his destiny, their eager prying and twisted interpretations of the privacies and dreams of the mind. Of course, they weren't popular! Of course, they were limited now to the operations of Psychological Service! And to admit that one had, oneself —

Duffold grimaced as he picked up the desk-speaker. He distributed sparse instructions to cover his probable period of absence from the Station, and left the office. There wasn't much time to waste, if he wanted to keep within Pilch's half-hour limit. In the twelve weeks he had been on Palayata, he had avoided direct contact with the natives after his first two or three experiences with the odd emotional effects they produced in human beings. But since he had been invited to the Service conference, it seemed advisable to confirm that experience once more personally.

The simple way to do that was to walk out to Ramp 19, instead of taking the Station tube.

The moment he stepped outside the building, the remembered surges of acute uneasiness came churning up in him again. The port area was crowded as usual by sight-seeing Palayatans. Duffold stopped next to the building for a few moments, watching them.

The uneasiness didn't abate. The proximity of Palayatans didn't affect all humans in the same way; some reported long periods of a kind of euphoria when around them, but that sensation could shift suddenly and unaccountably to sharp anxiety and complete panic. Any one of several dozen drugs gave immunity to those reactions; and the members of the Station's human personnel whose work brought them into contact with the natives were, therefore, given chemical treatment as a regular procedure. But Duffold had refused to resort to drugs.

He started walking determinedly toward the ramp area, making no attempt to avoid the shifting streams of the Palayatan visitors. They drifted about in chattering groups, lending the functional terminal an air of cheerful holiday. If his jangling nerves hadn't told him otherwise, Duffold could have convinced himself easily that he was on a purely human world. Physically, Palayatans were humanoid to the nth degree, at least as judged by the tolerant standards of convergent evolution. They also loved Hub imports, which helped strengthen the illusion. Male and female tended to wander about their business in a haze of Hub perfumes; and at least one in every five adults in sight wore clothes of human manufacture.

But Duffold's nerves were yammering that these creatures were more alien than so many spiders — their generally amiable attitude and the fact that they looked like human beings could be only a deliberate deception, designed to conceal some undefined but sinister purpose. He broke off that unreassuring line of thought, and clamped his mind down purposefully on a more objective consideration of the odd paradoxes presented by these pseudo-people. Palayatans were even more intrigued, for example, by the Hub humans' spectacular technological achievements than by Hub styles and perfumes. Hence their presence in swarms about the Station where they could watch the space transports arrive and depart. But, in twelve years, they hadn't shown the slightest inclination to transplant any significant part of Hub technology to their own rather rural though semi-mechanized civilization.

At an average I.Q. level of seventy-eight in the population, that wasn't surprising, of course. What was not only surprising but completely improbable, when you really considered it, was that they had not only developed a civilization at all, but that it had attained a uniform level everywhere on the planet.

It simply made no sense, Duffold thought bitterly. Outposts' sociological experts had made the same comment over a year ago, when presented with the available data on Palayata. They had suggested either a detailed check on the accuracy of the data, or a referral of the whole Palayatan question to Psychological Service.

The data had been checked, exhaustively. It was quite accurate. After that, Outposts had had no choice —

"My, you're perspiring, Excellency!" Pilch said, as he stepped up on the platform of Ramp 19, "This is Wintan. You've met before, I believe. But you really needn't have hurried so!" She glanced at her timepiece. "Why, you're hardly even two minutes late!"

Wintan was a stocky fair-haired man, and Duffold did recall having met him some months before, when his credentials — indicating a legitimate scholarly interest in sociology — were being checked at the Station.

They shook hands, and Duffold turned to greet the other man.

Only — it wasn't a man.

Mentally, Duffold recoiled in a kind of frenzy. Physically, he reached out and clasped the elderly Palayatan's palm with a firm if clammy grip, shook it twice, and dropped it, his mouth held taut in what he was positive was an appalling grin. Wintan was saying something about, "Albemarl ... guide and traveling companion —" Then Pilch tapped Duffold's shoulder.

"The records you sent by tube have arrived, Excellency! Perhaps you'd better check them."

Gratefully, he followed her into the ship. Inside the lock, she stopped and looked at him quizzically. "Hits you pretty hard, doesn't it?" she murmured. "Great Suns, why don't you take one of those drugs?"

Duffold mopped his brow. "Don't like the idea," he said stubbornly. He indicated the two outside the lock. "Don't tell me you got a volunteer for the investigation?"

Pilch's gleaming black hair swung about her shoulders as she turned to look. "No," she smiled. "Albemarl came along to see Wintan off. You've been honored, by the way! He's an itinerant sage of sages among Palayatans — I.Q. one hundred and nine! He and Wintan have been working together for months. Of course, Wintan's immune to the emotional reactions —"

"I see," Duffold said coldly. "No doubt he's also had thorough psychological conditioning?"

Pilch grinned at him. "Not many," she said, "have had as much!"

The Psychology Service ship that swallowed up the transport a few hours later was a camouflaged monstrosity moving along with the edge of an asteroid flow halfway across the system. For all practical purposes, it looked indistinguishable from the larger chunks of planetary debris in its neighborhood, and from its size, it might have had a complement of several thousand people. Duffold was a little surprised that out of that potential number, only five Service members attended the conference, two of whom were Wintan and Pilch. It suggested an economy and precision in organization he had somehow failed to expect here.

The appearance of Buchele, the senior commander in charge of the conference, was almost shocking. He had the odd, waxy skin and cautious motion of a man on whom rejuvenation treatments had taken an incomplete effect, but there was no indication of the mental deterioration that was supposed to accompany that condition. His voice was quick, and he spoke with the easy courtesy of a man to whom command was too natural a thing to be emphasized. He introduced Cabon, the ship's captain, a tall man of Pilch's dark slender breed, who said almost nothing throughout the next few hours, and a red-haired woman named Lueral who was, she said, representing Biology Section. Then the conference was under way with a briskness that made Duffold glad he had decided to bring Outposts' full records on Palayata along for the meeting.

They went over the reasons why Outposts was interested in maintaining a Station on Palayata. They were sound reasons: Palayata was a convenient take-off point for the investigation and control of an entire new sector of space, the potential center of a thousand-year, many-sided project. Except for the doubtful factor of the natives, it was as favorable for human use as a world could be expected to become without a century-long conditioning program. The natives themselves represented an immediate new trade outlet for Grand Commerce, whose facilities would make the project enormously less expensive to Government than any similar one on a world that did not attract the organized commercial interests.

Buchele nodded. "Assuming, Excellency, that. the Service might be able to establish that the peculiarities of the Palayatan natives are in no way dangerous to human beings, but that the emotional disturbances they cause will have to continue to be controlled by drugs — would Outposts regard that as a satisfactory solution?"

Duffold was convinced that under the circumstances Outposts would be almost tearfully thankful for such a solution, but he expressed himself a little more conservatively. He added, "Is there any reason to believe that they actually are harmless?"

Buchele's dead-alive face showed almost no expression. "No," he said, "there isn't. Your records show what ours do. The picture of this Palayatan culture isn't fully explainable in the terms of any other culture, human or nonhuman, that we know of. There's an unseen controlling factor — well, call it 'X'. That much is almost definitely established. With the information we have, we could make a number of guesses at its nature; and that's all."

Duffold stared bleakly at him. No one in Outposts had cared to put it into so many words, but that was what they had been afraid of.

Buchele said softly, "We have considered two possible methods of procedure. With your assistance, Excellency, we should like to decide between them now."

With his assistance! Duffold became suddenly enormously wary. "Go ahead, commander," he requested affably.

"Very well. Let's assume that 'X' actually is a latent source of danger. The section of your records covering the recent deaths of two human beings on the planet might suggest that the danger has become active, but there is no immediate reason to connect those deaths with 'X'."

Duffold nodded hesitantly.

"The point that the Service and, I'm sure, Outposts are most concerned with," the gentle voice of the dead-alive man went on, "is that there is absolutely no way of estimating the possible extent of the assumed danger. As we sit here, we may be members of a race which already has doomed itself by reaching out for one new world that should have been left forever untouched. On the basis of our present information, that is exactly as possible as that the Palayatan 'X' may turn out to be a completely innocuous factor. Where 'X' lies on the scale between those two possibilities can almost certainly be determined, however. The question is simply whether we want to employ the means that will determine it."

"Meaning," said Duffold, "that the rather direct kind of investigation I understand you're planning — kidnaping a native, bringing him out to this ship, and subjecting him to psychological pressures — could start the trouble?"

"It might."

"I agree," Duffold said. "What was the other procedure?"

"To have Outposts and Grand Commerce withdraw all human personnel from Palayata."

"Abandon the planet permanently?" Duffold felt his face go hot.

"Yes," said Buchele.

Duffold drew a slow breath. A spasm of rage shook through him and went away. "We can't do that, and you know it!" he said.

Lusterless eyes hooded themselves in the waxy face. "If you please, Excellency," Buchele said quietly, "there is nothing in the records given us by your Department to indicate that this is an impossibility."

It was true enough. Duffold said sourly, "No need to underline the obvious! We're committed to remain on Palayata until the situation is understood. If there is no danger there, or only ordinary danger — nothing that reaches beyond the planet itself — we can stay or not as we choose. But we can't leave, now that we've brought ourselves to the attention of this 'X' factor, before we know whether or not it constitutes a potential danger to every human world in the galaxy. We can't even destroy the planet, since we don't know whether that would also destroy 'X,' or simply irritate it!"

"Is the destruction of Palayata being seriously considered?" the Service man said.

"Not at the moment," Duffold said grimly.

For the first time then, Buchele shifted his glance slowly about at the other Service members. "It seems that we are in agreement so far," he said, as if addressing them. He looked back at Duffold.

That was when the thought came to Duffold. It startled him, but he didn't stop to consider it. He said, "My Department obviously has been unable to work out a satisfactory solution to the problem. I'm authorized to say that Outposts will give the Service any required support in solving it, providing I'm allowed to observe the operation."

There was a momentary silence. It was bluff, and it wasn't fooling them; but the Service was known to go to considerable lengths to build up good will in the other Departments.

Pilch said suddenly, "We accept the condition — with one qualification."

Duffold hesitated, surprised. Buchele's gaze was on Pilch; the others seemed to be studying him reflectively, but nobody appeared to question Pilch's acceptance. "What's the qualification?" he asked.

"We should have your agreement," she said, "that you will accept any safety measures we feel are required."

"I assume those safety measures are for my benefit," Duffold said gravely.

"Well, yes —"

"Why," said Duffold, "'in that case I thank you for your concern. And, of course, you have my agreement."

The others stirred and smiled. Pilch looked rueful. "It's just that —"

"I know," Duffold nodded. "It's just that I haven't had any psychological conditioning."

Pilch was called from the conference room immediately afterwards. This time Duffold was not surprised to discover that she appeared to be in charge of the actual kidnaping project and that she was arranging to include him in the landing party. There seemed to be a constant easy shifting of authority among these people which did not correspond too well with the rank they held.

Others came in. He began to get a picture of unsuspected complexities of organization and purpose within this huge, ungainly ship. There was talk of pattern analysis and factor summaries at the table at which Buchele remained in charge; and Duffold stayed there, since they were dealing with material with which he was in part familiar. It appeared that Wintan, the service operator who had been working planetside on Palayata, had provided the ship's Integrators with detailed information not included in previous reports; and the patterns were still being revised. So far, Buchele seemed to feel that the revisions indicated no significant changes.

Somebody came to warn Duffold that the landing operation was to get underway in eighty minutes. He hurried off to contact the Outposts Station on Palayata and extend the period he expected to be absent.

When he came back, they were still at it —

There seemed to be no permanent government or permanent social structure of any sort on Palayata; not even, as a rule, anything resembling permanent family groups. On the other hand, some family groups maintained themselves for decades — almost as if someone were trying to prove that no rule could be applied too definitely to the perverse planet! Children needing attention attached themselves to any convenient adult or group of adults and were accepted until they decided to wander off again.

There were no indications of organized science or of scientific speculation. Palayatan curiosity might be intense, but it was brief and readily satisfied. Technical writings on some practical application or other of the scientific principles with which they were familiar here could be picked up almost anywhere and were used in the haphazard instruction that took the place of formal schooling. There wasn't even the vaguest sort of recorded history, but there were a considerable number of historical manuscripts, some of them centuries old and lovingly preserved, which dealt with personal events of intense interest to the recorder and of very limited usefulness to his researcher. It had been the Hub's own archeological workers who eventually turned up evidence indicating that Palayata's present civilization had been drifting along in much the same fashion for at least two thousand years and perhaps a good deal longer.

Impossible ... impossible ... impossible — if things were what they seemed to be!

So they weren't what they seemed to be. Duffold became aware of the fact that by now Buchele and Wintan and he were the only ones remaining at that table. The others presumably had turned their attention to more promising work; and refreshments had appeared.

They ate thoughtfully until Duffold remarked, "They're still either very much smarter than they act — smarter than we are, in fact — or something is controlling them. Right?"

Buchele said that seemed to be about it.

"And if they're controlled," Duffold went on, "the controlling agency is something very much smarter than human beings."

Wintan shook his short-cropped blond head. "That wouldn't necessarily be true."

Duffold looked at him. "Put it this way," he said. "Does the Service think human beings, using all the tricks of your psychological technology, could control a world to the extent Palayata seems to be controlled?"

"Oh, certainly!" Wintan said cheerfully; and Buchele nodded. "Given one trained operator to approximately every thousand natives, something quite similar could be established," the senior commander said drily. "But who would want to go to all that trouble?"

"And keep it up for twenty centuries or so!" Wintan added. "It's a technical possibility, but it seems a rather pointless one."

Duffold was silent for a moment, savoring some old suspicions. Even if the Service men had a genuine lack of interest in the possibilities of such a project, the notion that Psychology Service felt it was capable of that degree of control was unpleasant. "What methods would be employed?" he said. "Telepathic amplifiers?"

"Well, that would be one of the basic means, of course," Wintan agreed. "Then, sociological conditioning — business of picking off the ones that were getting too bright to be handled. Oh, it would be a job, all right!"

Telepathic amplifiers — Outposts was aware, as was everyone else, that the Service employed gadgetry in that class; but no one outside the Service took a very serious view of such activities. History backed up that opinion with emphasis: the psi boys had produced disturbing effects in various populations from time to time, but in the showdown the big guns always had cleaned them up very handily. Duffold said hopefully, "Does it seem to be telepathy we're dealing with here?"

Wintan shook his head. "No. If it were, we could spot it and probably handle whoever was using it. You missed that part of the summary, Excellency! Checking for tele-impulses was a major part of the job I was sent to do." He looked at Buchele, perhaps a trifle doubtfully. "Palayatans appear to be completely blind to any telepathic form of approach; at least, that's the report of my instruments."

"Or shut-off," Buchele said gently.

"Or shut-off," Wintan agreed. "We can't determine that with certainty until we get our specimen on board. We know the instruments would have detected such a resistance in any human being."

Buchele almost grinned. "In any human being we've investigated," he amended.

Wintan looked annoyed. From behind Duffold, Pilch's voice announced, "I'll be wanting his Excellency at Eighty-two Lock in" — there was something like a millisecond's pause, while he could imagine her glancing at her timepiece again — "seventeen minutes. But Lueral wants him first."

As Duffold stood up, she added, "You two had better come along. Biology has something to add to your discussion on telepathy."

"Significant?" Buchele asked, coming stiffly to his feet.

"Possibly. The Integrators should finish chewing it around in a few more minutes."

Duffold had been puzzling about what Lueral and the Biology Section could be wanting of him, but the moment he stepped out of a transfer lock and saw the amplification stage set up, with a view of a steamy Palayatan swamp floating in it, he knew what it was and he had a momentary touch of revulsion. The incident with the keff creature, which had cost the lives of two Outposts investigators, had been an unlovely one to study in its restructure; and he had studied it carefully several times in the past few days, in an attempt to discover any correlation with the general Palayatan situation. He had been unsuccessful in that and, taking the seat next to the stage that was indicated to him, he wondered what Biology thought it had found.

Lueral, the red-headed woman who had attended the earlier part of the general conference, introduced him to a fat, elderly man, whose name Duffold did not catch, but who was Biology's Section Head. He was operating the amplifier and remained in his seat. Lueral said into the darkened room:

"This is the record of an objective restructure his Excellency brought shipward with him. The location of the original occurrence was at the eastward tip of Continent Two; the date, one hundred thirty-eight standard, roughly one hundred hours ago. To save time, we would like his Excellency to give us a brief explanation of the circumstances."

Duffold cleared his throat. "The circumstances," he said carefully, "are that we have investigators working in that area. Ostensibly, they are archeologists. Actually, they're part of an Outposts project, checking the theory that Palayata is operating under some kind of secret government. There is a concentration of the deserted settlements we find all over the planet around those swamps. The two men involved in the restructure were working through such a settlement — or supposed to be working through it — when the accident occurred."

He added, "If it was an accident. I brought the record along because of the possibility that it was something else."

The Section Head said in a heavy voice, "The restructure appears to have been made within two hours after the actual incident."

"A little less than two hours," Duffold agreed. "There were hourly position checks. When the team failed to check in, a restructure heli began to track them. By the time they reached this keff animal, some natives already had killed it — with a kind of harpoon gun, as the restructure shows. Some portions of the bodies of our investigators were recovered. "

"Had the natives observed the incident?" Lueral inquired.

"They said they had — too far off to prevent it. They claim they kill a keff whenever they find one, not because they regard them as a danger to themselves but because they are highly destructive to food animals in the area. They hadn't realized a keff might also be destructive to human beings."

The Section Head said, "This is view of the keff some minutes after the killing of the two men. The promptness with which the restructure was made permits almost limitless detail."

Duffold felt himself wince as the colors in the amplification stage between them blurred and ran briefly and cleared again. The keff appeared, half-submerged in muddy water, a mottled green and black hulk, the eyeless head making occasional thrusting motions, with an unpleasant suggestion of swallowing.

"Weight approximately three tons," said the Section Head. "The head takes up almost a third of its length. Motions very slow. Normally, this would indicate a vegetarian or omnivorous animal with a limitless food supply, such as these mile-long swamp stretches would provide. Possibly aggressive when attacked, but not dangerous to any reasonably alert and mobile creature."

He added, "However, we were able to pick up tele-impulses at this point, which indicate that the natives' description of its food habits is correct. I suggest using tel-dampers. The impulses are rather vivid."

Pilch's voice said, "Hold still!" behind Duffold, and something like a pliable ring slipped down around his skull. Soft clamps fastened it here and there, and then he was aware of her settling down in the chair beside him. Her whisper reached him again, "If you don't like what you're getting, say so! They don't really need you for this."

Duffold made a grunting sound, indicating complete contentment with his situation and a desire not to be disturbed, but not entirely turning down the suggestion. There were crawling feelings along his spine.

He felt good. He felt drowsy but purposeful, because now there were only a few more steps to go, and then the great pink maw would open before him, and he could relax right into it. Relax and —

He jerked upright in his chair, horror prickling through his nerves. Pilch was tapping his arm.

"Outside!" she whispered. "Keep the damper on." They moved through the dim room; a door clicked ahead of Duffold, then clicked again behind him, and light flooded around them.

He pulled the tel-damper off his head like some small, unclean, clinging animal. "*Whew!*" he breathed. "Should have taken your advice, I think!"

"Well, you didn't know. *We* should have thought of it. There are ways of letting stuff like that come at you, and you —"

"Don't say it," he warned. "I'm learning my limitations." He was silent a moment. "Was that how it felt to them?" He described his sensations.

"They felt something like that," she said. "You gave the impulses your individual interpretations, of course, because you'd seen the restructure and knew what the keff was like. Cabon will be out in a moment, by the way. They got the Integrators' report back on this; I gather there's nothing definite enough in it to change our plans."

"I see," Duffold said absently. Mentally, he was reliving that section of the restructure in which the two investigators had come walking and wading right up to the keff, looking about as if searching for something, and apparently not even aware of each other's presence. Then they had stood still, while the huge head came slowly up out of the water before them — and the wet, pink maw opened wide and slapped shut twice.

Cabon stepped out of the room behind them. He grinned faintly. "Raw stuff," he remarked. "You've got a fine restructure team, Excellency."

"Any delays indicated?" Pilch inquired.

"No. You'd better go ahead on schedule. It's almost certain we'll still need our average Palayatan — and the one we've got spotted isn't going to hold still for us forever."

Yunnan, the average Palayatan, had finished the satisfactory third day of his solitary camping hike with a satisfactory meal composed largely of a broiled platterful of hard-shelled and hard-to-catch little water creatures, famed for their delicacy. The notion of refreshing his memory of that delicacy had been in his mind for some weeks and had finally led him up to this high mountain plateau and its hundreds of quick, cold streams where they were to be found at their best.

Having sucked out the last of the shells and pitched it into his camp fire, he sat on for a while under the darkening sky, watching the stars come out and occasionally glancing across the plateau at the dark, somber mass of the next mountain ridge. Two other camp fires had become very distantly visible there, indicating the presence of other soqua spearers. He would stay here two more days, Yunnan thought, and then turn back, towards the valleys and the plain, and return to his semi-permanent house in his semi-permanent settlement, to devote himself again for a while to his semi-permanent occupation of helping local unbannut-growers select the best seeds for next season's crop.

It was all a very pleasant prospect. Life, Yunnan told himself, with a sense of having summed it up, was a pretty good thing! It was a conclusion he had come to before under similar circumstances.

Presently he rebuilt the fire, stretched out on some blankets close to it, and pulled a few more blankets on top of him. He blinked up at the stars a few more times and fell sound asleep.

Far overhead, a meteor that was not a meteor hit the atmosphere, glowed yellow, and vanished. A survey heli of the Hub Station's Planetary Geographers outfit, which had been moving high and unobtrusively above the plateau all day, came in closer to a point almost directly above Yunnan's camp, remained there a few minutes, and moved off again across the plateau and on beyond the mountain ridges to the east.

A dark spherical body, the size of a small house, sank swiftly and silently toward the plateau and came to a halt finally a hundred yards above Yunnan's camp and a little more than that to one side of it. Presently a breeze moved from that direction across the camp, carrying traces of a chemical not normally found in such concentration in Palayata's air. Yunnan inhaled it obligingly. A few minutes later, the breeze grew suddenly into a smooth, sustained rush of air, like the first moan of an approaching storm. Sparks flew from the fire, and leaves danced out of the trees. Then the wind subsided completely, and three people came walking into the camp. They bent above Yunnan.

"Perfect reaction!" Pilch's voice said. She straightened and glanced up. The spherical object had come gliding along at tree-top level behind them and was now stationed directly overhead. Various and sundry clicking, buzzing, and purring sounds came out of its open lock. "Take them two or three more minutes to get a complete reproduction," she remarked. "Nothing to do but wait."

Duffold grunted. He was feeling uncomfortable again, and not entirely because of the presence of a Palayatan. Pilch had explained what had happened to Yunnan; the patterns of external sensory impressions that had been sifting into his brain at the moment the trace-chemical reached it through his blood stream were fixed there now, and no new impressions were coming through. He would remain like that, his last moment of sleep-sensed external reality extending itself unchangingly through the hours and days until the blocking agent was removed. What worried Duffold was that the action was a deliberate preliminary prod at the mysterious 'X' factor, and if 'X' felt prodded, there was no telling at all just how it might respond.

He looked down at their captive. Yunnan certainly looked quietly asleep, but the mild smile on his humanoid features might have expressed either childlike innocence or a rather sinister enjoyment of the situation, depending on how you felt about Palayatans.

And assuming Yunnan was harmless, at least for the moment, was somebody — or something — else, far off or perhaps quite close in the thickening night around them, aware by now that untoward and puzzling things were going on in a Palayatan mind?

Duffold knew they were trying to check on that, too. A voice began murmuring presently from one of the talkie gadgets Pilch wore as earrings. When it stopped, she said briefly, "All right." And then, to Duffold, "Not a pulse coming through the tele-screens that wouldn't be normal here! just animals —" She sounded disappointed about it.

"Too bad!" Duffold said blandly. His nerves unknotted a trifle.

"Well, it's negative evidence anyway!" Pilch consoled him. The voice murmured from the same earring again, and she said, "All right. Put down the carrier then!" and to her two companions, "They're all done in the shuttle. Let's go."

A grav-carrier came floating down through the dark air toward them, and the crewman who had accompanied them into the camp began to extinguish the fire. He was conscientious and thorough about it. Pilch stepped up on the carrier. Duffold looked at her, at the busy crewman, and at Yunnan. Then he set his teeth, wrapped the Palayatan up in his blankets, picked him up, and laid him down on the carrier.

"Hm-m-m!" said Pilch. "Not bad, Excellency!"

Duffold thought a bad word and hoped she wasn't being telepathic.

"Of course not!" said Pilch, reaching up for the earring that hadn't come into noticeable use so far. She began to unscrew it. "Besides, I'm shutting off the pick-up right now, Excellency —"

Almost two hours later, Yunnan awakened briefly. He blinked up at the familiar star-patterns overhead, gazed out across the plateau, and noted that one of the camp fires there had gone out. Thus reminded, he yawned and scratched himself, stood up, and replenished his own fire. Then he lay down again, listened for a half-minute or so to the trilling night-cries of two small tree creatures not far away, and drifted back to sleep.

"He's completely out of the sensory stasis now, of course," Wintan explained to Duffold as the view of Yunnan's camp faded out before them. "How did you like the staging job?"

Duffold admitted it was realistic. He was wondering, however, he added, what would have happened if the Palayatan had decided to go for a stroll and walked off the stage?"

"Well," Wintan said reflectively, "if he'd done that, we would have known he was ignoring the five or six plausible reasons against doing it that were planted in his awareness. In that case, we could have counted on his being an individual embodiment of the 'X' factor, so to speak. The staff was prepared for the possibility,"

Duffold knew that Psychological Service as such was, as a matter of fact, prepared for the possibility that they had hauled a super-being on board which conceivably could destroy or take control of this huge ship — and distant weapons were trained on the ship to insure that it wouldn't be under alien control for more than an instant. Even more distantly, out in the nothingness of space somewhere, events on the ship were being subjected to a moment to moment scrutiny and analysis.

Nor was *that* all. The Outposts patrol ships at Palayata had been relieved from duty by a Supreme Council order from the Hub; and, in their places, heavily armed cruisers of a type none of the patrol commanders could identify had begun to circle the planet.

"They won't break up Palayata unless they have to, of course!" Cabon had said, in reporting that matter to Duffold. "But that's no worry of ours at the moment. Our job is to trace out, record, and identify every type of thought, emotion, and motivation that possibly could go ticking through this Yunnan's inhuman little head. If we find out he's exactly what he seems to be, that eliminates one possible form of 'X'."

And if Yunnan was something other than the not too intelligent humanoid he seemed to be, they had 'X' neatly isolated for study. Whether or not they completed the study then depended largely on the nature of the subject.

Rationally, Duffold couldn't disagree with the method. It was drastic; the casually icy calculation behind the preparations made by the Service had, in fact, shocked him as nothing else had done in his life. But, at one stage or another, it would bring 'X' into view. If 'X' was both hostile and more than a match for man, man at least had avoided being taken by surprise. If 'X' was merely more than a match for man —

"Mightn't hurt us at all to learn how to get along with our superiors for a while," Wintan had observed thoughtfully.

It was a notion Duffold found particularly difficult to swallow.

He had noticed, in this last hour while they completed their preparations to invade the Average Palayatan's mind, occasional traces of a tingling excitement in himself — something close to elation. By and by, it dawned on him that it was the kind of elation that comes from an awareness of discovery.

He was engaged in an operation with the most powerful single organization of the Hub Systems. The despised specialists of Psychology Service, the errand boys of the major Departments, were, as a matter of fact, telling everyone, apparently including the Hub's Supreme Council, just what should be done about Palayata and how to do it.

Probably, it hadn't always been that way, Duffold decided; but the regular Departments of the Hub were getting old. For a decade, Outposts — one of the most brisk of the lot — had been gathering evidence that Palayatan civilization wasn't so much quaint as incomprehensible. For an equal length of time, it had been postponing recognition of the fact that the incomprehensibility might have a deadly quality to it — that, quite possibly, something very strange and very intelligent was in concealment on Palayata, observing human beings and perhaps only tolerating their presence here for its unknown purposes.

Even after the recognition had been forced on it, the Department had been unwilling to make any move at all on its own responsibility, for fear it might make the wrong one. Instead, it called in Psychology Service —

For the same reason that Psychology Service always was called in when there was an exceptionally dirty and ticklish job to be done — the Service People showed an unqualified willingness to see any situation exactly as it was and began dealing with it immediately in the best possible manner, to the limits of human ability. It was an attitude that guaranteed in effect that any problem which was humanly resolvable was going to get resolved.

The excitement surged up in Duffold again. And that, he added to himself, was why they didn't share the normal distaste for the notion of encountering a superior life form. The most superior of life forms couldn't improve on that particular attitude! Here or elsewhere, the Service eventually might be defeated, but it could never be outclassed.

He wondered at that difference in organizations that were equally human and decided it was simply that the Service now attracted the best in human material that happened to be around. At other times in history, the same type of people might have been engaged in very different activities — but they would always be found moving into the front ranks of humanity and moving out of the organizations that were settling down to the second-rate job of maintaining what others had gained.

As for himself — well, he'd gone fast and far in Outposts. He knew he was brainier than most. If it took some esoteric kind of mental training to get himself into mankind's real front ranks, he was going to take a look at it —

Providing, that was, that the lives of everyone on the ship didn't get snuffed out unexpectedly sometime in the next few hours!

Wintan: Pilch, your lad has just bucked his way through simultaneously to the Basis of Self-Esteem and the Temptations of Power and Glory! I'm a little in awe of him. What to do?

Pilch: Too early for a wide-open, I think! It could kill him. If we tap anything, we're going to have trouble. Buchele isn't —
Cabon: Make it wide-open, Wintan. My responsibility.
Pilch: No!
Voice from Somewhere Far Out: Agreement with Cabon's decision. Proceed!

Wintan had left the pick-up room for the time being; and Duffold had it all to himself.

It was an odd place. Almost the most definite thing you could say about it was that it was somewhere within the vast bulk of the Service ship. Duffold sat in something like a very large and comfortable armchair with his feet up on a cushioned extension; and so far as he could tell, the armchair might have been floating slowly and endlessly through the pale-green, luminous fog which started about eight feet from his face in every direction. The only other thing visible in the room was another chair off to his right, in which Wintan had been sitting. Even the entrance by which they had come in was indetectible in the luminosity; when Wintan left, he appeared to vanish in cool green fire long before he reached it,

There wasn't much more time before the work on the captured Palayatan began, and Duffold started running the information he'd been given regarding the operation and his own role as an observer through his mind. Some of the concepts involved were unfamiliar; but, on the whole, it sounded more comprehensible than he had expected. They were acting on the assumption that, with the exception of the 'X' factor, the structure of a Palayatan's mental personality was similar to the human one. They reacted to outside stimuli in much the same way and appeared to follow the same general set of basic motivations.

It was already known that there were specific differences. The Palayatan mind was impermeable to telepathic impulses at the level of sensory and verbal interpretations, which was the one normally preferred by human telepaths when it could be employed, since it involved the least degree of individual garbling of messages. Palayatans, judging by the keff creature's inability to affect them, were also impermeable to telepathed emotional stimuli. In spite of the effect they themselves produced on most untrained humans, it had been demonstrated that they also did not radiate at either of these levels, as against the diffused trickling of mental and emotional impulses normally going out from a human being.

At least, that was the picture at present. It might change when the ship's giant amplifiers, stimulators, and microscanners were brought into play upon Yunnan's sleeping brain. If 'X' was a concealed factor of the Palayatan's personality, it would show up instantly. In that case, the investigation as such would be dropped, and the Service would switch its efforts into getting 'X' into communication. It should at least be possible to determine rather quickly whether or not 'X' was hostile and how capable it was of expressing hostility effectively, either here or on the planet.

But if it was found that Yunnan, as he knew himself, was Yunnan and nothing else, the search would drop below the levels of personality toward the routine mechanisms of the mind and the organic control areas. Somewhere in those multiple complexities of interacting structures of life must be a thing that was different enough from the standard humanoid pattern to make Palayata what it was. They had talked of the possibility that the 'X' influence, if it was an alien one, did not extend actively beyond the planet. But the traces of its action would still be there and could be interpreted.

Duffold's impressions of the possibilities at that stage became a little vague, and he shifted his attention to a consideration of what Wintan had said regarding himself. There was apparently always some risk involved in an investigation of this kind, not to the subject, but to the investigator.

Or, in this case, to the observer.

The trouble was, according to Wintan, that the human mind — or any other type of mind the Service had studied so far, for that matter — was consciously capable of only a very limited form of experience. "A practical limitation," Wintan had said. "Most of what's going on in the universe isn't really any individual's concern. If he were trying to be aware of it all the time, he couldn't walk across the room without falling on his face. Besides, it would kill him."

And when Duffold looked questioningly at him, he added, "Did you ever go in for the Sensational Limitations vogue, Excellency?"

"No," Duffold said shortly.

"Well," Wintan acknowledged, "they get a little raw, at that! However, they do show that a human being can tolerate only a definitely limited impact of emotion — artificially induced or otherwise — at any one time, before he loses awareness of what's going on. Now, the more or less legitimate material the Sensationalists use is drawn from emotions that other human beings have at one time or another consciously experienced, sometimes under extreme stimulation, of course. However, as a rather large number of Sensationalists have learned by now, the fact that a sensation came originally from a human mind doesn't necessarily make its re-experience a safe game for another human being."

He was silent for a moment. "That keff animal," he said then. "You saw it. Can you imagine yourself thinking and feeling like a keff, Excellency?"

Duffold grinned. "I hadn't thought of it," he said. He considered and shook his head. "Probably not too well."

"It appears to be a fairly complicated creature," Wintan said. "Stupid, of course. It doesn't need human intelligence to get along. But it's not just a lump of life responding to raw surges of emotion. There are creatures that aren't much else, a good deal farther down on the scale. They haven't developed anything resembling a calculating brain, and what we call emotion is what guides them and keeps them alive: To be effective guides to something like that, those emotions have to be pretty strong. As a matter of fact, they're quite strong enough to wreck anything as complex and carefully balanced as a conscious human mind very thoroughly, if it contacts them for more than a very short time."

"How do you know?" Duffold inquired.

"So far, our Hub Sensationalists haven't learned how to bottle anything like that," Wintan said. "At least, we haven't run into any indications of it. However, Psychology Service did learn how, since it was required for a number of reasons. In the process, we might have discovered that emotion can kill the body by destroying the mind in a matter of seconds if we hadn't been made aware of the fact a good deal earlier —"

"Yes?" Duffold said politely.

"Excellency," Wintan said, "civilized man is — with good reason, I think — a hellishly proud creature. Unfortunately, his achievements often make it difficult for him to accept that his remote ancestors — and the remote ancestors of every other mobile and intelligent life form we've come across — were, at one period, specks of appetite in the mud, driven by terrors and a brainless lust for survival, ingestion, and procreation that are flatly inconceivable to the conscious human mind today. "

Duffold laughed. "I'll accept it," he said agreeably.

"In that case," said Wintan, "you might consider accepting that precisely the same pattern is still present in each of our intelligent life forms and is still basically what motivates them as organisms. Self-generated or not, emotions like that can still shock the mind that contacts them consciously in full strength to death. Normally, of course, that's a flat impossibility — our mental structure guarantees that what filters through into consciousness is no more than the trace of a shadow of the basic emotions … no more than consciousness needs to guide it into reasonably intelligent conduct and, usually, at any rate, no more than consciousness can comfortably tolerate. But in an investigation of this kind, we'll be playing around the edges of the raw stuff sooner or later. We'll try to keep out of it, of course."

Duffold said thoughtfully that he was beginning to see the reason for safeguards. "What makes it possible for you to get into trouble here?"

"Something like a cubic mile of helpful gadgetry," Wintan said. "It's quite an accomplishment."

"It is," Duffold said. "So it's not all conditioning then. Can you — conditioned — people get along without safeguards?"

Wintan said amiably that to some extent they could. On reflection, it didn't sound too bad to Duffold. The particular type of safeguard that had been provided for him in the pick-up room was to the effect that as he approached an emotional overload, he would be cut out of contact automatically with the events in the ship. Otherwise, he would remain an observer-participant, limited only by his lack of understanding of the progress of the operation.

Wintan: I've given him fair warning, Pilch.

Pilch, grudgingly: There's no such thing in this game! I suppose you did what you could.

Pictures moved now and then through the luminous mist. Some were so distinct that it seemed to Duffold he was looking straight through the bulk of the ship at the scene in question. Most were mere flickers of form and color, and a few a tentative haziness in which a single detail might assume a moment of solidity before the whole faded out.

"Cabon's checking the final arrangements," Wintan said from the chair to Duffold's right.

Duffold nodded, fascinated by the notion that he was observing the projected images of a man's mind, and disappointed that the meaning of much of it apparently was wasted on him. Buchele's waxy face showed up briefly, followed by the picture of a thick-necked man whose cheekbones and jaw were framed by a trimmed bristle of red beard.

"Our primary investigators, those two," Wintan said briefly. "The other one's Ringor — Head of Pattern Analysis." The mind-machines and their co-ordinators did what they could; they supplied power and analyzed a simultaneous wealth of detail no human mentality could begin to grasp in the same span of time. To some degree, they also predicted the course that should be followed. But the specific, moment to moment turns of the search for 'X' were under the direction of human investigators. Eight or nine others would trace the progress of the leading two but would not become immediately involved unless they were needed. Pilch was one of these.

The reconstruction of Yunnan's camp area came gradually into sight now, absorbing the pick-up medium as it cleared and spread about and behind the two observers. Presently, it seemed to Duffold that he was looking down at the sleeping figure near the fire from a point about forty feet up in Palayata's crisp night air. The illusion would have been perfect except for two patches of something like animated smoke to either side of Yunnan. He studied the phenomenon for a moment and was startled by a sudden impression that the swirling vapory lines of one of those patches was the face of the red-bearded investigator. It changed again before he could be sure. He glanced over at Wintan, suspended incongruously in his chair against the star-powdered night.

The Service man grinned. "Saw it, too," he said in a voice that seemed much too loud here to Duffold. "The other one is Buchele — or the projector's impression of Buchele at the moment. They're designed to present what they get in a form that makes some meaning in human perceptions, but they have peculiar notions about those! You'll get used to it."

He was, Duffold decided, speaking of one of the machines. He was about to inquire further when the scene became active.

Something a little like a faint, brief gleaming of planetary auroras ... then showers of shooting stars ... played about the horizons. For a moment he forgot he was watching a reconstruction. The lights and colors flowed together and became the upper part of the body of a blond woman smiling down over the distant mountains at the sleeping Palayatan, her hands resting on the tops of the ridges. Briefly, the face blurred into an unpleasantly grimacing mask and cleared again. Then the woman was gone, and in her place was a brightly lit, perfectly ordinary-looking room, in which a man in the uniform of the Service sat at a table.

"What's all this ?" Duffold breathed.

"Eh?" Wintan said absently. "Oh!" He turned his head and laughed. "Our investigators were tuning in on each other. They've worked together before, but it takes a moment or so — Ah, here we go!"

Duffold blinked. The universe all around them was suddenly an unquiet grayness, a vaguely disturbing grayness because there was motion in it which couldn't be identified. A rapid shifting and flowing of nothing into nothing that just missed having significance for him.

"About as good a presentation as the projector can manage," Wintan's voice said, almost apologetically — and Wintan, too, Duffold noticed now, was invisible in the grayness. He felt uncomfortably isolated. "You're looking at ... well, it would be our Palayatan's consciousness, if he were awake."

Duffold said nothing. He had been seized by the panicky notion that breathing might become difficult in this stuff, and he was trying to dismiss that notion. A splash of blue, a beautiful, vivid blue, blazed suddenly in the grayness and vanished. "They're moving," Wintan's voice murmured. "Dream level now!"

Breathing *was* difficult! If only that blue would come back —

It came. Duffold gasped with relief, as gray veils exploded about him and a bright blue sky, deep with cloud-banks, spread overhead and all about. Wintan spoke from somewhere, with a touch of concern, "If this is bothering you at all, I can shut you out of it instantly, you know!"

"No," Duffold said. He broke out laughing. "I just discovered I'm not here!"

It was true in a peculiar way. There wasn't a trace of Wintan or himself or of their supporting chairs in sight here. He looked down through empty space where his body should have been and laughed again. But he could still feel himself and the pressure of the chair against him, at any rate; so he hadn't become disembodied.

"Dreams are odd." Wintan's voice sounded as if he might be smiling, too, but the concern hadn't quite left it. "Especially when they're somebody else's. And especially again when that someone isn't human. Incidentally, this is a visual pick-up for you. All you have to do to break it is to close your eyes."

Duffold closed his eyes experimentally and patted the side of the chair. Then he opened them again —

Yunnan's dream had changed in that instant. He was looking down now into a section of a shallow stream, swift-moving and clear, through which a creature like a mottled egg darted behind a silver lure. Another one showed up beyond it, both flashingly quick, propelled by a blurred paddling of red legs.

"Mountain soquas," said Wintan. "Our friend was spearing them during the day." His voice sounded thoughtful. "No trace of anything that might indicate 'X', so far. I imagine they'll stimulate a different type of sequence —"

The scene flowed, as he spoke, into something entirely different again. This was, Duffold decided, apparently an angular caricature of a Palayatan town-street, presented in unpleasantly garish colors. Something that was in part a redlegged soqua and in part an extremely stout Palayatan was speaking excitedly to a small group of other Palayatans. The next moment, they had all turned and were staring straight at Duffold. Their eyes seemed to contain some terrible accusation. Involuntarily, he cringed — just as the scene flickered out of existence.

The green luminescence was about them again. From the other chair, Wintan grinned briefly at him.

"Tapped a nightmare layer," he explained. "It woke him up. So our little friends have bad dreams, too, occasionally!" He studied Duffold quizzically. "Did you get the guilt in that one?"

"Guilt?" Duffold repeated.

"He'd been killing soquas," Wintan said. "Naughty thing to do, according to his subconscious, so it punished him." He added, "No luck at all, so far, unless there was something I missed. An orderly, childish mind. No real guile in it — and it does fit the way they look and act!"

"Could it be faked?"

"Well," Wintan said, "we couldn't do it. Not to that extent. They'll hit the Deep Downs next, I imagine. Should become more interesting now."

A riot of color blazed up about them — color that was too rich and in meaningless flux and motion, or frozen into patterns that stirred Duffold uncomfortably. Something came to his memory and he turned and spoke in Wintan's direction.

"Yes," Wintan's voice replied, "it's not surprising that it makes you think of some forms of human art. We have a comparable layer." He was silent for a moment. "How do you feel?"

"Slight headache," Duffold said, surprised. "Why?"

"It might affect you that way. Just close your eyes a while. I'll let you know if we run into something significant."

Duffold closed his eyes obediently. Now that his attention was on it, the headache seemed more than slight. He began to massage his forehead with his fingertips. Wintan's voice went on, "It's a nearly parallel complex of mental structures, as one would expect, considering the physical similarities. This particular area originates when the brain's visual centers are developing in the zygote. It's pure visual experience, preceding any outside visual stimulus. Later on, in humans anyway, it can become a fertile source of art ... also of nightmares, incidentally." His voice stopped, then resumed sharply, "Buchele's tracing something — there!"

Duffold opened his eyes. Instantly, he had a sensation that *was* pure nightmare — of being sucked forward, swept up and out of his chair, up and into —

The sensation stopped, and a velvety blackness swam in front of him like an intangible screen. He was still in his chair. He drew in a quivering breath. The only reason he hadn't shouted in fright was that he hadn't been capable of making a sound.

"That —!" he gasped.

"Easy," Wintan said quietly. "I've shut you off."

"But that was that keff animal!"

"Something very like it," Wintan said, and Duffold realized that he could see the Service man again now. Wintan was watching something that was behind the area of screening blackness for Duffold, and if he felt any of the effects that had paralyzed Duffold, he didn't show it. He added, "It's very interesting. We'd been wondering about the keff!"

"I thought," Duffold said, "that Palayatans weren't bothered by the animal."

Wintan glanced at him. "Our present Palayatans aren't. Did you notice the stylized quality of that image and the feeling of size — almost like a monument?"

Duffold said shortly that he hadn't been in a frame of mind to observe details. His vulnerability was still irritating. "It looked like a keff to me. Why should it be in this fellow's mind?"

"Ancestral image," Wintan said, "or I miss my guess! And that means — it almost *has* to mean that at one time the Palayatans weren't immune to ... ah, wait!"

"Something new?" Duffold said quickly.

Wintan seemed to hesitate. "Yes," he said.

"Then cut me in again. I don't want to miss more than I have to."

For a moment, Duffold thought Wintan hadn't responded. Then he realized that the blackness before him wasn't quite what it had been a few seconds ago.

He stared uncomprehendingly. An eerie shiver went over him. "What's this?" he demanded, his voice unaccountably low.

"Something really new!" Wintan said quietly. "I think, Excellency, that they've found 'X'!"

For the moment, that seemed to have no meaning to Duffold. The pale thing swimming in the dark before them was roughly circular and quite featureless. He had a feeling it was nothing tangible, a dim light — but his hair was bristling at the back of his neck. The thought came to him that if this was what the projectors were making of the thing that had been tracked down, the mind-machines were as puzzled as he was. "Something really new —" Wintan had said.

He realized that the thing wasn't alone.

To right and left of it, like hounds cautiously circling a strange beast they had overtaken, moved two lesser areas of light. The human investigators hadn't withdrawn.

They're trying to make contact with it, he thought. And some of the sense of awe and oppression left him. If they could face this strangeness at first hand —

It happened quickly. One of the smaller areas of light moved closer to the large one, hesitated, and moved closer again. And something like a finger of brightness stabbed out from the large one and touched the other.

Instantly, there was only blackness. Duffold heard Wintan catch his breath, and started to ask what had happened. He checked himself, appalled.

A face swam hugely before them. It was Buchele's, and it was the face of a personality sagging out of existence. The eyes were liquid, and the mouth slid open and went lax. Across the fading image flashed something sharp and decisive; and Duffold knew, without understanding how he knew it, that Cabon had given a command and that it had been acknowledged.

In the next instant, as the scene of darkness and its pale inhabitant reshaped itself, he knew also by whom the command had been acknowledged.

"No!" he shouted. He was struggling to get up out of the chair, as Wintan called out something he didn't understand. But it was over by then.

Again there had been three areas of light, two small and one large. Again, a small one came gliding in towards the large one; and again light stabbed out to meet it.

This time, it was like a jarring dark explosion all around him. Dazed, Duffold seemed to hang suspended for a moment over a black pit, and then he was dropping towards it. It was, he sensed suddenly, like dropping into a living volcano. Its terrors, stench, and fury boiled up horribly to engulf him.

The office seemed stuffy. Duffold reached back and turned the refresher up a few notches, simultaneously switching the window view to the spaceport section where the shuttles and transports stood ramped. Since he'd got back, that was the only available outside view he'd cared to look at. Except for that guide of Wintan's — Albemarl or whatever his name was — four days ago, no Palayatan ever had been allowed into that area. They hadn't sense enough to insure they would remain un-cindered there.

He noticed the Service transport had landed at Ramp Thirteen. They were punctual, as usual. A few figures moved about it, too far off to be recognized. Duffold picked up the sheaf of Service reports from a corner of the desk, flicked through them, and hauled out a sheet. There were some points he wanted to refresh his mind on before the coming interview with — well, with whomever it was they'd decided to send down! He hadn't specified Pilch, though he imagined it was the kind of job she would be likely to take on.

He read hurriedly, skipping sections here and there. "... Originally, then, it was the class of creatures of which the present-day keff is the only surviving species that forced the divergence in mental development on the proto-humanoids. Their evolutionary response was a shift of the primary center of awareness from the level of sensory interpretation to that of organic control, which has remained a semiautomatic, unconscious area of mind in any similar species. The telepathic bands on which the keff-like carnivores operated could stimulate only the sensory-response areas of the brain. The controlling central mind of the humanoid was no longer affected by them. The continuing inflow of keff-impulses on the upper telepathic bands became a meaningless irritation, and the brain eventually sealed off its receptors to them ...

"To an observer of the period, it might have seemed that the Palayatan humanoid species now had trapped itself in an evolutionary pocket. Animal intelligence must isolate itself from the full effect of the primitive emotional storms of the unconscious if it is to develop rationality and the ability of abstract thought. In doing this, it reduces its awareness of the semiautomatic levels of mind which remain largely in the area of the unconscious. In this case, however, it was losing contact with the level of sensory interpretation which normally is the indicated area of intellectual development ... For many hundreds of thousands of years, the Palayatan humanoid remained superficially an animal. His brain was, in fact, continuing to evolve at a rate comparable to the proto-human one; but the increase in consciousness and potential of organization was being absorbed almost entirely by the internal mind to which he as a personality had retreated ..."

Duffold put that sheet down, shook his head, and selected another one.

"... The fairly well-developed civilization we now find on Palayata ... of comparatively recent date ... The humanoid being with whom we have become familiar conveniently might be regarded as a secondary personality, subordinate to the internal one. However, the term is hardly more justified than if it were applied to the human sympathetic nervous system ...

"The Palayatan superficial mind has become an increasingly complex structure because the details of its required activities are complex. It has awareness of its motivations, but is not aware that an internal mind is the source of those motivations. It has no understanding of the fact that its individual desires and actions are a considered factor in the maintenance of the planetary civilization which it takes for granted.

"On the other hand, the internal personality, at this stage of its development, is still capable of only a generalized comprehension of the material reality in which it exists as an organism. It employs its superficial mind as an agent which can be motivated to act towards material goals that will be beneficial to itself and its species. By human standards, the goals have remained limited ones since the possibility of achieving them depends on the actual degree of intelligence developed at present by the superficial minds. They are limited again by the internal minds' imperfect concept of the nature of material reality. As an example, the fact that space might extend beyond the surface of their planet has had no meaning to them, though it has been presented as a theoretical possibility by some abstract thinkers ..."

Duffold shoved the sheets back into the stack. He couldn't argue with the reports or with the Service's official conclusion regarding Palayata, and he didn't doubt that the Hub Departments would accept them happily. So we're dealing with a native race of split personalities this time — no matter, so long as the Service guarantees they're harmless! The emotional disturbance they caused human beings couldn't be changed, unfortunately; but any required close contacts could be handled by drug-fortified personnel.

Everybody was going to feel satisfied with the outcome — except Duffold. He was reaching for another section of the reports when the desk communicator murmured softly up at him.

"Oh!" he said. "Why, yes. Send her right in!"

He studied Pilch curiously after she was seated. Objectively, she looked as attractive as ever, with her long, clean lines and a profile almost too precisely perfect. Otherwise, she stirred no feeling in him this time; and he was a little relieved about that.

"I understand," she said, "that you weren't entirely pleased with our reports?"

"I did have a few questions," Duffold said. "It was very good of you to come. The original reports, of course, have been transmitted to my head-quarters."

She nodded briefly.

"Personally," Duffold said hesitantly, "I find all this a little difficult to believe. Of course, I blacked out before the investigation was concluded. The reports simply state what you found, not how you got the information."

"That's right," said Pilch. "How we got it wouldn't mean much to someone who wasn't familiar with our methods of operation. What part can't you believe? That the real Palayatan is so far inside himself that he hardly knows we're around when we meet him?"

"Oh, I'll accept that that's the way it is!" Duffold said irritably. "But how did you find out?"

"One of those inner minds told us," said Pilch. "Not the one inside Yunnan — he was scared to death by the time we got done with him and yelled for help. So another one reached out far enough from the planet to see what was wrong — a colleague of ours, so to speak. At least, he regards himself as a psychologist — a specialist in mental problems."

Duffold shook his head helplessly.

"Well, it's an odd sort of existence, by our standards," Pilch said. "I don't think I'd go for it myself. But they like it well enough." She thought a moment and added, "The feeling I had was as if you were a deep-sea animal, intensely aware of yourself and of everything else in a big, dark ocean all around you. Actually, there was a sort of richness in the feeling. I'd say their life-experience is at least as varied as the average human one."

"What scared Yunnan?" Duffold asked.

"He knew something was wrong. He didn't realize he'd been removed bodily from the planet, but to use our terms, he felt as if he had suddenly grown almost deaf — and invisible. He couldn't understand the other Palayatans very well anymore, and they didn't seem to be too aware of him. And then our investigators suddenly were *talking* to him! Do you know what human beings seem like to those inside Palayatans? Something like small sleepy animals that have mysteriously turned up in their world. I imagine our degree of organic intelligence can't be too impressive at that! So when two of those animals began to address him — conscious minds like himself, but *not* his kind of mind — Yunnan panicked."

"So he killed Buchele," Duffold said.

Pilch said impassively, "It would be correct to say that Buchele killed himself. There were sections of his mind that he had never been able to accept as part of himself. Buchele was an idealist in his opinion of himself, and in Service work that's a risk. Of course, he had a right to insist on taking that risk if he chose."

"Exactly what did happen to him?" Duffold said carefully.

"The Palayatan jolted a sealed-off section of Buchele's mind into activity, and Buchele met its impact in full consciousness. It killed him."

"No matter how you phrase it," Duffold said, "it seems that one human being, at least, has been murdered by a Palayatan!"

She shook her head. "Not if murder is in the intention. Because it was only trying to frighten Buchele off. It's the way they deal with another mind that is annoying them."

"Frighten him off?" Duffold repeated incredulously.

"Look," Pilch said, "every time you felt that anxiety you mentioned, you'd been jolted by some Palayatan in exactly the same way! Every human being, every intelligent life-form we know about, keeps that stuff out of awareness by layers and layers of mental padding. Our heavy-duty civilized emotions are just trickles of the real thing! It takes the kind of power equipment we have on the ship to drive ourselves down consciously, with full awareness, to the point where we're close enough to it that a Palayatan could topple us in. So it can't ever happen on the planet."

Duffold looked like a man who has suddenly come upon a particularly distasteful notion.

"Some people reported euphorias!" he said.

Pilch nodded. "I didn't mention that because I knew you wouldn't care for it. Well, I told you they've been regarding us as some sort of small strange animal. Some of them become quite fond of the little beasts. So they stimulate us pleasantly — till we take a nip out of them or whatever it is we do that annoys them. Tell me something," she went on before he could reply, "just before you blacked out during the investigation, what were the sensations you hit — terror, self-disgust, rage?"

He looked at her carefully. "Well — all of that," he said. "The outstanding feeling was that I was in in close contact with something incredibly greedy, devouring ... foul! I can appreciate Buchele's attitude." He hesitated. "How did it happen that I wasn't aware of what got Buchele?"

"Automatic switch-off for the instant it lasted. It was obvious that it was going over the level of emotional tolerance that had been set for you. We told you there'd be safeguards."

"I see," said Duffold. "Then what about the other thing?"

Pilch looked faintly surprised. "Wintan would have cut you out of it, if he'd had the time," she said. "But obviously you did tolerate it even if you blacked out for a while. That was still well within the safe limit."

Duffold felt a slow stirring of rage. "When you took Buchele's place, it seemed to me that the Palayatan struck at you in the same way he had at Buchele. Is that correct?"

Pilch nodded. "It is."

"But because of your superior conditioning, it didn't disturb you?"

"Not enough to keep me from making use of it," Pilch said.

"In what way?"

"I opened it up on the Palayatan. That," said Pilch, "was when he yelled for help. But it was too bad you picked it up!"

Duffold carefully traced a large, even circle on the desk top with a fingertip. "And you could accept *that* as being part of your mind?" he said with a note of mild wonder. "Well, I suppose you should be congratulated on such an unusual ability."

She looked a little pale as she walked out of the office. But, somehow, Duffold couldn't find any real satisfaction in that.

Wintan was leaning against the side of the central Outpost building as Pilch came out of the entrance. She stopped short.

"Thought you'd be at the transport," she said.

"I was," Wintan said. "Twelve slightly stunned keffs in good shape have been loaded, and I was making a last tour of the area."

"Albemarl?" she asked as they started walking back to the ramps. "Or the psychologist?"

"Both," Wintan said. "I'd have liked to say good-by to Albemarl, but there's still no trace of the old tramp anywhere. He'd have enjoyed the keff hunt, too! Too bad he had to wander off again."

"How about the other one?"

"Well, there's very little chance he'll actually contact us, of course," Wintan said. "However" — he held his right hand up — "observe the new wrist adornment! If he's serious about it, that's to help him locate me."

She looked at two polished black buttons set into a metal wrist-strap. "What's it supposed to do?"

"Theoretically, it sets up a small spot of static on *their* awareness band. Tech hasn't had a chance to test it, of course, but it seems to be working. I've been getting some vaguely puzzled looks from our local friends as I wander about, but that's as much interest as they've shown. How did it go with his Excellency?"

"Satisfactorily, I suppose," Pilch said grudgingly. "No heavy dramatics. But for a while there, you know, that little man had me feeling mighty unclean!"

"Self-defense," Wintan said tolerantly. "Give him time to shake it down. Basically, he already knows it was one of his own little emotional volcanoes he dropped into, not yours. But it'll be a year or two before he's really able to admit it to himself, and meanwhile he can let off steam by sitting around and loathing you thoroughly from time to time."

"I read the Predictor's report on him, too," Pilch said. "I still don't agree it was the right way to handle it."

Wintan shrugged. "Cabon can estimate them! If we'd jolted this one much heavier, it might have broken him up. But if the jolt had been a little too light, he could have buried it permanently away and forgotten about it again. As it is, he knows what's inside him, and eventually he'll know it consciously. When he does, he'll be ready for Service work without qualifications — and that means he won't go out some day like Buchele did!"

They walked on in silence for a while, through the drifting crowds of visiting Palayatans. Assorted Hub perfumes tinged the air, soft voices chattered amiably, faces turned curiously after the passing humans. "What makes you all so sure Duffold will be back?" Pilch said finally. "Even if he realizes what happened, the rap on the nose he got could be discouraging."

"It could be, for someone else," Wintan said. "But there're some you can't keep away, once they learn where the biggest job really is. For his Excellency, the rap on the nose will turn out eventually to have been Stage One of conditioning."

"Well, maybe. But an idealist like that," said Pilch, "always strikes me as peculiar! They never want to look at the notion that the real reason Man rates some slight cosmic approval is that he can act as well as he does, in spite of the stuff he's evolving from."

"Can't really blame them," Wintan remarked. "As you probably discovered in your own conditioning, some of that stuff just isn't good to look at."

"Now there for once," Pilch agreed darkly, "you spoke a fair-sized truth! Incidentally, that static you're spreading doesn't seem to meet with everyone's approval around here. I've been jolted three times in the last ten seconds!"

"Small boy about six steps behind us," Wintan reported. "He's scowling ferociously — but mama's leading him off now. I wonder what he made of it consciously?"

"He'll probably grow up with a vague but firmly held notion that Hub humans don't smell good!" Pilch estimated. They were coming up to a long, low wall from which the ramp-ways led into the sunken take-off section. The crowds were thinning out. "Have you noticed anyone acting as if he might conceivably be our psychologist?"

Wintan said he hadn't. "If he's in the area, as he said he would be, he's still got about ten minutes to make up his mind to go space-faring. Let's stop here and give him a last chance to show up before we go out on the ramp!"

They leaned back against the wall surveying passing natives hopefully. "He was excited about the idea at first," Wintan said, "but I imagine it seemed like too big a change when he'd had time to think about it. After all, he would have lost contact with all his kind before the ship was out of the system."

Pilch shivered. "Like a man living in a solitary dream for years, listening to the voices of strange entities. Isn't it odd — two intelligent races, physically side by side, but each blocked from any real contact with the other by the fears of its own mind!"

"It needn't have stayed that way!" Wintan said. regretfully. "Lord, the things we could have learned! We working down towards his awareness band, and he working up towards ours. Wish we had time to experiment here for a year or so! But the Great God Schedule has got us. It's likely to be a half century before the Service can spare another look at Palayata!"

Pilch glanced at her timepiece. "The same Schedule also says we start moving towards Ramp Thirteen right now, Wintan!"

They moved, reluctantly. As they came up the stairs to the locked platform gate, a lanky figure that had been sitting beside it stood up without unseemly haste.

Pilch darted a wild glance at Wintan. "Great Suns!" she said as they both came to a stop. Wintan was clearing his throat. "Ah, Albemarl —" His voice sounded shaky. "I greet you!"

"And I greet you, Wintan!" the elderly Palayatan said benignly. "I must ask your forgiveness for not having met you here as I promised, but I have had a very strange experience."

"Ah, yes?" Wintan said.

"Yes, indeed! For forty long years, I have wandered over the face of the world, welcome everywhere because of my great wisdom and the free flow of my advice. When you asked me some time ago whether I would like to enter your ship and go out of the world in it, into that strange emptiness overhead from which you people come, I laughed at you. Because — forgive me again, Wintan — we all think here that it is very foolish to leave a fair and familiar world and the comfort of many, many friends, in order, at best and after a long time, to reach another world that cannot be so very different, where friends must be made again. Also, you spoke of risks."

"Yes," Wintan said, "there are always risks, of course."

Albemarl nodded. "But on the night after you left," he said, "I had a dream. A strong voice spoke to me, which I know as the voice of my True Self" — Pilch gulped — "and it told me of a thing I had overlooked. I knew then it was true, but it disturbed me greatly. So for these days and nights I have been wandering about the hills, thinking of what it said. But in the end I have come here with a calm heart to ask whether I may now enter the ship and go wandering with you and your friends through all the years and the strangeness that is beyond the world."

"You may, indeed, Albemarl!" Wintan said.

"And we leave now? I am ready."

"We leave now!" Wintan gave Pilch a look, still incredulous but shining; then he stepped up to the gate and put the ball of his thumb against the lock that would open only to a human pattern.

"Albemarl," Pilch said gently, as the gate hissed open, "would you mind very much telling me what the thing was that you had overlooked?"

Albemarl blinked at her benevolently with his somewhat muddy Palayatan eyes. "Why, not at all! It is a simple thing but a great one — that wisdom accepts no limits. So when a wise man hears of a new thing that may be learned, beyond anything he knew before, it may not seem as comforting as the familiar things he knows, but he must learn it or he will never be content."

Wintan had moved back from the gate to let Pilch through. She put her hand on Albemarl's elbow and stepped up to the gate with him. Then she stopped.

"After you, brother!" Pilch said.

Goblin Night

There was a quivering of psi force. Then a sudden, vivid sense of running and hiding, in horrible fear of a pursuer from whom there was no escape —

Telzey's breath caught in her throat. A psi screen had flicked into instant existence about her mind, blocking out incoming impulses. The mental picture, the feeling of pursuit, already was gone, had touched her only a moment; but she stayed motionless seconds longer, eyes shut, pulses hammering out a roll of primitive alarms. She'd been dozing uneasily for the past hour, aware in a vague way of the mind-traces of a multitude of wildlife activities in the miles of parkland around. And perhaps she'd simply fallen asleep, begun to dream ...

Perhaps, she thought — but it wasn't very likely. She hadn't been relaxed enough to be touching the fringes of sleep and dream-stuff. The probability was that, for an instant, she'd picked up the reflection of a real event, that somebody not very far from here had encountered death in some grisly form at that moment.

She hesitated, then thinned the blocking screen to let her awareness spread again through the area, simultaneously extended a quick, probing thread of thought with a memory-replica of the pattern she'd caught. If it touched the mind that had produced the pattern originally, it might bring a momentary flash of echoing details and further information ... assuming the mind was still alive, still capable of responding.

She didn't really believe it would still be alive. The impression she'd had in that instant was that death was only seconds away.

The general murmur of mind-noise began to grow up about her again, a varying pulse of life and psi energies, diminishing gradually with distance, arising from her companions, from animals on plain and mountain, with an undernote of the dimmer emanations of plants. But no suggestion came now of the vividly disturbing sensations of a moment ago.

Telzey opened her eyes, glanced around at the others sitting about the campfire in the mouth of Cil Chasm. There were eleven of them, a group of third and fourth year students of Pehanron College who had decided to spend the fall holidays in Melna Park. The oldest was twenty-two; she herself was the youngest — Telzey Amberdon, age fifteen. There was also a huge white dog named Chomir, not in view at the moment, the property of one of her friends who had preferred to go on a spacecruise with a very special date over the holidays. Chomir would have been a little in the way in an IP cruiser, so Telzey had brought him along to the park instead.

In the early part of the evening, they had built their fire where the great Cil canyon opened on the rolling plain below. The canyon walls rose to either side of the camp, smothered with evergreen growth; and the Cil River, a quick, nervous stream, spilled over a series of rocky ledges a hundred feet away. The boys had set up a translucent green tent canopy, and sleeping bags were arranged beneath it. But Gikkes and two of the other girls already had announced that when they got ready to sleep, they were going to take up one of the aircars and settle down in it for the night a good thirty feet above the ground.

The park rangers had assured them such measures weren't necessary. Melna Park was full of Orado's native wildlife — that, after all, was why it had been established — but none of the animals were at all likely to become aggressive towards visitors. As for human marauders, the park was safer than the planet's cities. Overflights weren't permitted; visitors came in at ground level through one of the various entrance stations where their aircars were equipped with sealed engine locks, limiting them to contour altitudes of a hundred and fifty feet and to a speed of thirty miles an hour. Only the rangers' cars were not restricted, and only the rangers carried weapons.

It made Melna Park sound like an oasis of sylvan tranquility. But as it turned towards evening, the stars of the great cluster about Orado brightened to awesomely burning splendor in the sky. Some of them, like Gikkes, weren't used to the starblaze, had rarely spent a night outside the cities where night-screens came on gradually at the end of the day to meet the old racial preference for a dark sleep period.

Here night remained at an uncertain twilight stage until a wind began moaning up in the canyon and black storm clouds started to drift over the mountains and out across the plain. Now there were quick shifts between twilight and darkness, and eyes began to wander uneasily. There was the restless chatter of the river nearby. The wind made odd sounds in the canyon; they could hear sudden cracklings in bushes and trees, occasional animal voices.

"You get the feeling," Gikkes remarked, twisting her neck around to stare up Cil Chasm, "that something like a lullbear or spook might come trotting out of there any minute!"

Some of the others laughed uncertainly. Valia said, "Don't be silly! There haven't been animals like that in Melna Park for fifty years." She looked over at the group about Telzey. "Isn't that right, Pollard?"

Pollard was the oldest boy here. He was majoring in biology, which might make him Valia's authority on the subject of lullbears and spooks. He nodded, said, "You can still find them in the bigger game preserves up north. But naturally they don't keep anything in public parks that makes a practice of chewing up the public. Anything you meet around here, Gikkes, will be as ready to run from you as you are from it."

"That's saying a lot!" Rish added cheerfully. The others laughed again, and Gikkes looked annoyed.

Telzey had been giving only part of her attention to the talk. She felt shut down, temporarily detached from her companions. It had taken all afternoon to come across the wooded plains from the entrance station, winding slowly above the rolling ground in the three aircars which had brought them here. Then, after they reached Cil Chasm where they intended to stay, she and Rish and Dunker, two charter members of her personal fan club at Pehanron, had spent an hour fishing along the little river, up into the canyon and back down again. They had a great deal of excitement and caught enough to provide supper for everyone; but it involved arduous scrambling over slippery rocks, wading in cold, rushing water, and occasional tumbles, in one of which Telzey knocked her wrist-talker out of commission for the duration of the trip.

Drowsiness wasn't surprising after all the exercise. The surprising part was that, in spite of it, she didn't seem able to relax completely. As a rule, she felt at home wherever she happened to be outdoors. But something about this place was beginning to bother her. She hadn't noticed it at first, she had laughed at Gikkes with the others when Gikkes began to express apprehensions. But when she settled down after supper, feeling a comfortable muscular fatigue begin to claim her, she grew aware of a vague disturbance. The atmosphere of Melna Park seemed to change slowly. A hint of cruelty and savagery crept into it, of hidden terrors. Mentally, Telzey felt herself glancing over her shoulder towards dark places under the trees, as if something like a lullbear or spook actually was lurking there.

And then, in that uneasy, half-awake condition, there suddenly had been this other thing, like a dream-flash in which somebody desperately ran and hid from a mocking pursuer. To the terrified human quarry, the pursuer appeared as a glimpsed animalic shape in the twilight, big and moving swiftly, but showing no other details.

And there had been the flickering of psi energy about the scene ...

Telzey shifted uncomfortably, running her tongue tip over her lips. The experience had been chillingly vivid; but if something of the sort really had occurred, the victim had died moments later. In that respect, there was no reason to force herself to quick decisions now. And it might, after all, have been a dream, drifting up in her mind, created by the mood of the place. She realized she would like to believe it was a dream.

But in that case, what was creating the mood of the place?

Gikkes? It wasn't impossible. She had decided some time ago that personal acquaintances should be off limits to telepathic prowling, but when someone was around at all frequently, scraps of information were likely to filter through. So she knew Gikkes also had much more extensively developed telepathic awareness than the average person. Gikkes didn't know it and couldn't have put it to use anyway. In her, it was an erratic, unreliable quality which might have kept her in a badly confused state of mind if she had been more conscious of its effects.

But the general uneasiness Telzey had sensed and that brief psi surge — if that was what it was — fragmentary but carrying a complete horrid little story with it, could have come to her from Gikkes. Most people, even when they thought they were wide awake, appeared to be manufacturing dreams much of the time in an area of their minds they didn't know about; and Gikkes seemed nervous enough this evening to be manufacturing unconscious nightmares and broadcasting them.

But again — what made Gikkes so nervous here? The unfamiliar environment, the frozen beauty of the starblaze overhanging the sloping plain like a tent of fire, might account for it. But it didn't rule out a more specific source of disturbance.

She could make sure, Telzey thought, by probing into Gikkes' mind and finding out what was going on in there. Gikkes wouldn't know it was happening. But it took many hours, as a rule, to develop adequate contact unless the other mind was also that of a functioning telepath. Gikkes was borderline — a telepath, but not functional, or only partly so — and if she began probing around in those complexities without the experience to tell her just how to go about it, she might wind up doing Gikkes some harm.

She looked over at Gikkes. Gikkes met her eyes, said, "Shouldn't you start worrying about that dog of Gonwil's? He hasn't been in sight for the past half-hour."

"Chomir's all right," Telzey said. "He's still checking over the area."

Chomir was, in fact, only a few hundred yards away, moving along the Cil River up in the canyon. She'd been touching the big dog's mind lightly from time to time during the evening to see what he was doing. Gikkes couldn't know that, of course — nobody in this group suspected Telzey of psionic talents. But she had done a great deal of experimenting with Chomir, and nowadays she could, if she liked, almost see with his eyes, smell with his nose, and listen through his ears. At this instant, he was watching half a dozen animals large enough to have alarmed Gikkes acutely. Chomir's interest in Melna Park's wildlife didn't go beyond casual curiosity. He was an Askanam hound, a breed developed to fight man or beast in pit and arena, too big and powerful to be apprehensive about other creatures and not inclined to chase strange animals about without purpose as a lesser dog might do.

"Well," Gikkes said, "if I were responsible for somebody else's dog, if I'd brought him here, I'd be making sure he didn't run off and get lost —"

Telzey didn't answer. It took no mind-reading to know that Gikkes was annoyed because Pollard had attached himself to Telzey's fan club after supper and settled down beside her. Gikkes had invited Pollard to come along on the outing; he was president of various organizations and generally important at Pehanron College. Gikkes, the glamour girl, didn't like it at all that he'd drifted over to Telzey's group, and while Telzey had no designs on him, she couldn't very well inform Gikkes of that without ruffling her further.

"I," Gikkes concluded, "would go look for him."

Pollard stood up. "It would be too bad if he strayed off, wouldn't it?" he agreed. He gave Telzey a lazy smile. "Why don't you and I look around a little together?"

Well, that was not exactly what Gikkes had intended. Rish and Dunker didn't think much of it either. They were already climbing to their feet, gazing sternly at Pollard.

Telzey glanced at them, checked the watch Dunker had loaned her after she smashed the one in her wrist-talker on the fishing excursion.

"Let's wait another five minutes," she suggested. "If he isn't back by then, we can all start looking."

As they settled down again, she sent a come-here thought to Chomir. She didn't yet know what steps she might have to take in the other matter, but she didn't want to be distracted by problems with Gikkes and the boys.

She felt Chomir's response. He turned, got his bearings instantly with nose, ears, and — though he wasn't aware of that — by the direct touch of their minds, went bounding down into the river, and splashed noisily through the shallow water. He was taking what seemed to him a short cut to the camp. But that route would lead him high up the opposite bank of the twisting Cil, to the far side of the canyon.

"Not that way, stupid!" Telzey thought, verbalizing it for emphasis. "Turn around — go back!"

And then, as she felt the dog pause comprehendingly, a voice, edged with the shock of surprise — perhaps of fear — exclaimed in her mind, "Who are you? Who said that?"

There had been a number of occasions since she became aware of her abilities when she'd picked up the thought-forms of another telepath. She hadn't tried to develop such contacts, feeling in no hurry to strike up an acquaintanceship on the psionic level. That was part of a world with laws and conditions of its own which should be studied thoroughly if she was to avoid creating problems for herself and others, and at present she simply didn't have the time for thorough study.

Even with the tentative exploration she'd been doing, problems arose. One became aware of a situation of which others weren't aware, and then it wasn't always possible to ignore the situation, to act as if it didn't exist. But depending on circumstances, it could be extremely difficult to do something effective about it, particularly when one didn't care to announce publicly that one was a psi.

The thing that appeared to have happened in Melna Park tonight had seemed likely to present just such problems. Then this voice spoke to her suddenly, coming out of the night, out of nowhere. Another telepath was in the area, to whom the encounter was as unexpected as it was to her. There was no immediate way of knowing whether that was going to help with the problem or complicate it further, but she had no inclination to reply at once. Whoever the stranger was, the fact that he — there had been a strong male tinge to the thoughts — was also a psi didn't necessarily make him a brother. She knew he was human; alien minds had other flavors. His questions had come in the sharply defined forms of a verbalization; he might have been speaking aloud in addressing her. There was something else about them she hadn't noticed in previous telepathic contacts — an odd, filtered quality as though his thoughts passed through a distorting medium before reaching her.

She waited, wondering about it. While she wasn't strongly drawn to this stranger, she felt no particular concern about him. He had picked up her own verbalized instructions to Chomir, had been startled by them, and, therefore, hadn't been aware of anything she was thinking previously. She'd now tightened the veil of psi energy about her mind a little, enough to dampen out the drifting threads of subconscious thought by which an unguarded mind was most easily found and reached. Tightened further, as it could be in an instant, it had stopped genuine experts in mind-probing in their tracks. This psi was no expert; an expert wouldn't have flung surprised questions at her. She didn't verbalize her thinking as a rule, and wouldn't do it now until she felt like it. And she wouldn't reach out for him. She decided the situation was sufficiently in hand.

The silence between them lengthened. He might be equally wary now, regretting his brief outburst.

Telzey relaxed her screen, flicked out a search-thought to Chomir, felt him approaching the camp in his easy, loping run, closed the screen again. She waited a few seconds. There was no indication of interest from the other psi; apparently, even when he had his attention on her, he was able to sense only her verbalized thoughts. That simplified the matter.

She lightened the screen again. "Who are *you*?" she asked.

The reply came instantly. "So I wasn't dreaming! For a moment, I thought ... Are there two of you?"

"No. I was talking to my dog." There *was* something odd about the quality of his thoughts. He might be using a shield or screen of some kind, not of the same type as hers but perhaps equally effective.

"Your dog? I see. It's been over a year," the voice said, "since I've spoken to others like this." It paused. "You're a woman ... young ... a girl ..."

There was no reason to tell him she was fifteen. What Telzey wanted to know just now was whether he also had been aware of a disturbance in Melna Park. She asked, "Where are you?"

He didn't hesitate. "At my home. Twelve miles south of Cil Chasm across the plain, at the edge of the forest. The house is easy to see from the air."

He might be a park official. They'd noticed such a house on their way here this afternoon and speculated about who could be living there. Permission to make one's residence in a Federation Park was supposedly almost impossible to obtain.

"Does that tell you anything?" the voice went on.

"Yes," Telzey said. "I'm in the park with some friends. I think I've seen your house."

"My name," the bodiless voice told her, "is Robane. You're being careful. I don't blame you. There are certain risks connected with being a psi, as you seem to understand. If we were in a city, I'm not sure I would reveal myself. But out here ... Somebody built a fire this evening where the Cil River leaves the Chasm. I'm a cripple and spend much of my time studying the park with scanners. Is that your fire?"

Telzey hesitated a moment. "Yes."

"Your friends," Robane's voice went on, "they're aware you and I ... they know you're a telepath?"

"No."

"Would you be able to come to see me for a while without letting them know where you're going?"

"Why should I do that?" Telzey asked.

"Can't you imagine? I'd like to talk to a psi again."

"We *are* talking," she said.

Silence for a moment.

"Let me tell you a little about myself," Robane said then. "I'm approaching middle age — from your point I might even seem rather old. I live here alone except for a well-meaning but rather stupid housekeeper named Feddler. Feddler seems old from *my* point of view. Four years ago, I was employed in one of the Federation's science departments. I am ... was ... considered to be among the best in my line of work. It wasn't very dangerous work so long as certain precautions were observed. But one day a fool made a mistake. His mistake killed two of my colleagues. It didn't quite kill me, but since that day I've been intimately associated with a machine which has the responsibility of keeping me alive from minute to minute. I'd die almost immediately if I were removed from it.

"So my working days are over. And I no longer want to live in cities. There are too many foolish people there to remind me of the one particular fool I'd prefer to forget. Because of the position I'd held and the work I'd done, the Federation permitted me to make my home in Melna Park where I could be by myself ..."

The voice stopped abruptly but Telzey had the impression Robane was still talking, unaware that something had dimmed the thread of psi between them. His own screen perhaps? She waited, alert and quiet. It might be deliberate interference, the manifestation of another active psionic field in the area — a disturbing and malicious one.

" ... On the whole, I like it here." Robane's voice suddenly was back; and it was evident he didn't realize there had been an interruption. "A psi need never be really bored, and I've installed instruments to offset the disadvantages of being a cripple. I watch the park through scanners and study the minds of animals ... Do you like animal minds?"

That, Telzey thought, hadn't been at all a casual question. "Sometimes," she told Robane carefully. "Some of them."

"Sometimes? Some of them? I wonder ... Solitude on occasion appears to invite the uncanny. One may notice things that seem out of place, that are disquieting. This evening ... during the past hour perhaps, have you ... were there suggestions of activities ..." He paused. "I find I don't quite know how to say this."

"There was something," she said. "For a moment, I wasn't sure I wasn't dreaming."

"You mean something ugly ..."

"Yes."

"Fear," Robane's voice said in her mind. "Fear, pain, death. Savage cruelty. So you caught it, too. Very strange! Perhaps an echo from the past touched our minds in that moment, from the time when creatures who hated man still haunted this country.

"But — well, this is one of the rare occasions when I feel lonely here. And then to hear another psi, you see ... Perhaps I'm even a little afraid to be alone in the night just now. I'd like to speak to you, but not in this way — not in any great detail. One can never be sure who else is listening ... I think there are many things two psis might discuss to their advantage."

The voice ended on that. He'd expressed himself guardedly, and apparently he didn't expect an immediate reply to his invitation. Telzey bit her lip. Chomir had come trotting up, had been welcomed by her and settled down. Gikkes was making cooing sounds and snapping her fingers at him. Chomir ignored the overtures. Ordinarily, Gikkes claimed to find him alarming; but here in Melna Park at night, the idea of having an oversized dog near her evidently had acquired a sudden appeal —

So Robane, too, had received the impression of unusual and unpleasant events this evening ... events he didn't care to discuss openly. The indication that he felt frightened probably needn't be taken too seriously. He was in his house, after all; and so isolated a house must have guard-screens. The house of a crippled, wealthy recluse, who was avoiding the ordinary run of humanity, would have very effective guard-screens. If something did try to get at Robane, he could put in a call to the nearest park station and have an armed ranger car hovering about his roof in a matter of minutes. That suggestion had been intended to arouse her sympathy for a shut-in fellow psi, help coax her over to the house.

But he had noticed something. Something, to judge from his cautious description, quite similar to what she had felt. Telzey looked at Chomir, stretched out on the sandy ground between her and the fire, at the big, wolfish head, the wedge of powerful jaws. Chomir was not exactly an intellectual giant but he had the excellent sensory equipment and alertness of a breed of fighting animals. If there had been a disturbance of that nature in the immediate vicinity, he would have known about it, and she would have known about it through him.

The disturbance, however, might very well have occurred somewhere along the twelve-mile stretch between the point where Cil Chasm split the mountains and Robane's house across the plain. Her impression had been that it was uncomfortably close to her. Robane appeared to have sensed it as uncomfortably close to him. He had showed no inclination to do anything about it, and there was, as a matter of fact, no easy way to handle the matter. Robane clearly was no more anxious than she was to reveal himself as a psi; and, in any case, the park authorities would be understandably reluctant to launch a search for a vicious but not otherwise identified man-hunting beast on no better evidence than reported telepathic impressions — at least, until somebody was reported missing.

It didn't seem a good idea to wait for that. For one thing, Telzey thought, the killer might show up at their fire before morning ...

She grimaced uneasily, sent a troubled glance around the group. She hadn't been willing to admit it but she'd really known for minutes now that she was going to have to go look for the creature. In an aircar, she thought, even an aircar throttled down to thirty miles an hour and a contour altitude of a hundred and fifty feet, she would be in no danger from an animal on the ground if she didn't take very stupid chances. The flavor of psi about the event she didn't like. That was still unexplained. But she was a psi herself, and she would be careful.

She ran over the possibilities in her mind. The best approach should be to start out towards Robane's house and scout the surrounding wildlands mentally along that route. If she picked up traces of the killer-thing, she could pinpoint its position, call the park rangers from the car, and give them a story that would get them there in a hurry. They could do the rest. If she found nothing, she could consult with Robane about the next moves to make. Even if he didn't want to take a direct part in the search, he might be willing to give her some help with it.

Chomir would remain here as sentinel. She'd plant a trace of uneasiness in his mind, just enough to make sure he remained extremely vigilant while she was gone. At the first hint from him that anything dangerous was approaching the area, she'd use the car's communicator to have everybody pile into the other two aircars and get off the ground. Gikkes was putting them in the right frame of mind to respond very promptly if they were given a real alarm.

Telzey hesitated a moment longer but there seemed to be nothing wrong with the plan. She told herself she'd better start at once. If she waited, the situation, whatever it was, conceivably could take an immediately dangerous turn. Besides, the longer she debated about it, the more unpleasant the prospect was going to look.

She glanced down at Dunker's watch on her wrist.

"Robane?" she asked in her mind.

The response came quickly. "Yes?"

"I'll start over to your house now," Telzey said. "Would you watch for my car? If there is something around that doesn't like people, I'd sooner not be standing outside your door."

"The door will be open the instant you come down," Robane's voice assured her. "Until then, I'm keeping it locked. I've turned on the scanners and will be waiting ..." A moment's pause. "Do you have additional reason to believe —"

"Not so far," Telzey said. "But there are some things I'd like to talk about — after I get there ..." She didn't really intend to go walking into Robane's house until she had more information about him. There were too many uncertainties floating around in the night to be making social calls. But he'd be alert now, waiting for her to arrive, and might notice things she didn't.

The aircar was her own, a fast little Cloudsplitter. No one objected when she announced she was setting off for an hour's roam in the starblaze by herself. The fan club looked wistful but was well trained, and Pollard had allowed himself to be reclaimed by Gikkes. Gikkes clearly regarded Telzey's solo excursion as a fine idea ...

She lifted the Cloudsplitter out of the mouth of Cil Chasm. At a hundred and fifty feet, as the sealed engine lock clicked in, the little car automatically stopped its ascent. Telzey turned to the right, along the forested walls of the mountain, then swung out across the plain.

It should take her about twenty minutes to get to Robane's house if she went there in a straight line; and if nothing else happened, she intended to go there in a straight line. What the park maps called a plain was a series of sloping plateaus, broken by low hills, descending gradually to the south. It was mainly brush country, dotted with small woods which blended here and there into patches of forest. Scattered herds of native animals moved about in the open ground, showing no interest in the aircar passing through the clusterlight overhead.

Everything looked peaceful enough. Robane had taken her hint and remained quiet. The intangible bubble of the psi screen about Telzey's mind thinned, opened wide. Her awareness went searching ahead, to all sides ...

Man-killer, where are you?

Perhaps ten minutes passed before she picked up the first trace. By then, she could see a tiny, steady spark of orange light ahead against the dark line of the forest. That would be Robane's house, still five or six miles away.

Robane hadn't spoken again. There had been numerous fleeting contacts with animal minds savage enough in their own way, deadly to one another. But the thing that hunted man should have a special quality, one she would recognize when she touched it.

She touched it suddenly — a blur of alert malignance, gone almost at once. She was prepared for it, but it still sent a thrill of alarm through her. She moistened her lips, told herself again she was safe in the car. The creature definitely had not been far away. Telzey slipped over for a moment into Chomir's mind. The big dog stood a little beyond the circle of firelight, probing the land to the south. He was unquiet but no more than she had intended him to be. His senses had found nothing of unusual significance. The menace wasn't there.

It was around here, ahead, or to left or right. Telzey let the car move on slowly. After a while, she caught the blur for a moment again, lost it again ...

She approached Robane's house gradually. Presently she could make it out well enough in the clusterlight, a sizable structure, set in a garden of its own which ended where the forest began. Part of the building was two-storied, with a balcony running around the upper story. The light came from there, dark-orange light glowing through screened windows.

The second fleeting pulse of that aura of malevolence had come from this general direction; she was sure of it. If the creature was in the forest back of the house, perhaps watching the house, Robane's apprehensions might have some cause, after all. She had brought the Cloudsplitter almost to a stop some five hundred yards north of the house; now she began moving to the left, then shifted in towards the forest, beginning to circle the house as she waited for another indication. Robane should be watching her through the telescanners, and she was grateful that he hadn't broken the silence. Perhaps he had realized what she was trying to do.

For long minutes now, she had been intensely keyed up, sharply aware of the infinite mingling of life detail below. It was as if the plain had come alight in all directions about her, a shifting glimmer of sparks, glowing emanations of life-force, printed in constant change on her awareness. To distinguish among it all the specific pattern which she had touched briefly twice might not be an easy matter. But then, within seconds, she made two significant discoveries.

She had brought the Cloudsplitter nearly to a stop again. She was now to the left of Robane's house, no more than two hundred yards from it, close enough to see a flock of small, birdlike creatures flutter about indistinctly in the garden shrubbery. Physical vision seemed to overlap and blend with her inner awareness, and among the uncomplicated emanations of small animal life in the garden, there was now a center of mental emanation which was of more interest.

It was inside the house, and it was human. It seemed to Telzey it was Robane she was sensing. That was curious, because if his mind was screened as well as she'd believed, she should not be able to sense him in this manner. But, of course, it might not be. She had simply assumed he had developed measures against being read as adequate as her own.

Probably it was Robane. Then where, Telzey thought, was that elderly, rather stupid housekeeper named Feddler he'd told her about? Feddler's presence, her mind unscreened in any way, should be at least equally obvious now.

With the thought, she caught a second strong glow. That was not the mind of some stupid old woman, or of anything human. It was still blurred, but it was the mind for which she had been searching. The mind of some baleful, intelligent tiger-thing. And it was very close.

She checked again, carefully. Then she knew. It was not back in the forest, and not hidden somewhere on the plain nearby.

It was inside Robane's house.

For a moment, shock held her motionless. Then she swung the Cloudsplitter smoothly to the left, started moving off along the edge of the forest.

"Where are you going?" Robane's voice asked in her mind.

Telzey didn't answer. The car already was gliding along at the thirty miles an hour its throttled-down engine allowed it to go. Her forefinger was flicking out the call number of Rish's aircar back at the camp on the Cloudsplitter's communicator.

There'd been a trap set for her here. She didn't yet know what kind of a trap, or whether she could get out of it by herself. But the best thing she could do at the moment was to let other people know immediately where she was —

A dragging, leaden heaviness sank through her. She saw her hand drop from the communicator dial, felt herself slump to the left, head sagging down on the side rest, face turned half up. She felt the Cloudsplitter's engines go dead. The trap had snapped shut.

The car was dropping, its forward momentum gone. Telzey made a straining effort to sit back up, lift her hands to the controls, and nothing happened. She realized then that nothing could have happened if she had reached the controls. If it hadn't been for the countergravity materials worked into its structure, the Cloudsplitter would have plunged to the ground like a rock. As it was, it settled gradually down through the air, swaying from side to side.

She watched the fiery night sky shift above with the swaying of the car, sickened by the conviction that she was dropping towards death, trying to keep the confusion of terror from exploding through her ...

"I'm curious to know," Robane's voice said, "what made you decide at the last moment to decline my invitation and attempt to leave."

She wrenched her attention away from terror, reached for the voice and Robane.

There was the crackling of psi, open telepathic channels through which her awareness flowed in a flash. For an instant, she was inside his mind.

Then psi static crashed, and she was away from it again. Her awareness dimmed, momentarily blurred out. She'd absorbed almost too much. It was as if she'd made a photograph of a section of Robane's mind — a pitiful and horrible mind.

She felt the car touch the ground, stop moving. The slight jolt tilted her over farther, her head lolling on the side rest. She was breathing; her eyelids blinked. But her conscious efforts weren't affecting a muscle of her body.

The dazed blurriness began to lift from her thoughts. She found herself still very much frightened but no longer accepting in the least that she would die here. She should have a chance against Robane. She discovered he was speaking again, utterly unaware of what had just occurred.

"I'm not a psi," his voice said. "But I'm a gadgeteer — and, you see, I happen to be highly intelligent. I've used my intelligence to provide myself with instruments which guard me and serve my wishes here. Some give me abilities equivalent to those of a psi. Others, as you've just experienced, can be used to neutralize power devices or to paralyze the human voluntary muscular system within as much as half a mile of this room.

"I was amused by your cautious hesitation and attempted flight just now. I'd already caught you. If I'd let you use the communicator, you would have found it dead. I shut it off as soon as your aircar was in range ..."

Robane not a psi? For an instant, there was a burbling of lunatic, silent laughter in Telzey's head. In that moment of full contact between them, she'd sensed a telepathic system functional in every respect except that he wasn't aware of it. Psi energy flared about his words as he spoke. That came from one of the machines, but only a telepath could have operated such a machine.

Robane had never considered that possibility. If the machine static hadn't caught her off guard, broken the contact before she could secure it, he would be much more vulnerable in his unawareness now than an ordinary nonpsi human.

She'd reached for him again as he was speaking, along the verbalized thought-forms directed at her. But the words were projected through a machine. Following them back, she wound up at the machine and another jarring blast of psi static. She would have to wait for a moment when she found an opening to his mind again, when the machines didn't happen to be covering him. He was silent now. He intended to kill her as he had others before her, and he might very well be able to do it before an opening was there. But he would make no further moves until he felt certain she hadn't been able to summon help in a manner his machines hadn't detected. What he had done so far he could explain — he had forced an aircar prowling about his house to the ground without harming its occupant. There was no proof of anything else he had done except the proof in Telzey's mind, and Robane didn't know about that.

It gave her a few minutes to act without interference from him.

"What's the matter with that dog?" Gikkes asked nervously. "He's behaving like ... like he thinks there's something around."

The chatter stopped for a moment. Eyes swung over to Chomir. He stood looking out from the canyon ledge over the plain, making a rumbling noise in his throat.

"Don't be silly," Valia said. "He's just wondering where Telzey's gone." She looked at Rish. "How long has she been gone?"

"Twenty-seven minutes," Rish said.

"Well, that's nothing to worry about, is it?" Valia checked herself, added, "Now look at that, will you!" Chomir had swung around, moved over to Rish's aircar, stopped beside it, staring at them with yellow eyes. He made the rumbling noise again.

Gikkes said, watching him fascinatedly, "Maybe something's happened to Telzey."

"Don't talk like that," Valia said. "What could happen to her?"

Rish got to his feet. "Well — it can't hurt to give her a call ..." He grinned at Valia to show he wasn't in the least concerned, went to the aircar, opened the door.

Chomir moved silently past him into the car.

Rish frowned, glanced back at Valia and Dunker coming up behind him, started to say something, shook his head, slid into the car, and turned on the communicator.

Valia inquired, her eyes uneasily on Chomir, "Know her number?"

"Uh-huh." They watched as he flicked the number out on the dial, then stood waiting.

Presently Valia cleared her throat. "She's probably got out of the car and is walking around somewhere."

"Of course she's walking," Rish said shortly.

"Keep buzzing anyway," Dunker said.

"I am." Rish glanced at Chomir again. "If she's anywhere near the car, she'll be answering in a moment ..."

"Why don't you answer me?" Robane's voice asked, sharp with impatience. "It would be very foolish of you to make me angry."

Telzey made no response. Her eyes blinked slowly at the starblaze. Her awareness groped, prowled, patiently, like a hungry cat, for anything, the slightest wisp of escaping unconscious thought, emotion, that wasn't filtered through the blocking machines, that might give her another opening to the telepathic levels of Robane's mind. In the minutes she'd been lying paralyzed across the seat of the aircar, she had arranged and comprehended the multidetailed glimpse she'd had of it. She understood Robane very thoroughly now.

The instrument room of the house was his living area. A big room centered about an island of immaculate precision machines. Robane rarely was away from it. She knew what he looked like, from mirror images, glimpses in shining instrument surfaces, his thoughts about himself. A half-man, enclosed from the waist down in a floating, mobile machine like a tiny aircar, which carried him and kept him alive. The little machine was efficient; the half-body protruding from it was vigorous and strong. Robane in his isolation gave fastidious attention to his appearance. The coat which covered him down to the machine was tailored to Orado City's latest fashion; his thick hair was carefully groomed.

He had led a full life as scientist, sportsman, man of the world, before the disaster which left him bound to his machine. To make the man responsible for the disaster pay for his blunder in full became Robane's obsession and he laid his plans with all the care of the trophy hunter he had been. His work for the Federation had been connected with the further development of devices permitting the direct transmission of sensations from one living brain to another and their adaptation to various new uses. In his retirement in Melna Park, Robane patiently refined such devices for his own purposes and succeeded beyond his expectations, never suspecting that the success was due in part to the latent psionic abilities he was stimulating with his experiments.

Meanwhile, he had prepared for the remaining moves in his plan, installed automatic machinery to take the place of his housekeeper, and dismissed the old woman from his service. A smuggling ring provided him with a specimen of a savage natural predator native to the continent for which he had set up quarters beneath the house. Robane trained the beast and himself, perfecting his skill in the use of the instruments, sent the conditioned animal out at night to hunt, brought it back after it had made the kill in which he had shared through its mind. There was sharper excitement in that alone than he had found in any previous hunting experience. There was further excitement in treating trapped animals with the drug that exposed their sensations to his instruments when he released them and set the killer on their trail. He could be hunter or hunted, alternately and simultaneously, following each chase to the end, withdrawing from the downed quarry only when its numbing death impulses began to reach him.

When it seemed he had no more to learn, he had his underworld connections deliver his enemy to the house. That night, he awakened the man from his stupor, told him what to expect, and turned him out under the starblaze to run for his life. An hour later, Robane and his savage deputy made a human kill, the instruments fingering the victim's drug-drenched nervous system throughout and faithfully transmitting his terrors and final torment.

With that, Robane had accomplished his revenge. But he had no intention now of giving up the exquisite excitements of the new sport he had developed in the process. He became almost completely absorbed by it, as absorbed as the beast he had formed into an extension of himself. They went out by night to stalk and harry, run down and kill. They grew alike in cunning, stealth, and savage audacity, were skillful enough to create no unusual disturbance among the park animals with their sport. By morning, they were back in Robane's house to spend most of the day in sleep. Unsuspecting human visitors who came through the area saw no traces of their nocturnal activities.

Robane barely noticed how completely he had slipped into this new way of living. Ordinarily, it was enough. But he had almost no fear of detection now, and sometimes he remembered there had been a special savor in driving a human being to his death. Then his contacts would bring another shipment of "supplies" to the house, and that night he hunted human game. Healthy young game which did its desperate best to escape but never got far. It was something humanity owed him.

For a while, there was one lingering concern. During his work for the overgovernment, he'd had several contacts with a telepath called in to assist in a number of experiments. Robane had found out what he could about such people and believed his instruments would shield him against being detected and investigated by them. He was not entirely sure of it, but in the two years he had been pursuing his pleasures undisturbed in Melna Park his uneasiness on that point had almost faded away.

Telzey's voice, following closely on his latest human kill, startled him profoundly. But when he realized that it was a chance contact, that she was here by accident, it occurred to him that this was an opportunity to find out whether a telepathic mind could be dangerous to him. She seemed young and inexperienced — he could handle her through his instruments with the slightest risk to himself.

Rish and Dunker were in Rish's aircar with Chomir, Telzey thought, and a third person, who seemed to be Valia, was sitting behind them. The car was aloft and moving, so they had started looking for her. It would be nice if they were feeling nervous enough to have the park rangers looking for her, too; but that was very unlikely. She had to handle Chomir with great caution here. If he'd sensed any fear in her, he would have raced off immediately in her general direction to protect her, which would have been of no use at all.

As it was, he was following instructions he didn't know he was getting. He was aware which way the car should go, and he would make that quite clear to Rish and the others if it turned off in any other direction. Since they had no idea where to look for her themselves, they would probably decide to rely on Chomir's intuition.

That would bring them presently to this area. If she was outside the half-mile range of Robane's energy shut-off device by then, they could pick her up safely. If she wasn't, she'd have to turn them away through Chomir again or she'd simply be drawing them into danger with her. Robane, however, wouldn't attempt to harm them unless he was forced to it. Telzey's disappearance in the wildlands of the park could be put down as an unexplained accident; he wasn't risking much there. But a very intensive investigation would get under way if three other students of Pehanron College vanished simultaneously along with a large dog. Robane couldn't afford that.

"Why don't you answer?"

There was an edge of frustrated rage in Robane's projected voice. The paralysis field which immobilized her also made her unreachable to him. He was like an animal balked for the moment by a glass wall. He'd said he had a weapon trained on her which could kill her in an instant as she lay in the car, and Telzey knew it was true from what she had seen in his mind. For that matter, he probably only had to change the setting of the paralysis field to stop her heartbeat or her breathing.

But such actions wouldn't answer the questions he had about psis. She'd frightened him tonight; and now he had to run her to her death, terrified and helpless as any other human quarry, before he could feel secure again.

"Do you think I'm afraid to kill you?" he asked, seeming almost plaintively puzzled. "Believe me, if I pull the trigger my finger is touching, I won't even be questioned about your disappearance. The park authorities have been instructed by our grateful government to show me every consideration, in view of my past invaluable contributions to humanity, and in view of my present disability. No one would think to disturb me here because some foolish girl is reported lost in Melna Park ..."

The thought-voice went on, its fury and bafflement filtered through a machine, sometimes oddly suggestive even of a ranting, angry machine. Now and then it blurred out completely, like a bad connection, resumed seconds later. Telzey drew her attention away from it. It was a distraction in her waiting for another open subconscious bridge to Robane's mind. Attempts to reach him more directly remained worse than useless. The machines also handled mind-stuff, but mechanically channeled, focused, and projected; the result was a shifting, flickering, nightmarish distortion of emanations in which Robane and his instruments seemed to blend in constantly changing patterns. She'd tried to force through it, had drawn back quickly, dazed and jolted again ...

Every minute she gained here had improved her chances of escape, but she thought she wouldn't be able to stall him much longer. The possibility that a ranger patrol or somebody else might happen by just now, see her Cloudsplitter parked near the house, and come over to investigate, was probably slight, but Robane wouldn't be happy about it. If she seemed to remain intractable, he'd decide at some point to dispose of her at once.

So she mustn't seem too intractable. Since she wasn't replying, he would try something else to find out if she could be controlled. When he did, she would act frightened silly — which she was in a way, except that it didn't seem to affect her ability to think now — and do whatever he said except for one thing. After he turned off the paralysis field, he would order her to come to the house. She couldn't do that. Behind the entry door was a lock chamber. If she stepped inside, the door would close; and with the next breath she took she would have absorbed a full dose of the drug that let Robane's mind-instruments settle into contact with her. She didn't know what effect that would have. It might nullify her ability to maintain her psi screen and reveal her thoughts to Robane. If he knew what she had in mind, he would kill her on the spot. Or the drug might distort her on the telepathic level and end her chances of getting him under control.

"It's occurred to me," Robane's voice said, "that you may not be deliberately refusing to answer me. It's possible that you are unable to do it either because of the effect of the paralysis field or simply because of fear."

Telzey had been wondering when it would occur to him. She waited, new tensions growing up in her.

"I'll release you from the field in a moment," the voice went on. "What happens then depends on how well you carry out the instructions given you. If you try any tricks, little psi, you'll be dead. I'm quite aware you'll be able to move normally seconds after the field is off. Make no move you aren't told to make. Do exactly what you are told to do, and do it without hesitation. Remember those two things. Your life depends on them."

He paused, added, "The field is now off ..."

Telzey felt a surge of strength and lightness all through her. Her heart began to race. She refrained carefully from stirring. After a moment, Robane's voice said, "Touch nothing in the car you don't need to touch. Keep your hands in sight. Get out of the car, walk twenty feet away from it, and stop. Then face the house."

Telzey climbed out of the car. She was shaky throughout; but it wasn't as bad as she'd thought it would be when she first moved again. It wasn't bad at all. She walked on to the left, stopped, and looked up at the orange-lit, screened windows in the upper part of the house.

"Watch your car," Robane's voice told her.

She looked over at the Cloudsplitter. He'd turned off the power neutralizer and the car was already moving. It lifted vertically from the ground, began gliding forward thirty feet up, headed in the direction of the forest beyond the house. It picked up speed, disappeared over the trees.

"It will begin to change course when it reaches the mountains," Robane's voice said. "It may start circling and still be within the park when it is found. More probably, it will be hundreds of miles away. Various explanations will be offered for your disappearance from it, apparently in midair, which needn't concern us now ... Raise your arms before you, little psi. Spread them farther apart. Stand still."

Telzey lifted her arms, stood waiting. After an instant, she gave a jerk of surprise. Her hands and arms, Dunker's watch on her wrist, the edges of the short sleeves of her shirt suddenly glowed white.

"Don't move!" Robane's voice said sharply. "This is a search-beam. It won't hurt you."

She stood still again, shifted her gaze downwards. What she saw of herself and her clothes and of a small patch of ground about her feet all showed the same cold, white glow, like fluorescing plastic. There was an eerie suggestion of translucence. She glanced back at her hands, saw the fine bones showing faintly as more definite lines of white in the glow. She felt nothing and the beam wasn't affecting her vision, but it was an efficient device. Sparks of heatless light began stabbing from her clothing here and there; within moments, Robane located half a dozen minor items in her pockets and instructed her to throw them away one by one, along with the watch. He wasn't taking chances on fashionably camouflaged communicators, perhaps suspected even this or that might be a weapon. Then the beam went off and he told her to lower her arms again.

"Now a reminder," his voice went on. "Perhaps you're unable to speak to me. And perhaps you could speak but think it's clever to remain silent in this situation. That isn't too important. But let me show you something. It will help you keep in mind that it isn't at all advisable to be too clever in dealing with me ..."

Something suddenly was taking shape twenty yards away, between Telzey and the house; and fright flicked through her like fire and ice in the instant before she saw it was a projection placed a few inches above the ground. It was an image of Robane's killer, a big, bulky creature which looked bulkier because of the coat of fluffy, almost feathery fur covering most of it like a cloak. It was half crouched, a pair of powerful forelimbs stretched out through the cloak of fur. Ears like upturned horns projected from the sides of the head, and big, round, dark eyes, the eyes of a star-night hunter, were set in front above the sharply curved, serrated cutting beak.

The image faded within seconds. She knew what the creature was. The spooks had been, at one time, almost the dominant life form on this continent; the early human settlers hated and feared them for their unqualified liking for human flesh, made them a legend which haunted Orado's forests long after they had, in fact, been driven out of most of their territory. Even in captivity, from behind separating force fields, their flat, dark stares, their size, goblin appearance, and monkey quickness disturbed impressionable people.

"My hunting partner," Robane's voice said. "My other self. It is not pleasant, not at all pleasant, to know this is the shape that is following your trail at night in Melna Park. You had a suggestion of it this evening. Be careful not make me angry again. Be quick to do what I tell you. Now come forward to the house."

Telzey saw the entry door in the garden slide open. Her heart began to beat heavily. She didn't move.

"Come to the house!" Robane repeated.

Something accompanied the words, a gush of heavy, subconscious excitement, somebody reaching for a craved drug ... but Robane's drug was death. As she touched the excitement, it vanished. It was what she had waited for, a line to the unguarded levels of his mind. If it came again and she could hold it even for seconds —

It didn't come again. There was a long pause before Robane spoke.

"This is curious," his voice said slowly. "You refuse. You know you are helpless. You know what I can do. Yet you refuse. I wonder ..."

He went silent. He was suspicious now, very. For a moment, she could almost feel him finger the trigger of his weapon. But the drug was there, in his reach. She was cheating him out of some of it. He wouldn't let her cheat him out of everything ...

"Very well," the voice said. "I'm tired of you. I was interested in seeing how a psi would act in such a situation. I've seen. You're so afraid you can barely think. So run along. Run as fast as you can, little psi. Because I'll soon be following."

Telzey stared up at the windows. Let him believe she could barely think.

"Run!"

She whipped around, as if shocked into motion by the command, and ran, away from Robane's house, back in the direction of the plain to the north.

"I'll give you a warning," Robane's voice said, seeming to move along with her. "Don't try to climb a tree. We catch the ones who do that immediately. We can climb better than you can, and if the tree is big enough we'll come up after you. If the tree's too light to hold us, or if you go out where the branches are too thin, we'll simply shake you down. So keep running."

She glanced back as she came up to the first group of trees. The orange windows of the house seemed to be staring after her. She went in among the trees, out the other side, and now the house was no longer in sight.

"Be clever now," Robane's voice said. "We like the clever ones. You have a chance, you know. Perhaps somebody will see you before you're caught. Or you may think of some way to throw us off your track. Perhaps you'll be the lucky one who gets away. We'll be very, very sorry then, won't we? So do your best, little psi. Do your best. Give us a good run."

She flicked out a search-thought, touched Chomir's mind briefly. The aircar was still coming, still on course, still too far away to do her any immediate good ...

She ran. She was in as good condition as a fifteen-year-old who liked a large variety of sports and played hard at them was likely to get. But she had to cover five hundred yards to get beyond the range of Robane's house weapons, and on this broken ground it began to seem a long, long stretch. How much time would he give her? Some of those he'd hunted had been allowed a start of thirty minutes or more ...

She began to count her steps. Robane remained silent. When she thought she was approaching the end of five hundred yards, there were trees ahead again. She remembered crossing over a small stream followed by a straggling line of trees as she came up to the house. That must be it. And in that case, she was beyond the five-hundred-yard boundary.

A hungry excitement swirled about her and was gone. She'd lashed at the feeling quickly, got nothing. Robane's voice was there an instant later. "We're starting now ..."

So soon? She felt shocked. He wasn't giving her even the pretense of a chance to escape. Dismay sent a wave of weakness through her as she ran splashing down into the creek. Some large animals burst out of the water on the far side, crashed through the bushes along the bank, and pounded away. Telzey hardly noticed them. Turn to the left, downstream, she thought. It was a fast little stream. The spook must be following by scent and the running water should wipe out her trail before it got here ...

But others it had followed would have decided to turn downstream when they reached the creek. If it didn't pick up the trail on the far bank and found no human scent in the water coming down, it only had to go along the bank to the left until it either heard her in the water or reached the place where she'd left it.

They'd expect her, she told herself, to leave the water on the far side of the creek, not to angle back in the direction of Robane's house. Or would they? It seemed the best thing to try.

She went downstream as quickly as she could, splashing, stumbling on slippery rock, careless of noise for the moment. It would be a greater danger to lose time trying to be quiet. A hundred yards on, stout tree branches swayed low over the water. She could catch them, swing up, scramble on up into the trees.

Others would have tried that, too. Robane and his beast knew such spots, would check each to make sure it wasn't what she had done.

She ducked, gasping, under the low-hanging branches, hurried on. Against the starblaze a considerable distance ahead, a thicker cluster of trees loomed darkly. It looked like a sizable little wood surrounding the watercourse. It might be a good place to hide.

Others, fighting for breath after the first hard run, legs beginning to falter, would have had that thought.

Robane's voice said abruptly in her mind, "So you've taken to the water. It was your best move ..."

The voice stopped. Telzey felt the first stab of panic. The creek curved sharply ahead. The bank on the left was steep, not the best place to get out. She followed it with her eyes. Roots sprouted out of the bare earth a little ahead. She came up to them, jumped to catch them, pulled herself up, and scrambled over the edge of the bank. She climbed to her feet, hurried back in the general direction of Robane's house, dropped into a cluster of tall grass. Turning, flattened out on her stomach, she lifted her head to stare back in the direction of the creek. There was an opening in the bushes on the other bank, with the clusterlight of the skyline showing through it. She watched that, breathing as softly as she could. It occurred to her that if a breeze was moving the wrong way, the spook might catch her scent on the air. But she didn't feel any breeze.

Perhaps a minute passed — certainly no more. Then a dark silhouette passed lightly and swiftly through the opening in the bushes she was watching, went on downstream. It was larger than she'd thought it would be when she saw its projected image; and that something so big should move in so effortless a manner, seeming to drift along the ground, somehow was jolting in itself. For a moment, Telzey had distinguished, or imagined she had distinguished, the big, round head held high, the pointed ears like horns. *Goblin*, her nerves screamed. A feeling of heavy dread flowed through her, seemed to drain away her strength. This was how the others had felt when they ran and crouched in hiding, knowing there was no escape from such a pursuer ...

She made herself count off a hundred seconds, got to her feet, and started back on a slant towards the creek, to a point a hundred yards above the one where she had climbed from it. If the thing returned along this side of the watercourse and picked up her trail, it might decide she had tried to escape upstream. She got down quietly into the creek, turned downstream again, presently saw in the distance the wood which had looked like a good place to hide. The spook should be prowling among the trees there now, searching for her. She passed the curve where she had pulled herself up on the bank, waded on another hundred steps, trying to make no noise at all, almost certain from moment to moment she could hear or glimpse the spook on its way back. Then she climbed the bank on the right, pushed carefully through the hedges of bushes that lined it, and ran off into the open plain sloping up to the north.

After perhaps a hundred yards, her legs began to lose the rubbery weakness of held-in terror. She was breathing evenly. The aircar was closer again and in not too many more minutes she might find herself out of danger. She didn't look back. If the spook was coming up behind her, she couldn't outrun it, and it wouldn't help to feed her fears by watching for shadows on her trail.

She shifted her attention to signs from Robane. He might be growing concerned by now and resort to his telescanners to look for her and guide his creature after her. There was nothing she could do about that. Now and then she seemed to have a brief awareness of him, but there had been no definite contact since he had spoken.

She reached a rustling grove, walked and trotted through it. As she came out the other side, a herd of graceful deerlike animals turned from her and sped with shadowy quickness across the plain and out of her range of vision. She remembered suddenly having heard that hunted creatures sometimes covered their trail by mingling with other groups of animals ...

A few minutes later, she wasn't sure how well that was working. Other herds were around; sometimes she saw shadowy motion ahead or to right or left; then there would be whistles of alarm, the stamp of hoofs, and they'd vanish like drifting smoke, leaving the section of plain about her empty again. This was Robane's hunting ground; the animals here might be more alert and nervous than in other sections of the park. And perhaps, Telzey thought, they sensed she was the quarry tonight and was drawing danger towards them. Whatever the reason, they kept well out of her way. But she'd heard fleeing herds cross behind her a number of times, so they might in fact be breaking up her trail enough to make it more difficult to follow. She kept scanning the skyline above the slope ahead, looking for the intermittent green flash of a moving aircar or the sweep of its searchbeam along the ground. They couldn't be too far away.

She slowed to a walk again. Her legs and lungs hadn't given out, but she could tell she was tapping the final reserves of strength. She sent a thought to Chomir's mind, touched it instantly and, at the same moment, caught a glimpse of a pulsing green spark against the starblaze, crossing down through a dip in the slopes, disappearing beyond the wooded ground ahead of her. She went hot with hope, swung to the right, began running towards the point where the car should show again.

They'd arrived. Now to catch their attention ...

"Here!" she said sharply in the dog's mind.

It meant: "Here I am! Look for me! Come to me!" No more than that. Chomir was keyed up enough without knowing why. Any actual suggestion that she was in trouble might throw him out of control.

She almost heard the deep, whining half-growl with which he responded. It should be enough. Chomir knew now she was somewhere nearby, and Rish and the others would see it immediately in the way he behaved. When the aircar reappeared, its searchbeam should be swinging about, fingering the ground to locate her.

Telzey jumped down into a little gully, felt, with a shock of surprise, her knees go soft with fatigue as she landed, and clambered shakily out the other side. She took a few running steps forward, came to a sudden complete stop.

Robane! She felt him about, a thick, ugly excitement. It seemed the chance moment of contact for which she'd been waiting, his mind open, unguarded —

She looked carefully around. Something lay beside a cluster of bushes thirty feet ahead. It appeared to be a big pile of wind-blown dry leaves and grass, but its surface stirred with a curious softness in the breeze. Then a wisp of acrid animal odor touched Telzey's nostrils and she felt the hot-ice surge of deep fright.

The spook lifted its head slowly out of its fluffed, mottled mane and looked at her. Then it moved from its crouched position ... a soundless shift a good fifteen feet to the right, light as the tumbling of a big ball of moss. It rose on its hind legs, the long fur settling loosely about it like a cloak, and made a chuckling sound of pleasure.

The plain seemed to explode about Telzey.

The explosion was in her mind. Tensions held too long, too hard, lashed back through her in seething confusion at a moment when too much needed to be done at once. Her physical vision went black; Robane's beast and the starlit slope vanished. She was sweeping through a topsy-turvy series of mental pictures and sensations. Rish's face appeared, wide-eyed, distorted with alarm, the aircar skimming almost at ground level along the top of a grassy rise, a wood suddenly ahead. "*Now!*" Telzey thought. Shouts, and the car swerved up again. Then a brief, thudding, jarring sensation underfoot ...

That was done.

She swung about to Robane's waiting excitement, slipped through it into his mind. In an instant, her awareness poured through a net of subconscious psi channels that became half familiar as she touched them. Machine static clattered, too late to dislodge her. She was there. Robane, unsuspecting, looked out through his creature's eyes at her shape on the plain, hands locked hard on the instruments through which he lived, experienced, murdered.

In minutes, Telzey thought, in minutes, if she was alive minutes from now, she would have this mind — unaware, unresistant, wide open to her — under control. But she wasn't certain she could check the spook then through Robane. He had never attempted to hold it back moments away from its kill.

Vision cleared. She stood on the slope, tight tendrils of thought still linking her to every significant section of Robane's mind. The spook stared, hook-beak lifted above its gaping mouth, showing the thick, twisting tongue inside. Still upright, it began to move, seemed to glide across the ground towards her. One of its forelimbs came through the thick cloak of fur, four-fingered paw raised, slashing retractile claws extended, reaching out almost playfully.

Telzey backed slowly off from the advancing goblin shape. For an instant, another picture slipped through her thoughts ... a blur of motion. She gave it no attention. There was nothing she could do there now.

The goblin dropped lightly to a crouch. Telzey saw it begin its spring as she turned and ran.

She heard the gurgling chuckle a few feet behind her, but no other sound. She ran headlong up the slope with all the strength she had left. In another world, on another level of existence, she moved quickly through Robane's mind, tracing out the control lines, gathering them in. But her thoughts were beginning to blur with fatigue. Bushy shrubbery dotted the slope ahead. She could see nothing else.

The spook passed her like something blown by the wind through the grass. It swung around before her, twenty feet ahead; and as she turned to the right, it was suddenly behind her again, coming up quickly, went by. Something nicked the back of her calf as it passed — a scratch, not much deeper than a dozen or so she'd picked up pushing through thorny growth tonight. But this hadn't been a thorn. She turned left, and it followed, herding her; dodged right, and it was there, going past. Its touch seemed the lightest flick again, but an instant later there was a hot, wet line of pain down her arm. She felt panic gather in her throat as it came up behind her once more. She stopped, turning to face it.

It stopped in the same instant, fifteen feet away, rose slowly to its full height, dark eyes staring, hooked beak open as if in silent laughter. Telzey watched it, gasping for breath. Streaks of foggy darkness seemed to float between them. Robane felt far away, beginning to slip from her reach. If she took another step, she thought, she would stumble and fall; then the thing would be on her.

The spook's head swung about. Its beak closed with a clack. The horn-ears went erect.

The white shape racing silently down the slope seemed unreal for a moment, something she imagined. She knew Chomir was approaching; she hadn't realized he was so near. She couldn't see the aircar's lights in the starblaze above, but it might be there. If they had followed the dog after he plunged out of the car, if they hadn't lost ...

Chomir could circle Robane's beast, threaten it, perhaps draw it away from her, keep it occupied for minutes. She drove a command at him — another, quickly and anxiously, because he hadn't checked in the least; tried to slip into his mind and knew suddenly that Chomir, coming in silent fury, wasn't going to be checked or slowed or controlled by anything she did. The goblin uttered a monstrous, squalling scream of astounded rage as the strange white animal closed the last twenty yards between them; then it leaped aside with its horrid ease. Sick with dismay, Telzey saw the great forelimb flash from the cloak, strike with spread talons. The thudding blow caught Chomir, spun him around, sent him rolling over the ground. The spook sprang again to come down on its reckless assailant. But the dog was on his feet and away.

It was Chomir's first serious fight. But he came of generations of ancestors who had fought one another and other animals and armed men in the arenas of Askanam. Their battle cunning was stamped into his genes. He had made one mistake, a very nearly fatal one, in hurtling in at a dead run on an unknown opponent. Almost within seconds, it became apparent that he was making no further mistakes.

Telzey saw it through a shifting blur of exhaustion. As big a dog as Chomir was, the squalling goblin must weigh nearly five times as much, looked ten times larger with its fur-mane bristling about it. Its kind had been forest horrors to the early settlers. Its forelimbs were tipped with claws longer than her hands and the curved beak could shear through muscle and bone like a sword. Its uncanny speed ...

Now somehow it seemed slow. As it sprang, slashing down, something white and low flowed around and about it with silent purpose. Telzey understood it then. The spook was a natural killer, developed by nature to deal efficiently with its prey. Chomir's breed were killers developed by man to deal efficiently with other killers.

He seemed locked to the beast for an instant, high on its shoulder, and she saw the wide, dark stain on his flank where the spook's talons had struck. He shook himself savagely. There was an ugly, snapping sound. The spook screeched like a huge bird. She saw the two animals locked together again, then the spook rolling over the ground, the white shape rolling with it, slipping away, slipping back. There was another screech. The spook rolled into a cluster of bushes. Chomir followed it in.

A white circle of light settled on the thrashing vegetation, shifted over to her. She looked up, saw Rish's car gliding down through the air, heard voices calling her name —

She followed her contact thoughts back to Robane's mind, spread out through it, sensing at once the frantic grip of his hands on the instrument controls. For Robane, time was running out quickly. He had been trying to turn his beast away from the dog, force it to destroy the human being who could expose him. He had been unable to do it. He was in terrible fear. But he could accomplish no more through the spook. She felt his sudden decision to break mind-contact with the animal to avoid the one experience he had always shunned — going down with another mind into the shuddering agony of death.

His right hand released the control it was clutching, reached towards a switch.

"No," Telzey said softly to the reaching hand.

It dropped to the instrument board. After a moment, it knotted, twisted about, began to lift again.

"No."

Now it lay still. She considered. There was time enough.

Robane believed he would die with the spook if he couldn't get away from it in time. She thought he might be right; she wouldn't want to be in his mind when it happened, if it came to that.

There were things she needed to learn from Robane. The identity of the gang which had supplied him with human game was one; she wanted that very much. Then she should look at the telepathic level of his mind in detail, find out what was wrong in there, why he hadn't been able to use it ... some day, she might be able to do something with a half-psi like Gikkes. And the mind-machines — if Robane had been able to work with them, not really understanding what he did, she should be able to employ similar devices much more effectively. Yes, she had to carefully study his machines —

She released Robane's hand. It leaped to the switch, pulled it back. He gave a great gasp of relief.

For a moment, Telzey was busy. A needle of psi energy flicked knowingly up and down channels, touching here, there, shriveling, cutting, blocking ... Then it was done. Robane, half his mind gone in an instant, unaware of it, smiled blankly at the instrument panel in front of him. He'd live on here, dimmed and harmless, cared for by machines, unwitting custodian of other machines, of memories that had to be investigated, of a talent he'd never known he had.

"I'll be back," Telzey told the smiling, dull thing, and left it.

She found herself standing on the slope. It had taken only a moment, after all. Dunker and Valia were running towards her. Rish had just climbed out of the aircar settled forty feet away, its searchbeam fixed on the thicket where the spook's body jerked back and forth as Chomir, jaws locked on its crushed neck, shook the last vestiges of life from it with methodical fury.

Bibliography

This bibliography is extracted from the Whole Science Fiction
Database. See the acknowledgments page for ordering details.
Wordcounts are in thousands of words (K). *ASF* stands for *Analog*
or *Astounding Science Fiction*, depending on date.

Agent of Vega (25K)
ASF, Jul 49;
Agent of Vega;
Space Police (ed. Andre Norton, 56)

Agent of Vega (collection)
hb: Gnome Press 60; pb: Permabooks, Jun 62; Mayflower, 64; Tempo, 73;
Ace 82.
contains: Agent of Vega; The Second Night of Summer; The
Truth About Cushgar; The Illusionists

The Altruist (7K)
Galaxy, Sep 52

Attitudes (8K)
F&SF, Feb 69

Aura of Immortality (5K)
If, Jun 74

Balanced Ecology (8K)
ASF, Mar 65;
Above the Human Landscape (ed. W. E. McNelly, 72);
Analog 5 (ed. J. W. Campbell, 67);
Analog: The Best of Science Fiction (ed. Editors of Analog, 85);
Bug-eyed Monsters (ed. A. Cheetham 72);
Countercommandment (ed. J. W. Campbell, 67);
Nature's Revenge (ed. S. Manley, 78);
Nebula Award Stories (ed. D. Knight, 66);
A Nice Day for Screaming and Other Tales of the Hub (65);
The Best of James H. Schmitz (ed. M. Olson, 91)

Beacon to Elsewhere (27K)
Amazing, Apr 63;
Most Thrilling SF, Spring #12

The Best of James H. Schmitz (collection)
hb: NESFA Press, 91.
contains: Balanced Ecology; The Custodians; Grandpa; Goblin
Night; Just Curious; Lion Loose…; Novice; The Second Night of
Summer; Sour Note on Palayata;

The Big Terrarium (15K)
Saturn, May 57

Captives of the Thieve Star (12K)
  Planet Stories, May 51
Caretaker (5K)
  Galaxy, Jul 53;
  The Galaxy SF Omnibus (ed. H. L. Gold, 54);
  The Second Galaxy Reader of SF (ed. H. L. Gold, 54)
Child of the Gods (18K)
  ASF, Mar 72
Clean Slate (10K)
  Amazing, Sep 64;
  Great SF, Fall #12
Company Planet (16K)
  ASF, May 71;
  The Telzey Toy and Other Stories (73)
Compulsion (21K)
  ASF, Jun 70;
  The Telzey Toy and Other Stories (73)
The Custodians (14K)
  ASF, Dec 68;
  The Best of James H. Schmitz (ed. M. Olson, 91)
The Demon Breed (novel)
  originally titled *The Tuvela*
  hb: SFBC, 68; pb: Ace, 68; hb: MacDonald, 69; UK SFBC, 71; pb: Orbit, 74.
The End of the Line (12K)
  ASF, Jul 51;
  Space Pioneers (ed. A. Norton, 54);
  To the Stars (ed. R. Silverberg, 71);
  Tomorrow 1 (ed. R. Hoskins, 71)
The Eternal Frontiers (novel)
  hb: Putnam, 73; pb: Berkley, 73; Sidgwick & Jackson, 74.
Faddist (story)
  Bizarre Mystery, Jan 66
Glory Day (15K)
  ASF, Jun 71
Goblin Night (13K)
  ASF, Apr 65;
  Incorporated into *The Lion Game*
  On Our Way to the Future (ed. T. Carr, 70);
  The Best of James H. Schmitz (Ed. M. Olson, 91)
Gone Fishing (18K)
  ASF, May 61;

Five-Odd (ed. G. Conklin, 64);
Possible Tomorrows (ed. G. Conklin, 64)

Grandpa (9K)

ASF, Feb 55;
The Arbor House Treasury of Modern Science Fiction (ed. R. Silverberg, 80);
The Astounding-Analog Reader, V2 (ed. H. Harrison, 73);
Caught in the Organ Draft (ed. I. Asimov, 83);
Decade the 50's (ed. B. W. Aldiss, 76);
Great Science Fiction of the 20th Century (ed. R. Silverberg);
The Infinite Web (ed. R. Silverberg, 77);
Isaac Asimov Presents the Great SF Stories: 17 (ed. I. Asimov, 88);
Penguin Science Fiction (ed. B. W. Aldiss, 61);
Penguin Science Fiction Omnibus (ed. B. W. Aldiss, 73);
A Science Fiction Reader (ed. H. Harrison, 73)
Spectrum V (ed. K. Amis, 66)
Time Probe: The Sciences in Science Fiction (ed. A. C. Clarke, 66)
The Best of James H. Schmitz (ed. M. Olson, 91)

Greenface (11K)

Unknown, Aug 43
The Circus of Dr. Lao and Other Improbable Stories (ed. R. Bradbury, 56)
A Pride of Monsters (70)
Things Hunting Men (ed. D. Drake, 88)
Unknown Worlds: Tales from Beyond (ed. S. Schmidt, 88)

Ham Sandwich (10K)

ASF, Jun 63

Harvest Time (10K)

ASF, Sep 58

The Illusionists (21K)

retitled from "Space Fear" in *Agent of Vega* (60)

An Incident on Route 12 (2K)

IF, Jan 62
101 Science Fiction Stories (ed. M. H. Greenberg, 86)
The Best Science Fiction from If (ed F. Pohl, 64)

Just Curious (4K)

Alfred Hitchcock's Mystery Magazine, Dec 68
Alfred Hitchcock's Fatal Attractions (ed. E. Lore, 83)
SF Author's Choice 2 (ed. H. Harrison, 70)
The Best of James H. Schmitz (Ed. M. Olson, 91)

Left Hand, Right Hand (13K)

Amazing, Nov 62

Legacy (novel)

retitled from *A Tale of Two Clocks*; pb: Ace, 79

The Lion Game (novel)

The stories "Goblin Night" and "Sleep No More" along with
considerable additional material were incorporated into this novel.
pb: DAW 73; Sidgwick & Jackson, 76; Hamlyn, 79; Ace, 82.

Lion Loose... (24K)
ASF, Oct 61
A Pride of Monsters (70)
The Best of James H. Schmitz (Ed. M. Olson, 91)

The Machmen (6K)
ASF, Sep 64
A Nice Day for Screaming and Other Tales of the Hub (65)

A Nice Day for Screaming (6K)
ASF, Jan 65
A Nice Day for Screaming and Other Tales of the Hub (65)

A Nice Day for Screaming and Other Tales of the Hub
(collection)
hb: Chilton 65.
contains: Balanced Ecology; A Nice Day for Screaming; The
Tangled Web; The Machmen; The Other Likeness; The Winds of
Time

Novice (12K)
ASF, Jun 62
incorporated into *The Universe Against Her*
Analog 2 (ed. J. W. Campbell, Jr., 64)
Analog's Children of the Future (ed. S. Schmidt, 82)
Mind to Mind (ed. R. Silverberg, 71)
Tomorrow's Children (ed. I. Asimov, 66)
The Best of James H. Schmitz (Ed. M. Olson, 91)

One Step Ahead (3K)
IF, Apr 74

Oneness (7K)
ASF, May 63

The Other Likeness (7K)
ASF, Jul 62
A Nice Day for Screaming and Other Tales of the Hub (65)

Planet of Forgetting (13K)
Galaxy, Feb 65
World's Best Science Fiction: 66 (ed. D. A. Wollheim, 66)

Poltergeist (story)
ASF, Jul 71

The Pork Chop Tree (32K)
ASF, Feb 65
A Pride of Monsters (70)

A Pride of Monsters (collection)
  hb: Macmillan, 70; pb: Collier, 73.
  contains: Greenface; Lion Loose...; The Searcher; The Pork Chop Tree;
  The Winds of Time.
Research Alpha (19K)
  IF, Jul 65 (co-authored with A. E. Van Vogt)
Resident Witch (15K)
  ASF, May 70
  The Telzey Toy and Other Stories (73)
  This Side of Infinity (ed. T. Carr, 72)
Rogue Psi (11K)
  Amazing, Aug 62
  Strange Fantasy, Summer 70
  The Best from Amazing (ed. T. White, 73)
The Searcher (28K)
  ASF, Feb 66
  A Pride of Monsters (70)
The Second Night of Summer (10K)
  Galaxy, Dec 50
  significantly revised version: incorporated in *Agent of Vega* (60)
  Possible Worlds of SF (ed. G. Conklin, 51)
  The Best of James H. Schmitz (ed. M. Olson, 91)
Sleep No More (8K)
  ASF, Aug 65
  Incorporated into *The Lion Game*
  The Analog Anthology #1 (ed. S. Schmidt, 80)
  6 Decades: the Best of Analog (ed. S. Schmidt, 86)
Sour Note on Palayata (14K)
  ASF, Nov 56
  The Best of James H. Schmitz (ed. M. Olson, 91)
Space Fear (21K)
  ASF, Mar 51
  retitled to "The Illusionists"
Spacemaster (9K)
  New Writings in SF 3 (ed. J. Carnell, 65)
The Star Hyacinths (15K)
  Amazing, Dec 61
  retitled to "The Tangled Web"
Summer Guests (11K)
  IF, Sep 59
The Symbiotes (20K)
  ASF, Sep 72

A Tale of Two Clocks (novel)
hb: SFBC/Torquil 62; pb: Belmont, 65
retitled to *Legacy*

The Tangled Web (15K)
retitled from "The Star Hyacinths"
A Nice Day for Screaming and Other Tales of the Hub (65)

The Telzey Toy (22K)
ASF, Jan 71
The Telzey Toy and Other Stories (73)

The Telzey Toy and Other Stories (collection)
pb: DAW, 73; Sidgwick & Jackson, 76; Ace, 82 ; Hamlyn, 83.
contains: Company Planet; Resident Witch; The Telzey Toy;
Compulsion.

These Are the Arts (6K)
F&SF, Sep 62
14 Great Tales of ESP (ed. I. P. Stone, 69)

The Ties of Earth (24K)
Galaxy, Nov 55 - Jan 56

Trouble Tide (16K)
ASF, May 65
Elsewhere and Elsewhen (ed. G. Conklin, 68)

The Truth About Cushgar (16K)
ASF, Nov 50
Agent of Vega (60)

The Tuvela (novel)
ASF, Sep-Oct 68
retitled to *The Demon Breed*

Undercurrents (35K)
ASF, May-Jun 64
incorporated into *The Universe Against Her* (64)

The Universe Against Her (collection)
pb: Ace, 64; Ace, 79; hb: Gregg Press, 81.
contains: Novice; Undercurrents

The Vampirate (8K)
Science Fiction +, Dec 53

Watch the Sky (9K)
ASF, Aug 62

We Don't Want Any Trouble (25K)
Galaxy, Jun 53
50 Short Science Fiction Tales (ed. I. Asimov, 63)
Assignment in Tomorrow (ed. F. Pohl, 54)

Where the Time Went (4K)

IF, Nov 68
Androids, Time Machines, and Blue Giraffes (ed. R. Elwood, 73)

The Winds of Time (13K)

ASF, Jul 62
A Nice Day for Screaming and Other Tales of the Hub (65)
A Pride of Monsters (70)

The Witches of Karres (14K)

ASF, Dec 49
expanded to *The Witches of Karres* (novel)
Analog's Children of the Future (ed. S. Schmidt, 82)
The Astounding Science Fiction Anthology (ed. J. W. Campbell, Jr., 51)
The First Astounding Science Fiction Anthology (ed. J. W. Campbell, Jr., 54)
Isaac Asimov Presents the Golden Years of Science Fiction: Sixth Series (ed. I. Asimov, 88)
Isaac Asimov Presents the Great SF Stories: 11 (ed. I. Asimov, 84)
Isaac Asimov's Magical Worlds of Fantasy: 2 Witches (ed. I. Asimov, 84)
Isaac Asimov's Magical Worlds of Fantasy: Wizards and Witches (ed. I. Asimov, 85)
Science Fiction Hall of Fame Vol. 2B (ed. B. Bova, 73)
The Second Astounding Science Fiction Anthology (ed. J. W. Campbell, Jr., 65)
Toward Infinity (ed. D. Knight, 68)

The Witches of Karres (novel)

expansion of "The Witches of Karres"; hb: Chilton, 66; pb: Ace, 66; Gollancz, 88.

Would You? (3K)

Fantastic, Dec 69

Schmitz created two series, the "Agent of Vega" series and the "Federation of the Hub" series. The Federation of the Hub series comprises about 29 stories and novels, the majority of which have an interlocking set of characters. The table on the next page shows the stories in which each major character appears.
Telzey: Telzey Amberdon
Trigger: Trigger Argee
Quillan: Heslet Quillan
Tate: Holati Tate
Kyth: Kyth Detective Agency
Pilch: Pilch
Etland: Nile Etland
Hub: The Federation of the Hub
Vega: Agent of Vega

Telzey	Trigger	Quillan	Tate	Kyth	Pilch	Etland	Hub	Vega	
								•	Agent of Vega
							•		Attitudes
			•				•		Aura of Immortality
							•		Balanced Ecology
							•		Beacon to Elsewhere
•							•		Child of the Gods
•							•		Company Planet
•	•				•		•		Compulsion
						•	•		The Demon Breed
•	•						•		Glory Day
•							•		Goblin Night
	•		•				•		Harvest Time
								•	The Illusionaires
		•					•		Lion Loose…
							•		The Machmen
							•		A Nice Day for Screaming
•							•		Novice
							•		The Other Likeness
•							•		Poltergeist
	•		•				•		The Pork Chop Tree
•				•			•		Resident Witch
				•			•		The Searcher
								•	The Second Night of Summer
•							•		Sleep No More
					•		•		Sour Note on Palayata
			•				•		The Star Hyacinths
•	•						•		The Symbionts
	•	•	•			•	•		A Tale of Two Clocks
•							•		The Telzey Toy
						•	•		Trouble Tide
								•	The Truth About Cushgar
•				•			•		Undercurrents
							•		The Winds of Time

Acknowledgments

I would like to thank the following people for the help they have provided in producing this book: Boskone 27 for letting me do a panel on a "Neglected Author" which proved that Schmitz still has fans out there. Janet Kagan and Mark Owings, whose long out-of-print article, and bibliography of Schmitz inspired me to re-read him and to do the panel. Ben Yalow, Beth Meacham, Ginjer Buchanan and Stanley Schmidt for help in locating the agent for the Estate of James H. Schmitz. David Hartwell for advice on small-run, hardbound, reprint publishing. Ben Yalow and Rick Katze for help in obtaining the right to use the cover art (which is from the collection of Rick Katze). Ben Yalow and Janet Kagan for advice on selecting stories. Merle Insinga for the three interior illustrations. Joseph Aspler for information on acid-free paper. Kurt Baty and Tony Lewis of Whole Science Fiction Database for building an amazingly complete Schmitz bibliography. Kenneth R. Johnson for contributions to the bibliography. Frank and Lisa Richards and their company, QuickScan, for scanning the stories and saving us a *lot* of typing. Kelly Persons, Rick Katze, Ann Broomhead and Dave Anderson, for doing the initial proofreading. George Flynn, preefroader extraordinarie, for proofing and copyediting this book. Sarah Prince for invaluable assistance in book design. Rick Katze and Peggy Thokar for assistance in writing the book contract. Greg Thokar and Mark Dulcey for assistance with PageMaker. Greg Thokar, Chip Hitchcock, George Flynn, and Jim Mann for teaching me much about publishing a book. Thanks to you all.

- Mark L. Olson
February 1991

QuickScan can be reached at PO Box 71, Marlow, NH 03456 (603) 446-7307.

The Whole Science Fiction Database is publishing a complete bibliography of SF in quarterly installments. Write to them at PO Box 90006, Oak Hill, TX 78709-0006.

This book was edited on a Macintosh SE/30 using Microsoft Word 4.0. Page layout was done using Aldus PageMaker 4.0 and printed at 115% on a HP Laserjet III with the PacificPage PE postscript emulator cartridge.

The book is set in Palatino on 60# acid-free Booktext natural.